Liz-Cat

Best

hope you enjoy, darlin'!

Rivi ♡

Seeking JUSTICE

RIVI JACKS

First Print Edition: April 2015

Cover design: Double J Book Graphics
Formatting: Streetlight Graphics

A loving thank you to my husband for always being here for me.

SPECIAL THOUGHTS

Thank you to my Street Team, Rivi's Rebels! Y'all are amazing women and I thank you for your friendship and constant support. It means the world to me.

My PA Laurie Schmidt Lee, Michelle Engler, Jessica Johnson Welch, Jacquie Denison, Leigh Ann Panorelli, Melissa McCarty, Suzette Warren, Lisa Molina, Kristie Farrell Root, Crystal St. Clair, Melanie Harrell, Michelle Berndt, Nancy Young, Linda Delaney, Rachel Rae Palmer, and Lea Winkelman. Y'all are kick-ass pimpers!

Thank you, Jessica Johnson Welch, Jacquie Denison, Michelle Engler, and Rachel Rae Palmer for your killer teaser designs. I love them.

An additional thank you for the support from these ladies, Teo Reaman, Joanna Hoover, and Tonya Ridener.

CHAPTER ONE

"CAIT!"

I jump, dribbling tea down the front of my blouse. I frantically brush the drops away before they seep into the fabric.

"Where have you been? Valerie's on the war path, and she's looking for you."

"What?" I set my teacup down and stand, reaching to close my laptop, grabbing up my phone. "Why didn't you call me, Paul?"

He follows me out the door. "I did. It went straight to voicemail."

I look down at my phone to see that I haven't turned it back on since my interview that morning. "Shit!"

"Yeah, she's fit to be tied."

"She's always fit to be tied," I mumble.

"Yeah, but this time she's been shut up in her office all morning with people. Something's up."

I look over at my close friend and co-worker, Paul Sims. We hired on at Query Magazine the same day and struck up an immediate friendship, smart enough to see allies in each other. Two years later, Paul and his wife are my best friends.

We round the corner and come face to face with Valerie's secretary.

"It's about time!" she hisses. "Next time you decide to disappear, do me a favor and do it on my day off."

"I'm here now, Pat."

She steps quickly over to Valerie's office and knocks softly. "Cait's here, Valerie."

"I'll talk to you in a bit," Paul says as he heads on down the hallway.

I step into the editor of Query Magazines office, leaving the door open, hoping she'll yell less if she knows people can hear her.

"Shut the door, Caitlyn."

So much for that idea. I do as bid and then sit in the chair facing her desk.

Beating me to the punch before I have a chance to apologize, she asks, "Did you lose your phone?"

"Sorry, I forgot to turn it back on after my meeting with Adams."

She gives me a raised eyebrow as she shuffles papers lying on her desk. "How did that go?"

"Not well. I think he's a—flake." She cocks her brow a notch higher. I shrug in answer as if that says it all. At her continued scrutiny, I fess up. "He's a disgusting pig." She'll just have to take that answer and leave it as I'm not about to repeat what the slime ball said to me.

"Tell Paul I said he's now on Adams. I have a new assignment for you."

I sit up straight at once feeling apprehensive. Valerie is acting out of character. One: she never pulls you off an assignment since she expects you to do your job. No matter what. Two: She's not yelling at me. She always yells especially if she's waited half the day to do so. And three: Valerie is never out of character.

She reaches across the desk to flop a file down in front of me.

"Liam Justice." I reach and pick up the file as she continues. "Owner of one of Chicago's most elite private clubs. Patronized by politicians and world dignitaries alike." Her tone is slightly mocking.

I flip through the information she's provided which includes a batch of pictures of various people. "Which one is Justice?"

"We don't have a good image of him." She stands and leans across the desk to sort through the photos, sliding one away from the rest. It's a long distance shot of an individual on a sailboat. It's hard to discern anything about the man in the grainy picture. "There doesn't seem to be *any* clear photos of Mr. Justice. He's afforded a level of privacy that is certainly attributed to the company he—entertains."

"Yeah, but still, in this day and age, it's unusual—" I gasp softly, and my head jerks up. "He's Mafia?"

Valerie rolls her eyes. "No, Caitlyn. He is a legitimate business man."

"So, you just want to do a story on the mysterious Mr. Justice? Find out what makes him tick."

"There are rumors about his background but nothing definite. In the last twelve years, he's made quite a name for himself and his club. Membership to The Justice is highly coveted."

I look up from the file when she doesn't say more. "So, do you want me to investigate those rumors or why membership is so highly coveted?" I'm a little confused; Valerie usually gets right to the point.

She leans forward in her chair her fist coming down on her desktop making me jump. "I need someone in there who can keep an eye on what's happening, watch to see who is coming and going, and find the hell out about Justice's past!"

O-kaay, she's in Valerie mode now. I feel a little less apprehensive. A little.

"Valerie, what's going on here? You evidently have plenty of resources available on Liam Justice." I hold up the extensive file.

"I've waited a year, and now a position has become available at The Justice." She pulls a paper from her desk drawer. "They advertise for their kitchen, restaurant, and nightclub help in the newspaper. He's an equal opportunity employer." She smirks as she slides the paper to me.

Wow. There's a nightclub?

"I've made an interview appointment for you." She hands me a business card. "Tomorrow at three, the position is for a hostess."

I take the card and glance at it briefly. "Anyone else I'm looking for?" I know there's something more here.

"Not, in particular. You'll be undercover on this one, Caitlyn."

"You're kidding," I scoff.

"Not at all. Here's your cover." She slides another file to me. "It'll be like a vacation, Caitlyn, you won't have to come into the office," she says wryly.

"Will I have to move?"

"That won't be necessary."

My eyes run over the cover information she's given me. "This is my real info!"

"Except, for where you've previously been employed.

Read the info, Caitlyn. We've covered all the bases in case someone gets inquisitive about you."

"Why would... " I take a deep breath to control my irritation. Something is setting off the little voice that tells me not all is kosher here. I've learned to trust that little voice. "Valerie—" I pause knowing I need to be careful how I say this. "You've never knowingly sent me into a dangerous situation, but you're making me nervous here."

Sighing heavily, she stands and moves to her small liquor cabinet in the corner where she pours a measure of her favorite bourbon into two glasses. We've had drinks in her office before, but usually it's after hours.

She hands me a glass, reclaiming her chair before downing her drink. She sets the empty glass down.

"The Justice House is a sex club."

I give her a long blink. "Excuse me?" My voice comes out in a squeak.

"You heard me, Caitlyn."

I set my untouched drink on her desk. An equal measure of shock, anger, and dread roll over me. "I'm not the person for this assignment, Valerie. I don't do sex clubs. I can't even begin to tell you how little I know about that scene."

"Oh, come now, I know you go out clubbing with Paul and a few of the others."

"Not to sex clubs!" I stand, shaking my head. "Get Tish, she'll do a better job."

"Sit down, Caitlyn. The Justice isn't the type of place that Tish frequents. It's a class act, and you my dear girl are the investigator for the job. End of discussion!"

I hate it when she says that. "Valerie, I know nothing about—"

"The position is for a hostess... nothing more. Even if Justice allowed his employee's access to that part of the club, they wouldn't be able to afford the membership. Rumor has it joining can set a person back sixty thousand a year."

Shit.

My mind scrambles. "Valerie, I know nothing about being a hostess—"

"Oh, for heaven's sake, Caitlyn! You greet people. I'm sure you can handle it. I need info on Justice and who frequents Justice House. I need someone who is quick on her feet, can fit in, and can retain information to bring back to me. You." She stands to pour herself another drink.

If she thinks to convince me by stroking my ego, she's mistaken. "I can't do it, Valerie. I wouldn't be comfortable in that type of environment."

She turns slowly, her expression smug. "You will if you want to continue working here."

My mouth opens in surprise. I enjoy working at the magazine, but if that's how it has to be, then I will start looking for another job tomorrow. I think she reads my mind as her next words finish that idea.

"Do you think you would like working at a fast food chain? Because, with one phone call from me, that will be the only type of work you will find in this town. And I can definitely make sure you will never work in journalism anywhere in this country."

I know she's serious. She has those types of connections. I pick up my neglected drink and down the contents in one gulp. The fiery liquid makes me choke, and my eyes tear.

Damn it! I'm going to work in some sleazy sex bar.

I close Valerie's office door behind me, taking a moment to pull my jumbled thoughts together.

"You okay?" Pat asks as she looks up from her computer.

"Yeah." I step to her desk. "Pat, who did Valerie have in her office this morning?" I ask quietly.

She casts a glance toward the closed door. "Two suits. And she was expecting them," she whispers back.

My eyes widen in surprise. "Cops?"

Pat nods. "Maybe. She had me hold all of her calls." She raises her brow indicating how unusual that was in itself. "They were in there three hours, and when they left she started trying to contact you."

I nod. "Thanks, Pat. I'll talk to you later, I need to find Paul."

"Sounds like you may need to drag out the ol' whip and practice a bit."

"That's not funny, Paul!" I give him the evil eye, and then smile at his wife Julie when she giggles. We're having drinks at our favorite little corner bar, not far from Paul and Julie's place.

"It'll be okay, Cait," Julie says. "It kind of sounds like it might be a good time." Now it's my turn to giggle at the look on Paul's face. "You know... with all the gorgeous people." She gives me a wink. "I've heard it's one swanky place. One of the girls in the office had the chance to have dinner there, and she said the whole estate was incredible. Although I am now wondering just what she was doing there, but since you're only hiring in as a hostess for the restaurant... why not have fun with it?" She shrugs. "Easy-peasy."

I give her a long blink. She makes it sound so simple,

and I wish she were right. I look at Paul and shake my head slightly, motioning to Julie with my thumb.

"I know. Why do you think I fell in love with her?" He leans over to give her a kiss, and I smile fondly at them. They were only a couple when I first met Paul, but they've been married a year now, and I will be forever grateful to Julie for not being jealous of the friendship between her husband and me.

Julie steps away to speak to an acquaintance, and it doesn't take Paul long to bring up my new assignment.

"Cait, all kidding aside, you're not really worried about this assignment are you?" He meets my gaze, his eyes full of concern.

"I think this whole expose' Valerie wants to do on Justice is a coverup."

"You think she's lying to you?" Paul finishes his beer and holds the bottle up to catch the waitress's attention.

I shift in my chair. "Maybe not lying exactly—but there's more to this than her wanting to uncover the guy's background. She has quite a file on him even though she insists that he's shielded by the big shots he knows. She insists she has no good photos of him, but I don't believe her."

Paul shrugs. "So something's throwing up a red flag. You know how Valerie is. Look him up on the web."

I laugh. "I thought about that, I've just not had the chance yet."

"Cait, I am a little worried about her asking you to report on who comes and goes. If it's as she told you, and there are all manner of people utilizing the Justice for their nefarious needs, some of those people might be willing to do anything to keep their squeaky clean reputations intact."

I inhale deeply. He's not saying anything I haven't already said to myself.

"You know, we all just keep assuming that I'm going to be hired for this job."

Paul gives me a raised brow as he accepts a fresh beer from our waitress. "You'll get hired, Cait. You said Valerie has a cover for you, and I'm sure it's a doozy. She wants you there; she won't leave anything to chance." I know he's right. "I've told Valerie I'm helping you on this one."

I give a sharp laugh. "You did! What did she say?"

He grins. "She said I'd best be worried about Adams, that you said he was some kind of ballbusting predator."

We're both laughing, our party mood restored when Julie rejoins us.

"Oh, Cait!" Julie grins mischievously. "Myles asked about you the other day. Kind of hinted around that he was going to call you."

With raised brow, I shake my head. "Not going to happen, Julie."

She laughs. "That's what I told him, but he acted like he didn't hear me. Just kept on talking about what a fun time the two of you had and how he couldn't get you out of his head. So, look out."

Crap. Myles Lee worked for the same advertising firm as Julie, and she fixed us up on a blind date, not knowing his true nature. I spent the entire time at the restaurant where we had dinner, fighting him off. It was embarrassing. The night finally ended when I hauled off and slapped him in the taxi on the ride to the theater. He demanded that the cab driver pull over and then kicked me out of the cab. That was two months ago, and if he thought I'd go on another date with him, he was crazy.

"Stay away from that guy," Paul says before turning to his wife. "You too! It would take little provocation for me to punch him."

"Oh, my hero," Julie says, batting her eyelashes at him.

I call it an early night since I have a job interview to prepare for.

Paul nudges my shoulder as we wait for my cab. "You'll be just fine, Cait as long as you don't catch the eye of some Dominatrix." I frown. "A female dominant," he explains, rolling his eyes.

"I told you I don't know anything about that kind of... stuff!" I playfully punch his arm.

"Paul, stop teasing Cait." Julie gives me a hug. "Call, and let us know how the interview goes."

"Yeah, I want to hear *all* about it," Paul teases, his arm going around my shoulder for a quick squeeze. "You'll be fine, kid."

My cab arrives, and we say our good-byes. I settle in for the short ride home, watching out the window as the city lights stream by. I wish it could be as easy and painless as Julie would have me believe and if it were just a new job as a hostess—maybe. But it's not. I will be snooping and lying to people, doing what I do best, uncovering their secrets.

And that little voice that I usually listen to is still nagging at me.

CHAPTER TWO

THE TAXI PULLS TO THE curb in front of an imposing three-story, limestone residence. A freaking *huge* stately home. The pictures Valerie showed me of the Justice House were a poor representation of this elegant building. With its old world charm, it looks as if it might have been transported from some European country. I pay the driver and step out onto the sidewalk, looking up and down the street. The neighborhood is a mix of old mansions and high-rise apartments. This is some serious real estate. Surely this isn't right. Before shutting the door, I lean down looking back into the taxi.

"Are you sure this is the address I gave you, the right street?"

"Yes miss. North State Parkway."

Damn.

I close the cab door and turn back to the imposing house. A wrought iron fence that is probably eight feet high encloses the large corner double lot that the estate occupies. I press the intercom located by the gate. I hear a click and then raise the latch that lets only one side of the double iron gates open and I slip through before latching it back. I take a deep breath and look up. This is an incredible home. Well, actually—sex club. I don't think anyone is using it as a home. I look around again, wondering how many of the neighbors are aware of the kinky sexcapades that happen here. I feel a little uneasy thinking about how my boss has involved me in this crap. And not for the first time I wonder what exactly does go on in a place such as this. I snort. A place such as this!

My eyes take in the magnificent building. It's a beauty with its Palladian and stained glass windows. Wide steps fan out from the large, imposing double front doors, and it's these steps I ascend to the top. A large brass plaque states that this is *The House of Justice*. I roll my eyes. There's a smaller plaque that says, *Ring Bell,* which I do, and I wait.

After several minutes, I'm considering if I should ring the bell again when the door opens. A young woman steps forward, smiling pleasantly. She's very pretty. I guess a few years older than me and dressed smartly in a black pantsuit with a pristine white blouse. Her short blonde corkscrew curls are held back on either side of her head with clips, and her hazel eyes are bright and friendly as she holds her hand out to me.

"Caitlyn?"

"Yes."

"Hi! I'm Holly Phillips," Her soft drawl is appealing and her handshake firm. I immediately like her.

"I'm so sorry to leave you standing out here." She holds the door wide, motioning for me to enter. "I was all the way at the back of the house with a delivery." She turns and strides across the large entrance hall, her heels clicking on the highly polished wood floor. "I'm not sure where Liam is, probably upstairs, and heaven forbid that he would tear himself away from his video game. One of these days, I'm going to blow that Xbox up, and then we'll have three grown men crying in their beers!" She laughs as if that is a pleasant thought. "If you'll follow me we'll go back to where we can sit and visit."

I follow slowly as I gaze around the impressive entrance hall that opens up into a rotunda. Looking up, I see railing that goes around each of the upper levels. My gaze then continues up to the stained glass dome. *Damn*. The halls crowning glory though is its massive staircase with intricate wood carvings that leads up to the next level.

Taking in the décor as I follow Holly, we travel deeper into the interior of the grand old home. I find it rich and over the top extravagant. Deep-jeweled colors used throughout are visually appealing and the original woodwork gleams with a beautifully aged patina.

We come to the area where the restaurant is located, and the décor is no different here.There is an abundance of dark wood, rich wall tapestries, and floor to ceiling windows that look out onto the immaculate grounds of the estate. A large crystal chandelier, hangs from the ceiling in the middle of the room, with additional crystal sconces placed at intervals along the walls of the dining room. To the right of the doorway, is the bar area, sectioned off from the dining room by the positioning of four large wooden pillars. It gives the illusion of the bar being its own room but still part of the dining area. Catty corner of the bar is an area with comfortable looking chairs positioned near a large fireplace and a lovely baby grand piano.

There are two men sitting at the bar talking to who I assume is the bartender since he's behind the counter. He looks up, and I return his smile.

There are no diners in the dining room at this time of

day. The tables have already been set up for the evening meal with long white tablecloths, sparkling crystal, gleaming silverware, and what I am sure is fine china. There are candles everywhere waiting to be lit, and I can imagine the effect when the lights are low with dozens of candles giving off their romantic ambiance. It is a beautiful room.

I look around as I follow Holly to a cleared table, noticing three men at a table farther back near the windows. Holly sits and motions for me to do the same.

"Would you like something to drink?" she asks politely.

"No, thank you."

I sit facing the men at the back table, and I look up to notice that they have stopped their conversation and are looking our way. My gaze meets the most incredible blue eyes, and at that moment, my world flips topsy-turvy. I think I forget to breathe as his intense, clear blue gaze holds mine captive. He is unbelievably attractive, model-gorgeous even. His dark hair, cut short and left a little longer on top, looks as if he just runs his fingers through it to style. I have the immediate thought that I'd like to run my fingers through his hair, my fingernails against his scalp. Light stubble covers his jawline, and I wonder if it's soft. It looks soft. How would it feel against my neck, my...

Someone needs to flip the switch to my brain back on as I hear Holly say my name. I can tell when I reluctantly pull my gaze to hers that she has said my name more than once.

"Are you okay?" Her voice sounds more amused than concerned.

I glance back to the far table and I'm aware that two

of the men stand to leave, but I only have eyes for the guy that remains seated, still looking intently at me. He speaks to the other two, but his gaze never leaves mine.

"Caitlyn." Holly reaches over to touch my arm, and I start guiltily. I've been caught staring at the pretty for too long.

"I'm sorry! Sorry." I feel myself blush. Holly's expression is now amused. She scoots her chair over a little, effectively blocking a clear view of the far table, and I dare not look past her. I need to pull myself together before I royally screw this interview up.

"You can call me, Cait." I clear my throat. "I go by Cait."

"Okay, Cait, tell me a little about you." Holly looks up from her iPad, her expression friendly and sincere, my indiscretion forgiven.

I can't help myself. I glance over Holly's shoulder taking a quick peek at the exceedingly handsome man who seems very interested in our conversation. My eyes collide with his bright blue orbs. *He is freaking gorgeous!* I tear my gaze away and take a deep breath, mentally shaking myself.

"Well... I grew up an only child in a suburb outside of St. Louis. I attended college—Washington University—decided I needed something more than how my life seemed planned out for me and... here I am. I discovered with my last position that I enjoy working in the restaurant and hotel industry, so I'm planning to start restaurant management classes in the fall."

"Well, this would be a good experience for you." Holly gives me an encouraging smile.

"Yes it would," I murmur, noticing over Holly's

shoulder that the blue-eyed charmer has a slight smile on his lips. I wonder what he finds amusing.

"I contacted your previous employer, and he had nothing but good things to say about you." I smile, amazed once again at Valerie's far reach. "How did you like working for Peter Yarsdale?"

Oh no! How well does she know the guy? Not that it matters, I'm sure my cover is secure.

"I enjoyed working with Peter very much. I learned a lot in my time at The Carriage House."

"The Carriage House is a wonderful restaurant," Holly replies.

"Yes, it is."

Holly has several more questions to ask, and I do my best, but it is disconcerting, feeling the eyes of the man on me. He seems to be listening to everything we say, and my gaze frequently strays in his direction. At one point, Holly has to repeat the question and then she looks over her shoulder, back at Mr. Beautiful.

I'm able to control myself for a bit, but then my gaze slides over Holly's shoulder and flicks right back when I see that he is still watching me. What the hell is his problem?

"The position of hostess is a little different here at the Justice." Holly pulls my attention back. "You would be expected to be more of a Concierge assisting our members. Your various duties would involve taking reservations, overseeing the restaurant and entry into the nightclub. You would also make certain that our members receive the best dining experience The Justice has to offer. Any request from a member, you would address directly or relay the request to the appropriate department."

"What type of request might that be?" I hope I sound

curious and not suspicious. I need to make sure that their idea of hostess duties are the same as mine.

"It could be anything from acquiring theater tickets to making hotel reservations for an out of town member."

Okay, I can do that sort of thing.

"You will rotate shifts with Tansy."

I like the way she says, you will.

Holy crap! Has he moved his chair?

He *has* moved his chair, giving us a clear view of each other once again. He's still staring, and for some unfathomable reason, as I look into those intense blue eyes, I feel myself blush.

"The day shift covers breakfast and lunch, although breakfast is room service only."

Room service?

Holly continues, unaware of the guy's chair games. "The evening shift covers dinner and the nightclub. You and Tansy will work closely together, and with a bit of luck, you'll provide for most of our members needs before they have to ask." She looks up at this point to witness my flushed face.

With a heavy sigh, she turns in her chair. "Dude! Do you mind? We're trying to do an interview here."

Blue eyes raises his hand and makes a gesture for her to continue, his eyes still locked on mine.

Holly turns around with a sigh. "I'm sorry. I've known him forever, and sometimes I forget the effect he has on women."

I glance quickly at him. He takes a sip of his drink, holding my gaze over the rim of the glass. I want to ask how she avoids drooling all over him, but maybe she has her own drool-worthy hunk at home since she wears a set of wedding rings.

"Would you like to trade places with me?"

Riiight. I'm so aware of this guy, I'm not sure that would even help.

When he suddenly stands, my eyes follow him up. He's tall and broad-shouldered but lean. His t-shirt fits close, outlining an awe worthy chest with pecs defined against the thin material. His arms are nicely muscled, his stomach flat, and his snug jeans hint at muscular legs. When he's abreast of our table, I look up into sharp blue eyes. He breaks eye contact to look at Holly, and I catch his slight headshake.

What? What's he shaking his head for?

As he passes our table, I catch a whiff of his masculine scent, and my stomach muscles clench. I watch him walk away; the fit of his jeans snugs his ass just right. He looks like something you'd want to lick and savor on all day.

What the hell is wrong with me? I mentally shake myself. I don't usually have thoughts like this, but this guy is causing a reaction in me that's definitely out of character.

"Cait." I turn my attention back to Holly. "I need to step away for just a moment. Do you mind?"

"No, it's fine." I watch as she follows in the direction of the blue-eyed Adonis. Holy crap! Who is that guy? A member? My tummy feels funny at that thought. Surely he's not a member since Holly called him *Dude*. I read up a little the night before about sex clubs, and if he is a member he probably has sex with any number of women every day. Kinky sex. Someone who looks like him...

The clicking of Holly's heels announces her return, and she's not alone. They stop at the bar where she and Mr. Good-looking exchange words, and then she's headed my way with an annoyed expression on her face.

"Sorry about that, Cait."

"No problem," I answer, looking back toward the bar. I gasp softly when my eyes connect with vivid blue. *Damn.*

"Cait, I really don't want to interview anyone else, I think you're perfect, and I'd like to offer you the hostess position."

Wow. Could it really be that easy?

"Thank you, Holly. I would love to work here." *I hope my nose doesn't grow.*

"Perfect." She opens a file that has been lying on the table and pulls out a sheaf of papers. "First off, you will need to sign a nondisclosure agreement."

Son-of-a-bitch! I hope she doesn't notice my dismay as I quickly compose myself. Is this something Valerie has considered? Does an NDA hold up in court if you're an investigator on a story? Will the NDA apply to Liam Justice or just members?

"I hope that's not a problem?" Holly asks, watching me closely.

"Not at all," I respond. "But I am a little surprised. Why would a hostess need to sign a nondisclosure agreement?" Of course, I know why, I just want to hear what she has to say.

"We have members whose privacy is extremely important to them, so our top priority is to protect that privacy. After you sign, I will go into more detail." She gives me a steady look. "At that point, you may choose to reconsider the job offer."

I raise my eyebrows. I wonder how many have "reconsidered" after discovering what type of establishment the Justice House really is.

"Fair enough."

"Good. So we'll move on to Lara Bruen's office, and let her notarize your signature."

Holly shuffles the papers back into the file, and as we walk across the room, I glance at the bar to see that another guy has joined blue eyes. They both watch our progress as we leave the beautiful dining room.

Lara Bruen's office is back the way Holly led me earlier on our way to my interview. As we make our way, we see several individuals who I assume are employees from the way they are dressed. They greet Holly and smile with friendly ease at me. Holly points out her office and Liam Justice's office catty-corner across the hall from hers. Two massive wooden doors bar entrance to his private domain, and I wonder when I'll get to meet the elusive Mr. Justice. I glance around and ponder which of the other doors might lead to the private club. The little bit of research I had time to read about sex clubs, suggests a main room for members to engage in sexual activities with each other. I shudder, hoping I never have to see any of that.

"Lara is our notary and records gal. She keeps all the membership files and health records current and up to date."

Health records?

"Sounds like an important job. How long has Lara worked here?"

"Ten years, and she's very adept at what she does." Holly smiles and knocks lightly against an open doorway.

"Hi, Lara." I follow Holly into the room. "This is Cait Shaw, she's our new hostess. Cait, this is Lara."

Lara, who looks to be in her fifties with soft graying

hair, glances up from her computer with a distracted smile. "Welcome, Cait. I hope you'll enjoy working here."

"Thank you, it's nice to meet you, Lara."

"We need to get Cait's signature on a few things," Holly says as she flips through her file and pulls out the NDA form, laying it on Lara's desk. Lara hands me a pen, and I glance over the agreement before signing. I guess it doesn't really matter, because regardless of what it says I'm signing it.

As Lara signs and does her official duties, Holly leads me to a smaller table in the room. We sit on damask covered chairs to go through the rest of the paperwork. This room follows much of the same décor as the other rooms I have seen with their dark gleaming woodwork but this one has paneled walls, deep, plush carpeting, and a high fresco painted ceiling. It is simply lovely.

I sneak a quick look at the tall antique file cabinets that line one wall. That's a lot of storage space. I imagine that Lara keeps a lot of member information on her computer too.

After signing all the new hire paperwork, we say goodbye to Lara, and Holly leads me to her office.

"Lara seems nice."

"She's a peach. We'll all have to go in for a drink after work soon."

"In?"

"It's a private joke, what we say when we're having drinks here at the nightclub, very handy." She grins.

Holly's office is larger than Lara's and has a fireplace with a gorgeous hand carved mantle. She also has a painted fresco ceiling but of a different design, more pastel colors.

She motions for me to sit in one of the chairs before her desk. "Would you like something to drink, iced tea?"

"No, thank you, I'm good."

"Well, what do you think so far?" Holly asks as she sits behind her desk.

I turn and let my eyes travel around the room again. So far, nothing is as I imagined it to be. There's nothing sleazy about any of this. Of course, there is a lot I haven't seen.

"I think this is one of the most beautiful buildings I have ever been in, and it will be heaven working here." The funny thing is I mostly mean it. The place is gorgeous, and the atmosphere seems upbeat. Everyone, I've seen or met, seems happy and friendly. Except maybe for Blue Eyes and he just seems… I shift uncomfortably in my seat.

"I'm glad to hear you say that because what I'm going to tell you about Justice House may… surprise you." I try for an interested expression. "The Justice, to a great extent, is extremely elite, but we pride ourselves on being more than an upscale club. We have a 5-star restaurant, a state of the art spa and fitness center. Our nightclub, while smaller than most around town, is extremely popular, and Liam has a highly coveted wine cellar. We offer many benefits that other clubs don't even think about offering."

Yeah, like kinky sex.

"Our members pay a yearly fee for all of these exclusive perks; therefore we cater to *all* of their needs." I wonder why she just doesn't say it. "Our upper floor consists of rooms equipped to meet the diverse needs of our members." She speaks slowly. "Each room is appointed a particular theme and—"

"The Justice is a sex club," I say bluntly, hoping she

doesn't think I figured it out too easily, but I just can't pretend any longer. I can only go so far on my acting skills.

She takes a moment, and I think she's nervous. "I don't want it to scare you away," she admits.

"Why are you afraid this will scare me away?"

"Cait, you just seem so young and..." She fans her hands out.

"I'm not that young, Holly, I'm twenty-four."

Her grin spreads across her face. "I know. Your birthdate's listed on your job application."

Which Valerie filled out.

"Holly, as long as I don't have to participate, I have no problem with what consenting adults do."

She gives a choked laugh. "No, your participation is not required. Your position as one of our hosts means you only deal with our members in the restaurant and nightclub. The Justice has strict rules separating floors." She smiles and I give her one back. "Do you have any questions?"

"Just one for now. How many members does The Justice have?"

She purses her lips. "Umm... around twenty-one hundred."

"You have two thousand freaking members?" I blurt.

She laughs at my reaction. "They don't all come to Justice House at the same time, Cait."

"I should hope not." My mind does a quick calculation. *Holy hell!* That's a lot of money coming into this place. I'm beginning to understand why Valerie is so interested in Mr. Liam Justice.

"A good number of our members are out of state and another healthy portion lives outside the country."

"Wow."

Holly laughs again. "Okay, I'll show you around, and we'll get your locker located." She pulls open a drawer, pulls out a set of keys and removes one, sliding it across the desk to me. "One thing we didn't discuss, was the fact you wrote on your application that you could begin work immediately."

"Yes."

"Tomorrow's not too soon?"

"No. I've already finished out my notice at The Carriage House."

"That's great because next week is going to be crazy around here. There's an Entertainment Expo happening, which will bring in out of town members," she says as we head out of her office to the hallway. "The rest of this week you'll train with Tansy while Joni and I continue covering the other shift. Joni is head of our waiting staff and, needless to say, she and I have our own duties, so we're more than ready for you to be able to take over your shift."

"Hostesses wear black and white. You can wear all black but not all white. Slacks are permissible, but Liam prefers dresses. If you need an advance to buy something to wear, that's not a problem."

"Thanks, but I wear a lot of black, so I'll be fine."

She glances at me. "I imagine you look good in black with all of that dark hair. You have beautiful hair, by the way."

I'm touched by her kind words. "Thank you." I wave my hand toward her. "You don't look so bad in black either." She grins at me, and I feel a little uncomfortable with the knowledge that a few weeks from now she will probably hate me. That's sad because I have a feeling that Holly and I could become good friends.

We head for the restaurant, with Holly pointing out the purpose of different rooms. We pass several members along the way, some dressed casually, some not so casually and some dressed in business apparel. Holly stops to speak to each of them and introduce me.

The dining room is busier at this time of day as servers bustle about seeing to the readiness of everything for the evening meal. Holly's telling me an amusing story as we move toward the bar. The smile slides right off my face though when I see the handsome blue-eyed man.

"Liam?" Holly says softly.

What? No. Freaking. Way!

He turns slowly on his bar stool, and I see a spark of surprise in those incredible blue eyes. What? Did he think I'd run when I learned what type of club the Justice House really is?

"I'd like to introduce our new hostess, Caitlyn Shaw. She goes by Cait."

We stop right in front of him, and he suddenly moves his long legs out on either side of mine. I'm not that close, but close enough that I am now standing between his legs. Nervous anyway at discovering that *he* is Liam Justice, I'm immediately overwhelmed by his scent and close proximity. I want to take a step back, but I can't seem to function. He stares at me with those intense blue eyes, and he doesn't look happy. I realize now what that little headshake meant earlier. He doesn't want me here.

"Caitlyn, I am Liam Justice." Whereas Holly's voice has only a hint of a southern drawl, this guy's voice is like slow, sweet molasses. He holds out his hand to me, and I just stare at it. I don't want to touch him. It might be hazardous to my state of mind. This guy just does something for me and standing this close to him...

He reaches out and grasps my hand, pulling me closer. My thigh brushes against his, and I jump. He grins at my discomfort, and I try to pull my hand free, but his hold tightens. "I am your new... master."

I give him a long blink, and he laughs outright. *Oh my...*

"Liam! Don't tease Cait," Holly scolds. "Ignore him, Cait."

"What?" He gives her a grin. "I am the master of Justice House." I tug my hand, but he's not letting go, and those blue eyes swing back to me, sliding over my body. I know my color has heightened at his inappropriate behavior because I feel my face heat.

"Leon," Holly calls, and the bartender steps over to us. I'm only aware of this from my peripheral vision as I can't seem to tear my gaze from the man that still grips my hand. Every feature on his face is perfect. A blend of masculine and sensual. He's lightly tanned and... just healthy looking. He also radiates a strength and power that's appealing but also a little intimidating.

He leans toward me as he gives a tug on my hand forcing me to take a step forward. "Do I make you nervous, Miss Shaw?" His voice is soft, sensual even.

With a will of its own, my gaze drops to his beautifully sculpted mouth, and I wonder how it would feel on mine.

Good grief, Cait! Get a grip. I can't remember ever being this attracted to a man. *No!* I am not attracted to him; he is the subject of my investigation. It's just... he is too damn good looking. With resolve, I take a step back and jerk my hand from his.

"No, Mr. Justice, you don't make me nervous."

One side of his mouth slowly lifts and then goes into a full-blown smile.

Oh hell – His smile takes my breath away, and I'm shocked to feel a tingling in my lower extremities. I wonder how many hearts he's broken with that smile.

He stands and steps close enough that I have to tip my head back to see his face, and his expression has me wanting to take another step back, but I stand firm.

Rule number one – don't let them intimidate you.

He reaches out to run his finger down my arm, taking hold of my hand again. I gasp softly at his audacity and the hot burn that trails down my arm.

"You are a very beautiful girl, Miss Shaw." His lopsided grin is lascivious as he raises my hand to his lips. I try to tug my hand away, knowing what he's about to do, but he clamps down with his fingers. His hot mouth moves over my knuckles, and it's all I can do to not pool into a puddle right at his feet.

I search blue eyes that bore into mine, trying to grasp what's going on here. I glance over at Holly, who's watching our exchange, her brow wrinkled with a frown.

My attention is suddenly drawn to a muscular dark haired guy as he walks into the bar area.

"Liam, I need to talk to you."

Liam at once drops my hand, taking a step back.

"Is it going to irritate me," he asks the big guy. I glance up to see his eyes on me once again.

"Probably."

Liam's eyes drop to my chest and then travel down my body. I'm startled when my nipples tighten, pushing hard against my bra. I quickly cross my arms over my chest before he can see how he affects me, but I catch his smirk. Okay. So he knows he has an effect on me.

He steps around me. "Okay, Mike let's talk." As he

walks by Holly, I hear him say, "She won't last two weeks." He walks on, and I glare at his back.

What was that? Was he testing me in some way?

Holly mutters softly under her breath, "Damn dominant male."

I glance at her, looking back to where Justice and the other man stand talking. "And here I thought he was just an arrogant ass."

Holy gasps, quickly looking at me. I uncomfortably realize I've just said my thoughts out loud. Holly and the bartender roar with laughter.

"Oh, Cait, you and I are going to get along just fine," she informs me as she struggles to compose herself. Liam turns to look at us, and this seems to set her off again.

The bartender chuckles and holds his hand out to me. "Hi, Cait, I'm Leon." I detect a slight foreign accent in his voice.

I return his friendly smile. "Hi, Leon."

"Cait is starting tomorrow, and she'll be working with Tansy the rest of the week," Holly says.

"Well, we're glad to have you. Welcome," Leon says, shaking my hand.

Mr. Liam Justice isn't pleased for me to be here, evidently. After the little stunt he just pulled, I would love to tell him to shove his job where the sun doesn't shine. I would too if I didn't want to continue working at Query Magazine.

"Leon will be a good source of help, Cait. He knows all the members."

"Anytime," he says, and I give him a grateful smile.

"I also have a directory with all the members' photos and specifics that you can take a look at," Holly adds.

"How about a drink ladies?" Leon asks.

"Maybe later, after work," Holly says.

"How about you, Ms. Cait?" He winks at me.

"Thanks, but I need to keep my wits about me."

"Okay," Holly says. "Let's take you around for the rest of the tour."

I call Valerie as soon as I return home, right after I pour a glass of wine.

"I'm in. Did you know they'd require me to sign an NDA?" I ask as soon as she answers.

"I knew they would hire you and yes, I imagined they would require you to sign an NDA. Don't worry about it, Caitlyn."

I snort softly.

"Did you meet Liam Justice?"

"Yes. You didn't tell me he was so young." Or so unbelievably beautiful. "He offers quite an employee benefits package."

"What do you think about the Justice House, Caitlyn?"

"The place is gorgeous and reeks of money. Did you know they have over two thousand members?"

"No, Caitlyn, I don't have privy to that type of information. That's why I have you there."

I roll my eyes. "Well, that figures out to a lot of kinky people."

"That figures out to a lot of zeros," Valerie adds. "Any idea where they keep their files?"

"Oh, yeah. It won't be easy getting a look, though. I noticed cameras in every room. Discreet, but there."

"You'll figure something out," Valerie says.

"I *will* have access to the member's directory which is

supposed to have photos and specifics. Maybe there will be enough information in the directory."

"We'll see."

I take a sip of wine. "I wish you'd tell me who I'm looking for." She doesn't say anything for a moment.

"Just familiarize yourself with the members and find me some info on Justice."

"Valerie, you do know they have private investigators for this type of thing."

"Yes, but why pay someone else when I have a perfectly good investigative reporter who's happy to do it. Just think of the great byline. Keep in touch," she says before hanging up.

Valerie Sharp gave me a job when no one else would even interview me. I never have figured that one out. I'm not a great reporter, but I am a good investigator. I'm tenacious, and I've even surprised myself at how resourceful I can be at getting the information I want. Now, Paul is a great reporter, an excellent writer. He can tell a story in a way that touches readers. We've been lucky that Valerie lets us work together, and some of our articles have been good. I owe Valerie, she and I both know it.

But I also know that Liam Justice is not why she has me at Justice House.

I eat a light supper and then call Paul to give him the lowdown.

"So how are things in the BDSM community?" he asks.

"I have no idea, and maybe you should be doing this story since you seem to know so much about the lifestyle."

He laughs. "Did you get the position?"

"Yes, and after talking to Val earlier, I now know there was never any doubt."

I hear Paul grunt. "What the hell's going on with this, Cait?"

"I don't know yet, but I do know it's not only about Liam Justice. How the hell did she get me hired?"

"She must have someone on the inside."

Holly?

"Holly Phillip's interviewed me, and I have a feeling it's because of her I was hired, and from the way Justice acted earlier, it wasn't with his blessing."

"Well, there you go."

"No, she said they've known each other a long time, and I'm sure they're from the same place, same southern accent."

"Well, I'm keeping an eye out at the office."

"Sounds good. Tell Julie I said hello. I'm going to bed."

"You be careful, and don't forget we're going out to dinner Thursday night."

"Okay, love you. Good night."

It's not so easy falling asleep; I toss and turn a bit. Why does Liam Justice think I won't last two weeks? And why does just thinking about him cause my libido to kick in? No man has ever caused a reaction in me as he does, and honestly, it's a little unsettling. He definitely intimidates me. He's so—naughty. I blush at my own thoughts of just how naughty Mr. Liam Justice could be. The man owns a sex club, I bet... *Forget it Cait!* I roll over and punch my pillow before settling back down. He's not my type.

A little voice deep down says, *Yeah, but he's the type you've always wanted.*

I fall asleep recalling the smile he gave me that almost melted my panties.

"Do I make you nervous, Miss Shaw?"

His warm breath caresses my ear as one large hand splays across my belly holding me tightly against his front. His other hand, wrapped around my throat, tips my head so it rests back against his chest. His hard erection presses against my lower back.

"Answer me!" he says sharply.

"No," I breathe.

His laugh is faintly sinister.

My knees nearly buckle when he brings his mouth to my neck, sucking and biting at my tender flesh.

"I want to do bad things to you," he murmurs, his voice raspy against my ear. I whimper in response.

He spins me around to face him, and I look up to see his eyes glowing with an unnatural blue brilliance. Delving his hands into my hair on either side of my head, he holds me in place as his mouth lowers to mine. He nips and sucks at my lips as his tongue makes its way in, skillfully exploring my mouth.

I gasp when he lifts me to the tabletop, setting me on the edge. "Back you go," he says as he pushes on my chest until I'm lying with my back resting on the table.

I'm naked, and I see my breasts quiver with every struggling breath I take.

He leans over me, and I want to touch his face but discover my hands tied, stretched across the table above my head.

"Now for your legs," he growls. "I'm going to spread

them, open you wide and see how much of me you can take."

I sit straight up in bed, my heart pounding, my body slick with sweat.

A sex dream with Liam Justice?

"Fuck!"

I fall straight back onto the mattress.

CHAPTER THREE

I'VE SWATTED THE SNOOZE BUTTON one time too many by the time I pull myself out of bed, and I have to hurry so I won't be late.

I rush to the shower, and now I'm studying my reflection in the full-length mirror that sits in my bedroom. My eyes are a deep chocolate brown, and I've been told they are very expressive. Right now, they just look tired, and it feels as if there is sand under my lids. My waist length hair is that dark brown that looks almost black, and I'm lucky that it's always looked thick and healthy, but of course today of all days, it just looks unruly. I finally decide to put it in a side braid hanging down over my shoulder.

Holly said Liam preferred his hostesses to wear dresses, so out of some perverse need to needle him, I'm wearing black slacks and a black V-necked sweater. I apply my makeup, and I'm just slipping into my heels when I hear my cab driver's horn.

As instructed by Holly, I have the driver let me out at the back entrance. Justice House sits on a large corner lot completely enclosed by a tall wrought iron fence. There's a large closed gate barring access to the driveway, which circles around the back of the house to allow guests to disembark from their vehicles, under the large columned Porte cochere. The driveway also forks off toward a five-car garage that sits a short distance from the main residence.

I, however, enter through a smaller gate, using the keycard Holly gave me to gain access. I look around as I head toward the back entrance. This view of the imposing estate is just as impressive as the front. I notice there's no one about as I enter and then hurry to the restaurant. I discover why as soon as I enter the dining room. Dozens of faces turn to look at me and I hesitate, seeing Liam Justice. I haven't let myself think about my dream, but seeing him now, I blush recalling every detail.

"You're late, Miss Shaw," he drawls.

I know I'm not, but I keep silent as I head for the young woman who is standing, waving to me. I smile gratefully, sitting in the chair she's saved for me.

"Hi, Cait, I'm Tansy," she whispers.

Lara, sitting at the next table smiles a greeting, and I give a quick look around but don't see Holly. Several of the men in the room turn to look at me, interest in their eyes. I feel like the new girl in school all over again.

"In case you didn't meet her yesterday,"—Liam gestures toward me—"Miss Shaw is our new hostess for the restaurant." Several people smile and nod a greeting to me.

"As I was saying—" Liam flicks a quick look my way. He's standing a short distance away from the tables where most of the employees sit. He's dressed in sweats and a sleeveless T-shirt. The T-shirt looks a little damp as if he exercised before the meeting. His hair is sexy-messy, and he has the shadow of scruff on his jaw. I don't think I've ever seen a more alluring man. "Next week is upon us, and the rest of this week, I want everyone to pay close attention to what needs to be done. If you see something out of place—put it where it goes. If you see anything that needs attention—act on it. If you can't fix the problem tell me, Holly or Mike."

Liam nods toward the muscular guy he spoke to yesterday in the bar. The big guy stands leaning against the wall near the hallway that leads to the kitchen. The chef, who I also met yesterday, stands beside him. I glance over and catch the eye of Leon, who leans against the bar counter. He grins, and I give him a smile. I quickly look back to see Liam frowning at me.

Why?

He looks away, sending his gaze around the room, before continuing. "Y'all may be asked to do something outside of your normal duties, but it will only be for a short time."

A slim, dark-skinned man sitting across from me calls out. "So, if I'm asked to clean the toilet, does that mean I get extra pay?"

"No, it means you don't get fired," Liam shoots right back.

Everyone laughs. Liam smiles, and I think I hear the sigh of every woman in that dining room. That smile is truly devastating.

"Y'all know I give quarterly bonuses, you will get your recompense then."

Tansy looks at me and wiggles her eyebrows.

So Liam Justice gives bonuses, cares enough to give excellent employee benefits, and if this meeting is any indication, his employees like him. I look around the room and observe how everyone is relaxed and seems happy to be here. I shift uncomfortably. I don't like this feeling that I'm experiencing like I'm a sneak doing something wrong.

"Okay." Liam claps his hands together. "We do our best, and our guests next week will receive the best possible experience the Justice House has to offer."

"Not any different than any other day at the Justice," Tansy whispers.

I look back at Liam as he stands with his legs braced apart, arms crossed over his chest. The meeting allows me the freedom to check him out, and I watch as he listens attentively to the big guy Mike and the chef as they discuss a problem. Without warning, as if he senses me watching him, those deep blue eyes connect with mine. I drop my gaze immediately, feeling my cheeks heat. I need to quit drooling over Mr. Gorgeous and pay attention to what's going on around me.

In a bid to get back on track, I ask Tansy about the muscular Mike holding up the wall.

"Mike Bowen, he's head of security. He and Mr. Justice went to the same school and started Justice House together," she says quietly.

That's interesting. Another childhood friend.

"Okay," Liam says. "If y'all have nothing else for me, let's all get to work. I have a meeting."

"If it's with one of your toy distributors, I'd be happy to help you out with that."

Toy distributor?

The whole room erupts in laughter. Heads turn to look toward the back of the room. I look too and see a tall, thin guy with flaming red hair. He's standing with his hands stuffed in his front pockets and a sheepish grin on his freckled face.

"Well now, Barry, I'd take you up on that offer,

but I do believe you'd embarrass me in front of my distributors." Another ripple of laughter sounds around the room, and Liam smiles good-naturedly. His gaze slides to mine, holding it for a moment before sliding on to his friend Mike. "And my distributors don't like drool on their samples."

Mike looks like he chokes, and I almost choke right along with him realizing they are talking about *sex toys*. The laughter is almost deafening. Liam is laughing, and I sit there like an idiot staring at the handsomest man I have ever seen. My heartbeat quickens, and I swallow with difficulty.

Oh, hell.

"Okay, okay." Liam, still chuckling, holds up his hands in a bid for silence. "Y'all are going to cause me to make a new house rule,"—there is an immediate chorus of exaggerated groans around the room—"no morning meetings lasting over thirty minutes." He smiles. "Go to work."

Everyone seems to rise at once, slowly heading for their duties. I notice a woman stop to talk to Liam, leaning into him. She's blonde, beautiful and looks like she could be a Victoria Secret's model. She's wearing a skintight dress that plainly shows she's not wearing any underwear.

"That's Miranda, she's got the hots for Liam, but it doesn't do her any good," Tansy says.

I turn my attention to her. "Why's that?"

"He doesn't date employees."

I look back at the couple. "Oh."

"Tansy Lewis." I turn back to the pretty brunette.

"Cait Shaw. Pleased to meet you, Tansy." I take her proffered hand.

"Would you like to meet the servers?"

"I would."

As we maneuver around the tables and other employees, a couple of the men stop us to introduce themselves, blatantly checking me out. When we get close to Liam and the blonde, Liam looks up, nailing me with those dark blue eyes.

"Miss Shaw, a moment, please."

The blonde turns, looking completely annoyed.

Sorry honey, but there's no need to get your nonexistent panties in a wad. He's probably just going to use his "moment" to fire me for being late, even though, I wasn't.

The blonde flips her head back around, blond hair flying.

"I'll come back in a few minutes, Cait," Tansy says.

Liam says something to the blonde, and she flounces off. Then he looks at me and crooks his finger in a come here motion. I take tentative steps toward him.

"Follow me, please."

I do, and just as we reach the entrance to the restaurant, Mike calls to him.

"Wait here, please." His eyes flick momentarily to mine before he turns and follows Mike from the room.

Okay.

I glance around and see Leon at the bar. I decide to visit with him while I wait.

"Hi, Leon." I sit on one of the stools as he looks up from slicing limes.

"Young Cait, how are you this fine day?"

"I'm great. How about yourself?"

He smiles. "I am always good." He does seem like a happy person, always smiling. He's a slim man, dark complected, with a head full of shiny black curls. I guesstimate he's in his late thirties.

"Where are you from, Leon, you have a pleasant accent."

He beams at me. "I come from a village in Greece called Portaria."

"Greece! Why are you here?" I blush realizing how rude that sounds. "I'm sorry, that came out wrong."

Leon laughs. "No worry. I frequently ask myself that question." He sets the sliced limes aside and wipes the counter. "I came to America with my parents when I was sixteen. I will go home someday but..." He shrugs.

"I would love to visit Greece. It's number one on my to-do list."

"I knew there was something special about you." His grin is infectious.

"How long have you worked here, at Justice House?"

"Almost ten years. Liam is a good boss."

"How long here in Chicago?"

"Twenty-two years. My parents and I settled, in Greektown."

"I've never been to Greektown." He looks at me as if I've just uttered something sacrilegious. "But I've always wanted to go," I hurriedly add.

"Miss Shaw, do you have a problem with following directions?"

I turn on my stool to look up into eyes that are as deep a blue as any picture I've ever seen of the Mediterranean Sea. "No. I was just—"

"I know what you were doing," he says tersely. "Let's go." He grips my arm, practically pulling me off the stool.

I give a startled glance at Leon. "I'll talk to you later, Leon."

Liam releases my arm as we step into the hallway, and I have to walk very quickly to keep up with his long-legged strides.

Damn it, he is going to fire me!

Reaching his office, he opens one of the double doors to allow me to precede him. Before entering, I glance anxiously at Holly's closed door, curious where she is this morning. Is he using her absence as a chance to get rid of me?

Liam's office is no different from the rest of Justice House with the décor being Rococo, but this room is decidedly masculine. His ceiling is done in fresco the same as Holly and Lara's, but where their ceilings are painted patterns, Mr. Justice has angels floating around on fluffy white clouds.

"Miss Shaw." His deep voice draws my attention from his ceiling. He's leaning against the front of a massive wooden desk, arms crossed over his chest with his long legs braced apart in front of him. Sexy as hell. His incredible blue eyes are watching me intently, and I nervously lick my lips. "I have a very busy schedule this morning, so I'll be brief."

I blink at him. Here it comes, I'm toast; Valarie is going to have a fit.

"You are a very beautiful young woman, Miss Shaw." My heart rate escalates. He sees me as a woman today whereas yesterday I was just a girl to him. His next words crush the exhilarating notion that he finds me attractive. "But I do believe you will be nothing but trouble here."

"Excuse me?" I bristle at his words.

"I observed you flirting with some of the men after the meeting." His slow drawl is accusatory.

What? I huff a breath. "Flirting with some of the men? They introduced themselves to me."

He gives me a condescending smile, which sets my teeth on edge. "Let's not ignore the little scene I just witnessed between you and Mr. Kallis." At my frown, he clarifies. "The head bartender, Leon."

I'm shocked at his ridiculous accusation. "We were just talking."

"You weren't coming on to him, angling for an invite?" His words hold a measure of disbelief.

"No!"

He regards me, his eyes speculative. "The fact is, Miss Shaw, you are a tad too young for this job. I don't think you have the experience or finesse to deal with our clientele."

Oh, forever more!

"Mr. Justice—I am fully capable of doing my job." I feel my body tense with anger, and I take a deep breath to calm myself as he stares impassively at me.

"Sorry, you simply look too young and innocent."

"Well, I'm not!" I snap. He raises an eyebrow. At my blush, he smirks.

"I'm afraid that some of our members might be tempted to—take advantage of that fact, Miss Shaw. In addition, with what I saw earlier... well, most of our members are wealthy. What you might consider a good catch."

I stare at him dumbfounded. He's accusing me of—I cross my arms over my chest, and I watch his eyes slide to my cleavage, which pushes up with my movement. I quickly unfold my arms.

He smirks again as if to say, "See, you won't be able to deal with the attention male members might give you."

My eyes narrow at him. I wish he weren't so good looking.

"One moment you're accusing me of blatantly flirting, trying to trap me a rich man, and the next moment you've decided I'm too young and—innocent. I am not innocent!" I want to stamp my foot, but I manage to refrain myself.

He at once pushes away from his desk, sauntering toward me. I swallow deeply. *Why does he have to be so freaking hot?* His nearness causes all kinds of reaction in my body. My stomach clenches, my breathing becomes hitched, and a tight tingling sensation moves across my skin. When he circles behind me, I bite my lip and squeeze my eyes closed, breathing in his incredible scent. He's close enough to my back that I can feel the heat of his body, and I'm annoyed when my nipples tighten. Right at my ear, his drawl more pronounced, he softly asks, "Is that in all things, Miss Shaw?"

My eyes fly open, every nerve ending in my body instantly sizzling. I can't imagine he doesn't feel it sparking off my body. Taking into consideration what he does for a living, his question takes on a whole new meaning, and I feel my face suffuse with heat.

He chuckles softly and moves to stand in front of me. When he laughs outright, my anger spikes again.

"Are you going to fire me?" I demand. If he's going to, I want him to get it over with. I'm ready to leave this room and his overwhelming presence.

He tilts his head as if he's considering my words, and I become increasingly uncomfortable under that stare. He breathes in deeply. "Not yet." He steps around me, moving to his desk and sits in the chair behind it. Resting an elbow on the chair arm, he strokes his chin with his long fingers as he stares at me. If he's not going to fire me then—what? I squirm uncomfortably under his penetrating gaze.

"You may go now," he finally says, and I inwardly growl at his insolence as I head for the door.

"Miss Shaw."

Oh no! Just when I thought I was getting away. My hand grips the doorknob as I turn around slowly.

"No more slacks. I'm making a new house rule, dresses only." He holds my gaze steadily. I shake my head in irritation and hurry out.

Out in the hallway, my heart is pounding as I lean against his closed office door. That had to be the most uncomfortable—I sigh heavily. This is not good. I am attracted to Liam Justice, unlike anything I have ever experienced. Which is totally crazy since he's like some kind of sex lord and probably has dozens of women in his life. He's so out of my league, not to mention I'm supposed to be investigating him.

I see Holly's door still closed as I hurry back to the restaurant to find Tansy.

The rest of the morning goes quickly as Tansy explains our duties, showing me the ins and outs of the job. I think she's shown me every storage room on the first floor, explaining our inventory and ordering responsibilities.

"We'll alternate shifts every other day. And you don't have to worry about coming in for the morning meeting when you pull the evening shift," Tansy says as we take a seat in the break room. "You didn't get into trouble for being late did you?" she asks quietly.

"No." I think she wants me to share why Justice

wanted to speak to me, but I'm not about to try to explain that. "I guess Holly forgot to tell me I needed to come in early. Is she off today?"

"No, she called to say something came up and she wouldn't be in until later. She's been working a lot of hours since Mel left."

"Mel?"

"Melanie Langford, you're filling the position she held. She just up and quit, no notice, which clearly put us in a bind." Tansy looks at her watch. "We'll go over the reservation procedures for the restaurant and nightclub after lunch. Right now we've got a few minutes, so let's go check in with the servers."

Lunchtime at Justice House is busy. Evidently the restaurant is popular with the members, and I ask Tansy about each one. She has a world of knowledge on each of them, and she thinks nothing of me asking questions.

I don't see Liam again during my shift, and at the end of the day on my way to get my bag from my locker, Leon calls to me as I pass by the bar.

"Young Cait, sit and tell me how your day went." I perch on a bar stool and smile at the friendly bartender. "What can I get you to drink?"

"I'd love a glass of white wine, please."

When he brings my wine, he asks, "Did you enjoy your first day?"

"I did, it was interesting. How was your day?"

He smiles as he plops strawberries into a mixer. "My days are always good, young Cait. I wouldn't have it any other way."

I take a sip of wine. Mmmm, this is not boxed wine. "This is an excellent wine."

"Only the best for Justice House," he replies as he pours his strawberry concoction into tall glasses.

"Do you live here at the bar?" I tease as I lean back, the wine helping me relax.

He grins. "Long hours keep me out of trouble."

"Uh-oh, were you a bad boy growing up, Leon?"

He laughs out loud as he sets the glasses on the counter. "I admit I gave my sweet Mama some sleepless nights." He looks over at a couple of club members who walk in and sit down at the bar. "Excuse me." He crosses to the other side to take their drink order.

I'm discreetly studying the members when a man sits on the stool right beside me.

"What's a beautiful girl like you doing in a place like this?"

I try not to smile at the corny pick-up line. "Does that actually work?" I ask as I slowly turn his way. *Oh! He's cute.* Longish blond hair, pretty blue-gray eyes, not as devastating as deep blue but…

"No, but once they look at me, I can usually reel them in." He gives me a roguish smile.

I laugh. "So, you're a good fisherman?"

His eyes glow with amusement. "I manage to catch a minnow or two every now and then." I giggle. "Now that's a pretty laugh."

"Mr. Bryce, no flirting with Ms. Caitlyn! She's new and doesn't know about you," Leon scolds as he returns.

"Now, Leon, I'm trying to remedy that. No one appreciates a new member like I do."

I sputter into my glass of wine. "I'm not a member!"

"No, she is not." A deep voice announces. "She's our new hostess, and I'd appreciate it if you didn't try to pick her up with your lame ass come-ons."

I swivel on my stool, meeting bright blue eyes. His hair looks as if he's run his fingers repeatedly through it, which just adds to his sexiness. Dark stubble on his jawline has me yearning to lean in and run my tongue along that jaw. *Is it soft?* The sleeves of his white dress shirt, rolled to his elbows, expose strong forearms. His tie is loose at the knot, and the top two buttons of his shirt are undone. He's wearing a silver chain that I noticed before, and I can almost see the shape of a medallion under his shirt. I chew my lip as I look him over, he is simply gorgeous, and he smells divine.

"Hey man!" The guy next to me says as he stands, and the two embrace briefly, slapping each other on the back. Then Liam laughs. A full rich laugh, his white teeth gleaming, eyes crinkling at the corners.

I swallow convulsively. *Oh, shit.*

"When did you get here?" Liam asks.

"Just now," Mr. Flirt says, looking at me. "And look what I found." He reaches over and fingers the end of my braid.

"Bryce." There's a note of warning in Liam's voice, and his friend turns back to face him.

"What?"

Liam sighs.

I decide to introduce myself since Justice doesn't seem inclined. "Hi, Bryce, I'm Cait." I give him a little wave, and he grasps my hand pulling it to his lips. I giggle nervously, glancing at Liam, and feel a blush steal over my face when I find him watching me.

"Look at that blush!" Bryce grins.

I see Liam shake his head, and then he glances down at my hand wrapped around my wine glass. "Miss Shaw,

I hope you're not planning to drive after you've been drinking."

My mouth opens slightly in surprise.

"Liam, she has more sense than that."

Yeah! I raise my eyebrow at Liam, and his eyes narrow.

Bryce reaches over to grasp my hand again. "I'm driving her home."

I glance quickly back at Liam. Great—next he'll be accusing me of scheming to trap his friend.

"Sorry, Bryce, there's something I need you to take care of for me. I'll drive Miss Shaw home."

What? I don't want him driving me home. The thought of being alone in a car with him has my stomach muscles clenching tightly. "No!"

Liam raises his eyebrows. "Excuse me?"

I know I don't imagine the hard glint his eyes take on, and I'm immediately intimidated. Well, *more* intimidated by the man.

"I-I mean, I've already called a cab and—"

"We'll dismiss the cab on our way out. Wait here please; I'll just be a moment." He turns to leave, and I look at Bryce, who seems puzzled.

"Bryce," Liam calls, turning to give his friend a look. "Coming?"

Bryce hesitates briefly, eyeing me. "Sure thing buddy." A slow smile moves over his face. "Cait, it was great to meet you." He starts to follow Liam and then turns back. "I'll take a rain check on driving you home."

I catch the frown Liam throws over his shoulder.

"Sure," I say softly.

As soon as they round the corner, I'm sliding off the stool and grabbing up my bag. "What do I owe you, Leon?"

"Nothing." When I start to object, he waves a hand. "No charge to employees."

Wow. Okay. "Thanks, I'll see you tomorrow. Please tell Mr. Justice I just remembered I have to be somewhere."

I hurry out, saying a prayer that my cab is still waiting.

CHAPTER FOUR

THE NEXT TWO DAYS AT the Justice House are extremely busy. Tansy keeps apologizing for the fact that I have to learn two weeks of training in four days. What she doesn't realize is that I have the ability to remember everything she tells me.

During lunch, I become familiar with the various members who eat at the Justice House restaurant, and it seems that some dine with us on a daily basis. It's interesting what some members request of the hostess. Anything from calling a cab for them, to calling and making an appointment for their dog at the groomer. Tansy seems to take it all in stride, though.

During our lunch break, after the dining room closes, I devour the information in the member directory. Afterward, Tansy takes me around to meet more of the house staff. Of course, when I work the evening shift, there's a new group of members and staff to meet and remember.

I get to know Bryce Fletcher better too. He frequently shows up wherever Tansy and I happen to be. Tansy informs me he's a huge flirt, but he's not so much flirting as he is prying for information. I recognize the techniques. He also seems to throw Liam's name about frequently.

Liam.

I can't get him out of my head. It's getting so bad, I can now sense when he's near, even before I see him. My body actually responds to his nearness. My heart rate increases, and I feel a tightening low in my belly. When he's close enough for me to pick up his delectable scent, my breathing becomes shallow, and it's difficult to catch a breath. I've even considered that I might be allergic to him, and I'm just having a reaction. I almost wish that were the case, but I know it's not. No, it's much more worrisome than that. I catch myself looking and listening for him. And I'm not the only one. When he walks into a room, every female within sight zeroes in on him. Club member and employee alike, they all suddenly seem to need his time and attention. He's charming and charismatic, and I'm sure he is the topic of many fantasies. I know he stars in my dreams, and that's beginning to freaking annoy me.

And he watches me. It's unnerving. He's not spoken to me since my first day when he offered to take me home after work. I am somewhat ashamed that I acted like such a coward. In all honesty, I am a little frightened of him.

I've only ever been with one man. We dated for three years, and I went to bed with Jeff because he pressured me. I thought having sex would bring me the type of relationship that I read about in books. I was young and naïve, and I wanted to be swept away by a lover who could satisfy all my yearnings. Someone who was adventurous and sexually enthralling. That someone was never Jeff. I knew it was a mistake the first time, but I kept hoping that my affection for him would grow into something more, but there was never any excitement with Jeff. I finally admitted to myself that I wanted—*needed* more, and I ended the relationship. The problem is—I've never felt that sexual attraction that I've heard so much about. Until now.

Until Liam Justice.

And that's messed up in so many ways because I'm here to do a job, not fantasize about a man who probably sleeps with a different woman every night. Even though Valerie says she wants information about Liam's past, I know she's looking for someone else. But that doesn't excuse my lusting after Liam.

So, I need to stop.

At the end of my shift on Thursday, I tell Tansy goodbye and decline Leon's offer of a drink as I hurry to my locker.

"Hey, Cait, how's it going?"

"Hi, Holly." I give her a bright smile as I retrieve my bag. "It's going great."

"I hear good things about you from the members."

It's crazy, under the circumstances, but I'm more than pleased to hear that people like me.

"I really like working here," I tell her, knowing it's the truth. She falls in beside me, and we walk down the hallway to the rear entrance.

"How about having a drink tomorrow night after your shift ends? We can stay here; it'll give you a chance to actually check out the nightclub."

So far, my only exposure to the club has been making reservations during the day and then checking members off the list as they arrive for an evening out at the trendy nightspot. Holly told me the nightclub, In Justice, was one of the city's busiest, and she wasn't kidding if the requests for reservations are any indication. Members are allowed to invite non-member guests to dine in the restaurant or join them in the nightclub but other than that, the rest of Justice House is off limits to non-members.

"That sounds like fun."

"Good. Tansy and maybe Lara are going too."

"I need a girl's night out."

"Me too," she says. "It's been a long week."

I slow my pace as we walk by the glass wall of the weight/gym room, making note of the members using the facilities. I'm now concentrating on learning the member's habits and routines.

"Tansy is amazed how quickly you've caught on with everything being dumped on you all at once," Holly says as we continue down the hall.

"I have a good memory, and I know that with the week coming up, I need to be ready."

"And I am very grateful for that."

I want to ask her if Liam is grateful or if he still wants me gone.

"Well, have a good night," she says as we reach the door. I can see my taxi waiting beyond the fence by the curb.

"You too, Holly. See you tomorrow."

I hurry out walking down the driveway to exit through the open gates, pulling my hair down from the casual up-do I've worn all day. I'm startled and falter when I look up and see Liam and Mike standing near the small guardhouse located just inside the gates. Mike is talking to the security guard Aaron while Liam listens, arms crossed over his chest.

He looks good. I lick my lips. Liam always looks good. He's wearing jeans that fit in a way that makes my stomach all flippy-floppy. His white V-necked T-shirt clings to every plain and ridge of his muscled torso with his biceps straining against the fabric of his sleeves. His amazing eyes are hidden behind sunglasses, so I can't see if he's looking at me—but I know he is.

"Night, Cait," Aaron calls to me. I tear my gaze from Liam.

"Night," my voice sounds breathy. I wonder if I'll ever get used to Liam's beauty so I can stop acting like an idiot anytime he's near.

Just at the moment I walk past them, Chicago's famous wind decides to blow up my dress and whirl my long hair all crazy. I give a little yelp as I know the three men get a clear view of my ass since I'm wearing a thong. I'm not certain but possibly the cab driver too, when I turn to stop flashing the three men, and just as quickly turn back, realizing the cabbie is probably getting an eyeful. I frantically try to hold my dress down with one hand and catch as much of my hair as possible with the other. I finally manage to re-instate my dignity and glance at Liam, catching his wide grin. I feel as if I blush beet red. Holding onto my skirt and hair, I scurry to my cab.

My cell starts ringing just as I'm unlocking my apartment door.

Damn it. I don't have time for her right now. "Hi, Valerie."

"Caitlyn, what have you found?"

I roll my eyes. "No more than yesterday when you called."

"I'm calling to let you know I'm going to be out of the country for a few days. I want you to stay on course with your assignment, and I'll call as soon as I'm back."

I frown. "A few days?"

"Possibly a week. You won't be able to reach me, but I will be checking in daily with Pat." I can tell she's moving around with the way her voice keeps fading in and out. "If something comes up call Pat, and let her know."

I shake my head in frustration. "Valerie, how am I going to know if something—comes up?" She really needs to clue me in here.

"Caitlyn, I'm boarding the plane now, so I need to go."

I stare dumbfounded at my cell after she hangs up.

"This is ridiculous," I mutter as I head for the shower.

I'm meeting Paul and Julie for drinks, and then we're meeting up with Paul's parents who are in town. We have plans to dine at the *Alinea*, one of my favorite restaurants. It's going to be a fun evening.

I put the finishing touch to my makeup and then stand back to check my dress. I'm wearing my red Asian silk, which I love and save for special occasions. I have a bit of an exotic look to me with my long hair and dark, almond-shaped eyes. My great-grandmother was pure Hawaiian, and I inherited a touch of her native look, so the dress suits me. The hem falls just below my knees with the skirt split up one side revealing quite a bit of thigh.

I'm so glad I've started paddleboarding again as it works wonders for my legs and ass. Apparently, that's a good thing if I'm going to be flashing people I work with. My stomach flutters with nerves at the thought of Liam looking at me. Did he like what he saw? I silently scold myself and finish with my preparations for the evening.

I've opted to leave my dark hair hanging down my back. Black strappy heels, large hoop earrings, and I'm ready.

I enter the trendy little lounge bar where I'm meeting my friends. It's already crowded, and it takes me a moment before I see Paul at the bar. Unnoticed, I walk up behind him. The guy next to Paul turns and checks me out and then gives me a cheeky grin. I ignore him, stepping up close to Paul's back.

In a teasing mood, I ask in my best seductive voice, "Would you like to buy me a drink, handsome?"

Evidently, men on the make can hear a woman's come on, even in a crowded bar. More than one turns to give me an appraising look.

Paul's grinning as he turns. "There you are," he says, handing me a glass of white wine. "You look nice."

"Thanks." I take a sip, glancing around the bar. "Where's Jules?"

"Defending our table. We're lucky we found one. Follow me."

Paul shoulders his way through the group waiting to order drinks as I follow close behind. Within a few steps, I feel the hair on my nape stand on end. I glance behind me and catch several men looking at my ass. Geez!

Julie sits at a table not too far away, thank goodness since it appears we'll have to get our own drinks from the bar. She stands to give me a hug.

"You look beautiful, Cait."

"Thank you, you do too." And she does. Julie has beautiful dark red hair, and the sapphire blue dress she is wearing compliments her vibrant coloring to perfection.

"I can say without a doubt that I am sitting with the two most beautiful women in this place," Paul declares as he leans over to give Julie a quick kiss. He then whispers something in her ear that has her blushing a deep red color that rivals her hair. Her laugh is low and sultry.

"You're insatiable," she says.

I watch the two of them. I want that. Not with Paul, he's my best friend, and I've never had a romantic thought about him. I want my own man. I know I'm only twenty-four, but I feel a loneliness that at times makes me sad that I don't have someone to share special moments with. I seldom meet anyone I even want to date. Except for—I shake myself mentally and polish off my wine.

"Are there any waitresses working?" I ask, my eyes searching the area. I spot a young woman working the tables on the other side of the room.

"That was fast," Paul says, nodding at my empty glass. "Hard day?"

"Not too bad, just busy." I lean into the table. "I love your parents, Paul, you know that, but I almost wish we were going somewhere we could drink and dance."

"Me too!" Julie declares. "It's just one of those nights."

"It is, isn't it?" I agree.

Paul shakes his head. "If Julie and I didn't have to get up early in the morning, I'd say let's go out after we eat, but we have a long day planned with my folks."

We're interrupted as a waitress stops to set drinks down at our table. "Here you go," she says. The three of us look at the fresh drinks. "Compliments of the gentleman at the bar."

"Who?" I ask automatically looking toward the bar, then back to her. She just smiles and then hurries on to the next table.

Paul holds up his beer. "Don't look a gift horse in the mouth."

I hold my drink up to clink against his and Julie's as I glance around the room. I carefully scan the people standing at the bar.

Holy Shit!

I almost drop my glass when my eyes connect with sultry blue. He boldly holds my gaze, even though the statuesque blonde next to him leans in close to whisper in his ear. He looks—No man should be that good looking.

"Liam Justice."

"What?" Julie asks, following the direction I'm looking. "Where?"

"Far end, on the right."

"Who?" Paul asks.

"Oh, my…" Julie sounds stunned.

"Who?" Paul demands.

"Cait's, new boss," Julie answers as if she's annoyed to be distracted from her focus.

I break eye contact, a little stunned myself. *What is he doing here?* I turn to face Julie. She gives me a wide-eyed blink.

"So, that's Liam Justice. He doesn't look so special," Paul mutters.

Julie and I smile at each other and then burst out laughing. Paul playfully sticks out his lower lip.

"Oh, baby," Julie croons, leans in close and rubs his shoulder.

Paul says something, but I've tuned them out. *What the hell is Justice doing here?* I desperately want to turn and look at him; I can feel him watching me. Is he with that woman? *Of course, he is.* I don't recall seeing her at Justice House. She's probably into the same type of kinky sex as he is. Not, for the first time I wonder if it goes beyond kink. Some of the stuff I read on the internet—I shudder.

"Earth to Cait," Paul quips.

"What? I'm sorry."

Julie grins knowingly.

"I asked if you ladies are ready to leave. It may take us a bit to get to the restaurant."

Julie stands. "We'll go freshen up first. Cait," she says and jerks her head, handing me my clutch bag.

As we head for the bathroom, I look back toward the bar. He's gone. So is the blonde. I look around, my body still buzzing with the feeling of him watching me.

"Oh. My. Gosh!" Julie grabs my arm as soon as we enter the bathroom. "He's gorgeous!"

I sigh deeply. "You ought to hear him talk." She lifts an eyebrow. "Slow, southern sexy."

"Ahhh... the kind of voice that can melt a girl's panties right off," she says.

I nod, taking my lipstick from my bag.

"The way he was staring at you... What's going on with him, Cait?"

I blot my lips with a tissue. "Trust me, there's nothing going on."

"Why was he looking at you like that?"

"I don't know." I rub the center of my forehead. Why *does* he look at me like that? I turn to her. "He stares at me like that at work."

She grins. "He does?"

"There's no need to grin like that." I move toward the door. "I think he wants to fire me."

She snorts. "He wants to do something to you all right."

I shake my head. "He chewed me out my first day and told me I was too young and—inexperienced to work there." I bite my lip recalling his question regarding my innocence.

"I guess getting together with him would be a little awkward with you investi—"

I quickly shake my head, holding my finger to my lips as Julie slaps her hand over her mouth. I give a quick scan of the bathroom stalls.

"Sorry," she mouths as I turn back to her.

"It's okay. We'd better get back out there."

As we leave the bar, I keep searching for Liam. I know he's left though because I no longer feel that little tingle of awareness in my body that he inspires. I actually feel despondent, which is silly, and I scold myself. Yeah, no reason to be down about being attracted to the man I'm supposedly investigating. I sigh. Why do I have to be so attracted to him?

CHAPTER FIVE

"UGH, MY FEET ARE KILLING me," I moan as Tansy, and I sit at one of the dining room tables. The restaurant has closed, and we're sharing a sandwich, finalizing our shift report. I kick off the heels I should not have worn to work no matter how good they look with my dress. I wasn't sure what to wear since we have plans to hit the nightclub after our shift ends. I settled on a very short black tank dress with an overlay of black lace that supplies sleeves and a little extra length at the hem but still shows plenty of leg. Hence the need for killer heels.

"You did not give me adequate warning about Friday nights."

She laughs. "Wait until next week, both shifts will be crazy." She glances at me. "Don't be nervous, remember I'll be in early and stay late."

"I hate that you have to do that."

She shrugs. "Just goes with the job."

I nod, pushing down the guilt I feel at the deception I'm carrying on here. I'm starting to think of it as nothing short of dishonesty. And that's not sitting well with me. I like the people I'm working with, and I have to admit, it bothers me to deceive them.

A couple stops in the doorway of the restaurant, and I slip my shoe's back on.

"I'll go," Tansy offers.

"No, I've got them." I cross the room conscious of the man watching me.

"Mr. and Mrs. Grant," I say in greeting. "I have the table for four you requested. If you'll follow me, please." Seeing that they are alone, I ask, "Do we need to wait for the rest of your party?"

"No. Phyllis and Ron will be along shortly," Mr. Grant informs me.

"Very well. This way, please."

I smile at Leon as we pass the bar on our way to the nightclub's outer room. Once there, I turn them over to the attendant who will seat them in the nightclub. Holly explained the reason for the formality of us escorting members and keeping track of who goes into the nightclub. Liam evidently, runs a tight ship, making sure that the rules and regulations of Justice House are fully adhered to. Apparently, he insists on knowing the location of any member at any given moment while they are in the mansion. There is an outside entrance to the nightclub, and all members and their guests go through the check-in process at that door too.

"Have a lovely evening." I give Mr. Grant a weak smile when he winks.

"I'm ready for a drink," Tansy says as I return to my seat.

"Me too. Who might Ron and Phyllis be?"

"The Eldridge's." I frown still not recalling the members. "Holly might not have their specs in the book yet, they're new." She leans a little closer and whispers, "He's the one from earlier who said you had a nice ass."

"Oh! That guy."

"Yeah, a real charmer."

"Besides being rude, that was really crass of him to say it in front of his wife."

"I don't think she minded." Tansy has her head down, but I see her smirk.

"What?"

"They're swingers," she whispers.

Okay. I don't want to think too much on that. "The Grants too?"

"Yep."

I study her for a moment. "You certainly know a lot of information about the members that's not in the book."

"At times, more than I want to."

I decide this is a good moment to pump her for information. "You also seem to know a lot about all the people who work here."

She looks thoughtful. "I guess I do. I've been here eight years, and I've gotten to know some of the staff and members very well." She grins. "A person can hear quite a bit of gossip here in the dining room."

That's what I'm counting on.

"How did the Justice House get started? Did Mr. Justice just decide to move here, bringing all his school chums? He must have been fairly young."

"I know very little about him personally. Mr. Justice is a very private person, but from what Holly has told me, the four of them went to school together. When Mr. Justice bought this place to open up a private club, the other three joined him here." She looks over at the entrance. "Oops."

I glance up to see the Eldridge's.

"Let me get them," she says.

I watch as Tansy walks with the couple across the room. Mr. Eldridge looks back at me, and I quickly avert my gaze. Music filters out from the nightclub as the door opens, and I look up as Holly joins me at the hostess stand.

"Cait, would you take this list to Leon? The Edwards are in the nightclub, and they would like to purchase a few bottles of wine." Holly hands me a list that I look over.

"I can do that."

"It's not something we usually allow, but Liam okayed it so..." she shrugs. "Just make sure Leon has it all and that he puts the bottles in a wine box. We'll take the wine with us on our way to the club, and the Edwards can pick it up as they leave."

"No problem."

Leon has several customers sitting around his bar, and I take a stand at the end of the counter. When he notices me, he smiles a welcome and holds a finger up, signaling he'll be right with me.

"What can I do for you, young Cait?"

"We have a member who would like these bottles of wine." I hand him the list and watch as he scans it.

"Hmmm, has Liam approved this?"

"Yes."

He glances behind him as a small group walks up to the bar. "Let me take care of these folks, and I'll get the wine for you."

"Do you have a spare wine box?"

"I'm sure I do." He smiles, then heads for the other side.

As I stand waiting for Leon, I'm aware when Liam enters the bar area. His heady scent permeates the air, and I feel the powerful energy that seems to emanate from him. When he sits on the bar stool right next to where I'm standing, I toss him a quick look to find him staring at me.

"Miss Shaw." His voice is deep and oh so sexy. My lower extremities tighten in reaction.

I can't stop myself, I glance his way again. He looks so good my mouth goes dry. He's in dark jeans and a white linen shirt, loose at the waist with the top two buttons undone. I see the outline of his pendant under the material of his shirt and decide he must wear it all the time. His sleeves, rolled up to his elbows, expose a light smattering of dark hair on his tanned forearms. Taking a deep breath, I look away.

"Mr. Justice." My voice comes out all breathy.

His chuckle is soft, and I glance at him again, this time making the mistake of direct eye contact. His intense blue gaze holds mine for a moment before I'm able to look away. *How can one man be so freaking hot?*

"I hope you had a pleasant… time last night." Something in his voice has me looking at him again.

"Yes." I lick my lips, praying for Leon to hurry. "Um… thank you for the drinks."

"My pleasure," he says with a caress in his slow drawl. My stomach muscles clench tightly, and I bite my lip. *Oh hell!* I frantically look for Leon, who's still busy on the other side of the bar.

"The couple you were with—" I look at him again when he leaves his sentence hanging.

"My friends." His eyes. *Shit!* His eyes are almost hypnotic to me, and I now notice he has a thin, darker band of blue around the outside of the iris.

"I thought they might be your lovers."

"What?" I give a choked laugh, and I know I blush bright red if my heated face is any indication. I look away. "No, we're just friends." I glance at him again, his expression thoughtful. "Paul and Julie are married." I'm not sure why I'm explaining this to him.

"Do you often tag along with your... friends?"

What the hell, he thinks I'm lying? "Yes, I guess I do *tag* along with them as we are good friends."

"Good friends." He says it as if he's trying to decide if there is hidden meaning in my words, or maybe I'm talking in code. Are *his* friends lovers? Is that why he's wondering about mine?

I sigh. "Mr. Justice, Paul, and his wife Julie and I are nothing more than friends. We enjoy spending time together." I look at him and then turn back.

"So, you had no date?"

I glance again. He's leaning back with his arms crossed over his chest, facing me. I just now realize his legs, stretched out wide, are on either side of mine so that I'm standing between them. Why does he do that? I want to step away, but because I'm right at the end of the bar, against the wall, I have nowhere to step. I'm trapped.

I clear my throat in nervousness. "No. Paul's parents are in town, we met them for dinner."

"Ahhh. Do you usually have a date when you tag along with your married friends?"

I blush again. Why is he pursuing this? "No," I say softly, genuinely embarrassed. He probably thinks I'm a loser. *Where the hell is Leon!*

"Caitlyn, I do believe you've lied to me."

I look at him in surprise. "What?"

He unfolds his arms and leans forward on the stool, moving in close. Too close. "You told me I didn't make you nervous, darlin'."

My breathing is shallow, and I nervously lick my lips at his nearness. I don't say anything I just look at him, at his mouth so close all I need to do is...

He suddenly sits back, effectively moving his lips from my reach. I blush again. He knows I almost kissed him, and with the realization that he didn't want me to, I'm mortified. *I have to get the hell out of here.*

I frantically look around for Leon, who seems to have vanished. I feel panicked, desperate to get away.

"Cait—"

I turn, facing away, and when he pulls his legs in, I head away from him as fast and as far as I can manage. Of course, the *far* is only to the ladies' bathroom in the main hallway.

I lock the stall door leaning back against it.

Damn! Damn, damn, damn!

I know I've made matters worse by running. I should have stood my ground, acted as if nothing happened. I cover my face with my hands. But it did happen, and I will never be able to look him in the face again. I would have kissed him; except he made it perfectly clear he's not interested. I pull my hands from my face, tucking my hair behind my ears. Why him? Why do I finally desire a man who is so far out of my reach, so incredibly beautiful that he would never be interested in someone like me? A man who is probably some kind of libertine who only dates women as sexually liberated as he is.

Not someone—like—me.

Compared to the women I'm sure he sleeps with, he'd probably laugh me right out of bed.

I wonder why he thought Paul and Julie were my lovers. Is that what he's used to? He lives in a world so different from mine. The man doesn't just frequent sex clubs; he freaking owns one.

Okay, enough of this, I need to get back to work before Tansy comes looking for me asking questions. Exiting the stall, I dampen a paper towel, lifting my hair to place the cool towel on my neck. Looking at my reflection in the mirror, I look flushed. As I exit the bathroom, I say a prayer that I don't see Liam Justice for the rest of the night.

Finishing our shift, Holly joins Tansy and me as we head for *In Justice,* picking up the bottles of wine Leon has left sitting on the bar top. We stop at the employees' bathroom near the break room to freshen up.

"Where's everyone been all day?" Tansy asks Holly as she brushes her hair.

"You mean Liam and Bryce?" I tense slightly at the mention of Liam's name. Holly snorts, rolling her eyes. "The idiots, my husband being one of them, have been upstairs all day playing that stupid game."

Upstairs? Playing? I'm shocked that Holly says this so casually. I now know that all of the nefarious activities of Justice House happen on the second level. Holly must see something in my expression because she's quick to explain.

"Not upstairs, upstairs! I'm talking about Liam's apartment."

Liam's apartment?

Holly laughs. "I'd kill Ryan if he messed around upstairs, and he knows it, being the smart lawyer that he is. Y'all ready?"

I pick up the box of wine bottles, and we head out the

door. I stop just outside finally making the connection. "Wait, your husband is Ryan Phillips? *The* Ryan Phillips?"

Holly beams at me. "Heard of him, have you?"

"Who hasn't?" Ryan Phillips is an up and coming lawyer connected to one of Chicago's most prestigious law firms. The past two years he's been in the news often with his court cases. He doesn't like to lose.

"Wow, I'm impressed."

"Thanks," she says, giving me a wide grin as she pushes against the door that leads into the small outer room that we pass through to the nightclub. This is where we escort and leave the Justice's club members. Holly pulls the inner door open, and we walk into a noise level that could rival a loud rock concert.

We step just inside, and I'm surprised at the number of people. I had no idea the club was so large. Holly had previously informed me that it was the mansion's old ballroom. It's a long room with a two-story domed ceiling running its length. At the end of the room, steps lead up each side of the far wall to meet in the middle near the top where a balcony is located. From under the point where the two stairways meet, multiple rays of flashing teal colored light shoot out across the room like laser beams. It's definitely awe-inspiring. Below the flashing lights, and the balcony and stairs, is the nightclubs bar.

I grin at Holly and Tansy.

Holly makes a motion for us to follow, leading the way through the throng of people as she skirts the crowded dance floor located in the middle of the room. The Sohodolls, *Stripper* plays over the sound system, and the overhead teal lights pulsate to the beat. Holly leads us to the bar, where one of the bartenders is a good-looking guy I've seen around Justice House. He looks up and grins when Holly gives him a sign that he evidently understands as he immediately reaches for glasses.

I lean close to Tansy, hoping she can hear me when I ask her if we are going to try to find a table.

"What?" she mouths, holding her hand to her ear. I try again, speaking louder. She grins and shakes her head then shrugs.

The hot bartender reaches toward me and hands me a glass with a salted rim and a lime wedge. Mmmm. Just what I need, a margarita. I lick the salt from my upper lip and nod my thanks to the guy. He grins and winks. Holly taps my shoulder and points up. I look up realizing she means we are going up to the balcony. There are quite a few steps, and after a couple of margaritas, I imagine it won't be as easy coming back down as it will be going up.

As we reach the landing, we step into the balcony area. I'm surprised that the noise level drops to a decibel where conversation is an option.

"This is a private area, invitation only," Holly says as I look around.

We're up above the crowd, and we stand at the railing for several minutes checking the people out down below. The sight is awesome with the lights flashing across the room.

I turn to follow Holly and Tansy when I see Liam bounding up the steps. My legs go weak at the knees. *Oh, no!* I don't want to see him this close to my moment of weakness. I knew I wouldn't be able to avoid him for long since he is my boss, but I had hoped for a little time. Why did I not realize he would probably be here tonight?

About halfway he looks up, and our eyes meet. He holds my gaze, and then his eyes move over me looking me up and down. My body tightens in response to that heated look. I suddenly feel as if I can't take a deep enough breath, finding it difficult to swallow.

Holy hell!

My heart is pounding. JT's *SexyBack* is blasting over the sound system, and I can't think of a more appropriate song, for the sexiest man I have ever seen. There is something in his expression as his eyes meet mine again, but it passes quickly and then Tansy is pulling on my arm.

We join Bryce, Holly's husband Ryan, who I'd met the day before and muscular Mike sitting at a large table. There are other people seated too. Two older gentlemen with younger women. A couple of members that I've seen around the club and two very beautiful women, one of them being Miranda, the tall blonde who is interested in Liam. I know she mostly works upstairs, so I don't see her too often. Tansy said her job was similar to ours. I made a joke and said I couldn't imagine how, unless she took reservations for sex. Tansy laughed saying that was exactly what Miranda did, that and taking care of the members requests. Evidently, members have to reserve the suites available upstairs. I remember Holly telling me there are different themed rooms for the club members enjoyment. I don't even want to think about what goes on in those rooms, and I can only imagine what requests they might have.

Holly introduces me to the ones seated who I don't know, and I make a mental note of the two older men. Ryan stands, walking around the table to greet us. He's tall, dark headed, not exactly handsome but very striking in appearance. After sharing pleasantries with Tansy and me, he latches onto his wife bending her back over his arm for a very juicy kiss. Bryce shouts at them to get a room.

"I have just the room," Liam answers right behind me. I swing around in surprise meeting his dark gaze. He's close, too close for comfort, and I want to step back but the table is right behind me. A slow, wicked smile lifts one side of his mouth as if he knows my thoughts.

Oh, hell. That smile could be my downfall.

"Have a seat, Miss Shaw." He pulls out a chair, and I sit. When he places his hand right where my neck and shoulder meet, I gasp and jump in surprise. *What is he doing?* I see Bryce watching with a knowing smile and Miranda scowling. Just when I think his fingerprints will be forever branded into my skin, he removes his hand, and I reach for my margarita, downing it. A fresh drink appears in front of me, and I watch as the waitress returns to a small corner bar.

I pick up my glass as Liam sits directly across the table from me, his eyes watching me. Miranda immediately stands, swaying her hips seductively as she walks around the table to sit in the empty seat beside him. She gives me a smug smile before leaning close to whisper in his ear. She places her hand on his chest as she whispers and looks at me from the corner of her eye. It looks as if she's saying something about me to him. He frowns slightly and then turns toward her to say something. She laughs and glances quickly at me. I feel my cheeks heat.

One of the club members at the table asks Tansy to dance, and as she vacates her chair beside me, Bryce slides right in. I give him a smile.

"How are you tonight, Cait?" he asks as he leans his arm across the table in front of me and places his other hand on the back of my chair. I'm a little uncomfortable with his closeness, but he is effectively obstructing my view of Liam and Miranda, so I guess that's probably a good thing.

"I'm fine. How are you?"

He laughs. He really is quite good looking. "Drink up, and we'll dance." He shifts slightly, and I get a glimpse of Miranda rubbing up against Liam.

"That sounds like a great idea." I down my second strong margarita, and right on cue, another drink appears in front of me. Oh, this kind of service could be a dangerous thing.

"Come with me," Bryce says as he stands. "Bring your drink."

I stand, looking across the table to see Liam glaring at me. *What's his problem?* He could have asked me to dance just as easily as Bryce did. A part of me wishes it had been Liam who'd asked.

"Let's go too, Ryan." I hear Holly say, and they join us as we make our way down the stairway. I'm grateful for the handrail and Bryce's hand at my elbow as we descend.

Bryce shoulders his way to a table near the dance floor that is empty save for a reserved sign sitting in the center of the table.

"Take a sip," he shouts near my ear and then takes my glass, setting it down on the table next to his beer. He takes my hand leading me out onto the dance floor. It's crowded, so there's not much room for anything but swaying our bodies. Holly and her husband stand beside us, and Holly wraps her arms around her husband's shoulders. He pulls her tight against him, one hand resting on her bottom.

The music is great, and we quickly manage to work up a sweat. I'm grateful when Bryce leads me from the dance area to our table. The ice in my drink has melted, diluting the alcohol, but it doesn't matter, it's deliciously wet and cold. We stand, not bothering to sit as we finish our drinks. I am so hot I feel as if I'm melting. I gather my long hair and hold it up off my neck.

Bryce grins and then fishes in his pocket, pulling out a hair tie which he promptly holds out to me. I hesitate. I hope he didn't just pick it up off the floor. Gripping my shoulders, he spins me around and gathers up my hair. When I try to pull away, not liking how personal this feels, he tightens his hold on my hair and tugs. *Okay, damn!*

As he braids my hair, I look up. Liam is standing at the balcony's railing looking down watching us. His eyes burn into mine, their vivid blueness striking even from this distance. I don't know what comes over me. Possibly it's the effects of the strong drink, or maybe it's just that I want him to be the one down here, the one with his hands in my hair. I sing the words of the Katy Perry song playing, looking into those blue, blue eyes, making my statement that I want him, that I'm capable of anything.

His eyes take on a blazing heat, and he steps back from the rail. I know he's coming for me, and my heart pounds in anticipation. Miranda takes that moment to sidle up next to him. Seeing the two of them like that, their beauty together almost breathtaking, has the same effect as dousing me with ice water. Tansy said they weren't dating, but something is going on between them, and I'd do well to remember that. I quickly turn and catch Bryce watching them too. He drops his gaze to me, and his frown quickly disappears replaced with—pity?

Oh, hell no!

I need to get a grip and remember why I am here

at Justice House. I would leave right now with my determination to get myself back on track, but that would look too much like I am running, and I've already done that once tonight because of Liam. There's a fresh drink sitting on the table, I pick it up and down half of it in one long drink. Taking Bryce's hand, I pull him with me onto the dance floor. We dance nonstop until closing time.

CHAPTER SIX

I'M NOT IN A VERY pleasant mood when the alarm goes off way too early Saturday morning. I have plans to go paddleboarding with Paul on Lake Michigan, and lack of sleep plus my overindulgence of margarita's the night before, has me ponder giving him a call to postpone. Our plans are to put in near Navy Pier and paddle out to the lighthouse. It's a four-hour round-trip in open water, and I'm not sure I'm up for it. On second thought—it is probably just what I need to get my mind off Liam Justice.

When Bryce led me back up to the balcony the night before, at closing time, Liam and Miranda had already left. It was probably a good thing so I can remind myself that they are an item. My jealous mind conjured up all kinds of scenarios between them, however. Even though Tansy said Liam didn't date employees, it was plain to see that he and Miranda had something going on. Now if I could just stop dreaming about him. And why are they always freaking explicit sex dreams?

Getting dressed for my outing, I put my two-piece swimsuit on. It's not as skimpy as a bikini and perfect for paddleboarding. I slip into shorts and a tank top over the suit, tuck sunscreen into my waterproof fanny pack and head out the door, pulling my hair up into a high ponytail as I wait for the elevator. I have just enough time to get coffee and a muffin at the coffee shop across the street before Paul arrives.

I'm standing in line waiting my turn when my cell rings. I fish it out of my pocket, frowning when I see the main number for the magazine. I almost don't answer, figuring it's Valerie back from her trip. I've not spoken to her since she called to tell me she was leaving.

"Hello."

"Cait?"

"Hey, Pat. I figured it was Val calling, what's up?"

"Have you spoken to Valerie?"

"Nope. She said she'd talk to me when she got back. Why?"

"Well, I haven't spoken to her either." I can hear the concern in Pat's voice.

"She told me that if I needed to talk to her, I was to call you," I say as I step forward in line.

"Yeah, well, I haven't been able to reach her."

"She's probably busy or... whatever she's doing," I say.

"She was supposed to call me, but I haven't heard a thing from her."

"Did you try calling the hotel where she's staying?"

"I don't know where she's staying. She was so damn secretive about the whole trip."

"No one in the office has spoken with her?"

"No. She said she would only stay in touch with you or me. Do you think I should call the police?"

I frown. That might be jumping the gun a little. This *is* odd for Valerie, but I think it a little premature to call the police in. Would they even consider Valerie missing until the time for her return passed?

"I'm not sure, Pat. Maybe, you should call her lawyer. I can't imagine she would do anything without his knowledge." Joseph Case has been Valerie's lawyer and good friend for years. If anyone knew what she was up to, it would be Joseph.

"He's out of town until Monday. I called him yesterday; his secretary said he was on a business trip."

"Maybe he's with Valerie."

"I don't think so. His secretary wasn't very helpful, but she surely would have said after I told her my concerns about Valerie."

"You're probably right," I say thoughtfully.

At the same moment that I feel a sensation lifting the hairs on my nape, I breathe in his unique scent. Scanning the room as I turn, I just about jump out of my skin when I encounter Liam standing directly behind me in line, deep blue eyes boldly staring.

"I guess I'll wait until Monday to call the police," Pat says in my ear.

I just look at Liam, unable to speak. How much has he heard? My mind quickly replays what I've said, trying to recall if I've mentioned the magazine or—*Shit!* What is he doing here?

"Cait? Are you still there?"

Pat's question finally registers, and I drag my attention back to her, my eyes held captive by Liam's.

"Um… yeah, sorry."

"What do you think about waiting until Monday to call the police?" Pat asks.

"That's… probably the best option. Let me know. Hey… sorry, but I need to go."

"Okay, I'll talk to you later."

I stare at Liam warily. "What are you doing here?"

He raises an eyebrow. "I reckon the same thing as you, Caitlyn." Saying my name in that slow as molasses voice causes a fluttering low in my belly.

I pull my gaze from his, swallowing uncomfortably, still thrown off by his presence. I'm not sure what to say. When he suddenly leans in, his head bending close to mine, I give a soft gasp, my eyes flashing back to his. I see humor lurking in those beautiful orbs as his lips twitch slightly at the corners as if he's suppressing a smile.

"I like you being nervous around me, Caitlyn," he says softly, his warm breath flowing across the side of my face. I have to steel myself not to lean toward him.

"Why?" I ask in a whisper.

His eyes gleam with some unknown emotion. "It increases the anticipation."

I frown slightly. "Anticipation?"

"Of the inevitable."

What? My eyes search his, and for some inexplicable reason, I blush, becoming aware of the connection that seems to pulsate between our bodies. What does he mean, inevitable? He straightens and smiles that full megawatt, heart-stopping smile of his.

"You're next, darlin'," he says.

I'm next? Is he warning me? I exhale sharply. I don't think he's talking about firing me any longer. Is he? My eyes narrow at him. Surely he's not suggesting—*No, don't be stupid Cait.*

Liam nods toward the counter. "You're next."

"Oh!" I quickly turn, my face heating with embarrassment. The back of my neck prickles while I give my order and then move down the line to pick it up. I hear Liam order two coffees. Of course, he's with someone. I want to look, but I don't as I grab up my breakfast, making a hasty retreat out of the coffee house without a backward glance.

Paul drops me off at my apartment, late afternoon. I'm a little sunburned, wind-blown, and starving. We had a good day out on the lake, and it helped keep my mind off Liam if only somewhat. I've not shared with Paul my confused feelings about Liam. I'm embarrassed that I'm not able to control my attraction to the man I'm supposed to be investigating. I did voice my concern that I like the people I work with, and I worry about all this affecting their jobs. After all, neither Paul nor I have a clue what Valerie is searching for or what the outcome will be when she finds it. To be more precise—when I find it for her.

Being out on the open water gave me time to reflect on the position I'm in. What if I tell Valerie I can no longer snoop around Justice House and she fires me? Paul said I might not find another job with a newspaper or magazine, but insurance companies hired good investigators.

We discussed my phone conversation with Pat, but unlike us, Paul doesn't seem too worried about Valerie's lack of communication.

I use the rest of the weekend to catch up on housework and laundry.

Monday morning starts out with the usual morning meeting, except Bryce is the one to give us our pep talk, going over the schedule for the busy week. Liam is absent, and I'm disappointed but relieved at the same time. I look around for Miranda, but she's absent too. I wonder if they are together. I need to keep reminding myself that they are an item and to stay out of Liam's way.

"Are you nervous about being on your own?" Joni the head waitress asks as the meeting breaks up.

"Not too much, you'll be here to help." I smile.

"Yes I will and don't forget it."

"We missed you Friday night." I hate bringing the night up, but I feel I need to let her know we thought about her.

"Yeah, I had something I couldn't get out of. I'll make it next time. Did you enjoy yourself?"

"Of course, she did. She danced with me all night," Bryce answers her question as he walks up.

"I hope someone told you how big of a flirt this guy is," Joni says, nodding at Bryce. He grins at her.

"Don't be listening to any derogatory gossip about me, Cait."

"Oh, I don't need to listen to gossip *or* warnings about you. I think I've got your number." He dramatically holds his hand over his heart, and Joni and I laugh.

Bryce is so cute and boyishly charming, but he's not Liam. Not that there's a need to compare them, neither one has made a pass at me. I think Bryce is just being nice and Liam? Who the hell knows with him? He has me confused. My fragile confidence, where he is concerned, refuses to let me consider he might be interested. But there is something about the way he looks at me...

The three of us look toward the door when we hear Liam. He enters the dining room with two other men, his eyes colliding with mine before moving on to Bryce, giving him a slight nod.

"The day begins, ladies." Bryce flashes us a smile and moves to join Liam. Half way across the room he turns back and calls to me. "Cait, let's do lunch later."

I see Liam frown in Bryce's direction, then his gaze cuts to mine. The intent, I see in those blue eyes, has me taking a step back. Then he's turning away as he says something to the other men, and they all laugh as they continue toward the bar.

The morning is busy as we gear up for a larger lunch crowd than normal. The double doors that join the dining hall to the conservatory are propped open wide with tables set up in the beautiful sunroom to accommodate the extra guests.

At first I am a little overwhelmed, but with Joni and Holly's help, I make it through my first day on my own. Relieved once the dining room closes for the afternoon, I sit at one of the tables going over my paperwork when Bryce arrives with a pizza box.

"Hey, Cait, ready for lunch?" He turns one of the dining chairs across from me around and straddles it, opening the box.

"Mmmm, I am now," I say appreciatively, realizing how hungry I am when the aroma of the pizza hits me.

"Quite a morning, huh?" he asks as he flops a slice of pizza on a napkin, handing it to me. "I looked in earlier, but you were busy, so I figured a pizza would be okay."

"Perfect," I mumble around a bite.

Bryce suddenly stands. "I'll be right back."

I've devoured my slice of pizza by the time he's back with two wine glasses and a bottle of red wine.

"Um... I don't think—"

"One glass won't hurt you," he says as he pours the ruby red liquid into the glasses before handing me one.

I desperately want it. "I don't think the *master* of the house would appreciate me drinking on the job... but thanks."

"The *master* of the house won't begrudge you one glass of wine, darlin', not after the day you've had."

Liam's deep voice has me spinning around in my chair to see him standing behind me. *Now how did he sneak up on me?* Just as quickly I feel myself blush when I realize he heard what I said.

Liam pulls out the chair next to me and sits, sprawling out so that his leg brushes against mine. It feels like he shocks me, and I jump, pulling my leg away. He reaches over lifting the lid of the pizza box and scarfs a slice. I glance at him warily when he stands and takes a water goblet from the next table. Filling it nearly to the brim with wine, he raises the glass as Bryce lifts his. Liam arches a brow at me, and I hastily raise my glass.

"To many more," Bryce says.

I take a sip and close my eyes, savoring the delectable nectar and give an appreciative, "Mmmm". When I open my eyes, Bryce is staring at me with an amused expression. I glance at Liam and catch him watching me with those immensely sexy blues of his.

"Do you like the wine?" he asks, his lips twitching.

"Very much." I take another sip.

He reaches into the pizza box again and flops a slice down on my napkin before taking another one for himself.

"No thanks, I'm full." I push the napkin and pizza to Bryce, who picks it up.

"How many tonight," Bryce asks as he chews. I unconsciously sit up straighter with his words.

"Holly said there would be around seven hundred combined with the nightclub and dinner. She hasn't gotten back to me with just the totals for upstairs."

Seven hundred?

From the corner of my eye, I see Liam looking at me. After several moments of feeling his eyes on me, I glance over at him. He's turned to face me, his elbow resting on the table with his head propped upon his hand.

"Did you enjoy your weekend, Caitlyn?"

I gulp at the use of my name. "I did, *Mr. Justice.*" Liam laughs out loud and then he's looking toward the bar area.

"Bryce." When Bryce looks at him, Liam nods toward the bar, and Bryce turns to look, standing abruptly. He takes off in that direction as Liam pulls on the leg of my chair with his foot.

"Still not embracing the inevitable?"

I turn to him with annoyance. "I don't know what you're talking about. What's inevitable?"

Liam stands and leans in close, bracing a hand on the table and one on the back of my chair. I lean away from him slightly, and he grins wolfishly as my heart rate accelerates into overdrive.

"Me fucking you." He steps away as my mouth drops open. "Remember, only one glass of wine, *Miss Shaw,*" he calls over his shoulder as he saunters off to join Bryce at the bar.

Tansy calls to say she has a family emergency and will be late, so I agree to stay and cover for her. I've finished my paperwork and have a little free time before the dinner crowd starts coming in, so I decide to chat with Leon. I need to stay busy and keep my mind off Liam. Every time I think about what he said, my heart starts racing, and I find it difficult to breathe.

The bar is crowded, and Leon is moving about definitely multi-tasking, but he seems to be enjoying himself.

"Young Cait, what can I get for you?"

"Oh, nothing. I'm still on the clock, just thought I'd visit for a minute."

He gives me a smile as he pours a concoction out of a blender into a tall hurricane glass.

"Do you need any help? I can slice limes or something."

He sticks a pineapple spear into the glass and places the drink on a tray along with a bottle of beer and another glass. "Do you mind taking this to the table in the corner?"

"Not at all." I'm back at the bar in a matter of minutes.

He looks up from mixing another drink and says,"Efharisto." At my puzzled expression, he translates, "Thank you."

"You're welcome."

He glances across the room as more members walk in the bar. "Do you mind going to the storage room down the hall and getting me a couple packages of bar napkins?"

I slide off the stool. "I'll be right back."

I head down the hallway, past the kitchen to the supply room. The door is stuck, and I give it a bump with my hip, reaching around the doorframe for the light switch. The door closes softly behind me as I take a moment looking around for the cocktail napkins. The light in here is dim, but I finally spot the container. Pulling the sliding library ladder along the shelf rail, I climb carefully in my heels until I'm level with the box I want, delving inside to pull out a couple of the napkin packs. As I step down a rung, hands close around my waist startling me, and I step back off the ladder. With a little shriek, I fall into strong arms. I know surprise is registering on my face, but the angry eyes of Liam Justice, glaring down into my own, puzzles me.

"What the fuck do you think you're doing?"

I push against his chest. "Put me down!"

Oh, this is too embarrassing. Not the fact that I feel a fool for falling into his arms or the obvious fact that he's not happy about it, but because I'm suddenly panting. My chest feels tight, my lungs compressed, and I'm struggling for every breath I take. My lips part as desire coils low in my belly. His eyes flick to my mouth, and then back to my eyes with intent, slowly letting my legs slide down the length of his body. Standing in front of him, my heels bring me closer to his mouth, which plays havoc with my equilibrium. I sway slightly. Snaking his arm around my waist, he anchors me to his front as his other arm reaches up to the back of my head, his hand grabbing a fistful of my hair, pulling my head back. An involuntary gasp escapes at his sudden move, and I grasp his broad shoulders, fingers curling into the fabric of his shirt.

"Are you trying to break your fucking neck?" His voice is soft, his breath fanning across my face. I struggle for a deep breath, his scent infusing every cell of my body. This man could make a serious dent in the cologne industry if he bottled his mind-numbing scent. His lashes cast shadows on his cheekbones as my eyes move across his face down to his lips.

"No." I breathe, looking back up to his incredibly blue eyes. I hope he never lets me go—

He leans over me slightly, pressing me against his arm causing my back to bow. There's some kind of pulsating, vibrating energy passing back and forth between us. I can feel it, and I wonder if he does.

I lick my dry lips. "You... startled me."

Before I can take another breath, his mouth comes crashing down on mine, his tongue sweeping in to quickly stroke mine. His mouth is hot, and he tastes incredible. With a mind of their own, my hands move from his shoulders to delve into his thick, soft hair as he presses his rock hard erection into my lower belly. His mouth moves over mine, sucking my bottom lip between his teeth where he bites down gently. He keeps me anchored against his front, and I moan softly when I feel his hand slide up under the skirt of my dress, stroking my thigh, moving up to my hip. His hand is unbelievably warm as his fingers splay around my hip and dig into my bare bottom.

"Your skin is so soft," he murmurs as his lips move along my jaw to take my tender earlobe between his teeth, biting down. I whimper at the slight pain.

"Shhh."

I jerk and almost yelp, grabbing hold of his upper arms when his hand moves from my hip and cups me between my legs. He looks up to meet my eyes. Before I have a chance to decipher his wicked grin, he's twisting the fabric of my thong in his hand, his fingers shredding the delicate fabric as he rips it from my body. I do yelp at the burning sensation where the elastic bites into my skin.

"Darlin' you need to keep quiet," he breathes as he bends me back further, placing his mouth in the hollow of my throat, his hand once again cupping my sex. I squeak at the contact and feel his smile against my skin.

"You're already hot and wet for me." He raises his head to look into my face. "I do like that, sugar. I like that very much."

I'm quivering in his arms as one of his long fingers slides deep inside of me, my head dropping back weakly, a long, low moan escaping my throat.

"Fuck, you're tight."

Oh hell.

His words cause an uncontrollable reaction in me as I clench my inner muscles tightly around his finger, pressing more firmly into his hand.

I need more.

"Fuck!" He growls, gripping my waist tighter, almost cutting off my ability to draw a breath as he grinds his hand against me, his finger moving widely, rubbing against my vaginal walls. We're both panting now, and he suddenly straightens, pulling me up more fully against his chest. I'm on my toes as one of his hard-muscled legs wedges between mine, nudging until I step my legs farther apart. He's moving his finger in and out of me roughly now, and I'm finding it impossible to keep quiet. In a bid to silence me, he brings his mouth back down on mine.

There's a sensation building deep inside, unlike anything I've ever experienced. It's causing every muscle in the most intimate part of me, the part he has his finger buried in, to tighten. This in turn makes his strokes feel rougher, more abrasive, and the friction is about to make me lose all coherent thought. When his thumb comes down on my clit, the sensation is exquisite, causing my legs to stiffen and my toes to curl against the insoles of my shoes. I grip his upper arms as his mouth continues to devour mine, my tongue tangling with his.

When he yanks his mouth from mine and pulls his finger from me, I do cry out. He spins me around, effectively shielding me from the bright light that suddenly streams in from the now open door.

"Cait... Liam! What are you doing in here?" Holly's voice holds a note of surprise.

Liam's looking down into my face, his eyes holding mine captive. He raises his wicked finger and pops it into his mouth, pulling it out slowly. "Mmmm," he hums softly, grinning wickedly as my eyes widen. My blush scorches me as it moves over my skin. My legs are shaking, and I feel like I could be one of those massive firework displays that have just had the lit fuse yanked out, the grand finale stolen. My breathing is still ragged as is Liam's.

He tugs my skirt in place and turns to face Holly. I move slightly and bend on shaking legs to pick up the packages of cocktail napkins I dropped when Liam snatched me off the ladder.

"Oh hell no!"

I look up at Holly's sudden outburst.

"No! No, no, no, no." I glance up at Liam to find him watching me. "Liam! She'll leave us—and I don't want to lose her. I like her!" Liam continues to hold my gaze. "You have rules, Liam!" Holly's voice has raised an octave in her tirade.

"Rules are made to be broken, Holly." His voice is raspy, and the timbre of it causes my still racing heart to skip a beat. My breath catches when his eyes move to my lips.

"Huh-uh." Holly moves further into the storage room and nudges against Liam, reaching for my arm, pulling me away from him. She wraps her arm protectively around my shoulders. "I don't—want her—to leave."

Liam reaches out and rubs *that* finger across my bottom lip. "She's not going anywhere," he murmurs, his eyes boring into mine as if daring me to disagree. Then he's striding toward the door. Stopping, he turns back. "New house rule. No climbing ladders in fuck me heels." He gives me a pointed look, and then he's gone.

Holly looks at me with raised brows, and I feel my face heat again.

"Leon's waiting for his napkins," she says softly. I can tell she's now wondering just what did happen between Liam and me.

I am too. Did I honestly just let him—

Shit!

I am so screwed. And fired. I'm at once not so much worried about Valerie firing me as I am about the fact that I do want Liam to finish what he started. I'm still tightly wound, my core continuing to quiver in a state of sexual tension. My body is screaming for me to hunt him down and demand—*What?* What the hell is the matter with me? I can't think that. He's the subject of my investigation, not to mention that he might be involved with Miranda. How did I let this happen? *So not cool, Cait, so not cool.*

Realizing Holly is still studying me, I mentally shake myself. I need to get back to work. Then I have a disquieting thought. Where is my thong? I don't dare look down to the floor for it. If it's lying at our feet, Holly hasn't noticed it yet, and I want to keep it that way.

I take a deep breath. "Holly, do you mind taking the napkins out to Leon and giving me a moment? I'll be right out."

She frowns slightly. "Cait..."

"It's okay, Holly." I give her a reassuring smile. "I have no illusions about Liam."

She eyes me warily. "O-kay." She reaches over to take the napkins. "Don't be long." One more backward glance, and then she's out the door, propping it open behind her.

I lean against one of the shelves. *Holy crap!* How am I going to face Liam? Crap, crap, crap! This is all his fault. His dirty mouth at lunch has kept me on edge all afternoon. Thank goodness Holly interrupted us. There's no telling what might have happened.... Who am I kidding? I know exactly what would have happened if she hadn't walked in on us. Evidently I lose all common sense with that man, not to mention my inhibitions.

The number one problem right now though, is where is my thong? I hurriedly scan the floor to no avail.

As I walk back to the dining room, I feel like my whole body is one scalding, guilty blush. I feel like every person that glances my way, knows what I've been up to, knows that I am in desperate need of release and knows I don't have underwear on!

I'm expecting Liam's smug, knowing smirk when I see him, but mercifully, he's nowhere in sight.

The first diners of the evening walk in the door, and I greet them, leading the way to their table. It's a little unsettling in my state of undress. The thought of Liam having my thong makes me uneasy. Knowing how much I want him makes me worried. The fifteen minutes of passion he ignited in the storage room surpassed my entire relationship with my ex. I snort softly. The fumbling in the dark Jeff and I shared had no passion—it was just his quest for an orgasm, never concerned about mine.

Liam Justice has awakened an emotion in me that I want to explore. I don't care that it will be nothing more than sex for him. Just as I told Holly, I have no illusions on that end.

Tansy arrives about nine, apologizing and promising to make it up to me. I tell her not to worry as I'm the one who gets to sleep in the next day.

The dinner shift has been crazy, with the dining room and conservatory full to capacity all evening. I've stayed to help Tansy, and the last of the evening's guests are just finishing up as I leave. One advantage of being so busy is I've not had much time to think about what happened in the storage room. But I know I'll replay the entire scene later. I can still smell Liam on me. That in itself has kept my body in a tightened state all evening, ensuring that I have this constant ache deep down inside of me that I know only he will be able to alleviate.

But then, maybe the state I'm in is just because I have no underwear on.

I walk back to Holly's office to leave my shift paperwork and glance toward Liam's closed door. Maybe he has someone in there with him, someone who is helping to ease his ache. Or maybe—he's upstairs. I worry my bottom lip as I process that thought. I need to remember who he is and what he does for a living.

And if what Valerie says is accurate, he is a powerful man with connections. Money, power, and prestige are all attributes that draw women in like a magnet. Add all that to the fact that he's drop dead gorgeous, and I'm sure he never lacks for female companionship in or out of bed.

I need to keep my perspective here, I tell myself as I walk out the back door.

I stand outside the gates to wait for my cab, glad I have a jacket since the spring evening is a little chilly. This entrance to the property is on a mostly quiet street, except for the traffic entering and leaving Justice House. There are cars still pulling through to let club members out for a night of fun at the mansion's nightclub. But it seems especially dark tonight in between the coming and going headlights. I could wait at the guard stand, but my cab should be along any moment.

My thoughts naturally drift back to Liam, he's increasingly taken them over since the first day I saw him. I know I have to stop my—interest in him as nothing can ever come of it. If he ever finds out why I am here... he will hate me.

An SUV slows to enter the driveway but instead pulls to a stop at the curb in front of me. As the driver's side window slides down, I find myself staring into Liam's darkened features.

"Miss Shaw, what do you think you're doing standing out here in the dark?"

I swallow against the sudden dryness in my throat. How does he do that to me? How does he cause me to feel this way with just a look or just the tone of his voice? I've spent my entire adult life wondering why no one interested me sexually, if maybe there was something wrong with me. Then one look at Liam Justice, and I'm ready to throw away everything I've made for myself, knowing that I want to be with him. All because he said, we were inevitable. Well, not us... just his fucking me.

"I'm waiting for my cab," I say softly.

I catch a hint of his scent as it flows gently out of the car's interior. Deeply breathing in his essence, I close my eyes only to open them to find him watching me intently. His eyes are like pools of dark water that seem to glow just below the surface, and there's something in his expression, but it's hard to discern in the glow of his dash lights. Turning his head, he speaks to someone in the car.

The passenger side door opens, and muscular Mike steps out, leaving the door ajar.

"Get in," Liam's voice is deep, husky even.

I watch as Mike heads toward the gates before I turn back to look at Liam. I need a moment to control the sudden rush of need and longing for him that I feel, which scares the hell out of me.

I swallow. "No thank you. My cab should be here any minute."

He doesn't say anything for a moment, and I shift nervously.

"It wasn't a request." His expression is unreadable in the dim light, but there's no mistaking the deadly quiet in that voice.

I inhale sharply and consider running for the safety of the mansion.

"I *will* come after you." He drawls softly.

"I have a cab coming and—"

"Mike canceled your cab."

What? Of all the—

"I'm on the brink of not being happy here, Caitlyn, now get in the fucking car."

I give a choked laugh, his words surprising me. Well, I wouldn't want to make him *unhappy*, and as if I have no will of my own, I walk around the front of the SUV and climb in.

"Good girl. Now buckle up."

All I'm aware of as I settle into the seat, is his overwhelming, mind-blowing scent, the strange energy pulsating between us, and the fact I have no panties on.

He pulls away from the curb, making a U-turn in the street heading back toward State Parkway.

I'm supposed to be on my way to meet Paul and Julie, so when he turns in the direction of my apartment, I consider if I should just go on home and call them from there to cancel. I really need to think some things over; I have a decision to make.

"Um... I'm supposed to meet my friends... for drinks."

He glances over at me, and my heart skips a beat. He is so handsome. It's dark in the car, but with the dash lights, I can see the blue of his eyes. They meet mine, holding my gaze for a moment. His hair is mussed, and I feel a sudden yearning to run my fingers through it. The shadow of scruff frames his sensuous mouth and firm jaw line, giving him a bit of a dangerous look. He's dressed in jeans and a white button-down shirt with the sleeves rolled up.

"What's the name of the bar?" He glances at me again catching me still looking at him.

"Oh, um..." I dig into my jacket pocket for my phone, pulling up Paul's text for the address. "I've never been there..."

"What's the name of the bar, Caitlyn?"

I give him the name, and he's suddenly pulling off another U-turn, causing me to latch on to the grab handle above the door.

"Shit! You drive like a maniac!" He flashes me a wide grin, and my heart stutters.

"Don't worry, I promise to get you there in one piece."

"Maybe you should let me drive," I gasp when he suddenly changes lanes, whipping around a car.

He laughs. "I'm sure I've been driving longer than you."

I snort softly. "How old are you?" I ask, knowing full well how old he is, from the info in Valerie's file on him.

"Old enough."

"That old, huh?" I look at him and catch his grin.

"Older and wiser than you," he teases as he pulls up in front of a building that displays architecture clearly from another era then the other buildings on the block.

"Crap." There's a long line stretching back down the sidewalk. I sit back in dismay. *I'll never get in.*

"Don't worry little girl, I'll get you in." He does another U-turn, as a car pulls out of a parking space across the street.

I reach for the grab handle. "Stop doing that!"

He deftly backs into the spot and kills the engine.

I exhale loudly as I open the door. "You must be a teenager, you certainly drive like one."

I look up in surprise when he exits the SUV too. He further surprises me when he takes my hand, my heartbeat spiking as we cross the street.

I eye the overly large bouncer that stands in front of the door with his arms crossed over his chest. With his shiny bald head, he reminds me of a genie I once saw in a movie. All he needs is baggy pants and shoes with the toes curled to be the perfect genie. He's huge, and I can see that the first few people in line are watching him carefully, intimidated by the man's size.

"What the hell are you doing back here?" The genie's voice booms out, clearly directed at us.

I try to let go of Liam's hand, but his fingers tighten around mine as he pulls me along with him.

"Just thought I'd come slumming," Liam growls, and I look at him as if he's crazy.

The next thing I know the two men are shaking hands, and the genie is pounding Liam on the shoulder.

"How the hell have you been?" The genie asks his face breaking into a huge grin.

"I'm good. Is Jimbo here?"

"Does he ever leave?" The genie looks down at me. He really is intimidating up close, and I sidle a little closer to Liam.

"Darius, this is Caitlyn. Caitlyn, Darius. He's the meanest, ugliest bouncer in the city, and one of these days he's going to acquire some sense and come to work for me."

The big guy snorts as he holds out his hand to me. "Nice to meet you, Caitlyn. What's a pretty little girl like you doing with this low-life?"

"I'm... not really sure," I answer as I tentatively put my hand in his large one.

Darius throws back his head and guffaws, loud and boisterous, his laughter echoing off the buildings around us. I look up at Liam, and he smirks down at me.

"She's a smart one," Darius says, and I wince as he squeezes my hand. When he lets go, I hide it behind my back as I flex the life back into my fingers.

Darius opens the door, motioning for us to enter,

and Liam pulls me along with him as he walks briskly through the lobby.

"Hello, Mr. Justice." The coat check girl calls to Liam, and he raises his hand in greeting, but I don't think he even looks her way. She's certainly looking at him though.

Another bouncer, positioned at the entry into the club greets Liam. "Mr. Justice, good to see you again, sir."

Liam shakes his hand. "Thanks, Gary. We have friends inside."

"Good luck finding them; it's a packed house tonight."

Liam leads the way, shouldering through the crowd.

I suddenly see Paul as he stands waving his arm. When we reach the table Paul gives me a hug, and I catch his puzzled expression.

"Where's Julie?" I ask loudly near his ear as he squeezes my waist. Garbage's *I Think I'm Paranoid* is blasting over the sound system, and I know the music will be so loud we won't be able to have any kind of conversation.

"She's running late," he says loudly near my ear and shrugs.

He looks at Liam, and Liam steps closer. Paul doesn't hesitate before shaking his hand and then motions for us to sit. I know he's dying to know what Liam is doing here. Me too.

I sit, and as I slip my jacket from my shoulders, Liam reaches to help, draping the jacket on the back of my chair. I look up to tell him thanks, but the dark glare he turns on me, lodges the words in my mouth.

What?

A waitress with long, dark blonde hair stops at our table. She has a tray full of drinks, and she sets one down in front of each of us. I'm a little puzzled and glance at Paul. He shrugs.

She's bending down close to Liam so he can hear her, and she puts her hand on his arm as she leans against him.

How does everyone working here seem to know him?

She laughs when Liam says something and swats him flirtatiously on the arm.

He's slept with her.

I don't know how I know this, but I have no doubt. Maybe it's their body language. I'm not sure why this bothers me, but it does. When he glances at me, I quickly look away.

Damn! I don't like the idea of him with someone else. I know I'm totally out of line, considering the reason he's in my life to begin with, but—I want him. And as impossible as it would seem, with him being who he is and how he looks, I think he wants me too.

Maybe.

A little.

At least sexually.

From the corner of my eye, I see Paul looking at me, and I give him a small smile. He lifts his eyebrow, and I shake my head. I really need to talk to him, find out if anyone from the magazine has heard from Valerie but obviously, not here.

The annoying waitress picks up her tray, preparing to leave, and I read her lips as she tells Liam to, "call me". She then runs her hand up his arm before turning and walking away.

I watch her go. What a bitch. I'm sure she's aware that I'm here with Liam; she just doesn't need to know why, that's not the point. The point is you don't come on to a man who is clearly with another woman.

When Liam suddenly stands, I expect it's to follow her, so I'm more than surprised when he grips my arm pulling me up from my chair. He pulls me along with him as he heads into the crowd.

Whoa!

I look back, but Paul's already hidden from view by the mass of people.

I almost trip in my heels and Liam stops, pulling me to his side, his arm encircling my waist before moving on. My heart is pounding as we step into the lobby. *Where's he taking me?* Before I have a chance to ask, Liam pushes me against the wall. Stepping close, he glares down at me.

"Don't you *ever* fucking lie to me again." His voice is hard, his eyes narrowed.

"What?" *What the hell is he talking about?* "I don't know what you're talking about." My voice sounds breathy.

He glowers down at me. "You told me he wasn't your lover." His vibrant blue eyes blaze into mine.

"Who?" I frown, confused. "Paul?" My eyes widen, realizing whom he's talking about. Geez, I thought we'd cleared that up. "Paul's not my lover, I told you that! Why would you think—"

He moves quickly, claiming my lips, pressing me hard against the wall with his body. Pleasure spikes through me as his mouth devours mine. I kiss him back, arching against him. I want to reach up and delve my hands into his hair, but he holds my arms down against the sides of my body. I moan as his tongue explores my mouth, and he grinds his erection into my lower belly.

Sounds of laughter pull us from our lustful moment,

and Liam presses his forehead to mine as we both try to catch our breath.

"Fuck!" he whispers forcefully. "I knew you were trouble, the moment I saw you." He steps back, releasing my arms. Feeling a little dejected by his comment, I bring my arms up to wrap protectively around my middle.

"What about you?" I mutter.

"What about me?" His voice sounds stern, and I can't make eye contact with him, knowing his answer might be the end of us before we even begin.

"Do you have a girlfriend?" I need to hear him say that he's not involved with Miranda.

He doesn't answer, and my heart sinks.

When he uses his finger to tilt my face up, I meet his eyes.

"You don't have a very high opinion of me do you?"

I frown. "What does that have to do with you having a girlfriend or not?" His breath exhales with a startled laugh. "And what does it say about your opinion of me, when you think I'm involved with Paul?"

He shakes his head and then runs a hand through his hair. "This isn't the place to have this conversation."

I look over at a group as they enter the club laughing, looking for a good time. When I look back at Liam, he's watching me intently. As if he makes a decision, he suddenly grips my hand and leads me back toward the nightclub's main room. Just before we reach the entrance where the bouncer stands, there's a doorway and this is the direction Liam takes.

We walk down a dark hallway, and then Liam is opening a door for us to step into a small room that looks to be someone's office. Filing cabinets, a couple of chairs, and a desk occupy the space. As soon as the door shuts, Liam is pushing me back against it.

He grips my hands and raises them above my head, bringing them together to hold in one large hand that's like a manacle around my wrists. Pressing his hard body against mine, he holds me firmly in place as his free hand smooths the hair off my face and then encircles my throat.

I moan softly as he holds me securely. I like the feeling of him controlling my body like this. My nipples pucker in reaction, chafing against my suddenly too confining bra, and I squirm as much as he allows.

"I can feel your nipples harden, sweetheart." He releases my throat to slide his hand down over my breast and tweaks my nipple through my clothes as he grinds his erection into me.

He leans in to nuzzle my ear, inhaling deeply. "You think I'd be chasing after you if I had someone in my life?"

Chasing after me?

His hand slides down over my belly, to cup me between my legs.

I mewl and try to press against his hand. The desire I felt for him earlier is back in full force, and I need relief.

"You've been hurting all evening, haven't you darlin'? Needing me to satisfy that ache I started earlier." His voice is low, erotic as he rubs the soft scruff on his jaw against my cheek. He applies more pressure between my legs, gripping me firmly.

I squeeze my eyes shut and cry out with pleasure. Oh! That feels good, but I need more.

His chuckle is dark and knowing. I gasp softly when he releases my hands to fist a handful of my hair, his other hand still gripping my sex. He pulls my head back, arching my neck.

"The thought of you with no panties, has kept me in a fucking state all night too," he growls softly.

My eyes spring open in surprise at his admission.

He's horny? Because of me?

His mouth comes down on mine then, and he kisses me hard, his tongue pushing into my mouth.

I've never been kissed like this. Consumed. With abandon, I give myself over to his sweet possession.

"Mmmm," I hum. His mouth tastes like cinnamon, warm and spicy as my tongue tangles with his. Suddenly not able to get enough of him, my hands slide from his shoulders to the back of his neck, up into his thick hair. He releases his hold on my hair and moves his hand from between my legs. He wraps me in his arms as he pulls me close, one hand splayed across my bottom, holding me tightly against his rock hard erection.

By the time, he lets me come up for air we're both breathing hard and gasping. He presses his mouth against my neck, nipping and sucking at my sensitive skin. One hand molds around a breast, squeezing firmly, the other works its way up under the skirt of my dress, sliding over my skin to the junction of my thighs.

I cry out, startled at the spark that seems to flow from his fingers straight to my clit.

He emits a dark, self-satisfied chuckle. His fingers move lightly over me, exploring with the barest of touch, and I tremble against him.

"Move your legs apart," he orders as his knee nudges between them. This opens me more fully to him, and I hold onto his shoulders for support. His fingers continue to stroke me lightly as he watches me.

"I like this," he says as his fingers move over me. "Neat and trimmed."

I feel my cheeks heat.

When his fingers delve between my lips, my breathing escalates. I feel myself dampen as he slides a finger along my slit. He strokes back and forth, swirling his finger at my entrance, and then wraps his arm around my waist, inserting his finger slowly into me. I moan at the friction against my sensitive tissues.

"You're swollen," he moans against my throat. "I like how you're swollen from me finger fucking you hard earlier."

I blush at his crude words and immediately cry out when he thrusts a second finger deep inside of me.

"Fuck! I can't get over how tight you are." My core muscles tighten reflexively around his fingers as he moves them widely around inside of me. "I can't wait to fuck you," he growls, pinching my nipple again.

I want him to take me. I need him to take me, now. I lay my forehead against his chest as everything inside of me starts to tighten. My breathing becomes ragged, and when he pulls his fingers from me, I cry out in despair.

"No! Please, Liam," I beg, clutching at his shoulders.

"Hold on." He walks me backward until my backside meets the large desk.

He's going to fuck me on the desk! A part of me quivers in anticipation. What girl hasn't fantasized about being taken hard, bent over a desk?

"Look at me, Caitlyn."

In my dazed state, I find his bright blue eyes particularly mesmerizing. I want him more than I've ever wanted anything. I smooth my hands down across his well-defined pecs, over the medallion he wears, sliding lower to his flat stomach. I can feel the ripple of muscles beneath his shirt in response to my touch.

He quickly grasps my hands pulling them to the small of my back, locking one large hand around both wrists. He brings his free hand up to cup my face.

"Do you want me to fuck you, Caitlyn?"

Is he blind? I give an impassioned moan, turning my face into his palm.

"Yes!" I whisper.

"Look at me," he demands firmly.

I meet his eyes.

"You need to be sure, darlin'." He holds my gaze steadily. "I don't make nice when I fuck."

Holy shit. I swallow convulsively at his erotic words. I nod my head in the affirmative.

"I need a verbal response, sugar." His eyes move down to my lips.

"Yes, please," I whisper.

He raises an eyebrow as he continues to look at my mouth.

"I want you to… fuck me… but not nice," I say breathlessly and can't stop my blush.

There's a salacious gleam in his eyes as he meets my gaze. "Well, in that case—"

He releases my wrists, and I feel his hands as they work the zipper on the back of my dress, slipping it off my shoulders to pool at our feet. He stares down at me, and my nipples pucker hard against the abrasive lace of my bra. He grips the straps and yanks them off my shoulders, roughly pulling my bra down, exposing my breasts. I gasp at the suddenness of it.

My nipples jut out, and my breasts seem to quiver as he reaches out to run a finger around my areola.

"Well now, that looks real nice. All pink and pretty." His eyes slide down my body. "I'm anxious to see if your sweet little nub is all pink and pretty."

I moan softly and sway.

He grasps my arm and spins me around to face the desk.

"Hands on the desk," he orders as he presses into the back of me, and I feel his erection hard against my bottom. He unclasps my bra, slips the straps down my arms and drops it to the floor. Bringing his hands up to cover my breasts, he squeezes as he presses me hard into the edge of the desk. His mouth finds my shoulder, nibbling to my neck. When he comes to the spot where my neck and shoulder meet, he bites down.

"Aargh!" *Shit that hurt!* I buck against him, but he holds me firmly licking away the sting. I'm sure there will be a mark.

He turns me back around to face him and grips my waist to lift me up onto the desk.

"Hands behind your head."

I quickly do as he says. This makes my breasts thrust forward, and I moan softly as he brings his fingers to my nipples again. But that moan quickly gives way as I gasp, crying out sharply as he exerts pressure, extending my nipples further—pinching, twisting and pulling on them. I'm a throbbing mess when he finishes.

"Very nice, darlin'." I blush when he grins at me and flicks a nipple. "Let's see that pretty little nub now." He encircles my shoulders with his muscled arm and pushes against my chest to lay me back on the desk.

It's cold, and I feel goose bumps rise on my skin.

He pushes my legs apart, and I close my eyes, hoping to hide my embarrassment. No one has ever looked at me down there. I jerk when his fingers spread me open. His thumb rubs over my sensitive clit, and I cry out.

"Easy, darlin'." He places a hand on my stomach and rubs gently. "You're red and swollen. But not as much as you're going to be," he murmurs.

I moan as my core tightens at his words.

When he leans in and licks the length of my slit, I almost come off the desk.

"Liam!"

When his mouth closes over my clit and he sucks, my whole body bows off the desktop.

I cry out as I feel my core tighten painfully.

"What the hell!"

"Fuck!" Liam shouts. "Get out!" He pulls me up from the desk as he shields me with his body from the view of the man standing in the open doorway.

"Close the fucking door!" Liam yells again. "Give me a moment!"

I hear the click of it closing, and I feel faint with embarrassment.

"You didn't lock the door?" I push against him. Oh, this is so embarrassing. "Please let me go," I beg.

He steps back, bends and picks up my dress to hand to me. I clasp it to my chest as I look accusingly at him.

He laughs softly and runs his hand over his mouth, down his chin.

I turn my back to him and work at untangling my dress. I wonder what he finds so funny; he still has all his clothes on. Maybe that's what he finds so amusing.

He dangles my bra in front of me, and I snatch it from his hand. I slip the straps up my arms, and before I can reach around, Liam is fastening it. When he finishes, he cups my bottom, a cheek in each hand.

"You have a beautiful heart-shaped ass, darlin'," he murmurs near my ear.

I close my eyes and breathe in his scent. When he smacks my bottom hard, I give a yelp.

"Get dressed," he says harshly.

I give him a disgruntled glare as I rub my bottom.

When Liam opens the office door, I want to die on the spot as the tall, slim man waiting outside saunters in. I blush bright red when he looks me over and then turns to Liam.

"You came all the way over here to use *my* desk?"

Liam sits on the edge of the desk and reaches to grip my arm, pulling me in between his legs. I try to resist, but he settles me against his bulging hard-on.

"You have a nice desk," Liam answers lazily. His hand smooths my hair behind my shoulder. I look up to meet his eyes, silently pleading with him to let me out of this room. He frowns slightly.

"Well, I'm glad you enjoyed it. But I won't be able to sit and work here again, without imagining your lovely young lady draped across it."

I feel Liam's body tense. "Fuck you!"

Liam stands abruptly and pulls me to the door. "Go join your friend, and I'll be there in a few minutes." He opens the door. "Can you find your way?"

"Yes," I whisper, too embarrassed to look at him.

"Hey." He tips my chin up, and I meet his eyes briefly, before looking away. "You okay?"

I swallow and then nod.

"Good. Stay at the table with Paul."

I nod again, and he lets go of my arm.

Once I hit the lobby, I make haste to reach Paul inside

the nightclub. Julie has arrived, and they sit cuddled together, looking up as I reach them.

"I'm going," I shout over the music as I grab up my jacket and bag. I step around to their side of the table to give Julie a quick hug.

"Wait. What?" Paul looks concerned and slides his chair to stand. I wave him back down and lean in close.

"I'll come by the magazine in the morning."

He spreads his hands in a "what's up" gesture. I shake my head, wave goodbye and turn to get out of there before Liam returns.

Luck is with me when I step out the door, and a cab pulls up. I breathe a sigh of relief as the cabbie pulls away from the curb, and I give him my address.

What in the hell am I doing? I bring my hands up to cover my face. I don't even know the man and what, I almost let him screw me in some stranger's office?

I need to rethink this situation. Is this what I want? For years, I've longed to meet someone who makes me feel the way Liam does. Someone whom I can be intimate with, who fills me with desire. I *want* that. But I also know I've always thought of having those things in the context of a relationship. And I don't need Liam Justice to tell me that that's not going to happen.

But I do want him sexually and if that's the only way…

I lean my head back against the seat, and it's all I can do to stop my nervous giggle. That's twice now that he's had me on the brink of an orgasm and we've been interrupted. It's beyond embarrassing, caught like that, and the only thing that keeps me from dying of actual embarrassment, is that I'll never again have to see the guy whose office we were in. I do have to face Holly though, and the questions that I know are coming.

Desire pools low in my belly just thinking about Liam touching me. When I recall his warning that he doesn't make nice when he fucks, I have to squeeze my legs together as my head lolls weakly back and forth on the seat.

What is he doing to me?

I sit up straight as the cab driver slams on his brakes and lets loose with a string of expletives as another driver pulls out in front of us. Normally the cab drivers vivid language would make me blush, but I think Liam's dirty mouth is rubbing off on me.

Liam's dirty mouth.

Mmmm.

Liam's mouth on me...

"Did you say something, Miss?" I look up to catch the cabbies eyes in the rearview mirror.

"No. Wait! This is my stop."

I clamber out of the cab, pay the driver and quickly enter my apartment building. I'm tired and glad to be home.

I don't waste any time, stripping out of my clothes and stepping under the shower. My breasts and nether region are supersensitive from Liam using my body as he did. Drying off in front of the mirror, I see the bite mark on my neck. Shit. What is he an animal? I smile at that thought, and a shiver runs through me. I doctor the spot and head for bed.

CHAPTER SEVEN

Entering the foyer of Query Magazine the next morning, I'm greeted by friends and colleagues. It's good to see the people I've worked with for the last two years, but I'm here for two purposes, and I head for Valerie Sharp's office first.

I see Pat before she sees me, and I notice she seems stressed. I'm afraid I'm about to add to that stress.

"Cait!" Pat stands and walks around her desk.

"Hi, Pat. Have you heard anything?"

"Not a thing. Cait, I'm really worried."

"Yeah, I've been thinking a lot about Valerie, and her going off the radar like this is..." I look over and wave at a couple of copy girls who call a greeting. "It's just not good," I say quietly. Pat nods in agreement.

I point to Valerie's office. "Can we go in?"

"Yes." Pat opens the door, and I follow her in.

It's strange, but the room seems oddly quiet. I've been in Valerie's office on occasion when she's been gone, and it never felt like this.

When my cell rings, I jump, and Pat gives a little squeak. I dig it from my purse and see *Liam Justice* displayed with a phone number on the screen. Oh. This can't be good his calling me this early in the morning.

The morning meeting must be over by now, and I feel certain what he's calling about is not work related. I quiet the ringer and drop the cell back in my bag pulling out the envelope I prepared earlier that morning.

I walk to Valerie's desk and hold the envelope up for Pat to see. "I'm leaving this for Valerie… but I need to let you know this is my letter of resignation."

"What?" Pat wrings her hands together. "Cait, Valerie is coming back…"

"I know she is, Pat, and I will help any way I can until she returns. But I'm not on the payroll any longer, and you need to be aware of that." I reach into my bag and pull out another paper. "This is a copy of my resignation, I don't want there to be any confusion about this matter. I want it official."

Pat looks at me strangely. "Okay. But I don't think you should consider this until Valerie returns."

"No. It has to be now," I insist firmly.

Pat shakes her head as she takes the paper. "I'll submit it to Personnel."

"Today."

"Yes, Cait, today."

"Thank you. Now have you heard from Joseph?"

"Yes. He is stopping by this afternoon." We walk out of Valerie's office back to Pat's desk.

"I feel better knowing he's coming by."

"I do too," Pat says.

"As a friend, you'll let me know what he thinks?"

She smiles. "Of course."

"Good. I'll give you a call tomorrow afternoon, but I need to go for now. Please, call me if you hear anything from Valerie."

"Oh, I imagine she'll be calling you as soon as she

hears you've quit," Pat says with a laugh. Then she surprises me when she gives me a hug.

"I'll talk to you soon, Pat."

My step is lighter as I head to Paul's office. I feel as if there has been a weight lifted from my shoulders. It's been hard the last few days, coming to this decision, though. Valerie gave me a chance when no one else would, and she's taught me a lot. But I can't have a relationship with Liam, even a purely sexual one, not if I'm still on Valerie's payroll. I can't continue to deceive him. I just pray that when I tell him how I came to be at Justice House, he will understand.

"What the hell was that last night?" Paul asks as we sit drinking coffee at the coffee shop across the street from Query Magazine headquarters. It's one of our favorite places for lunch and morning coffee. It's small and not overly busy since there's one of the big coffeehouse franchise chains with a drive-thru not a block away. Paul and I prefer this little café, it has excellent coffee and those fried donuts that are the current rage.

I look around before answering. I knew this line of questioning was coming, but I'm still not sure what to say to him.

"I..." I laugh. "I'm not sure, Paul. He was giving me a ride home, and then I remembered I was supposed to meet you and Julie and... he just came along."

Paul studies me for a moment. "I'm not talking about how you got to the nightclub, Cait. I want to know where you two disappeared to and why you ran out on him. What happened? Did he do something to upset you?"

"No, he didn't upset me. Well, kind of, but..."

"Son-of-a-bitch!"

I bite my lip.

"Cait..." He leans in close so he's not overheard. "You're investigating the guy; you can't let yourself become involved with him."

"I know Paul. That's why I quit."

His eyebrows lift. "You quit Justice House?"

"Nooo," I say slowly.

He frowns and then looks astounded. "You quit the magazine!"

"Shhh!" I quickly glance around the room.

Paul sits back in his chair, his body language displaying his shock. "I can't believe you're doing this. Julie said you were attracted to the guy but..." He shakes his head in utter confusion.

"Paul..." I lean in close. "I'm not doing this just because of Liam. I told you I wasn't comfortable with this whole investigation." I reach over and take his hand. "You know I've not felt at ease for a while now, about the damage done to innocent people who happen to get caught in the crossfire of our expose's."

"I know but..."

"I think whether I had met Liam or not this is the decision I was headed for."

"But we're good together."

I laugh and squeeze his hand. "Yes we are. But you are a great reporter, you don't need me."

"You are a great investigator, and I'm not letting you off the hook."

"I'll always help you, Paul."

He shakes his head and gives a resigned sigh. "I cannot believe you're doing this."

"It's the right thing to do."

"Are you sure of that, Cait? I just hate to think of you throwing away your career..."

"I'm not throwing away my career! I just can't work at the magazine any longer."

"Because of Liam Justice."

"Not... entirely," I say weakly.

Paul's gaze is intense as he continues to look at me. "Let's get out of here," he says at last.

We take our coffee with us as we head outside to walk before Paul has to go back to work. The sun is shining, and though it's a little cool, it's a beautiful spring morning.

"So, what's going on with Justice?"

I take a deep breath. "A lot of heat." I laugh a little shyly. "We want each other."

"I told you, you'd eventually find someone you'd be interested in." He stops and takes hold of my arm pulling me to a stop. "I just wish it wasn't someone who owned a sex club."

I nod, uncomfortable with this subject. "I know." My eyes meet his. "Me too," I whisper.

He releases my arm, and we continue to walk. "So, you have it bad for him?"

I smile. "Yeah. But it's just sex, Paul."

He looks down at me and smirks. "And here I thought it was just men who believe it's only about the sex at the start of a relationship."

I smile up at him. "Is that what you thought when you met Julie?"

"Hell, yeah! I immediately started plotting how soon and where I could nail her."

"Paul!"

"What?" He grins and shrugs. "It's true."

He takes my arm as we cross the street. "I want you to be careful, Cait. Are you going to tell him?"

I know he's talking about me telling Liam of the investigation. "I'll have to, but I think I'll wait until Valerie gets back."

Paul stops again. "Cait, I don't think that's a good idea. You should tell him before he finds out elsewhere."

"I think it's only fair to let Valerie know in advance before I tell Liam she's having him investigated. Besides, how's he going to find out? There are only six of us who know what I was doing and one of those people is unattainable."

"And Julie has limited knowledge," Paul inserts.

I frown. It is disturbing that Valerie has not been in contact with anyone. She has to know people are worried. "None of the rest of us will say anything. Valerie will be back soon, and I'll tell Liam then," I assure him.

"There's no secret in the world that doesn't come out eventually." Paul quotes one of Valerie's favorite sayings. "I have to get back to the magazine. Julie's off this weekend, want to go paddleboarding?"

"Yeah, sounds like fun." I give him a hug. "Call me."

"Hey, Cait. Are you early, or am I late?" Holly looks at her watch.

"You're not late, I'm a little early." I walk into her office. She has papers and ledgers scattered across the top of her desk.

"Thank goodness, I need to get the balance sheets for the month ready before Liam gets back."

Liam's gone?

"What's up?" she asks as she leans back in her chair and raises her arms above her head, stretching.

"Nothing, I finished my errands early, so I thought I'd come on in and help Tansy out. I just wanted to say hi. I'll let you get back to it."

"Cait, you're working Friday night, right?"

"Yeah."

"It may be a little wild with the expo ending and people headed home the next day. They're planning a special event upstairs, and we're certain to catch a bit of the celebratory attitude down here and at InJustice."

I nod.

"I just wanted to give you a heads up. I'll be here to help, and I may shift things around, so Tansy works the evening shift with you. Maybe we can have a drink afterward?"

"Sounds like fun."

She grins. "Okay, it's a plan. Oh, and Liam's issued a new house rule."

I raise my eyebrow in question.

"Female employees, working the late shift, will wait inside the gates until their mode of transportation arrives."

Oh!

"I must say, sometimes his house rules get a little tedious but this is a good one. It's way too dark out there on that street." She gives me a steady look. "I wonder what motivated him on this house rule."

I shrug and smile. "I'll talk to you later. Good luck." I nod toward her paperwork.they

She immediately starts sifting through papers, and as I turn to leave I hear her mumble, "I'll probably need a drink once I get finished here."

I'm finishing up with my afternoon tasks in preparation for the evening ahead when I walk past the bar area, and Leon calls out to me.

"Hey, Leon, how's it going?"

"Too busy, and Rafe called to say he's running late. I need you to take this tray upstairs to room number twenty-two for me please, Miss Cait."

What? Hell no!

That's the first thought that goes through my mind. I don't want to go anywhere near the upstairs!

Leon looks up when I don't make a move to pick up the tray, which holds two wine glasses and an ice bucket with a bottle of champagne.

"You only need to knock on the door, Miss Cait. You don't need to go in."

It's not in my job description.

"I'm sorry to ask you but there's no one else." He picks up the tray and holds it out to me.

I swallow convulsively and reach out to take it. *Only because I know I have to.*

"Okay, Leon, but I'm not going into any room," I say firmly. I can't get my legs to move, so I just stand and stare at him. I really don't want to go up there.

"Miss Cait? I really need you to take the tray upstairs, now."

I take the back service stairs, and when I reach the landing, I mentally scold myself for not asking directions.

Wow. No expense spared up here I notice as I look around at the opulent furnishings. The landing is lovely, rich and luxurious, larger than I imagined. And to top it off, the beautiful rotunda with the stained glass dome.

Two hallways split off from this area, and after checking I decide to take the one closest to the main stairway. It's a long corridor with doors on both sides, each one numbered. I just hope that room twenty-two isn't going to be all the way near the end.

I'm increasingly nervous as I commence down the hall. *Are these all bedrooms?*

I pass a couple who have come out of one of the rooms, both of them giving me a nod. I hear the woman giggle and look back to see the man groping her ass. O-kay. I hear laughter as another door opens. Well, whatever they do up here, they certainly seem to enjoy themselves.

I am almost to the end of the hallway when the door I am near, suddenly opens. A man steps out and almost collides with me. He's tall and thin, swarthy in appearance with a face scarred from a severe case of acne. He immediately makes me feel uncomfortable. There is just something—menacing about him.

"Oh! I'm so sorry!" My tray wobbles and he reaches out to help me steady the glasses.

"Sorry about that, sweetheart."

I don't like him calling me sweetheart or the look in his eyes when he looks me over.

"That's alright," I tell him and then continue down the hallway more than ready to deliver the tray, which is getting heavier by the minute. When I hear him following behind me, I glance back nervously. *Shit!*

I breathe a sigh of relief when one of the last two doors is number twenty-two. I balance the tray and knock as I glance at the man now leaning against the doorjamb on the opposite side of the hall from me. *What is he doing?* Please. Please hurry and answer the door.

I'm more than a little surprised when Miranda, dressed as a French maid, finally answers my knock. I think she's surprised too. She looks past me at the strange man and then back at me. When she steps aside, I don't hesitate to scuttle in. She closes the door behind me.

"You can set the tray on the table."

Holy Shit!

I don't know what I was expecting, but it wasn't this. The room looks as if it belongs on a stage or movie set. It *is* a staged set as most of the room is elevated. There are even white brocade curtains, intricately woven with gold threads that hang down to frame the whole effect. I've stepped into a boudoir, which looks similar to something that might belong in a French queen's chambers. The walls and frilly, delicate looking furniture are all in white and gold, and there's fluffy white carpeting, which looks too pristine to walk on. A chandelier hangs from the ceiling, its crystals reflecting light back and forth between the mirrored walls on opposite sides of the room. The room's dramatic effect is a little overwhelming. It's the most luxurious and done-up room I could ever imagine.

I look at Miranda in her little French maid costume, and I start to giggle. She looks annoyed as my giggling continues, and the glasses on the tray start to rattle.

"I'm glad you find this so amusing," she says as she takes the endangered tray from my shaking hands. As she flounces across the room in her short maid outfit to deposit the tray on one of the fragile looking tables, I'm laughing outright.

I wrap my arms around my middle trying to control my laughter. It's no use though as I double over losing it.

Oh! This is too funny. I thought I would be walking into some type of a torture chamber and here I've stumbled into a frilly, girly boudoir—with its own French maid!

"I'm so sorry," I manage to get out between bouts of laughter. "It's... just not... what... I imagined." I start on a new round of deep belly laughs. I point at her and howl with laughter. It's even made funnier with Miranda's *I-am-so-not-amused* expression.

"Oh... oh..." I try to control myself, fanning my face with both hands. Maybe if I don't look at her...

"You can go now." She opens the door and that sobers me. I peek out looking for my stalker. Seeing that the coast is clear, I step out into the hallway and turn.

"I really am sorry. I was nervous about coming up here and when I—"

My apology is abruptly cut off as she slams the door in my face.

"How *rude*," I mutter.

I descend the stairs still chuckling. I consider my uncontrollable laughter may have been a bit hysterical. I had been terrified of going upstairs expecting torture devices and men with whips; instead I get the equivalent of a room full of puppies.

Looking behind me and not paying attention as I hit the bottom step, I walk right into a solid wall with piercing blue eyes.

I make a little "oomph" sound and step back. "Sorry," I mumble. His masculine scent inundates my senses, and I take a deep breath before I look up, noticing he's not smiling.

"Miss Shaw, have you managed to get yourself into trouble?" he drawls.

I swallow nervously. "Um... no?" His expression tells me yes. I'm not sure why though, but something tells me he's about to set me straight on that question.

He crooks his finger at me, "Come with me, please." He turns and heads down the hallway, not waiting to see if I follow or not. I wonder how his arrogance would take my heading in the opposite direction.

I follow, a slow burn starting deep in my belly as I watch him walk ahead of me. He moves with an easy grace that arouses me.

Everything about him arouses me.

He holds the door to his office open, and as I pass, he watches me with an enigmatic expression, which suddenly makes me nervous. His words come back to me, and I wonder what kind of trouble I might be in.

He comes up behind me as I enter the room, placing his hand on the small of my back. I gasp softly at the contact.

"Would you care for something to drink?" he asks as he guides me to the center of the room and leaves me there as he continues to his liquor cabinet.

"No, thank you." I look away, hoping to calm my racing pulse, but when I hear the clink of ice hitting glass, it sets my nerves on edge.

"Mr. Justice, I really need to get back to work. The dinner hour will be starting soon."

He comes to stand in front of me, drink in hand. He has a wicked gleam in his eye as he looks down at me. He looks so fine in his soft gray suit. Something about the color makes his deep blue eyes appear even clearer, brighter than normal. There's a hint of dark stubble on his handsome face, and his tousled hair has me weak in the knees. His scent as he stands near washes over me again, and all the need and yearning I've felt in the last two days has me biting my lip.

I struggle to draw a breath, and I can see the movement of my knit dress over my chest. Is he able to see it too, the rapid beating of my heart?

"Mr. Justice," he says softly. "I like the way that sounds when you say it. Very—respectful."

I frown at his tone. The first stirrings of unease take up residence in my nervous stomach.

He settles on the edge of his desk, his long legs spread out in front of him. Even in his smart suit, all respectable, conservative even, he manages to exude a raw sexual energy.

I want him to kiss me, take me into his arms, and make love to me. No. Not love. I've had slow, "treat her like a lady" lovemaking. I want hard pounding raw sex, and I think Liam Justice is just the man for the job. Everything about him screams sex. His hard, toned body promises countless orgasms, and I want him to give them to me. I wonder what he would think of me if he knew my thoughts, if he knew my limited sexual experience, that I've never had an orgasm. I blush at my own thoughts.

"Now that's right pretty, sugar." He pushes away from his desk and is in front of me in two strides.

I gasp when he reaches out to stroke my flushed cheek with his finger, sliding it down my neck, across my collarbone, then over my chest. His finger continues down to delve into the V of my neckline and ends up between my breasts. My body flushes, and my skin feels on fire where he's touched me. Does he have any idea what his touch does to me? I look up to see his knowing smile. Yes, he knows exactly how he affects me and any other woman he fancies. That thought alone should douse the heat running through my veins, but it doesn't. I want this man. I know it will only be sex and that's okay because that's all I want from him.

"Your skin is incredibly soft." His low, deep voice

sends chills through me, and my breath comes in soft little pants.

When his warm hand slips inside my bra to pinch my nipple, I whimper, closing my eyes. I grab hold of his arm in reflex as he rubs his thumb over the throbbing peak.

He brings his face close to mine. "What do you want, Caitlyn?" His voice is raspy and causes my core to clench almost painfully.

"You." My voice comes out sounding parched.

"I know you want me baby, but *what* do you want?"

I lay my hand against his chest and it happens to rest on the medallion under his shirt. It feels hot from his body heat.

"Do you want me to fuck you?"

My face grows warm. "Yes," I whisper.

He doesn't say anything, and I glance up, meeting that intense blue gaze.

Without warning, he jerks me against his body, his hand fisting in my hair as he brings his mouth to mine. I moan as he kisses me as if he'll consume me. Pleasure quakes deep in my core.

Lifting his lips from mine, I whine softly when he takes a step back. He holds my arms, so I can't move those few inches back into his arms.

"No expectations, darlin'."

"What?" I'm dazed from his kiss, uncertain what he's saying, but I know I want his mouth back on mine.

"No expectations—between us." He holds my gaze steadily.

Okay. I got it this time. I consider his intense blue gaze. The skin looks tight around his eyes, and I realize as my head clears, he's concerned about my answer. Or maybe it's my actions he's worried about. I smile slightly to put him at ease.

"I have no expectations of us, Liam." I reach to run my hand down his chest. *Hell, am I ever going to see this man naked?* I see the relief in his eyes, and my self-esteem is a little piqued. "Your reputation precedes you, darlin'," I say, smugly.

He frowns, and I feel his body tense under my hand. "What the fuck is that supposed to mean?" His voice is angry as his eyes blaze down at me.

"Just that I... have no expectations... of us," I answer softly. His tone, and the way he suddenly looms over me leaves me not quite as brave as when I hurled the insult.

His eyes glare into mine, and once again, I wonder at his mood.

And then he's jerking me back into his arms. His mouth comes down on mine almost violently, grinding against my lips in a punishing kiss. His tongue forces its way into my mouth plunging deeply as his hand grips my hair, keeping my head pulled back.

Excitement courses through me at his assertiveness, and I gasp for breath when he releases me.

His warm breath sends a shiver down my spine when he nuzzles my ear. "I'm almost out of my mind with wanting you. I've had to wait for you far too long," he growls.

He's about out of his mind wanting me?

He spins me around toward the desk and presses his body in tight against my back. Bending over me, he pushes me down onto the desk. His erection feels hard... and huge against my bottom.

"I've been denied what I want so now" —his breath is hot against my ear as he moves my hair to the side, exposing the back of my neck—"all I want to do is fuck you hard, raw," he murmurs darkly. He bites down on the back of my neck, and I tremble beneath him.

Holy hell! He wants to fuck me raw? I whimper.

He releases my neck licking the spot as goose bumps break out on my skin. He lifts off me and grips the shoulders of my dress, yanking the bodice down to my waist. I pull my arms out of the soft knit as he unfastens my bra, slipping it off.

"Hands flat on the desk," he orders.

My nipples are so hard they ache, and my breasts feel heavy and swollen as he cups them, testing their weight as I lean over the desk. When he brushes his fingertips across my taut nipples, I grit my teeth. They are so sensitive.

"I'm afraid, darlin', I will be quite rough with you when I make you mine." He gives me this dark warning in his erotic voice, right before he rucks the bottom of my dress up around my waist. Arousal, deep and primal slams into me, and I can't stop the shiver that runs down my spine, or my soft, shuddering gasps.

Smoothing his hands over my bottom he then digs his fingers into my skin, and I cry out at the sharp pain that pierces straight to my core.

"Quiet." He pinches my nipples, and I moan loudly. A sharp smack on my bottom smarts enough to bring tears to my eyes.

Fuck, that hurt!

"Stand still," he orders when I fidget from the sting.

Wedging his leg between mine, he runs his hand over the abused cheek. "You have a perfect ass, sugar, and it looks even better wearing my hand print," he says roughly, and I feel a slight unease. There's an underlying anger in his voice.

When he leans down to kiss and then bite the abused cheek, I moan softly trying hard to be quiet. "Very good, darlin'."

He abruptly pulls me up and turns me to face him. As he smooth's my hair away from my face, tucking it behind my shoulder, I try to calm my erratic breathing. I blush slightly, bared to his gaze as I am. He frowns down at me before tipping my chin up.

"Caitlyn... " His eyes search mine. "I want you, but I won't be gentle with you. I will fuck you hard, and I will fuck you often. I'll expect certain things from you, but I will offer you little more than sex. If you aren't sure or comfortable with that, you need to say right now because if we go any further—I will not stop."

Holy crap. He'll fuck me often? So how has casual sex just turned into... an affair? He just warned me about no expectations, and now he's saying that he'll expect things from me. What am I to make of that?

"Liam—" I want this. I want him—desperately. I don't know why I feel as I do about this man, but his words, his dominant personality—everything about him excites me in a way I could never have imagined. I inhale deeply. "I don't want you to stop." My voice sounds breathy.

His eyes darken, and for just a moment I think I see a gleam of satisfaction. His gaze slides down my body, and everything south of my neck tightens with anticipation. When his hand molds around my breast, I sway slightly.

"Caitlyn?" He rolls my nipple between his forefinger and thumb.

"Yes," I gasp.

"Do you know what I'm talking about when I say I will expect certain things from you?"

I meet his direct gaze and nod slowly. "Yes," I say softly. He's talking about doing to me, the things he enjoys doing upstairs. A slight tremor courses through my body.

One corner of his mouth lifts slightly.

"But—" I quickly insert. I need to make my feelings clear too. "I—don't want to go upstairs."

Bright blue eyes widen in surprise for a moment, and then he regards me steadily, his expression impassive.

My stomach twists into a bundle of nervous tension at his silence. "But I do want to be with you." My voice sounds a little anxious.

"Well, here's the deal, darlin'... if you are with me... you *will* go upstairs."

Oh.

Can I do that? Do I want him bad enough that I'd be willing to subject my body and possibly my soul—to his lifestyle? In just a few days' time, Liam has awakened desires that have lain dormant deep inside of me. I am suddenly needful of his seductive, licentious nature, and I don't want how he makes me feel to stop. I've yearned for an intimate relationship for years, not that Liam and I are entering into a relationship per se, but no one else has ever made me feel this way. And we're just getting started.

Yes. I want to have sex with Liam, so I guess I will do whatever is necessary to be with him. I just pray it doesn't lead to anything too dark. I've managed to convince myself that if I can stay detached from what happens upstairs I'll have some sense of control.

"I can always say no if the situation gets to be too much for me. Right?" I bite my lip in nervousness.

"Cait—" He runs his fingers through his hair, mussing it further. His action has me wanting to run my fingers through his hair too. "We can go into details later."

"Liam..." I worry my bottom lip. "I... I don't... I *can't* be with anyone else." My breath rushes out, knowing I have to be firm about this point but worried what he'll say.

He looks surprised again. "Darlin', I have no intention of sharing you."

I take a deep breath. "But I'll have to share you?"

His eyebrows raise, and I know he's trying not to smile. "Not if all my needs are met."

"What about my needs?" I breathe.

A roguish grin curves up one side of his mouth. "Oh, Miss Shaw, they will be met." I gasp as sharp arousal courses through my body.

He pushes me against the desk. "I think it's time to shut up now, Cait." His deep voice no longer sounds amused, it holds an edge, and when he looks at me as he is, I forget how to breathe.

He slips his thumbs under the silky material of my thong, following the material down in front, and I gasp. Using his thumbs he pulls up until the G-string tightens against my sensitive clit.

"Ahhh!"

He pulls tighter, and I grip his arms.

I'm up on my toes trying to alleviate the pressure when he releases the material, sliding the thong off my hips and down my legs as he squats in front of me.

Damn.

"Let's save this pair, shall we?" He looks up his gaze catching mine, and I see a sparkle in the blue depths.

He does have my thong from the storage room. I knew it!

Running his hand over my hip and down my leg, he lifts first one foot and then the other laying my thong on top of my bra.

I'm naked save for my dress bunched around my waist and my heels. He's still in his suit, but when he stands, he slips off his jacket, loosens his tie and begins rolling up his sleeves.

When I shift my weight, desperately wanting to cover myself, he orders, "Stand still."

"Okay," I whisper.

He steps back in front of me so close there's barely any space between us. When his shirtfront lightly brushes my nipples, I bite my lip. "Spread your legs." When I comply, he runs his middle finger along my slit, pressing in to rub against my clitoris.

I reach for his waist, but he grabs my wrists placing my hands beside me on the desk.

"Grip the edge, and don't let go. Do you understand?"

"Yes," I breathe.

"Do not. Let. Go." His expression is stern as he looks down at me.

I nod. My breasts rise and fall with each labored breath as I lick my lips.

His finger rubs over me again. "I want your legs farther apart." He uses his foot to push against mine until I spread them to his satisfaction.

His finger slides over me swirling around my opening as his eyes watch me intently.

I moan, and my head falls back.

"You are so fucking sexy." Something in his deep voice calls to me, and as his finger swirls back over my clit, I cry out softly.

Repeatedly stroking me, he rubs firmly over my clit with each pass through my wetness. He raises his free hand to grasp a nipple between his fingers, rolling and pinching. The added stimulation causes a tightening deep inside of me, almost painful with its intensity, and I grip the desk edge so tightly my fingers feel numb.

"You're so wet for me, sugar." He raises his fingers and licks them, his wicked eyes gleaming.

My eyes widen. *That's so – hot.*

"You taste as sweet as honey, darlin'." He leans in and takes my mouth in a slow, deep kiss returning his fingers between my legs.

I'm not so sure I taste like honey…

"Let's see if we can make you wetter," he says against my lips and grins when I whimper. He pushes two fingers deep into my slick channel, and I cry out.

"Ahhh – Liam!" I almost let go of the desk edge, I want to touch him so desperately, but I catch myself in time.

"So swollen and tight." He presses into me hard, twisting and grinding his hand against me as he moves his fingers widely stretching my tender tissues.

I have to grit my teeth to stop from screaming, and when he bends down and takes a nipple between his teeth, biting gently, I whine. It's too much. I can't control my body as the pressure builds inside of me. It is so overwhelming I begin to shake. I've never felt anything close to how this feels.

"Liam!" I press against his hand, unable to hold still as his fingers stroke me forcefully. I shudder violently, and it's as if the tension deep inside of me radiates out in the most unbelievable sensation that is so pleasurable, it's painful. I feel a gush of warmth between my thighs as I scream. Liam wraps his arm around my back, pulling me hard against his chest and covers my mouth with his, silencing my cries as his fingers repeatedly thrust into me.

I clutch his shoulders, and my body writhes against his as my inner muscles grip his fingers. All I can do is hang on, my body shaking as I ride out my orgasm. I don't think it will ever end.

"Fuck!" He laughs hoarsely. "Fuck, Cait." He pulls his fingers from me, and I collapse against him.

Wrapping his arms around me, he holds me close, stroking my hair down my back, his touch gentle. When my body finally stops quivering, he leans back, tipping my chin up with his finger.

"Look at me." I meet his smoldering eyes. "You—are fucking amazing." I blink, and he kisses my forehead. Threading his fingers through my hair, he holds my head in place while he takes my mouth in a soft kiss.

He chuckles at my dazed expression when he releases me. I feel languid, needing a nap.

"You're late for work." He says as he smacks my bottom. I give a small yelp and jump.

Work!

"Shit!" I pull my dress up over my breasts and down over my bottom.

Shit!

He hands me my underwear, and I blush. "Bathroom." He points across the room.

Thank goodness, I don't have to dress before I have a chance to clean up. I hurry across the room on shaking legs, feeling his eyes on me.

I'm not surprised to find his bathroom is stylishly elegant and fully equipped. I bite my lip as I clean between my legs, I'm sore. Then I smile. I had an orgasm!

A freaking amazing one, even Liam thought so. I grin like an idiot. I've long been afraid that there was something wrong with me, but Liam's shown me differently.

I knew he was the man for the job!

Liam knocks on the door. "Let's go."

"One moment."

I use the hairbrush lying on his counter and then rinse my mouth with mouthwash I find in a drawer. I'm spitting it out into the sink as the door swings open.

Geez.

"I've only been a few minutes," I inform him. He raises an eyebrow at me, and I hurry out.

"Come here, Caitlyn."

I turn to look at him, and he quirks his finger at me. *Why is it so intimidating when he does that?* I take a deep breath and then go to stand in front of his desk as he sits behind it. His sleeves, still rolled, set off his muscular forearms, and his tie remains loose at the knot. The top two buttons of his shirt are undone to expose a tantalizing expanse of skin. He looks incredibly handsome, and I feel a tightening in the pit of my stomach. I wonder what he would do if I walked around his desk to sit in his lap.

"We have a couple of things to discuss before you go back to work."

I look anxiously at his wall clock.

"Don't worry; everything is taken care of until you return." He leans back in his chair, and the look he turns on me has me swallowing uncomfortably.

"I don't appreciate how you ran last night. It was very disrespectful."

I don't know what to say other than, "I'm sorry." He continues to hold my gaze, and I squirm under the piercing blue heat.

"A more pertinent question is what the fuck you thought you were doing upstairs earlier."

The quick change of topic throws me for a moment. "I-I was delivering a tray that Leon asked me to take up there."

"And did he tell you to go into the room?"

I frown. "No, but—"

"There are no buts, Caitlyn." He fixes me with an implacable stare, and I immediately close my mouth, feeling hurt.

"You stepped into a scene taking place, totally disrupting and disrespecting the people involved in that scene. You upset and humiliated Miranda, and this in turn upset Dante, who was only in town for the day and looking forward to spending time with Miranda."

Miranda must have called him as soon as I left the room upstairs. My post-orgasm buzz has totally dissipated, and I feel as though I am a child receiving a scolding for misbehaving. He isn't even giving me a chance to explain.

And what the hell is a *scene?*

"We have rules upstairs that everyone has to follow. I realize you don't know what those rules are, and I do believe that is why you were told to knock and leave the tray."

He continues to watch me, but I don't make eye contact with him, and I'll be damned if I say I'm sorry. I already told Miranda I was. She didn't want to hear my explanation and clearly, neither does Liam. I am surprised Miranda didn't say anything about the man in the hallway, though.

"Am I fired?" That would be a shitty piece of luck, fired from the job I quit the magazine for.

He sighs deeply. "Not this time, but under normal circumstances, a person disrupting a scene would receive a punishment."

My eyes finally meet his. *What? Like hell!* I'll quit before I let him punish me for something that was an accident. Maybe I didn't need to laugh the way I did, but I put that down to nerves. Besides, I didn't know there was a *scene* in progress, and Miranda certainly didn't explain.

"I'll make a decision and let you know."

I huff a laugh and shake my head.

"Do you have something to say Miss Shaw?"

We're back to Miss Shaw? After what just happened between us? Why didn't he inform me of this before he took off my clothes?

"If you're not going to fire me, I need to get back to work." Plus I need to get out of here before I cry.

His eyes narrow. "You can go, but when your shift ends, I want you back here. I'm not finished with you yet—I plan on fucking you tonight."

My mouth drops open, and my face heats with embarrassed anger.

"Go to hell!" I turn and head for the door.

He moves fast, quickly beside me, pushing me up against the wall.

"Let go of me!" I struggle with him, but it's pointless. He leans his weight against me, and when I try to slap him, he grabs my wrist and jerks me around, forcing the front of my body up against the wall. He pulls my hands to the small of my back and presses his body into mine.

"Let go of me!" I cry again, angry that the tears start to fall. I never cry, and for him to reduce me to this, makes me hate him at that moment.

"Not until you calm the fuck down!" His voice is rough.

I struggle against him, and he pushes me even harder into the wall.

"Fucking stop! I don't want to hurt you, Cait."

I'm sobbing at this point, all the fight gone out of me. He eases back slowly and releases my wrists turning me around. I cover my face with my hands.

"Hey." He pulls me into his arms and holds me against his chest. He kisses the top of my head and murmurs soothing words, all the time just holding me.

I don't know how long we stand there before he leans back slightly, looking down at me.

"Better?"

I look up at him, and I know I probably look a mess.

"I need to go home."

He's quiet, watching me.

"I... can't work this way." I feel like crying again. *What the hell's wrong with me?*

"Forget about work, it's covered." His voice is soft. "Look at me, darlin'." He grips my chin and tips my face up.

My breath catches at his expression, but before I have a chance to analyze it, the phone on his desk rings. He almost seems reluctant to let me go as he leads me back toward his desk.

He picks up the phone. "What?" he says impatiently, his eyes on me.

"Too late," he replies curtly. Sighing he looks away and rubs the spot between his eyebrows. "Will it piss me off?"

Whatever the caller says on the other end of the line has his gaze flashing back to mine. His eyes move slowly over me as he continues to listen to the caller, and I can't stop my response to his heated look. I want him. As upset as I am, the need and longing I feel for him is overwhelming.

"Okay, but it'll be a bit." Evidently, the caller has something to say about that as Liam continues to listen. "All right."

He hangs up the phone and stares at me, his expression at once both assessing and enigmatic.

I take a deep breath, uncomfortable under his scrutiny. "Since you have someone covering for me... I'm going home."

He slowly shakes his head. "No."

I frown. "What?"

He silently walks toward me. My heart is pounding by the time he stops in front of me. His hand lifts the dark hair that hangs over my shoulder. He seems to study the curl before his eyes lift to meet mine.

"I'm needed in security, and I would like for you to wait here."

I narrow my eyes at him. "Why... so you can fuck me tonight?"

The sudden anger that comes over his features has me taking a step back, but I can't go too far since he has a handful of my hair. He begins to wrap that hair around his hand, effectively reeling me in. "I should give you warning, Caitlyn." He continues wrapping his hand until I'm up against his front, blue eyes blazing into mine. "It's not wise to rile me."

"I just want to go home," I whisper.

"I don't want you to." He frowns as if he's not certain why.

"You... don't want me to go home?" *Why?*

He doesn't say anything for a long moment. "I don't want you to leave."

Oh. Pleasure surges through me at his words.

A frown flits across his face, and his mouth tightens visibly. "And it's not just because I want to fuck you tonight. I reckon that's off the agenda at this point anyway, don't you?" He releases me abruptly and returns to his desk.

What? All of this suddenly frustrates me. I still want to go to bed with him. Tonight.

"How about you wait in the bar?" He looks at me. "You can have a drink, and when I'm finished, I'll come for you."

If he doesn't want to have sex, why does he want me to stay?

He runs a hand through his hair, and I realize how tired he looks. I take a deep breath and move across the room to him, lifting my hands to cup his face. He looks a little bemused by my action. I go up on tiptoe, lean into him and place my lips on his. I mean for it to be a quick kiss, but his hands grip my arms pulling me firmly against his chest, and the kiss becomes anything but quick. His lips mold to mine, his tongue pushing against my lips to gain entry, stroking my tongue with his. He releases an arm to grasp the nape of my neck, kissing me deeply.

Oh, this man can kiss! My body responds, and I can feel his reaction too as he boldly presses the rigid length of his erection into my lower belly.

Oh my. I wonder what his response would be if I reached out to grasp him. Almost as if he knows my thoughts, he ends the kiss, putting distance between us. My breathing is erratic, and hot desire pools in my belly.

"Let's go," he says his voice suddenly cool and detached. His sharp blue eyes glance at me before he turns and heads for the door.

I'm embarrassed at how easily he turns me on, whereas he seems able to turn his emotions on and off at will. But I know he was as aroused as I was. He pressed his erection against me to let me know how he felt.

"C'mon, sugar." He holds out his hand as he stands in the open doorway. I take his hand, and he pulls me close, his nose brushing against my ear. "You're going to drive me fucking crazy," he croons gently, and then he's leading me down the hallway.

CHAPTER EIGHT

I LAUGH AS LEON SWATS AT his cousin Tony with a bar towel. Tony's too fast though and moves back out of the line of fire, grinning at me.

"You won't be smiling if Mr. Justice sees you flirting with his employee." Leon scowls at him.

Tony shrugs in a nonchalant manner. There's no reason to be concerned, Mr. Justice is nowhere to be seen. It's been over an hour since Liam left me here at the bar, warning me to stay put. I remind myself to inform him that I don't stay on command.

I've probably had too much wine to drink, but Tony keeps refilling my glass. He zeroed in on me as soon as Liam left, right after telling Leon to keep an eye on me. I was a little annoyed at first but then amused. Would he keep me here by force?

I do venture over to speak with Shelly, one of the weekend hostesses whom Liam called in. She seems nice and says she needs the extra hours, which makes me feel better about her having to cover for me.

I return to the bar, and Tony immediately steps away from the two club members he was waiting on. Both women look at me and frown. Tony is a handsome devil and charming as all hell with his sexy accent and sparkling black eyes. I can understand how he's probably a favorite around here with the female members. He told me he comes in to work for Liam a couple times a month, doing whatever Liam needs him to do at the time.

I feel a sudden tingling along the back of my neck. I know it's Liam even before I turn to see him standing beside one of the pillars between the restaurant and the bar watching me.

Damn he's gorgeous. He stands with his legs braced apart, his arms crossed over his chest. With his shirt sleeves still rolled to his elbows, his muscular forearms make me feel weak remembering the strength in them. His dark hair is in its usual sexy disarray, making my fingers positively itch to pull at the silken strands. And even from across the room as I look into the most unbelievable blue eyes I've ever seen, I'm in danger of melting into a puddle right where I sit. A dull throb starts low in my belly.

The two women sitting across the bar from me wave to him. He looks their way, and then gives me a quick glance before moving across the room with that easy grace that causes the dull throb to turn into an all-out ache.

Tony leans in and taps his finger against the rim of my wine glass.

"I'm out of here in a couple hours. We could go see other bar, maybe dance," he says in his thick accent.

I tear my gaze from Liam, who's laughing with the women, to look up into Tony's anxious eyes. He's sweet, and I hope my being friendly with him hasn't led to a misunderstanding.

"I'm sorry, Tony. Mr. Justice wants to speak with me that's why I've been here, waiting for him."

Tony looks disappointed for a moment, and then his face breaks out into a bright smile. "Soon we will go out. You won't say no."

I bite my lip. How do I do this? "Tony, I don't think—"

"Miss Shaw, are you ready?"

I'm startled, not realizing Liam's standing behind us.

"Mr. Justice," Tony greets.

Liam shakes Tony's hand. "How's it going Tony?" Liam grips my elbow and draws me up from the bar stool.

"It goes good, Mr. Justice."

As Liam leads me away, I glance back to see Tony's confused expression.

"I can't leave you alone, for two minutes," Liam mutters, looking down at me from the corner of his eye.

I huff a soft breath. "Two minutes?" I give him a raised eyebrow.

He leans down, his mouth close to my ear. "I was in the security office, darlin'. I could see you on a monitor," he says softly. I blush slightly and feel warm from the idea of him spying on me.

"Like a peeping pervert?"

He doesn't say anything for a moment and then he's laughing out loud.

We garner several glances as he leads me from the bar through the restaurant to the door going out into the hallway. I'm surprised when he directs me to the security office.

"Right this way, Miss Shaw." He opens the door and gestures for me to precede him.

He stands in the doorway, and I breathe in his intoxicating scent as I brush past him. My reaction to his nearness makes me tense all over. I chance a look up, and he gives me a cursory glance. I'm at once nervous, wondering why we're here.

I've never been in the security room, and I look around with interest. Mike Bowen sits before a wall of monitors and glances up to give me a nod. I've seen plenty of cameras located around Justice House, and here is proof of surveillance coverage for every room. Including the bar.

My gaze immediately settles on one monitor, in particular.

The space the surveillance camera is covering is an extensive area. Is the location upstairs? It almost resembles a—dungeon. The walls appear as if they are stone, and the lighting is subdued, flickering light coming from wall sconces. There seem to be several activities going on around the large room, but my attention centers on one. There's no volume, thank goodness as the visual alone is enough. I'm not sure that if I were able to hear the woman's screams, I'd be any more alarmed by the scene than I am. She's tied, naked, to a large wooden cross while a man stands behind her wielding a wicked looking whip. And she is definitely screaming.

Holy shit!

I feel the air suck right out of my lungs. I look at Liam, and he's watching me intently.

"Miss Shaw." Mike draws my attention as he reaches over and hits a button on his console of buttons and switches. Every monitor goes blank, save for one. He taps another button, and I appear on the screen. As he taps, I see myself from different angles as I walk down a long hallway, carrying a tray with glasses and champagne. It's evident that I'm looking for a particular room, and when a dark-haired man steps out into the hallway and nearly collides with me, Mike freezes the frame. Looking up he asks, "Have you ever seen this man before?"

I take a deep breathe. I wonder what Liam is thinking. "No."

"Are you sure? Look carefully."

"I am positive. I already looked at him when we were in the hallway. I've never seen that man before."

Mike's gaze holds mine for a moment longer and then he reaches to flip a switch, and we watch the scene from earlier that day replay. He again stops the video when I reach the room, glancing nervously at the stranger.

Both men remain silent, and then Mike asks, "Miss Shaw, why did the man in the hallway make you uncomfortable?" He looks up expectantly at me.

I frown and then shrug. "I'm not sure why... he just did. Sorry, I wish I could be more specific." I remember thinking at the time that I couldn't pinpoint my unease about the man.

He glances over at Liam.

"Cait." I look at Liam. He stands with his arms crossed, leaning against the wall. "Did you read the employee manual that Holly gave you when you first hired on?"

"Yes."

"And did you read the part that states if anyone says or does anything to make you feel uncomfortable, you are to report them?" He holds my gaze with that piercing blue stare of his.

Crap. I think I'm in trouble again. However, this time, Liam holds some of the blame. It's not as if he gave me any time to report anything. I don't really want to talk about it in front of Mike, though.

"Yes," I say softly.

He continues to hold my gaze, and then he sighs heavily. Pushing away from the wall he walks toward the door.

"Keep checking, Mike." He glances over at me. "Let's go." He holds the door open and then follows me out into the hallway.

"Liam— "

"Not here," he says firmly.

As soon as we enter his office, he heads to his liquor cabinet and pours a drink. "Can I get you something to drink?"

"No thank you."

He sits on the couch and pats the spot beside him. "Have a seat."

I sit but not right beside him. He quirks his eyebrow before taking a sip of his drink. "Would you care for a water? I keep bottles in the mini-fridge, help yourself."

"I'm fine thank you."

He crosses a leg over the other at the knee angling his body toward mine. Stretching his arm along the top of the couch, his intense gaze settles on me.

We sit for several minutes with him watching me. Finally, I decide to bring up the episode with the stranger upstairs, ending the nerve-racking silence.

"Liam, I didn't get a chance to think about reporting that man. I had just come down from upstairs when you... then when we were in here... I... "

Liam doesn't say a thing he just continues his unrelenting regard.

"You didn't... give me a chance to explain," I say softly. I know he's seen the rest of the surveillance footage and now knows, at least in part, Miranda's neglect in telling him about the man. I venture another glance to find him still watching me.

He takes a sip of his drink and then places the glass on the small table that sits in front of the couch.

"How many lovers have you had?"

"What?" I manage to gasp out.

"I want to know how many men you've slept with." His arm still lies across the back of the couch, but now his arm's bent at the elbow, his chin resting on his hand while one of his long fingers strokes his bottom lip.

I look away. "One." My face heats with my blush.

For several moments, he doesn't say anything else, and I try hard not to squirm under his scrutiny.

"And what did your lover do for you that you enjoyed?"

I huff. "What?" Why is he asking me this? What would he think about me asking how many women he's slept with? That's probably a staggering amount. I sigh inwardly.

"I don't like repeating myself, Caitlyn." His hand drops from his face. "Now answer the question."

I flush again and look away. "Nothing."

"Excuse me?" I look back to see his frown.

"It's okay for *me* to repeat *myself*?"

He cocks his head and raises an eyebrow. "Your smart mouth is going to get you into trouble with me, darlin'," he drawls softly.

My breath catches at his tone. His eyes hold mine, intimidating me further.

"He wasn't... I don't think of him as my lover." I lick my lips in nervousness. "He was my first boyfriend and... " Shit, this is embarrassing.

Liam moves suddenly. Gripping my arm, he pulls me

over settling me on his lap. My stomach is set aflutter as I absorb his scent.

When I meet his gaze, he smooth's my hair behind my shoulder and gives me a small smile, his eyes staring into mine.

"I'm sorry."

"Me too." I sound breathless, and I can't look away from his stunning eyes. "I shouldn't have slept with him just because he was pressuring me, and all my friends were doing the deed."

A slightly amused, puzzled expression crosses Liam's face.

"I know, lame reason to have sex... and it wasn't that good. I mean, neither one of us knew what we were doing. And it didn't get any better over time." I take a deep breath. I'm not sure why I'm explaining this to him, probably because I'm nervous. "I finally realized he wasn't what I wanted... or needed," I say softly. "I... I wanted the all-consuming passion where you can't keep your hands off each other. Where you need, the other person like you need your next breath." I blush, looking down. *Shut up, Cait.* A nervous laugh escapes my lips. "Did I mention I was only nineteen?"

"Cait."

I look up, and he smiles, his eyes alight with humor. "I was apologizing... for not letting you explain earlier."

"Oh." I gasp. *Oh!* Oh, shit! I bring my hands up to my mouth. In retrospect, I should have done that sooner. As my embarrassment grows, I move my hands up to cover my face wanting to be anywhere, but sitting here on his lap.

Liam laughs a deep full laugh and pulls my hands away from my face.

Damn it… why does my brain stop functioning around this man? I dramatically drop my upper body backward over the arm of the couch. *Floor open up and swallow me now.*

When his fingers stroke down across my chest, my breath catches, and my attention immediately centers on those long fingers. I raise my head.

There's a small frown between his brows, and those blue, blue eyes take on a sudden fervent gleam. His arm goes under my shoulders lifting me up to meet his mouth as he brings his down on mine, sucking and nipping at my lips. I reach up to run my fingertips over the soft stubble on his jaw. He deepens the kiss, and I turn more fully into him, my fingers skimming his sideburn and then back along his jawline. Arms tighten around me as his large hand fists in my hair, his kiss becoming possessive and dominant. A shiver runs down my spine as raw need settles in my lower extremities.

His tongue is forceful as I return his kiss with equal fervor. Cupping my face, his fingers skim my jaw trailing down my neck. As he encircles my throat with his large hand, I feel the pulse in my neck flutter against his palm. When his hand moves down to mold firmly around my breast, I moan as he plucks at my nipple with his fingertips. His hand continues down flattening over my stomach, and my muscles jerk in response to his touch.

As the palm of his hand presses against my mound, I gasp against his mouth and moan loudly as hot desire pools in my belly.

"Shhhh," he says against my lips.

His hand smooths up my thigh, under the skirt of my dress, and then he's pulling my dress up and over my head. I try to sit up, but he pushes against my chest, pushing me back down until my head is resting on the arm of the couch, and my bottom rests on his lap. His hard erection throbs against my backside. My whole body is quivering as I lie there in my bra and panties, his eyes scorching my skin as they move over me.

Oh, I want this man.

He reaches down to stroke across my panties with the lightest touch, right over my sensitized clit. He does this repeatedly until I'm gasping with desire and arching up into his hand.

His eyes are blazing as they look into mine. "Are you ready for me to fuck you, Caitlyn?"

No one has ever spoken as crudely to me as he does, but it's a complete turn on with Liam.

"Yes!" I gasp as he slides my panties aside and enters two long, thick fingers deep into my slick passage.

"You're always so fucking wet for me," he growls.

I buck hard against his hand, and the sudden pressure against my sex, against my clit, causes my back to arch pressing me more firmly onto his fingers. My legs stiffen, my body tightens, and I cry out with my release.

"Fuck!" Liam cries out hoarsely.

My body convulses as I climax, pulsing around his fingers still buried deep inside of me. He holds me tightly against his body as I shudder in the aftershocks of my orgasm.

Shit! That was…

Leaning over me, Liam smooth's the hair off my forehead as he gazes down at me.

"Do you know what a fucking turn on that just was?" he laughs softly.

I'm embarrassed. He barely touched me, he must

think.... I turn to hide my face against his stomach, deeply mortified by my reaction.

"Hey," his deep voice takes on a gentleness I've never heard. It is incredibly sexy, and I feel an answer to his tone deep in my core. "Look at me, baby," he commands in the same tone.

I turn my face but can't meet his eyes. I feel so—

"Caitlyn, I told you to look at me." His voice is firm, this time using a tone that dares me to challenge him. I look up to meet his eyes.

"The way you respond to me—you have no idea how it affects me." His eyes are glowing, and I swallow deeply.

When he stands, I squeak and clutch at his shoulders. He just stands there holding me in his arms gazing across the room, a man in deep contemplation. I reach up to gently stroke his tense jaw.

He gazes down, a salacious gleam in his eyes. "Ready for wild, unrestrained fucking, darlin'?"

"What?" I squeak again. *Wild, unrestrained fucking?*

His answering smile is so wicked, my stomach muscles clench with potent need.

Holy hell! How does he do that to me? I'm quickly learning he wields a power over my body that is a little unsettling, immensely pleasurable but unsettling.

Liam releases my legs to let me slide down the length of his. He smiles widely before releasing me and striding toward his desk. Picking up the phone, he holds up a finger in a "one moment" gesture.

"Hey, I'm headed upstairs," he says into the phone.

Upstairs? My eyes widen, and I quickly turn away. I grab up my dress and slip it over my head. I don't want to go upstairs! It's too soon. I'm not ready. I haven't had time to prepare myself. I take a deep breath trying to calm my racing heart.

"Try not to disturb me." Liam laughs at what the person on the other end of the call says.

Will he take me to a private room or—Where was that place I saw on the monitor in the security office? Will he take me there? What will he do to me?

My thoughts are racing as fast as my heart, and I jump when Liam takes hold of my elbow.

"Ready, darlin'?"

I don't say a word as he ushers me toward the back of his office. I've paid little attention to this area of the room, since it's partially blocked off by a screen, and I'm surprised when he leads me to a set of elevator doors. Instead of a call button, there's a slot where he inserts a card, and the doors open immediately. Inside, Liam touches the control panel as I take a much-needed deep breath. I'm apprehensive and almost paralyzed with indecision. And fear. I wonder what would happen if I say no. Just at the moment the doors close, I realize that my breathing is coming in short gasps. Liam notices too and reaches to touch the control panel again. The doors slide back open.

I feel him looking at me, but he doesn't say anything.

"I guess... I'm just a little nervous... about going upstairs," I say softly. I shrug and peek up from under my lashes when he doesn't respond. He's watching me intently, his expression unreadable.

Oh, shit! How badly do I really want him? I bite my lip, knowing my answer.

"Ready?" His tone is as unreadable as his face.

Am I? "Yes," I whisper.

The doors close again, and it only seems to take a

smooth moment before they re-open, presenting a long hallway before us. Liam takes my hand and leads me from the elevator. He stops, letting me look around. It's hard not to notice the beauty of the entryway, even in my nervousness. Hardwood flooring, crafted in a beautiful chevron pattern in light and dark stain, is the central focus of the room. The walls, and the two doors leading off the hall reflect the same shades of stain, with the woodwork and elaborate crown molding done in an eggshell white. Overhead, integrated lighting draws attention to the long domed ceiling. There's an antique table against one wall, with a gorgeous mirror displayed above it. The whole effect is lovely.

"Where are we?" I look at him, confused.

His expression is grave and the skin around his eyes, tight. "My apartment."

I frown as I look around again. "Your apartment? I thought—" My eyes widen in surprise. "You wanted me to think that we were going…" I suddenly find it hard to swallow. "Why would you do that? Make me assume…" I swallow convulsively. *I am not going to cry.*

"Maybe… I wanted to see if you would do it for me," he murmurs.

"Oh!" My breath whooshes out, and I feel a sudden anger. "Did I pass your fucking test?" I snap, glaring at him as his eyes narrow. Then he's sweeping me up into his arms with effortless ease.

"Put me down!"

His eyes collide with mine. "I don't think so." Without warning, he strides from the entryway, storming through one room after the other as I push against his chest, struggling in his arms. He abruptly stops before a closed door, reaching down to open it.

I have a short moment to register that we are in a bedroom before he's throwing me down on a large bed, quickly coming down on top of me, pressing me into the mattress. He easily captures my wrists before raising them above my head.

Oh, shit!

I suddenly understand the expression of *swooning* as I experience light-headedness when his erotic scent surrounds me. He feels so good, his hard body pinning me to the bed, my anger of a moment before quickly forgotten. I desperately want to move my legs apart, but his lie on either side holding mine firmly in place. With the amount of movement, he does allow, I arch my body against his, moaning with my arousal.

"Look at me, Caitlyn," he commands.

I bring my eyes to his, and his intense gaze delves into mine, immediately immersing me in blue.

"If you're going to be with me, *I* decide when and where I fuck you, darlin'."

I think I nod my head slightly.

"Do you want to be with me?" He demands.

"You know I do," I answer breathlessly.

"Well then, it doesn't matter where – does it now?"

"But – " I bite my lip and unwittingly turn my face.

Liam pulls my wrists into one large hand, gently gripping my chin with the other, turning my face back to his.

"I told you I have no intention of sharing you with anyone. That means," – he leans down to give me a quick, soft kiss – "no one else sees your delectable body but me. No one touches you but me, and most definitely, no one watches you come. But. Me."

His words are seductive and ignite an almost

unbearable yearning in me. I tug against his hold on my hands. "Liam," I gasp, desperate to touch him.

His laugh is husky and masculine. Tangling his hand in my hair, he holds my head in place as he kisses me long and hard. I'm breathless when he releases my lips. He lifts off me to stand beside the bed, and as he looks down at me, panting with my need for him, he removes his shirt.

Liam is breathtakingly handsome with clothes on but without—he's devastating.

His body is lean but impressively ripped. His chest is solid and well defined, his pecs impressive.

The round, silver medallion I have long wondered about lies nestled against his hard chest, and I find myself suddenly jealous of an inanimate object.

I kick off my heels before sliding back and sitting up on the bed, tucking my legs under me as he unbuttons his slacks. As he slides his zipper down, I look up, and his lips lift slightly as his pants drop to the floor. I inhale sharply as he kicks his slacks to the side. He's left standing in a pair of tight, white *Calvin Klein* boxer briefs that sit low on his hips. I swallow with difficulty as I take in the sexy lines of his sculpted V, which sets off his chiseled abs.

My eyes travel lower. I knew he was well endowed, very evident in the jeans that he wears and the feel of his erection whenever he presses it against me. But now his briefs blatantly display his package in vivid detail, and I get the idea that I might have underestimated a bit. I bite my lip. I look up again to see that he's watching me closely, his eyes full of sensual promise. I uncurl my legs and slowly crawl to the edge of the bed. I reach out with my need to touch, and he catches my hand.

"What do you want, darlin'?"

"I want to touch you."

"Do you?"

I look up, searching his face. "Don't you want me to?"

"Oh yes," he drawls.

He immediately jerks me off the bed to stand before him. I sway slightly with the suddenness of the move.

"Touch away."

Standing this close to him, I have to tilt my head back to meet his amused gaze. I reach up, and my fingers flex around his muscled shoulders. This is the first time I've had the chance to really touch him, and I feel a slow sizzle that begins low in my belly, my stomach muscles tightening.

I run my hands over his broad shoulders, down his arms loving the feel of the hard muscle beneath his skin. Smoothing my hands back up his arms, I angle them down across his chest. When I reach his rock-hard abs, I flatten my hands out, moving my palms down the rippled expanse, my bottom lip caught between my teeth.

Geez. I've never been more turned on. He's incredible. A freaking work of art!

When I reach the waistband of his briefs, I look up and gasp softly at the heat in his eyes.

"Don't stop now, darlin', we're having too much fun."

I look down. His erection juts out at me, and as I watch, it pulsates and twitches against the material of his briefs, jutting out further as if it's seeking contact with me.

Liam reaches down to grasp the hem of my dress. "Arms up." I glance nervously at the glass doors across the room from us. "They're tinted, no one can see in," Liam assures me.

I tentatively raise my arms as ordered, and I'm left standing in my underwear. When he hooks his thumbs in the waistband of his briefs, pulling them down, his erection springs free, slapping against my belly.

I squeak and step back, and then I'm embarrassed at my reaction. Liam laughs as he kicks his briefs toward his slacks.

He grips my arms and pulls me close again. "Careful, darlin'. It *will* bite."

I giggle.

He runs his fingers under the straps of my bra. "Now that's a sweet sound, sugar."

I look up to meet his amused gaze, quickly looking back down as his erection continues to extend upward, nudging against my stomach.

Oh, my...

I reach my hand between us and partially wrap my fingers around him. *He's huge!* He also feels like velvet-covered steel, throbbing in my hand, long and thick. I gulp, suddenly nervous about being able to take all of him.

"Turn around, darlin'."

I do as bid, and he unfastens my bra, slowly sliding the straps off my shoulders and down my arms.

The contrast of the cool air compels my nipples to stand painfully erect, and the heat of his body against my back, causes goose bumps to erupt on my skin.

He gathers my hair, pulling it to my back. "I can't wait for this to fall over my chest and stomach as you ride me."

I suddenly feel hot at that mental image.

His finger strokes down the side of my neck, sliding across my naked shoulder. I feel weak in the knees as both his hands cover my breasts, my breath hitching up a notch.

"I like that I affect you this way." His voice is low and raspy. My eyes widen in surprise at his admission. He leans close, his breath brushing my ear. "It'll make my fucking you all the more intense." I gasp softly, a jolt of sharp desire twisting my insides.

His hands move from my breasts, one to rest against my stomach, the other to encircle my throat.

Oh.

I tremble against him, and when his mouth moves to my ear, my head falls back against his chest. His lips nibble down the side of my neck, ending with his hot, open mouth on my bare shoulder. I cry out softly at the sensation.

"Fuck, Cait. I can't wait to be inside you," he says almost gutturally, and I wonder what's stopping him. I'm more than ready.

His fingers stroke across the front of my thong. "Do you want to save this?"

It takes me a moment to comprehend what he asks.

"Yes!" He's already destroyed one pair.

"Then let's get you out of it."

I start to step away, and he pulls me back against him. "Don't move." He grips my hair and tugs. "You don't move again unless I tell you to."

"Okay," I breathe.

He squats behind me, sliding his finger under the G-string, following underneath the elastic, down between my cheeks to my sex.

"Liam!" I gasp. *Oh.* There's no way I can be still as

he slides his finger between my slit, back and forth. "Please!" I cry out. He needs to stop teasing me, or I'm going to spontaneously combust.

I bite my lip, somewhat relieved when he withdraws his finger and pulls my thong down my legs.

He stands and reaching around me, he pulls the duvet down the bed. I practically salivate watching the muscles in his back ripple with his movements.

"On the bed, sugar." He smiles down at me.

I move to do as instructed as he reaches into the drawer of the bedside table, pulling out a foil packet. I pull the sheet up to my chin.

"You'll need to get on birth control, these aren't as reliable," he says as he lays the packet on the bed.

"How do you know I'm not?" He looks at me with raised brow. "I'm... not." I flush and look away.

Liam reaches over, yanks the sheet and grabs my ankles pulling me across the bed.

"How long has it been since you've had sex?"

Geez, he asks personal questions. "Two years." I know my face turns red, and I'm suddenly annoyed with him. "How long has it been since you've had sex? An hour?"

He blinks. At first he looks slightly surprised by my question, and then he narrows his eyes. He moves quickly, grasping my wrists, jerking me up flush against his body, my face level with his. I gasp softly, and then bite my lip to keep from crying out. He wraps an arm around my back and a hand across my bottom anchoring me tightly to his front. My breasts, pressed against his chest, swell with my arousal, and my stomach against his, clenches with need. It feels heavenly.

"You best learn to control that smart mouth, sugar." His voice is raspy. He gives me a quick kiss, and when he licks across my bottom lip, my stomach flutters. "I'd hate to start the night off by punishing you."

What?

I didn't think I could be any more aroused. But the combined sensations of skin on skin while pressed tightly against him, his tantalizing scent, and the sexy tone of his dominating voice almost makes me come.

Well, damn.

I press my legs tightly together, close my eyes and whimper softly.

His deep chuckle is full of satisfaction.

"I... I don't want you to hurt me." I manage to gasp.

After several moments when he doesn't say anything, I open my eyes to meet his gaze. His expression is unreadable.

"Well Caitlyn, I reckon you're just going to have to see things my way then."

I exhale sharply, and with my next breath, he's lifting me up and tossing me back onto the bed.

"Arms above your head," he orders, and I quickly comply. "Keep them there."

His gaze is intent, his eyes burning with blue fire as he grips my ankles and pulls me toward the spot he wants me. He runs his hands over the tops of my thighs down to my knees and then lifts one leg to place on his shoulder, smoothing his hand over the calf.

My breathing is affected, coming, in short, sharp gasps. I'm finding it hard to catch a deep breath.

He slides my leg off his shoulder and places it back on the bed. Leaning over he places his hands flat on the mattress on either side of me, looking down into my face. He's close enough his medallion lands on my chest, right between my breasts. It feels hot.

"We are going to establish a few rules, you and me."

My heart thuds against my chest. "But later, because right now,"—his voice is rough with arousal—"I'm going to show you I have ways to punish you, other than with pain."

Oh. Shit.

I swallow convulsively, and then he's on the bed, moving down between my legs, his medallion sliding down my body with his movement. Spreading my legs apart with his hands and shoulders, he lies between them, and I'm immediately embarrassed and apprehensive all in one.

"Please, Liam." I close my eyes, unnerved that I'm already begging.

His deep laugh causes my body to arch slightly.

He rubs his nose against my thigh, moving up as he inhales deeply, his scruff brushing against my sensitive skin, causing me to jerk. His hand comes down on my leg to hold it in place, and he bites the inside of my thigh up high where the skin is soft. I cry out.

"I love how you respond to me, darlin'."

I moan softly. I love what he does to me.

He comes up to his knees between my legs and uses his hands behind my knees to bend and raise my legs up and apart, spreading me open wide.

"No!" I squirm, scooting back across the bed, trying to pull my legs back together. This has to be one of the most exposed and vulnerable positions a woman can be in.

"Stop, or I'll tie you down."

My breathing stops along with the movements of my body. I rapidly shake my head.

"Then do as I say, and lie still." He pushes my legs open wider to lie between them again, and I squeeze my eyes shut.

When he drags his stubbled jaw roughly against my

thigh, I jerk and cry out. I warily look down the length of my body at him, but he seems unconcerned, staring between my legs.

Oh! My stomach muscles clench painfully.

He blows his hot breath right on my sex, and I mewl softly, clutching at the sheets under my hands.

"Did your boyfriend ever touch you here?" Liam asks his voice low and erotic.

"Um..." His question throws me for a moment.

He cups me with his large hand. I arch, pressing against that hand.

"Not like that," I answer breathlessly.

"Did he ever inhale your delicious scent, right here?" He taps a finger against my sex.

"No," I gasp.

Liam buries his nose between my legs. I clench my teeth to stop myself from coming up off the bed, but I'm unable to stop my whimper.

Holy hell!

"Please, Liam." My plea is long and plaintive.

"Did he ever taste your sweet essence?" Again he taps his finger against me.

I cry out even before he brings his mouth to me. I jerk when his tongue rasps over my sensitized clit, licking down to my entrance to enter me with a quick jab of his tongue before giving me a long lick back to my clit.

His hands keep my legs spread in place as I writhe and buck beneath his assault.

"You taste sweet as nectar, darlin'," he drawls lazily.

Oh, hell... his voice. His sexy voice alone could send me over the edge.

"Did he ever suck on this pretty pink nub, darlin'?" He flicks his finger against the bundle of nerves.

A tremor runs through my body, and my head thrashes back and forth on the bed. Placing his mouth over my clit, he sucks gently, pulling and lengthening it before sucking forcibly.

My legs stiffen, and my back arches up off the bed as I feel the internal tightening of my muscles. The intense pleasure causes the pounding of my heart to send my blood roaring through my veins. As he continues to suck, ruthless in his onslaught, I feel the familiar quiver low in my core.

And then he releases me. "Not yet, sugar."

"What?" I manage to gasp. "Please, Liam," I beg. Why is he stopping? I fist my hands until my nails dig into my palms. Rubbing my leg against his shoulder, I try to turn my body to gain a little advantage so I can press against him, anything to ease this unbearable ache that he's created.

He lifts up to his knees, and I shift my legs down. I want to cry out for him to continue.

"No. I don't think you are contrite enough, sugar."

What?

He begins at my ankles, taking his time, he slowly moves up my body, sucking and nipping, torturing me with his mouth until he's lying firmly on top of me again. His fingers twist tightly in my hair, and he takes my mouth in a searing kiss, his hold tightening as his kiss becomes more intense. When he releases my mouth, my senses are reeling. I'm gasping, my chest rising with each labored breath. He smiles down at me before latching onto my nipple, biting and pulling at the sensitive peak with his teeth.

"Ahhh!" I reach for him, but his hands grab mine keeping them held above my head.

"Did you forget I said I would tie you down?" His voice is gruff and his expression hard as he looks down at me.

"If it will make you hurry up and fuck me, then do it!" I snap.

His eyes crinkle at the corners and he laughs. "Sorry, darlin'—but I say when."

Ughhh! I'm not going to survive this. I see that now. Maybe I should plead for physical punishment as this is pure torture.

He threads his fingers back through my hair, gripping tightly, pulling my head to the side and bringing his mouth to my neck, biting the delicate skin. I cry out, but I'm determined, not to beg him again.

I hope I don't.

He continues to torment me, his fingers twisting and plucking at my nipples as his body holds me down against the mattress. The burn starts low in my belly, working its way up until I'm shaking uncontrollably.

When he releases my nipples, holding perfectly still as he watches me, I know I can't take it anymore, I feel as if I'm about to explode.

"Please, Liam!" I writhe beneath him and try to move my legs apart hoping that will entice him to end my torment. But he's got my body secured to the mattress with his, so I can't move them.

"I like you this way, sweetheart, tightly strung." He leans in and places his mouth against my ear. "I control your pleasure—only me," he murmurs.

I whimper softly.

He pushes my legs apart with his, his hand coming down to the top of my thigh. He slides his fingers between my legs, over my wetness, moving slowly over my clit, around and over, bringing me closer.

When he slides one long finger into me, he growls deeply, and every muscle in my body tightens and quivers as I arch against him. I cry out my pleasure, and his mouth covers mine in another searing kiss. His tongue mimics his finger, plunging deeply into my mouth as his hand presses against my sex, his finger probing farther into me. My moan sounds tortured when he slips a second finger in, and I gasp against his mouth as he stretches my swollen tissues. When he presses and relentlessly rubs his fingers against a spot deep within me, I think I'll pass out from the intense pleasure. It's so good—so good that the pleasurable sensation overwhelms me.

"Please Liam," I cry, not recognizing my own voice.

He shifts suddenly rising to his knees to cover himself with the condom. Bracing his upper body on his forearms, he moves my legs widely apart until he's lying with his erection pressed against my entrance. The medallion of his necklace lies hot and heavy against my breast.

"Are you ready for me, darlin'?" he asks, his voice strained.

"Oh, yes!" My voice quivers, and I nod as I tentatively move my hands down to his shoulders while his eyes stare into mine. I need to touch him.

He thrusts into me then, thick and hard, filling me beyond what's comfortable.

I cry out as a rough growl erupts from between his clenched teeth. I gasp and struggle for breath as he withdraws and once again plunges deeply into me. Pleasure pain.

"You're so hot and slick," he growls. "Tight." He pulls almost all the way out, then thrusts, much deeper. My cry sounds guttural this time, and I move my hands to his chest, pushing, instinctively trying to avoid the pressure and pain. It's too much.

"No." He grasps my wrists and pulls them above my head again, holding them against the mattress. "You will take all of me." His voice is raspy.

I whimper, not sure that I can. He's too big, and with that thought, he plunges hard and deep, sheathing himself to the hilt.

"Ahhhh!" My back arches off the bed. The pain is sharp. My first time never hurt like this.

He rests his forehead against mine, holding his body still above me. It gives me a chance to grow accustomed to his size.

"Fuck, Caitlyn!" His voice sounds raw. All I can do is whimper in answer.

Liam slowly withdraws only to push back deeply into me. He continues the pattern, a slow withdraw, a forceful plunge, over and over. I grip his upper arms gradually starting to meet his thrusts.

He picks up speed his shaft sliding deep and fast, creating a friction that's almost unbearable with its depth of pleasure. He brings his mouth to mine in a passionate kiss that only fuels the flames that are roaring inside of me as I race to keep up with each wild thrust.

The force of my orgasm hits me hard, and I cry out. My arms encircle his shoulders, and my legs wrap around his waist. The sensation is too much as I struggle to hold on, to save myself from the body-shattering intensity that will inevitably consume me.

Liam calls out my name as he finds his release, shuddering and thrusting as he empties himself. Collapsing on top of me, he's breathing hard, and then he rolls onto his back, pulling me on top of him. He buries his face in my hair as it falls around him.

"Fuck!" he exclaims as he wraps me in his arms.

CHAPTER NINE

I WAKE SLOWLY, LIAM'S AROUSING SCENT teasing me to consciousness. I stretch, arms above my head toes pointed. The soreness in my muscles brings me fully awake, reminding me of the intense pleasures of the night before. I sit up, the sheet tucked around me. I'm in the bedroom alone, and the en suite door is open, revealing its emptiness. A glance at the bedside clock, and I know that Liam is probably at the morning meeting. A sudden overwhelming shyness hits me, and I know I want to be gone before he returns.

I really do need to go home, I tell myself as I leave the rumpled bed. My face heats noticing pillows strewn about the bedroom floor, and one corner of the fitted sheet pulled away from the mattress as it sits a little cockeyed on the frame of the bed. The duvet is pooled on the floor at the end of the bed since there was no need for the cover during the night; the man sleeps hot. I awoke more than once, overheated and slightly sweaty wrapped in Liam's arms. I spot my shoes, but I don't see my clothes as I search the room. I pick up the duvet, pulling it up onto the bed. No clothes. What has he done with my clothes? I hope they aren't keeping company with my still missing thong.

I hurry to the bathroom to find my dress and underwear neatly folded on the counter. I glance up and catch my disheveled reflection in the mirror.

Oh no! I look as if I've spent the night having sex. Good sex. I smile and can't stop from grinning. Great sex. Sex, I definitely want to repeat. With Liam.

I need to hurry. Not only do I want to avoid Liam but co-workers too. I dress hurriedly, and as I walk through the apartment, headed for the elevator, I notice how large it is. Why does he need so much room? I wish I had time to look around. It's a beautiful apartment, spacious with lots of windows allowing the morning sunshine to stream in across the hardwood floors.

I'm relieved to discover I don't need a card to open the elevator doors from within the apartment. Once inside, I look at the control panel. Four numbers. Four floors? I know that the Justice has three levels, does it have a basement too? Then I know. It does. I saw it on the monitor in the security office. The area that looked similar to a dungeon.

Holy shit!

I definitely want to avoid that level. I touch the number two hoping it takes me back to Liam's office, and I'm relieved that when the doors slide open it has.

I stop long enough to use Liam's desk phone to call for a cab, and then I hold my breath as I hurry toward the back door of the mansion. I've never had a reason to do the walk of shame and immediately decide that I'm not a fan. I don't allow myself a good, deep breath until I sit back in the taxi cab.

Two hours later, I enter through the front doors of Query Magazine. I had just enough time to go home and shower before heading to the magazine.

Pat called me the day before requesting that I join her to meet with Valerie's lawyer, and Paul is going to sit in on the meeting too, at my request.

Sitting in Valerie's office, I study Joseph Case, a distinguished looking man in his early fifties. With a smattering of gray in his dark hair and his fit appearance, he looks as if he could grace the cover of GQ Magazine. Valerie once told me he enjoyed dancing, and I wonder if that's how he stays in shape. I've often speculated about Valerie's relationship with the lawyer.

"Thank you all for joining me this morning, I won't keep you long." Joseph Case begins. "I have contacted the authorities about the situation concerning Valerie, and I've instructed a private detective that works for me, to travel to her last known location."

I wait for him to say what location that is.

"Ms. Shaw, Pat tells me you are the last person Valerie spoke with, could you divulge that conversation, please."

"Um..." Caught off guard I glance at Pat. I was the last person to speak with Valerie? I clear my throat in nervousness.

"She wanted to know if I'd discovered anything at Justice House." The lawyer's gaze is direct and perceptive. Geez, no wonder I'm a little nervous. I clear my throat again. "Then she told me that she was going to be out of the country for a few days. She wanted me to stay on course with my assignment and she would call as soon as she returned. I asked her the meaning of a few days, and she said possibly a week. She informed me that I wouldn't be able to reach her, but that she would check in daily with Pat." I glance again at Pat. "She said if something came up, to call Pat and let her know. Then she said she needed to go, she was boarding the plane, and she hung up."

"And did you?" the lawyer asks.

"Did I?" I ask and glance at Paul.

"Discover anything new at Justice House?"

"Not to my knowledge." The lawyer gives me a long look.

"Did Valerie tell you where she was going?"

"No."

"Did you speak of her leaving to anyone, other than the people in this room?"

"No."

He nods, giving me a small smile. He turns his attention to Pat next.

"Did you know where Valerie was going?"

Pat shifts in her chair. "No."

The lawyer tilts his head. "You didn't make her travel arrangements?"

"No. She made those on her own, which I thought a little strange at the time," Pat says.

"Did you speak to anyone about her leaving?"

"No, I did not. And if someone asks where she is, I tell them she's had a family emergency."

"Mr. Sims?" The lawyer turns to look at Paul, including him in his line of questioning.

"No, I have not spoken to anyone about Valerie's absence, other than you three. My wife is aware that Valerie is out of town, but I haven't mentioned anything else to her. I had no prior knowledge of her leaving, so I am not aware of where she was traveling."

"Okay." Joseph Case stands. "My man will be in touch with me tomorrow, we may know something then. I know I don't need to remind you to call me immediately if any of you hear from Valerie." He hands us each a business card. "My personal cell number is on the back. Call anytime of the day or night." He moves to the office door. "And please, be very careful of who might overhear you if you speak of the situation to each other." He gives us a nod of dismissal.

That's it? That's all he has to say? I want to get him aside and grill him about what he knows, what he isn't telling us, although I'm sure he wouldn't crack easily under pressure.

"One thing Mr. Case," Paul says. "Will the police be contacting us?"

"Probably not you, Mr. Sims, but they may wish to speak with Ms. Shaw and Mrs. Williams." He looks at me and then Pat.

I look quickly at Paul and then back at the lawyer. "They won't be coming to Justice House, will they?" My heart jumps into my throat at the thought.

"No. I took the liberty of giving them your cell number and informed them that is how they need to contact you."

"Thank you." I sigh with relief. A visit from the police while at Justice House might be a little difficult to explain to Liam. I give the lawyer a quick look wondering how he has my cell number and then realize Pat must have given it to him.

Paul and I take our departure, leaving Pat with Mr. Case.

"Let's go grab a quick lunch, I have a meeting at noon," Paul says as we walk toward his office.

"Is it with Adams?" I grin.

"You think that's funny? Maybe I'll call him, and the three of us can do lunch together. You can sit in on our meeting. Adam's would enjoy that." Paul smirks.

"Ha! Not on your life." I reach into my jacket pocket for my phone so I can turn the ringer back on, noticing I have two missed calls from Liam's number. My heart gives a little thump.

"Problem?"

"Nope. Where are we going to eat?"

Paul stares me down.

"What?" I try my best to hold his gaze.

"How are things going with Justice?"

"I don't know what you mean." It's hard not to smile.

"Cait?"

"Hmm?"

Paul stops, takes my arm, and then he's pulling me into his office.

"You've slept with him," he states, not looking happy.

"Um... that's not really any—" I catch myself before I tell him it's not any of his business. "I'm a big girl, Paul."

"No you're not." I frown at him. "You're young and sweet, and a guy like Justice will eat you alive." He's glaring down at me, and my sudden red face at his "eat me alive" comment doesn't escape his notice.

"Fuck, Cait!"

I'm surprised at his vehemence. "Paul... I told you I'm not looking for a relationship with Liam Justice, and I meant what I said."

"Cait—"

"It's just sex, Paul," I say firmly. "I'm not some delusional little innocent here." I don't want to hurt his feelings, but... "I can take care of myself, and you need to understand that."

He looks surprised. "I understand that you're hooking up with a guy who owns a sex club. Are you using protection?"

"Shhh!" I glance toward his closed door. "That's none of your business, Paul! And why are we talking about my sex life instead of discussing our meeting about Valerie?"

"I'm worried about you!"

A sharp knock has Paul reaching over to open the door with a scowl on his face. We're both surprised to see Julie standing in the hallway.

"What are you doing?" Paul asks as he pulls her into the room.

"I could hear you two fighting out in the hallway, so I thought I'd better knock."

"We weren't fighting," I say, looking over at Paul. "Your husband was just trying to make sure I understood his point of view on a matter." My cell rings, and I pull it from my pocket. "Could you really hear us?"

"Yes, and I think the whole office is wondering, as am I, if you are practicing safe sex."

"What?" I screech. I give Paul a glare before checking my phone. Damn it! It's Liam calling again.

"I need to take a rain check on lunch, Paul."

"Don't be mad, Cait!"

"I'm not mad," I tell him and smile to reinforce my words. "I Promise. I need to go in to work early. It's going to be a big night."

"At the sex club?" he asks with sarcasm.

"Paul! That's not nice," Julie scolds. "Come on, Cait, I'll walk you out while Paul sorts out the office rumor that he's started." She gives her husband a pointed look.

No one looks at us as we walk through the outer office, a sure sign that I'll be the topic of conversation that afternoon.

"He's been worried about you," Julie says as we stand outside the building waiting for my cab.

"I know but..."

"So." She steps close, linking her arm with mine. "How is Justice in the sack?"

"Julie!" I laugh.

"That good? Hmm, I want to hear all about it."

I take a deep breath. "Do you think that I'm being foolish... about Liam?"

"Do you?" She turns to look at me.

"No, I don't."

"Well then.... Look, you know how overprotective Paul is, and how he drives me freaking crazy sometimes." I laugh when she makes a face. "But we're the only family he has close here."

"I know, and I love him for caring. I really don't want him to be mad at me."

"Here's your cab." She gives me a quick hug. "I'll line him out."

I give her another hug. "You are amazing," I tell her.

"I know, and that's why I deserve to hear what a great fuck Liam Justice is." She grins impishly.

I shake my head at her as I open the cab door. "We'll have to get together and share a bottle of wine."

"Sounds good. I'll talk to you sometime this weekend."

"Okay." I give her a wave as the cab pulls away from the curb.

I have no intention of going in to work this early, but Paul's comment about protection reminded me that I need to call my doctor for an appointment. I call her office, and as luck would have it, she has a cancelation right after lunch.

I see it as a good omen.

I enter through the back door of Justice House on Friday afternoon of the next day, eager to start my shift and even more eager to see Liam. He'd been absent the entire day before, called away on business. He'd left me a short message on my cell informing me that we were going to have a talk when he returned about my, "fucking habit of leaving without saying goodbye."

I walk briskly through the entrance to the restaurant and stop dead in my tracks. The first thing that catches my eye is Liam, laughing at the bar with two other men. Members I assume, a lot of new faces this past week. He's sitting on a stool, his back to the bar, long, muscular jean clad legs stretched out in front of him. He's wearing a white linen shirt, sleeves rolled to his elbows, and I can see the outline of his medallion under the fabric. He looks devastatingly handsome with his sexy day old scruff and disheveled hair. I follow his strong arms down to his hands as they grip the bare-assed cheeks of the woman standing between his legs.

Miranda.

She stands facing him, and it looks as if she's only wearing a bra and thong. It's plain to see she's enjoying the attention of the men, especially Liam as she leans in to kiss his cheek. A jolt of red-hot jealousy sears its way straight to my heart.

I pray I can back out, undetected, but at that moment, clear blue eyes look up to catch my gaze. I notice surprise and—something else in their depths but I'm not sure what. Why is he surprised? After all, it is the time of day for the evening shift to arrive.

Miranda and the men gathered, notice his attention diverted, and they all look in my direction. I decide to go for indifference and continue to cross the room. I feel eyes watching me, and I say another prayer that I don't trip or disgrace myself. When I almost reach the blessed cover of the hallway, Holly calls to me.

"Cait! Wait up."

I turn, keeping my eyes from looking over to the bar area. I paste a smile on my face and hold my head up, pretending that I'm unaffected by the fact that Liam has his hands on that woman's ass. When Holly reaches my side, she laughs softly. We continue down the hallway toward the employee room, where she begins to chuckle again, soon laughing outright.

"What's so funny?" I throw my purse and sweater in my locker, petulantly slamming the door shut.

"You should have seen Randi's face!"

Who? "Randi?"

"Miranda, the bitch."

Surprised at Holly's derogatory comment, I turn toward her.

"Don't look so shocked. Wait until you get to know her."

I nod in understanding. I already know enough about her. She wants Liam.

"You should have seen her face. Standing there with her coochie barely covered, and those men only had eyes for you. Especially Liam." She laughs with apparent glee.

"I don't think they were looking at me, other than I'd disturbed their little—" I shrug.

"Oh Cait, you are priceless!" She nudges my shoulder.

"Don't forget we're hitting the bar tonight. I'm headed back to work, see you later."

My shoulders slump with her exit, and the sudden panic that I feel, is overpowering. "No!" I whisper. I can't let this hurt me. What the hell am I thinking? This is supposed to be just sex. Remember that, Cait!

Why can't they keep their sexual shenanigans upstairs? I have the sudden realization that he wanted me to see him that way, effectively putting me in my place. The arrogant ass! Now I'm pissed.

I go out of my way back to the dining room, steeling myself against looking anywhere near the bar, so I'm not sure if Liam is still there groping Miranda's ass or not. I don't think he is, though; I don't have any sense of him being near.

I'm glad that he's reminded me of the fact that our—coming together is only about sex. Now if I could only get the ache in my chest to stop...

The next couple of hours is crazy with the extra members who join us for dinner before joining the sexcapades going on upstairs. Plus it's a Friday night, and that always seems to bring more people out.

Holly juggled the schedule around so that the weekend hostesses came in to work the early shift while Tansy and I are working the evening shift.

"Hey," Tansy says as she bumps my shoulder. "The guys I just seated at table twenty-four, want you."

"What?" I laugh, my eyes sliding across the room to the table in question. All four men are looking our way. "What do they want?" I ask cautiously.

"Mr. Evans said—"

"Oh, hell! I forgot to check on his cigars. Will you be okay for a few minutes?"

"No problem."

I head down the hall to Bryce's office. The door is ajar and a light is on inside the room. When there's no response to my knock, I slowly push the door open.

"Bryce?"

Bryce looks up from the redhead he's holding in his arms.

"Oh! I am so sorry." I back up, pulling the door with me as I step back.

"Cait, wait. What do you need?"

I stop and respond through the partially open door. "Um... did you happen to get those cigars for Mr. Evans?" I can't see into the room now, but I hear movement and then Bryce is opening the door wide.

"Yes, sorry. I forgot to let you know they came in." He hands me a wooden cigar box. "Remind Evans that he doesn't light up in the house or outside on the grounds."

"Okay."

"Tell him to speak to me if he has a problem with that."

"Okay, thanks." I start backing up.

"Hey, what's wrong?" Bryce leans against the doorframe looking down at me.

"Nothing." I take another step back and motion toward the restaurant. "I better get back."

"Are you sure?"

I smile. "Yes, I'm sure. Thank you."

"Okay. I'm going to claim you for a dance later. Holly told me you girls are stopping in at the club after your shift ends," he explains.

"Yes, well..." I motion down the hall again.

Bryce laughs. "Hey man."

I turn and walk smack dab into a solid chest. I look up into bright blue eyes. Damn it, how did he sneak up on me?

"Sorry." I step around him and head down the hall.

"Cait, wait," he calls. "Bryce, I need you to check upstairs for me, please."

"No problem, buddy."

"Caitlyn!" Liam calls.

I walk faster.

"Hey!" He grips my arm, having finally caught up with me just as I reach the dining room doorway. Pulling me aside, he scowls down at me. "What part of fucking wait, do you not understand?"

"I'm sorry, I'm just busy. What do you need?" I'm proud that my voice sounds so normal.

His eyes narrow. "I'd like to talk to you for a moment. Inform Tansy you're taking a break."

"Can you just say what you need to… here?"

"Excuse me?" He glares down at me.

"I need to get these cigars to a member, and the dinner rush is just starting."

Yes! I'm proud of myself, not letting on that I've been dwelling on him and Miranda for the last two hours.

"After the dinner rush, I expect you in my office." When I don't say anything, he gives me one of his stern looks. "Do you understand me?"

"Yes," I snap. "Won't you be busy?"

His eyebrows lift. "Busy?"

I can tell he's trying not to smile. So much for attempting to act as if I don't care about what I saw earlier.

I look away. "You might have employees to… grope."

"You sound a tad jealous, darlin'." He reaches out

to finger the curl lying over my shoulder, his finger brushing against my breast, which instantly causes my nipple to harden.

Oh! The arrogant ass!

I push his hand away. "Not at all, it's just..." I look up to meet his amused gaze and desperately want to wipe that smirk off his face. "I saw my doctor and she started me on birth control. But evidently—I think you need to continue using a condom." I turn quickly as I feel my face begin to warm. I don't want to blush in front of him. I gasp when he reaches out and grasps my upper arm, jerking me back around, pulling me up hard against his chest. His face moves close to mine, and I try not to breathe in his mind-numbing scent.

"And why the fuck is that?" he growls from between clenched teeth.

My heart ricochets off my rib cage. Wow, he can get mad fast. "Because... I don't want to sleep with everyone you sleep with." I try to jerk from his hold, but this only causes him to tighten his grip.

"You have a choice," his voice rasps. "You can walk with me to my office, or I can throw you over my shoulder and carry you. Choose."

I look up into his angry face, his blue eyes blazing. "You... wouldn't." I glance around; there are people everywhere. We're already garnering a few curious glances as it is. "People would see," I say breathlessly.

"I don't give a fuck," he hisses. "Choose."

I gape at him. He is really pissed. He probably wouldn't hesitate to throw me over his shoulder, not caring who saw.

I swallow against my dry throat. "I'll walk," I whisper.

I inform Tansy I'm taking a break as Liam waits for

me just inside the door. I cross the room to deliver to Mr. Evans his cigars, feeling Liam's eyes following me.

The men look up as I approach their table and Evans stands.

"Thank you, Cait. I appreciate you ordering these for me. I can never find them, but Bryce seems to have inside sources." He smiles.

"I'm sorry I didn't have these waiting for you when you arrived."

"That's no problem." He gives me an appreciative smile. "I know you are working right now, but would you like to have a drink with me later?"

"Sorry, Eric, but Caitlyn is busy later."

My back stiffens, and when Liam puts a possessive hand on my shoulder, I want to shrug it off. Why doesn't he just piss on me to stake his claim, I fume. Why is he doing this? The man is starting to confuse me.

"Sorry, Liam, I didn't realize." Evans bows his head slightly.

"No problem, Eric." Liam steps closer to Evans, his hand still gripping my shoulder. In an undertone I can hear, he says, "I'm sure you will find someone more to your liking downstairs, Eric. Ask for Clarissa."

"Thank you, Liam, I'll do that." Then Evans looks at me. "Miss Shaw."

Liam's hand slides down to my elbow as he guides me back across the dining room, and I'm uncomfortably conscious of the quiet that has settled over the room. Tansy stares at us with wide eyes.

Once we are out in the hallway, I shake off Liam's hand and turn to glare at him.

"What are you doing?"

"Trust me, darlin', you're not his type."

"What? What's that supposed to mean?"

I think he's about to answer me and then I see the shutters go down.

"Let's go." He grasps the nape of my neck, reminding me he's still angry.

We enter his office, and he shuts the door firmly as I move into the room. I turn and watch as he walks to the liquor cabinet, a slow burn starting deep inside of me.

"Would you care for something to drink?"

"No thank you, I'm working," I say pointedly. "What did you want to talk to me about?"

His eyes lift to mine, and he smiles, but the smile doesn't reach his eyes. He moves to his desk and leans against the front his long legs spread out in front of him. I breathe in deeply, my insides suddenly clenching with need. As frustrating as he is, I want him.

Stupid girl.

"Come here."

I bite my lip in nervousness and tentatively step closer. He reaches out to pull me between his legs, lifting his hand to caress the side of my face, letting his thumb stroke across my bottom lip.

"You're very beautiful, Caitlyn." His voice is soft.

My breath catches at the sexy timbre of his voice. "Thank you," I whisper.

He weaves the fingers of one hand through my hair. "Why so nervous, sugar?"

I shake my head slightly. I'm nervous because I'm... confused.

"As I told you the other night, we are going to go over the rules, but I thought we had already established a few basics." His soft drawl causes a quiver of need to vibrate through my body.

"I know what you think you saw in the bar today, but sometimes things are not as they appear." I frown slightly, and he reaches to smooth the frown line from my forehead.

I know what I saw.

"Are you involved with Miranda?" I hold my breath, afraid of his answer.

"No, I am not."

Okay, but I know I haven't imagined the sense of something going on between them.

"But you were."

He holds my gaze. "Yes."

"For how long?"

"Long enough." He runs his fingers through the length of my hair. "It was only fucking, Cait," he says softly.

Like us. Is that how he is going to explain me to his next conquest? Of course I'm not really a conquest, I have been a very willing participant, right from the start.

"Does she know that?"

He sighs and pulls his legs in. "Caitlyn—I never lied to or misled Miranda. She knew the score right from the start."

"Like me." Except now, I'm not certain. He is so confusing.

He frowns. "Cait—"

He's saved by the bell when his cell rings.

He stands, and we are so close I have to tilt my head back to see his face. He looks down at me while he digs his phone out of his jean pocket.

He frowns, as he looks down at the screen. "I have to take this," he says, and I step back.

"Justice," he answers. I mosey behind his desk and

move the curtain aside to look out the window that faces the front of the estate and the street beyond.

"What the fuck!" I turn to see Liam run his hand through his hair. "I thought you said you would take care of it, I don't call this taken care of." His eyes slash to mine, and he turns to pace across the room. "I'm coming over there, so you can explain to me what went wrong." He immediately ends the call and stuffs the cell back into his pocket.

"I have to leave." He holds out his arm, and his fingers curve in a "come on" motion.

O-kay.

"Let's go," he says impatiently.

I hurry across the room, and he ushers me out the door. As we walk down the hallway we meet several people that stop to speak, but Liam only gives them a short greeting as we continue. They each look startled, and I understand why when I peek up, faltering at the anger, I see when his cold, frigid gaze meets mine. He grips my arm tighter and pulls me along. There are sounds of laughter and conversation throughout the mansion as we pass through. Liam doesn't slow though until we reach the entrance to the dining room where he pulls me aside, out of view of the diners.

"Cait..."

I look up meeting his still angry gaze. I watch as his eyes soften as he looks down at me. Shaking his head he orders, "Stay out of trouble." Then he's off down the hall with quick strides, leaving me with my mouth open gazing after him.

"That was quick," Tansy says when I join her at the hostess stand. She looks over at the entrance and then back at me.

"Anything exciting happen while I was gone?" I glance around the dining room, relieved that Eric Evans and his group has left.

"If dealing with obnoxious drunks is considered exciting, then yeah, lots."

I laugh softly. "That bad?"

"Let's just say"—she looks up and smiles at the couple who walk thru the entrance—"I'll be ready to hit the bar as soon as we close."

Me too. What just happened with Liam? That phone call clearly did more than upset him, he was furious. I wonder who called him, and what could be going on in his life to anger him that way. Was his absence yesterday connected to that phone call? It did seem odd that he would have a business meeting during one of the busiest weeks for Justice House.

My thoughts on Liam's odd behavior will just have to wait until later I decide as I seat a group for dinner. The rest of the night follows suit as Tansy and I stay busy.

Everyone seems in high spirits, and I wonder at the antics going on upstairs. I do notice that Mike and Bryce both make several passes through the dining room on what I assume is a security check. Leon too keeps a close watch, frequently strolling into the dining room to speak with members.

I'm grateful when we close the doors at eleven. I don't know how many members we escorted to the nightclub, I'd long given up trying to keep count.

"Are you ladies ready to join the party?" Holly's voice sings out as she joins us. "Don't worry about tallying up totals, we'll do those later." She gathers up our paperwork. "Let's drop these off at my office and get this party started."

I grin at her enthusiasm. I want to ask Holly if Liam is back, but I don't. I need to quit thinking about him.

As we head back to the club, Miranda steps out from one of the rooms. She's still wearing only the bra and thong she wore earlier, but now she also wears a shimmery, transparent robe. She's tall, blonde, and beautiful, and I wonder why Liam would be interested in someone like me. I'm short, definitely not blond, and... okay, I'm not ugly, but she's the Greek goddess type, and she and Liam look—really good together. The goddess and the Adonis, I sigh inwardly.

"Oh, Holly," she coos. "Liam called me, and he wants you to remind security to stop incoming traffic at midnight."

My gut twists at her words, and I see Holly frown as she looks at Miranda.

"Okay," Holly says slowly.

"That would be great, thanks." Miranda smiles and sashays down the hallway with Holly glaring at her back.

"That bitch really gets on my third nerve," Holly snarls.

Tansy laughs. "Yeah but..." She quickly glances at me and closes her mouth, not finishing her statement.

Liam called Miranda?

"Come on." Holly loops her arm through mine. "We only have three hours to tie one on."

Yeah, that's what I need to do, get drunk and forget about Liam and his sexy, lying mouth.

It's a rowdy crowd at the club tonight and again, I'm surprised that Liam isn't present. He usually keeps a close watch on everything. Maybe I should ask Miranda if he plans on showing up anytime soon.

Enough Cait, I scold myself.

"I need a drink. Now," I shout over the music.

Holly motions for us to follow and we head for the bar. We're standing in line waiting, and I jump when a pair of hands encircles my waist.

I can tell that Bryce thinks he's funny, startling me that way, as I look up into eyes, filled with mischievous delight. As I shake my head in despair of his teasing, he reaches around me and taps Holly on the shoulder. When she turns, he motions for us to follow him.

Wherever he's taking us, I hope he has alcohol waiting.

We follow as he leads us through the crowd to the reserved table that we sat at the last time I was here. I wonder why we aren't going up to the balcony above, and I look up to see the railing lined with people looking down, watching the crowd.

Tansy, behind me, sees me looking and leans in close. "Private party," she says.

Oh. I start to look away when the shimmer of long blonde hair and the flash of skin catch my eye.

Miranda.

I hold my breath hoping I don't see Liam.

A guy suddenly appears before me, blocking my line of vision with his height. I focus on him; he's really tall, blond and good looking. I can't hear him, but I read his lips, and he asks me to dance. I think. I point toward Holly and Bryce's back and shrug as I move on to follow them.

When we reach the table, there's a stunning brunette already seated. I eye the two bottles on the table as I sit. I don't care what they're drinking as long as it makes me forget Liam.

Bryce takes the seat next to me, beside the brunette. He leans over to give her a kiss. Geez, two different women in one night. He and Liam have a lot in common.

Holly pours us each a shot of a clear liquid. I pick mine up and down it.

Shit!

The potent brew takes my breath away, burning a path straight to my stomach. I almost gag on the taste of it. My eyes swim and Bryce thumps me on the back.

"Moonshine," he yells.

"Vile," I yell back as I catch my breath. He laughs.

It is the nastiest tasting liquor I've ever tasted. Do people really enjoy drinking that?

When Holly goes to pour me another shot, I cover the glass with my hand and shake my head, pointing at the other bottle. I smell the drink this time. Tequila, I can handle. I down the shot and push my glass toward the bottle, but when Holly goes to pour another shot, Bryce slides the glass out of our reach and shakes his head. Holly says something, and Bryce holds up two fingers, and then makes a slash sign with his hand. What? He can't dictate my drinking to me; I'm not on duty.

I reach over and grab the tequila taking a swig right out of the bottle. Bryce grins and then shakes his head.

The same tall, blond guy from earlier appears before me and holds out his hand.

Why not? I'm here to have fun. I place my hand in his, and he leads me out onto the dance floor.

This is just the first of many dances with several different men. Bryce continues to take it upon himself to temper our alcohol consumption, which is probably a good move on his part. I'm quickly learning he is a control freak. I do manage to sneak a bit more than he's aware of, and overall I manage to catch a good buzz and have an excellent time.

The night is winding down, and I'm slow dancing with Mr.Tall and Blond when I feel Liam. I can feel his hot stare without even turning around to look for him. Where has he been all night? A part of me has worried about him, knowing something seriously upset him earlier and the other part of me wants to—What? We agreed, no expectations. But I now know that I am telling him I do have the expectation of no lies between us. Wait. Can I do that and not tell him the truth about why I came to work at the Justice House? I honestly believe the right thing to do is to talk to Valerie before I expose her to Liam. I owe her that. But I owe Liam the truth too. Oh, this is way too intense for my buzzed state.

"I believe this dance is mine," a deep voice interrupts my train of thought.

But it's not Liam, it's some handsy guy I danced with earlier, and I have no intention of repeating those moves.

The tall blond, Marc, smiles. "Sorry, friend, it's the last dance and it's mine."

Living up to his reputation, handsy guy grabs hold of my arm, but Marc quickly delivers a blow to his forearm that makes handsy release me. Then Marc pulls me behind his back and steps into the other guy's space, blocking the fist headed for his face.

"That's enough!" Liam shouts as he pushes his way between the two men.

Bryce grabs my arm, pulling me away.

"Get her out of here!" Liam yells, leveling an anger filled glare my way. The crowd parts, staring at us as Bryce pulls me toward the exit. I look back to see what happens next and there's already a security guard standing by Liam.

"Wait!"

"Shut up, Cait!"

Startled I look up to catch Bryce's hard expression. He leads me back into the mansion, and neither of us says another word until we reach Liam's office.

"What's going to happen now?" I ask as Bryce reaches into the mini fridge for two bottled waters, holding one out to me.

"No thanks."

"Drink it, Cait."

I take the proffered water and drink about half of it down while Bryce paces the room. My mind runs through several scenarios about what's happening out in the club.

"This isn't going to be good is it?" I ask softly.

Bryce's expression is grim. "No. I'm afraid not."

"So... what will be the outcome?"

Bryce studies me for a moment. "Both members will have their membership revoked."

"What? Marc didn't do anything!"

"It's the rule, any altercation in Justice House calls for expulsion of the individuals involved."

"But Marc didn't do anything, it was the other guy. Marc didn't throw a punch, he tried nice, but handsy guy wasn't taking "no" for an answer."

Bryce's eyebrow shoots up in a perfect imitation of Liam's. "Handsy guy?"

I blush as Bryce stares at me. "I danced with him earlier in the night and... he couldn't keep his hands to himself."

"You should have told me, Cait," Bryce says quietly.

"I didn't think anything about it; I just knew I wouldn't be dancing with him again."

Bryce sighs deeply and resumes his pacing.

"Bryce can't you intercede on Marc's behalf? You know how respectful he acted all night."

"Cait... it's not up to me. The rule about fighting is strictly enforced."

"Well, it's not fair, why would the guy defending the both of us against an attack be in trouble too?"

"The rules are clear, Cait. *Anyone*—involved in an altercation—" Bryce falls silent as the office door opens.

Liam walks in, and I can feel the anger roll off of him. Well, I'm not happy either. It doesn't help though that the now familiar tightening in my lower extremities and his spicy male scent, have me instantly wanting him.

"Everything sorted out?" Bryce asks.

Liam flashes me a quick hard glance. "Yes."

"Okay. I'm headed back out there." Bryce gives me a tight smile. "Liam." Bryce lays a hand on his shoulder as he passes by. "It's been a long night." I see him squeeze Liam's shoulder, and then Bryce is out the door.

I watch as Liam unloads his black leather jacket pockets, depositing everything into a desk drawer, shrugging out of the jacket before walking across the room to his liquor cabinet as my eyes hungrily follow him.

"Liam—" My breath catches when he turns eyes on me filled with an anger that rivals what I saw in them earlier in the evening. I instinctively take a step back, and then I'm instantly irritated at myself for letting him intimidate me.

"You know darlin'"—He knocks back the drink he

poured and sets the glass down to pour another—"I do believe you have some explaining to do."

Oh, good. I know I can make him understand the situation. "Well, I was dancing with Marc when the—"

"I don't want"—he says harshly and turns, his eyes ablaze with anger—"or need your explanation of what happened. I was there. I saw!" He practically shouts. I frown, determined to hold my ground in the face of his anger but not sure what to say. "I want you to explain what you were doing inciting members of my club to fight over you!"

What? My mouth drops open. "I didn't incite anything… I was dancing."

He levels his gaze on me, and I realize he's holding his temper under a tight reign.

"Yes, I'm well aware that you danced with every man in the fucking bar!"

"You're… mad because I was dancing with other men?" Wait. "How long have you been back? How long were you watching me dance?" The thought that he didn't join me in the club makes me think that he might have been up in the balcony area with Miranda.

"Were you with Miranda?" His eyes widen in surprise. "You told me you weren't involved with her, but clearly, there is something going on between the two of you."

I watch as his eyes narrow dangerously. "Excuse me," he says softly, his jaw clenching tightly.

Whoa! He's kind of scary when he's this angry. And why is he so angry?

"Liam, I can dance with whomever I want. You really don't have any say in the matter." There. If he thinks he can lie to me and then dictate whom I dance with, he's crazy. "And I did not cause that... altercation... and neither did Marc. The other guy was the problem."

Liam gently sets his glass down on the bar top and then slowly paces toward me, never taking his eyes from mine. His smile chills me. "You've made a mistake, darlin'." His voice is quiet, deadly quiet. His eyes, lit with a blue fire, generate stirrings of unease that flutter low in my belly. He slowly walks around me, and I have to steel myself from turning when he is at my back. "You don't seem to understand."

He's right; I don't understand him at all.

He leans close his lips at my ear. "Once I fucked you, you became mine." I suck my breath in sharply and tremble slightly as his warm breath flows across my face, down my neck. "And what is mine—I keep."

Oh.

"I won't allow another man to touch you." He pulls my hair back over my shoulder and one long finger strokes down the side of my neck. "To taste you." His open-mouthed kiss right below my ear makes my knees buckle, and his arm slides around my waist to hold me up. "Or take you from me." His large hand encircles my throat, and I close my eyes with a moan. "Do you understand what I'm saying?"

"Yes." I can barely whisper, his seductive voice weaves his sensual magic over me, robbing me of all coherent thought and reason.

He pulls against my neck, and I step back flush to his chest, his hand tilting my face up and to the side. His mouth comes down on mine in a punishing, possessive kiss that steals my breath. I turn in his arms, and he pulls me in tight against his front, never breaking our kiss. Pressing his hand against my bottom, he holds me against his rock-hard erection as he grinds against me. I mewl softly as I entwine my arms around his neck, my fingers running through his already messy hair.

When Liam breaks the kiss, pressing his forehead to mine, we're both breathing hard.

"I thought you said..." I swallow convulsively. "No expectations."

He lifts his head to lock eyes with mine.

"Do you want to belong to me, Caitlyn?"

I search eyes that have enthralled me from the moment I first caught a glimpse of them. The man totally captivates me, and I know there is nothing I want more than to be with him. But I'm frightened of what he wants from me and more so that I might give it to him.

"What does that mean?" I ask softly.

He brings his mouth close to my ear. "It means—that I can do with you—as I please." I almost feel faint at how my body reacts to his whispered words. He strokes the side of my face with his finger, and I inhale sharply as blatant need claws at me. "You're already mine, darlin'." His voice is mesmerizing as he caresses my ear with his nose. "You just need to accept the inevitable." He brings his lips to mine in a searing kiss that leaves me breathless.

"Tell me you belong to me." His voice is rough and demanding. His hand slides up underneath my jaw, pushing my chin up, head back. "Tell me."

"Yes," I breathe.

"Say it," he growls, his eyes ablaze with intensity.

"I belong to you," I gasp.

Complete satisfaction settles over his features, and his hand encircles my arm in a firm grip as he hauls me across the room.

I give a little squeak at the suddenness of his action.

Oh shit, is he taking me upstairs? My heart starts to beat erratically.

He doesn't stop until we reach the elevator and he slides his card. The door opens immediately, and he pulls me inside, stabs the floor button—and then he's on me, pushing me against the back wall of the elevator. He grasps my hands pulling them above my head to grip in one large hand as he buries the other in my hair fisting a handful as he jerks my head back. I cry out softly as his mouth comes down on mine almost violently, and I moan as his hot tongue delves into my mouth. When I mimic the movements of his tongue, a growl erupts from deep in his chest. He presses against my softness with his hard body, his erection thrusting against my belly.

Oh, please just take me right here, right now.

He suddenly steps back, releasing my hands, leaving me dazed. We're quickly out of the elevator, and he's pushing me against the wall of his entryway. I gasp, and my heart races at his bold assertiveness as he roughly grips both of my hands, raising them above my head, anchoring them to the wall. When he reclaims my mouth, I moan as he sucks and bites at my lips. His knee presses between my legs, nudging them apart as he ruts against me, hitting my clit. He's so hard and forceful that I cry out.

"There's not going to be anything gentle about tonight, darlin'," he rasps against my mouth. "I've waited all day for you, and watching you dance with those other men, letting them touch you, I'm going to punish you." My body quivers at his words. "I'm going to fuck you so hard you won't be able to walk tomorrow."

Holy shit!

The sharp bite of arousal causes my stomach to clench

in reaction as he grips my hand and pulls me through the apartment, not saying another word.

The bedroom door closes with a soft click behind us as Liam continues to grasp my hand as if he's afraid I'll run if he releases me. He looks down, nailing me with his intense blue gaze, and my breath catches.

"I have to call downstairs," he murmurs.

"Okay," I breathe.

His eyes are fervent as his gaze holds mine. He releases me, and I finally break eye contact, moving across the room to stand before the doors that open out onto a balcony.

"I'm upstairs."

I turn to find him watching me as he talks on the house phone. I turn back to look out the darkened window. I feel awkward, not knowing what I should be doing. Undressing? I'm out of my depth here. I don't have experience in this type of situation. Are men put off by a woman's lack of sexual knowledge? The thought that it might, flames my self-doubt, and I look back uneasily at Liam as I hear him say, "I'll talk to you in the morning."

He sets the phone down on the bedside table. Then he crosses the room in long strides, pulling his shirt up and over his head, tossing it aside.

Holy hell!

My eyes greedily devour every inch of his hard, muscular perfection. The fierce hunger in his eyes, almost savage in its intensity, spikes my desire, creating a raw need that hits me like a physical blow.

When he reaches me, he pulls me roughly against the length of his body as he wraps me in his arms and his spicy male scent. His mouth comes down on mine, and his tongue is forceful as he pushes it into my mouth. His kiss consumes, possesses and sucks every ounce of doubt from my thoughts. Our passion is almost tangible, and I strain to get closer as he grips my bottom, squeezing firmly. I smooth my hands across his broad shoulders, down his arms, loving the feel of his hard muscles as I run my hands over his firm chest.

"Fuck, Cait," he gasps against my lips. When he lifts me up into his arms, I press my mouth to his neck and suck against his skin. I nip and bite as he crosses the room to lower me beside the bed.

"Fucking clothes off. Now!" he snarls as he jerks the duvet and top sheet off the bed.

Our eyes lock as I hurry to pull my dress off as he slides his jeans and briefs down his legs, his erection springs free to stand tall and proud.

I still, my mouth going dry. He is so freaking beautiful, I can't take my eyes from him.

When he grips his erection and pumps his hand along the length, I look up to meet his knowing blue gaze.

"Is this what you want, darlin'?" he asks with a lascivious smile.

I swallow with difficulty. "Yes," I breathe.

He walks slowly, purposefully toward me.

"On your knees."

CHAPTER TEN

OH, SHIT.

I feel as if I'm going to pass out from the riotous emotions running rampant through me. My breathing has escalated, coming in short pants as I sink to the floor in front of Liam.

He reaches down to cup the side of my face, his thumb sliding over my bottom lip.

"You are very beautiful on your knees like this, sugar."

"Thank you," I whisper. I've never done this before. What if I'm not any good at it.

He runs the fingers of one hand through my hair. "I've dreamed of your luscious lips wrapped around my cock from the first moment I saw you," he murmurs.

Oh, hell. I close my eyes in a bid to control the sudden wanton image his words evoke. When I look up at him, the heat in his eyes, takes my breath away, and it's mind staggering to realize that this incredibly sexy man wants *me*.

I take his hard length in my hand, and partially wrap my fingers around his thickness, lightly stroking my hand up and down his length, mimicking his actions of a moment before. Bringing my face close, I lick, slowly drawing my tongue along his length and then back, ending on the underside of the tip where I let my tongue swirl around the engorged head.

Mmmm. I like this. I can tell he does too with the sudden flexing of his hips.

"Suck it, sugar," he says, voice husky.

I look up as I draw him into my mouth. His hand tightens in my hair, and he slowly pushes in further.

My tongue presses and swirls around him. I suck firmly, his erection sliding farther into my mouth.

He moans deeply, his head thrown back. My nipples harden, and I feel a sharp pain between my legs in reaction to his response. *Oh! This is good.* I'm going to drive him out of his mind with need, just as he does me.

With my newfound resolve, my tongue flattens along his hard length, and I suck him in deep.

"Fuck!" He bucks against my face.

His hands tangle in my hair, and he holds my head as he withdraws slightly and then pushes forward again, deeper. Repeating the move, his thickness forces my mouth open wide with each stroke.

"Fuck, Cait!" I look up to see his eyes flash with intense heat. His mouth is open, and he's breathing hard, labored. He flexes his hips and pushes against me as I suck him deeper. I relax the pressure and withdraw, letting him slide almost all the way out to the tip, my lips catch at the ridge, and I circle it swirling my tongue quickly and firmly around him. He grips my hair tighter and groans as if he's in pain.

"Suck harder," he growls through clenched teeth.

I do. I suck as hard as I can, slowly drawing him deep. I stroke his erection with my mouth and throat as I take him deeper, releasing to the tip only to suck him quickly back in, deep and hard. Over and over.

He's panting, and I raise my eyes, looking up the flat plane of his stomach to take in the magnificence of his beauty. He stands with his legs braced apart, head thrown back, biceps bulging as his hands fist in my hair, and I've never felt more powerful in my life.

For as long as I live, I will never forget this first time. The first time I caused Liam Justice to come apart, to lose control.

I quicken the strokes of my mouth, moving faster. His moans intensify as I feel his body stiffen. As I draw him as far to the back of my throat as I can, I bare my teeth against him and moan. The sharpness of my teeth, the vibration of my mouth has Liam gripping my hair, pumping his erection deeper.

He suddenly pulls himself free, bends to grip my arms jerking me up off my feet and roughly pulls me against his chest. His mouth comes down on mine almost savagely, his tongue plunging deep into my mouth, just as his erection did only moments before.

He breaks the kiss, grips my waist and throws me onto the bed. As my back hits the mattress, he comes down to his knees between my legs. Gripping my hips, he raises my lower body up off the bed as he enters me, burying himself balls deep in one hard thrust.

I cry out, and my back bows up off the bed.

Fuck!

He doesn't falter as he pulls my legs up over his shoulders, thrusting into me with a relentless intensity, each thrust deep, ruthless. I whimper at his roughness, and he slows, grabbing my hands to pin them above my head. His eyes smolder as they hold mine captive. "So fucking tight," he whispers hoarsely. He begins to move again, shifting his hips to hit a spot deep inside my core that soon has me coming apart, screaming his name with a mind-blowing orgasm. Liam continues to pound with vigor, each deep, hard thrust hitting that sweet spot that soon has my insides tightening, my inner muscles contracting around his hard length.

No! Oh, fuck! This second orgasm rips me apart, wringing cry after cry from me. Liam thrusts twice more and then roars with his release, collapsing on top of me.

I lie there under him, gasping for breath. Oh, my. That was... I nuzzle his shoulder, inhaling the musky scent of his sweat-dampened body. A fine sheen of sweat covers both of us, and it's sexy as hell. I almost purr with satisfied pleasure.

Eventually I'm able to speak, and I can't help but wonder...

"Did I do it okay?" I ask, hesitant, knowing that I thoroughly enjoyed what I did to him with my mouth. He seemed to enjoy it too but...

Liam lifts his head, giving me a quizzical look. I nervously bite my lip. He suddenly rolls to his back, taking me with him, slinging his arm over his eyes. "Fuck, Cait!" Then he's laughing. Hard. He pulls me up, tucking me firmly against his chest, and then rolls us over again until he's back on top of me, looking down into my eyes. His eyes crinkle at the corners, sparkling with his amusement, and he smiles widely. "I do believe, darlin' that you just might have a natural born talent there."

I blush, feeling shy. Damn, but he makes me feel the things I've always wanted to feel.

My after sex glow quickly dissipates when I realize Liam didn't use a condom. I'm horrified, but he seems unconcerned.

"You're on the pill."

"Liam," I push against his chest until he releases me, and I scoot across the bed, putting space between us. "I just started. We're supposed to use protection for at least two weeks."

He frowns. "It won't happen again," he murmurs. His lack of reaction to the situation annoys me.

"Well, that's just great, Liam." I look over at him.

He doesn't say anything for several moments and then he looks at me. "What can I say, darlin'? I was caught up in the moment." He smirks. "I guess that answers your question on whether you sucked me off the right way or not."

I blush profusely at his coarse language and glower at him when he laughs.

"Yeah?" I retort. "Well, what about the fact I've now, by association, most likely slept with half the women in this club, and whoever or *whatever* they've slept with."

Wow. That was harsh. But I don't have time to apologize as he quickly rises to his knees, looming over me. He grips my arms, jerking me up, and I land with a thud against his hard chest. I cry out, alarmed. Eyes that burn with blue fire glare down into mine. He lowers his face, so our eyes meet level.

"Just who the fuck, do you think you're talking to?" He asks quietly, but it's a scary kind of quiet. "You are precariously close to me beating your ass."

I swallow with difficulty.

He continues to glare at me, his eyes blazing with anger, and then he releases my arms and slides out of bed, walking toward the bedroom door, gloriously naked. "Go to sleep," he growls over his shoulder before exiting the room.

I stare at the closed door, contemplating getting up to dress and leaving. I'm too much of a coward though, not wanting to face Liam's anger.

I pull his pillow to me, burying my face to inhale his scent.

I moan. My back arching as fingers rub firmly, over and around my clit. I'm brought fully awake when Liam lies on top of me, pressing his erection against my sex, and I whimper softly as he rubs the head of his arousal into my wetness. Somewhere in the recesses of my mind, a tiny voice says I'm supposed to be mad at him. I hear the rip of a condom wrapper, and he pulls away from me for a moment. When he presses back into me slightly and then withdraws to rub over my clit, my body shudders in response. His laugh is dark, sexy, and my body reacts as my inner muscles clench uncontrollably. His thick shaft pushes in further, and I groan at the exquisite sensation. Firmly, he relentlessly presses deeper filling me, and I cry out at the feeling of being stretched, filled beyond capacity. "It's too much," I gasp as I writhe beneath him, desperate to free myself.

"Baby, we've already established you can take all of me." His voice is deep and raspy. When he thrusts into me, burying himself to the hilt, I cry out as he stretches me to the point of pain. My body strains to accommodate him, and I whimper as his hands hold my hips firmly so I can't pull away. He withdraws slowly, so slow, pulling against my throbbing nerve endings. My back arches, and I gasp.

"Fuck!" He growls. "I love how tight you are." His dark, sexy slow voice almost makes me come.

He withdraws completely, and then he's standing beside the bed, pulling me to the edge, rolling me onto my stomach. "Up on your knees." I'm dazed, still half-asleep and slow to respond. Impatiently, he grips my hips and pulls me up to my knees, delivering a stinging swat to my bottom.

"Ow!" My hand moves to cover my abused flesh, but he grips both my hands, placing them on the bed.

"On your hands and knees," he growls, and I quickly do as bid, knowing I'll receive another swat otherwise and again, he firmly grips my hips.

"Hold on baby, I'm going to fuck you hard now." His words cause my stomach to clench. He thrusts into me with long steady strokes that soon have my passage a slick slide allowing his shaft to create an unbelievable friction as he pumps in and out of me. When he pulls almost all the way out, I whimper. Without warning, he slams into me almost sending me down flat to the bed. I gasp for breath as he plunges deep again.

He takes me without an ounce of mercy, repeatedly slamming into me. Every muscle in my body strains to remain on my hands and knees, receiving his pounding. I feel the build-up of tension deep inside, winding me tightly, so tight that I hurt with the need for release.

He presses between my shoulder blades, pushing me down until my chest meets the mattress. Pulling my hips higher, he shifts, and then thrusts into me, deep and forceful. My cries are muffled against the mattress as he does indeed, fuck me hard.

The sky is beginning to lighten when he finally lets me rest. I'm exhausted, thoroughly spent as I drift into a deep sleep.

Bright sunlight brings me fully awake, and I roll to look at the bedside clock, groaning when I see the time. I'm supposed to meet Julie in two hours; we have plans to visit one of the local Farmer's Markets.

I sit up on the side of the bed and wince at the soreness between my thighs. My body heats remembering Liam's passion. I'm not sure where he is, but I really want to take a shower. I decide to find him first. I glance nervously over my shoulder as I open what I hope is his closet door.

Wow. His closet is as large as my entire bedroom. I wander in, letting my fingertips gently trail over his hanging clothes as I move to the back of the closet where there are built in shelves. Finding a T-shirt, I quickly slip it over my head.

I carefully close the closet door and then head out to the hallway. It's quiet, really quiet, and I instinctively know that I'm alone in the apartment. I peek in the closed doors as I walk down the hallway and discover two more en suite bedrooms, beautifully furnished and decorated. They too have French doors that lead out onto the balcony. When I open the door at the end of the hall, I'm a little taken aback. Dust covers drape across everything in the room, and that's not the only thing that's different from the other bedrooms. Although this room also has an en suite bathroom, there the similarities end. There are no windows, no outside door to the deck, and the floor is hardwood instead of soft, luxurious carpeting like the others. The room just seems so unfinished with its exposed beams running the length of the ceiling. A storage room? I close the door and retrace my steps back to the point where the hallway branches off to another long hallway that connects to the main rooms of the apartment.

Besides the three bedrooms and storage room, the apartment has a den, a family/media room, formal living/dining room, utility room and a kitchen. I remember the first time I was here, thinking that this place was too large for one person, but I really had no idea. The apartment is bright and open, a more modern design than the rest of the elegant mansion but equally as beautiful.

I walk back to the bedroom, and as I enter, the sunshine lures me to the French doors opening out onto a narrow deck. This side of the house is facing the gardens, and as I open one side of the double doors, I breathe in the sweetly scented spring air. It's a little breezy as I step out, but otherwise a gorgeous day. The deck, furnished with outdoor furniture, would be a lovely place to sit in the evening. I step to the railing. *Wow, it's really high up here.* I move back and stand just outside the door in the sunshine to bask in its warmth.

I take a deep breath and wonder where Liam is. I know there's no morning meeting on Saturday. My thoughts drift to the night before.

Last night! A small smile crosses my lips. Last night was simply amazing. Definitely unlike anything I've ever experienced. It still amazes me my response to Liam. The man is certainly attuned to my body, most assuredly more so than my previous experience with Jeff. And I know that nothing would ever have changed with Jeff if we had stayed together and possibly married. I never lusted after him as I do Liam. I couldn't have cared less if Jeff and I had sex, but with Liam... I'm turned on by the mere thought of him. I grin. I want sex all the time with Liam. The man makes me feel alive.

Of course, he did piss me off last night. But it wasn't entirely his fault that he didn't use a condom, I forgot too. That's what he does to me. Right from the start, I've wanted him and acted like a sex starved—I suddenly wonder how Liam sees me? I cross my arms, hugging my elbows. Maybe that's the answer for his reaction last night. I've never given him reason to respect me.

Stop it! I sound like my mother lecturing me. I'm a modern woman, and Liam is—well, he probably thinks no less of me than any other woman who drops her panties for him. Okay, that thought doesn't really make me feel any better.

A gust of wind whips my long hair around, and the door closes against my back. When I try to take a step forward, I find the door has closed on my hair. Caught up close, I'm unable to turn around. *Geez.* I reach for the doorknob behind me.

"Sonofa..."

It won't open.

A huff of laughter escapes me. Well, this is a first. I'm trying to decide my next move when I hear a door open. From the corner of my eye, I see someone walk to the railing farther down the deck from me, and I assume that it's Liam who has joined me. I immediately decide I don't want him to see me this way. I flatten my back against the door and close my eyes, saying a little prayer that he doesn't see me. For several moments, I listen to the birds chirping and the sound of the breeze ruffling leaves in nearby trees. There's also the sound of cars from the street below, and just when I think he hasn't noticed me—

"What are you doing, Cait?"

Oh, hell. "Enjoying the sunshine," I say weakly.

"Come here, darlin'."

I squeeze my eyes tightly closed. Maybe he'll just go away.

"Caitlyn." His voice holds a warning note.

"I... can't. I'm... stuck." I open my eyes to find him in my field of vision now.

Holy shit hotness!

My mouth drops open as he walks closer. He's dressed in a dark blue vested suit that brings out something in his eyes, which absolutely makes them a lethal weapon. His snowy white shirt highlights his dark hair, and the scruff on his jaw, just sets everything off to perfection. As I look back up to meet his eyes, I feel myself melt into their blue depths.

"You're stuck?"

I sigh. "Yes. The wind blew the door closed and... my hairs caught." The last ends on a plaintive note. His sensual lips turn up slightly at the corners.

"I see." Is all he says as he stands looking down at me.

I knew he'd enjoy this too much, that's why I didn't want him to see me here. Although just who I thought was going to free me from my predicament other than him, I don't know.

I give him an exasperated sigh. "Could you please go back in and open the door?"

He cocks his head to the side and brings his hand up to his face to stroke his jawline.

"Well now, I don't know about that." He steps right up against my front, and before I have a chance to bring my arms up, he's gripping both my wrists to secure them behind my back in one of his large hands.

Damn, he smells so good. I inhale his scent deeply, and the most unbearable burn develops low in my belly.

"Nice T-shirt," he says as he brings his free hand up to grip my chin, and his mouth comes down on mine in a soft kiss. Molding his mouth to mine, his tongue slowly parts my lips to slip inside. His hand releases my chin, caressing my jaw as it continues down my neck, sliding across my collarbone to cover my breast, squeezing firmly before his fingers pinch my nipple as he lazily explores my mouth. I moan, and the burn in my belly is now concentrated right between my legs.

He at once steps back, releasing me. I feel flush move over my body with my embarrassment. I'm panting with need, trapped on his deck dressed only in his T-shirt for anyone below to see, and he stands before me grinning.

"Yes," he gloats, "this has possibilities." His laugh is full of sensual wickedness, and I almost groan with the clenching of my well-used muscles. "But I have an appointment." He turns abruptly and walks back across the deck out of my line of vision.

"Liam." When he doesn't answer, I call again, this time louder.

The bastard leaves me standing, trapped, for a good ten minutes.

When he finally opens the door, I'm on the verge of being pissed. I glare at him before marching back into the room, picking up my clothes on the way to the bathroom. When I re-emerge, he's still in the room, standing in front of the balcony doors looking out. He turns to watch as I slip on my heels.

I'm trying to decide what to say to him. What do you

say to a man after an incredible night of lovemaking... no, not lovemaking, sex. *Thank you for the great sex?*

"I have something for you."

I look up and once more, his masculine beauty floors me. "What?"

He steps close and holds out a folder.

"What's this?" I ask as I take it. I open the folder and then look up as he steps even closer.

"It's the results of the physical I had a month ago. Clean bill of health, no STDs."

I frown and close the file. "Liam..."

"You're the only one I've been with since then, Cait."

I'm the only one he's been with?

He takes the folder, reaches over to lay it on the dresser, and then pulls me into his arms. My hands slide up his chest over his vest as I look up into intense blue eyes.

"Cait... last night..." He gives a slight shake of his head, his lips tilt up at the corners in a small smile. "I have *never* lost control in that way." His voice is low and reverberates throughout my body as his eyes search mine. "I apologize, darlin', for my appalling attitude last night, and for my inexcusable neglect in my responsibility to protect you. I was just as shocked as you were when I realized I hadn't used a condom."

Wow. This totally knocks me off balance. I feel a warm glow at his words. An apology is the last thing I expected. Maybe he doesn't think so badly of me.

"It would probably be a good idea to call your doctor, just to be on the safe side," he suggests, his gaze holds mine.

"Yes." I'd already decided to do just that. I'm sure

there's no reason to worry, but I'll let the doctor make that decision.

He tips my chin up and gives me a quick kiss before releasing me. "I have to go."

I follow him to the elevator.

"You don't need to leave because I am. There's food in the refrigerator," he says as he presses the call button. His cell rings, and he fishes it from his inside jacket pocket as the elevator doors open.

"Justice." Is all he says when he answers.

I step into the elevator and watch as he hesitates a moment before joining me.

"I'm on my way. All right, I'll," —he glances at me— "pick her up on the way."

Who?

"Yes, I'll bring it with me." He glances at me as the doors open, and I step out. I keep walking and head out of his office, down the hall.

There seem to be more people here on Saturday than there is through the week at this time of day. I nod and return greetings as I head toward the back of the mansion for the exit. I just want out of here before I have to see Liam again. I almost make it too, but as I reach the backdoor, he grabs my arm, halting my escape.

"Cait, It's not what you think." I can hear the amusement in his voice.

I steel my expression and then turn to look up into his sparkling eyes. "I don't know what you mean."

He grins. "Don't you, sugar?"

The door swings open and Liam drops my arm as we step back to allow the three female club members to enter. They all zero in on Liam, and I seize the opportunity to squeeze past them out the door. It doesn't take him long though to catch up, and he walks beside me in silence as we approach the guard stand.

"Can you call me a cab, please?" I ask the security guard. Normally he would have already called as soon as he saw me headed his way. I guess seeing Liam with me, has him confused. I'm confused too. I leave the estate through the gates to wait for my cab, with Liam right behind me. *What is he doing?*

"I thought you had a meeting."

"I do. You're making me late."

I stop and spin to look at him. "Then stop following me," I snap. My eyes narrow on him when he doesn't say anything. "Liam, it's broad daylight, I think I'll be perfectly safe on my own." I suddenly feel very vulnerable where he is concerned, and I feel a need to put into perspective how things stand between us. As if hearing his conversation earlier weren't enough.

"Liam." I look up into bright blue eyes. "It's only sex. I know that." I raise my shoulder in a small shrug. "No expectations."

He frowns staring down at me, and then he grips my arm, yanking me close. I have a moment to gasp before he takes my mouth in a hard kiss. My hands rest on his chest as my traitorous body leans into his. When he lifts his lips from mine, he meets my eyes. "Cait..." I wait patiently and then he says, "We'll talk about this later." He takes a step back and turns me around as my cab pulls up. He leans forward to open the door and then closes it behind me after I climb in. He says something to the driver and then he's walking away.

I look back as the cab pulls away from the curb. Liam has his phone to his ear, and when he turns, we make eye contact for just a moment before I turn back around. I settle back into the seat with an inexplicable need to cry.

Two things are perfectly clear to me. I'm falling in love with Liam Justice, and I have no idea what to do about it.

My cell rings just as I exit the cab in front of my apartment building.

"Hi Julie, I was just about to call you."

"Oh, Cait, I'm running late, I had to stop by the office."

I laugh. "Yeah, well I'm running late too, and I still need to shower."

"Maybe we should plan on going to the market next Saturday."

I feel relieved at her suggestion. "I think that's a good idea."

"Do you have plans, or do you want to do something tonight? We could check out a new club over off LaSalle Street. Some of the people at work will be there. Paul's not too keen on going, but I bet we could talk him into it, maybe get a bite to eat beforehand."

I take a deep breath, stepping into my apartment building's foyer. No way am I going to let myself sit at home, dwelling on Liam. "Sounds fun."

"Okay. You want us to pick you up?"

"Sure," I say as I check my mailbox.

"Okay, see ya!"

I let myself into my apartment and toss the mail onto the hall table as I pass by, headed for the shower.

My late night hours and increased physical activity take its toll on me by late afternoon, and I lay down for a nap. When I wake, it's almost dark. I stretch, feeling the soreness in my body. The thought of how Liam used me the night before causes my heart rate to speed up. I roll over onto my stomach burying my face into the pillow to smother my moan. I want him. Right now. I know he wants me too. He makes that perfectly clear. But, from his phone call earlier, he's possibly seeing someone else, and if he is to be believed, it is not Miranda. And, he wants me to trust, that he's not having sex with anyone but me. I roll over onto my back, closing my eyes tight as I envision his handsome face. I don't want to delude myself into believing that he cares for me just because he's not sleeping with anyone else. If I were smart, I'd stay away from him. But I know it's too late for that.

I sigh as I slip out of bed.

We decide to eat dinner at one of our favorite restaurants, not far from the new club we're checking out later. I'm determined to have a good time, having sworn off thinking about Liam. My second glass of wine helps with that.

"A couple of Chicago's finest came by the magazine yesterday," Paul says watching his wife as she steps over to another table to greet a client.

I sit forward in my chair. "What did they say?"

"Not much, they were there for *us* to do the talking." His eyes meet mine. "They asked questions, moseyed around a bit."

"They spoke with you?"

He nods. "They basically asked the same questions as Valerie's lawyer."

"Maybe I should go to them? I don't want a detective showing up at Justice House to ask me about the last time I spoke to Valerie."

We both look up as Julie returns to the table.

"What's up with the short skirt?" Paul asks his wife, frowning as his eyes roam over her again.

I snort softly.

"You didn't think it was short earlier." Julie smirks.

Paul gives her a surprised look, and I smile behind my glass of wine.

"That was in private, for the enjoyment of your husband."

"How about in the cab? You didn't think it was too short when you hiked it up around my waist." I sputter into my wine. "Cait's dress is short too," she continues, grinning over at me.

Paul doesn't take his eyes from his wife as she laughs and then leans in to whisper in his ear. His lips lift in a smile, quickly replaced with a scowl. Paul turns to look at me, nodding toward the entrance of the restaurant, and I turn.

Holy Shit!

What is he doing here?

Liam stands in the doorway, a proverbial feast as my eyes move over his blatant masculinity. He's still wearing the suit from earlier in the day, but now his jacket and tie are gone, with his shirt sleeves rolled to his elbows. Raw lust rears up inside of me, stealing my breath. But it's his eyes that hold me in their thrall. There's enough heat in the depths of blue fire to blister my soul.

As I stare, a woman swiftly walks up to him, clearly intent on engaging him in conversation, but he continues to hold my gaze before stepping away from her. With purposeful strides, he crosses the room to reach our table.

"Walk me to the restroom, Paul." I hear Julie say, but

I can't pull my eyes from Liam. She places her hand on my arm. "If you need to go we understand. Right Paul?"

I look up and catch Paul's frown. "Yeah. Stay safe and call us," he says before he leads his wife away with a backward glance. I look back at Liam just as he reaches the table.

"Hi," I say softly. Damn he looks good. My belly is aquiver with nerves. His eyes are intense, and I can tell something is wrong.

"Can you leave?" He asks his gaze holding mine.

"Yes," I say without hesitation.

He reaches down and grips my arm as he pulls my chair back. "Let's go." He leads me a few steps from the table when I remember my purse.

He releases my arm, and I walk back to the table, conscious of his eyes on me. As I walk back to him, his eyes roam over my body. He motions for me to precede him, and as we step outside the restaurant he firmly takes hold of my arm as he leads me down the sidewalk. He doesn't say a word, and I'm soon breathless trying to keep up with his long strides as we walk.

Liam abruptly stops beside a bright yellow, low-slung sports car, and pushes me against the door none too gently.

"Liam, what the—"

He forcefully pushes against me, and I look up in surprise into his blazing blue gaze.

"You, in this dress, is about to piss me off! I can't decide if I should beat your ass for wearing it out in public, or fuck you right here to show all the men who are looking at you—just who you belong to," he snarls. My mouth drops open, and then he's pulling me away from the car to open the door. "Get in."

I'm almost afraid to turn my back to him, fearful he'll decide to carry out his threat out here on the street. I sidle around him and edge into the sporty convertible. He closes the door firmly before stalking around the front of the vehicle to enter on the driver's side.

I watch as Liam starts his fancy car, the engine growling to life. He eases the car out of the parking spot onto the street before punching the accelerator, forcing me back against the seat with a gasp.

I decide I'm better off watching Liam than the other cars we are flying past, and I quickly notice that his whole body seems tense. What's happened to put him in such a state?

"What's wrong?" I ask softly. He glances over and then turns his attention back to the busy street not bothering to answer me. But then he surprises me by taking hold of my hand, raising it to his mouth to brush his lips across my knuckles before placing my hand back in my lap.

Well, at least he's not totally pissed at me. Although I know my short skirt is not entirely the reason for all this anger that I feel emanating from him. Something happened today, and not for the first time, I wonder where he spent his day. And with whom. I know he was with a woman from his phone conversation in the elevator. Did they spend the whole day together, or maybe—she stood him up? My eyes move over him, hard to imagine any woman breaking a date with Liam Justice. Something has him upset though, and maybe I'm a misguided fool, but… I know right now that he needs me, enough so that he came to the restaurant. I frown slightly.

"How did you know where I was?" He quickly glances at me. A disturbing realization comes to me. "You have a tracking device on me!" I gasp. I immediately want to start searching for the hidden object. *Oh, no!* "For how long?"

Liam turns to look at me again, his eyes questioning, his forehead creased with a frown line. "A tracking device?" He glances back to the road and then levels me with an intense look.

"A friend of mine, who happens to be your friend Julie's client, called me and mentioned seeing my new hostess at the restaurant where he was dining." Liam's look is too speculative, and I know I've sent up a red flag.

Shit!

"Why would you think I'd put a tracking device on you, Caitlyn?" he asks, once again his eyes back on the road.

How do I answer that? "Too many movies?"

He glances at me again, and I turn to watch the scenery fly by. He really does drive too fast and it seems really fast in this sweet little sports car.

"What kind of car is this?" I ask in a bid to distract him from my blunder.

"It's a Porsche 918 Spyder."

"It's nice. And fast."

"Well now, it's supposed to be fast."

"Oh, I can see that." I smile when he looks at me and then he grins. Boys and their toys!

He slows the Porsche, and I look out the front, relieved we've reached Justice House in one piece. When he eases the car to a stop in the street, for just a moment I think he's going to drive on, and then he's pulling in driving straight back to the garage. I look around. It seems quiet tonight after the busy week but then it's early yet. Liam pulls up in front of the garage so he can back in beside the Range Rover that he usually drives.

We both get out, and I stop in front of the Porsche as Liam retrieves something from the SUV. When he reaches me, he suddenly grasps my arms, and the next thing I know, I'm lying flat on my back on the hood of his fancy sports car with him on top of me. He levels his full body weight onto mine. Grasping my wrists, he raises them above my head, binding them together in one large hand as his other hand grips my chin and jaw. My heart rate kicks into overdrive as his mouth comes down on mine in a punishing kiss. I feel alarmed for a split second before a raw need claws at the pit of my stomach as Liam continues to ravish my mouth. I try to shift in some way as my body screams for his possession, but he has me thoroughly pinned, unable to move.

I feel inflamed with need as his tongue ruthlessly plunders the recesses of my mouth, moaning softly as he grinds his rock hard erection against my mound with a bruising pressure. Releasing my jaw, Liam shifts his large body, moving his hand between my legs. My thong is no barrier as he plunges two fingers deep within my core. My cry at his roughness, quickly smothered by his kiss.

I tear my mouth from his, gasping for a breath as he quickly thrusts his fingers in and out of me.

"So hot and slick," he growls against my throat. Abruptly, he releases me, removing his fingers as he stands. He pulls me up only to spin me around, once again flattening me against the hood of his car, his hard body pushing against the back of mine to hold me down.

I'm panting as I try to gain a little control of my senses. He's forceful moving against me, and when he rucks my dress up around my waist, the night air drenches my lower extremities in cooling relief.

When I hear Liam sliding his zipper, I panic, realizing anyone might walk back here to the garage.

"No, Liam!" I gasp, struggling to rise, but he presses me more fully onto the hood.

"Quiet," he growls near my ear. He angles his body to roll on a condom, and then wraps his hand in my braid, pulling my head back as he enters me.

My moan is long and plaintive. He feels so good that I whimper against the extreme pleasure of him thrusting into me. To my surprise, the added danger of discovery brings a measure of excitement to our licentious moment, heightening my state of arousal.

"I don't want you to come," he grounds out between clenched teeth.

What? Why?

I gasp as he drives each thrust home. Each one forceful enough to slide me across the car hood, only to have him grip my hip with his free hand, pulling me back onto his massive erection. I have a fleeting thought that I hope we're not scratching his expensive car because I feel as if his hard erection could probably pound holes into the metal hood. He certainly is giving me a hard, ruthless pounding as I bite my lip until I taste blood in a bid to stop my cries.

My body tightens with my impending orgasm, and Liam suddenly grips my hips with both hands, thrusting hard and deep as he growls with his release, quickly pulling out of me and stepping back.

Oh. I lie there for a moment until I realize he's not going to give me the release I so desperately need. I want to claw at the hood with frustration. He's never left me hanging this way before. I take a deep, shuddering breath and stand, turning on shaking legs as I adjust my thong and pull my dress back into place. Liam zips up and walks to a trash can where he deposits the used condom.

"Let's go," he says as he holds out his hand.

I move slowly as my legs feel weak and wobbly. When I reach him, he grips my hand and pulls me close. I want to ask him why he didn't let me come, but he seems too—distant.

Thank goodness there's no one about as we walk the driveway to the mansion, and I hold my breath as we make our way to Liam's office. We meet only one person, and he barely gives us a glance.

"Barton," Liam says in greeting as we pass. I can't hide my flush of embarrassment as I know I probably look just fucked. I sneak a peek up at Liam, and he looks down at me with a smirk.

Once we reach his office, he pulls me across the room to the elevator. As the doors slide closed, I look up. Blue eyes burn with an intensity that causes me to gasp softly as they delve into mine.

"Take off your dress."

"What?"

He moves quickly, grabbing me around the waist as his hand grips my braid, yanking my head back, just as the elevator doors open.

"I'm not in the fucking mood to repeat myself, darlin'." He glares down at me. "Now take off your fucking dress." He releases me and steps back, making no move to leave the elevator.

I stand there with my mouth open, staring at his implacable expression. What the hell is wrong?

Something certainly is. But under the anger that I sense coming from him, is an underlying need. I felt that need in the way he kissed me earlier, in the way he pressed his body to mine. There was almost—a desperation in his actions.

I slowly pull my braid and loose strands of hair over my shoulder and turn, presenting my back to Liam. After a moment, I feel him step close. As he lowers my zipper, his hot breath fans my neck and shoulders, eliciting goosebumps across my skin. He lightly slides his hands down my arms, slipping the dress off my shoulders and it falls, pooling at my feet. I stand perfectly still not turning to face him as I feel his eyes on me.

"Turn around," he says softly.

I breathe his scent in deeply before I turn. His eyes move over me, and my nipples harden further in response to that hot gaze.

He reaches out to run a finger across my shoulder, slipping it under my bra strap to follow it down to the swell of my breast.

"I like this," he murmurs as he drags his finger over the lace of my bra to my hardened nipple.

Desire curls low in my belly, and I close my eyes to the overpowering need he elicits as I sway slightly into his touch.

"Take it off," he orders hoarsely.

My eyes fly open. "Liam—"

"I said take it off." There's a latent threat in his tone as he steps back, his facial expression now impassive.

I don't want to strip in his elevator, and I certainly don't want to walk naked through his apartment.

"I'm losing my patience here, Caitlyn."

I snort softly, and his eyes take on a dangerous gleam.

I quickly reach behind me to unfasten my bra, holding it in place over my breasts as I slide out my arms. His eyes narrow when I hesitate.

Oh, hell! I'm suddenly irritated by his need to have me strip naked while he stays fully clothed. I let my bra drop to join my dress on the floor. I fight the unbearable urge to cover my breasts as they swell, and my nipples tighten into erect, hard points under his unnerving stare. I meet his blue gaze, lifting my chin in defiance.

"Now the thong," he murmurs.

I gulp. *The bastard!*

I grit my teeth and clench my hands into fists. I kick off first one high heel before kicking the other in his direction. It flies up and he catches it in his hand right before it makes contact with his face.

One finely arched black brow lifts.

I bite my lip. I'd probably laugh at that move under normal circumstances, but right now I'm too pissed.

"Finish," he commands, and I glare at him before angrily jerking my thong down over my hips. As I bend to slide it down my legs, Liam swiftly moves in front of me, gripping my upper arms, jerking me up and against his body. I cry out just before his mouth crashes down on mine, only to have him release my arms, wrapping his tightly around me to hold me close.

My hands slide up his chest and over his shoulders, my fingers twisting into his hair, loving the silky texture as his kiss slays me.

Effortlessly, Liam lifts me, and I wrap my legs around his waist as his mouth continues to devour mine. He walks with me in his arms from the elevator out into the apartment entryway to slam me up against the wall. He breaks the kiss, his gaze burning into mine as one large hand cups my bottom to support me against the wall as his other hand works to release his erection. I take the opportunity to unbutton his vest and pull at his shirt buttons, yanking his shirttail out of his slacks. My hands slide inside his shirt to his bare back, clawing lightly across his skin.

Liam growls as he rolls on a condom, and I lean in to bite and suck the skin over his heart. I grab the chain of his pendant with my teeth and pull until he leans in to reclaim my mouth, thrusting up to bury himself deep inside of me.

Shit! My back bows, involuntarily, as I tear my mouth from his, crying out his name. Maneuvering my legs over his arms, he spreads me wide for deeper penetration as both of his hands cradle my bottom. He surges into me with thrusts so powerful, I'm certain I'll never walk the same.

"Fuck!" he growls, his fingers digging into my soft bottom, and I mewl softly as he sets up a desperate rhythm that forces the breath right out of my lungs. When he buries his face against my neck, I feel a deep satisfaction that his breathing is harsh and uneven, his gasps as ragged as my own.

As the tension starts to build low in my belly, everything else begins to tighten in anticipation of my impending orgasm. I know it's going to be intense, and there's not a damn thing I can do to help alleviate the overpowering sensation.

I whimper as Liam widens my legs almost to the point of pain, grunting with each hard, almost violent thrust. My back feels raw from the repeated slams against the wall, and it's almost a relief when he stills, buried deep within. But then he releases a long drawn out, almost feral growl as he draws away from me.

No!

"Liam, please!" I cry as he pulls out, releasing my legs to let me slide down his length. If he weren't holding on to me, I'd slide right to the floor at his feet. I grip his shirtfront in desperation. Why is he doing this? It's torture.

He rests his forehead against mine, his breathing labored as I contemplate beating my fists against his chest.

"Are you hungry?" he finally asks, his voice husky.

What? "No, I'm horny, dying here." I run my hands up and down his chest, over the hard muscles of his stomach.

He laughs, smoothing my hair back behind my shoulders. He brings his hands to my breasts, and I arch my back, presenting them more fully to him. He pinches my nipples, and I gasp as he uses his body to press me back against the wall.

"You want me to fuck you again and let you come, darlin'?"

I mewl softly. His sexy drawl when he talks to me this way is almost my undoing. I'm still so tightly wound it won't take much to push me over the edge.

"Please, Liam!" I pant as he squeezes and pulls at my sensitized nipples.

"Answer me!" he says sharply.

"Yes! Please." I gasp, reaching up to grab his forearms in an attempt to stop the pressure he is exerting on my poor nipples.

He immediately releases me, stepping back. He smirks and then turns, stepping into the elevator he grabs up my dress, undies, and my purse before striding down the hallway.

"Kitchen. Now."

I look after him in shock and frustration. *The man is fucking crazy.*

He turns at the end of the hall, disappearing with my clothes.

To hell with this. I head down the hall toward his bedroom. I know where to find a shirt, and I know how to relieve this deep ache between my legs. Liam has taught me a lot in a few short weeks.

I turn in the direction of his room when I hear him call my name.

"Caitlyn." I feel so freaking vulnerable with no clothes on. "You are not to come." He sounds close.

I almost stop in my tracks, but instead, I take off running down his hallway to the bedroom and lock myself in his en suite bath. I move quickly, my heart pounding, to the back of the bathroom as if that will provide me with more security.

Maybe I'm the crazy one since I'm grinning like an idiot.

The doorknob rattles and my heart gives a lurch. After a few minutes when all remains quiet, and I'm fairly certain he's not going to bust down the door, I step toward the vanity to wash my hands and splash water on my face. Then I brush and rebraid my hair. I lean against the counter looking in the mirror. I'm still in need of relief, and it wouldn't take much to find the release I so desperately need. Do I dare? How would he know? All he'd have to do is touch me and I'd be ready to go again.

My nipples are still throbbing, swollen into hard, pouty points. My lips are swollen too from his demanding kisses, and I know that when I come, I want it to be by Liam's hand.

He's so much better at it than I am.

I wrap a towel around my body and slowly open the door. The bedroom is empty, and I stealthily move to the closet, slipping into one of Liam's T-shirts.

CHAPTER ELEVEN

I STOP ABRUPTLY IN THE KITCHEN doorway.

Wow.

Liam has changed out of his suit clothes. He's now wearing a black, short sleeve button down shirt, left undone to flap open as he moves with ease about his kitchen. I catch tantalizing glimpses of his perfect chest and rock hard abs while his low-slung jeans do little to conceal the defined V that dips beneath the well-worn fabric.

His feet are bare, and I decide, not for the first time, that he is the sexiest man I have ever seen. I smile. Barefoot and in the kitchen, hmmm...

The delicious aroma of whatever he's cooking causes my stomach to grumble. He looks up, dark blue eyes meeting mine. When his gaze travels down my body, I shiver in reaction.

"Sit." He nods toward the center island, and I slide onto one of the stools.

"It smells delicious in here," I say appreciatively. He smiles slightly as he sets plates and silverware onto the counter. "Can I help with anything?"

"No, it's nearly ready." He looks up and smiles. "It's only pasta."

Fuck. Will I ever get beyond melting for that smile?

He steps to the refrigerator and pulls out a bottle of white wine. I watch as he uncorks and pours two glasses, bringing one to the counter to sit in front of me.

Oh. I need wine. Lots of wine. As I reach for the glass, he looks back at me from the fridge.

"You only get two glasses of wine—so enjoy them wisely." His eyes linger momentarily.

"What?" I say softly. "Why?" He's not only going to control my orgasms but my alcohol consumption as well?

He turns to give me his full attention. "Because the evening is young, darlin', and I have plans for you."

A delicious tingle resonates across my skin.

"Oh."

He walks slowly toward me, his eyes holding mine. There's a wicked gleam in those blue depths. I gasp softly when he swiftly spins my stool and me around, his arm snaking around my waist to jerk me forward against his hardening erection.

Is this man always aroused? I blush, knowing that because of him *I'm* always ready too.

"Oh," he says softly in mimic, close to my ear. His warm breath against my neck teases a soft moan from me. The hand that rests on my bare thigh slides up under the hem of his T-shirt. My legs are open, splayed apart on either side of his, and there is no barrier to stop his fingers as they firmly stroke over me. My hands grip his upper arms, as I strive to remain on the stool. "You have no idea what the evening holds for you, darlin'," he croons against my ear as he inserts two fingers deep into my channel.

My back arches and my head goes back, a long low

moan pulls from deep down, letting him know just how much he affects me.

"I'll never tire of watching how you respond to me," he says, his voice gruff. He abruptly pulls his fingers from me and steps back. I almost spill off the stool, and he reaches out to steady me.

"Sit up, sugar. It's time to eat." He promptly pops the fingers he just had buried between my legs into his mouth. I can't stop my small gasp or the widening of my eyes, and he laughs outright, low and sexy. "Well now, I know what I'm having for dessert."

If the heat I feel radiating from my face is any indication, I know I'm blushing bright red. I turn back around, and with a trembling hand I reach for my wine glass, downing half the contents. When I look up, licking my upper lip, Liam is watching me, his blue eyes filled with a lascivious gleam.

My traitorous body responds to that look, and I squeeze my legs together, hoping to curb the riotous need coursing through me. My nipples harden further, jutting boldly against the thin material of the T-shirt, drawing Liam's knowing gaze, and I cross my arms over my chest.

I feel as if my whole body is a quivering shell. He enjoys keeping me on the edge this way, and I wonder why. His manipulations go beyond foreplay. This is torture.

Liam takes a long sip of wine, watching me over the rim before turning back to our dinner. I watch as he drains the pasta and then pours it into a large bowl.

"Where did you learn to cook?"

He hesitates a moment in the process of drizzling

olive oil over the pasta. "My mother," he says softly and picks up tongs to toss the pasta and oil.

"Is she a good cook?"

He glances up and smiles gently. "Yes. She was—an excellent cook."

I gulp the sip of wine I've just taken, not misunderstanding his answer. "Oh! I'm so sorry." I don't know what else to say, and the sudden sadness I feel in the room is not my imagination.

He turns back to the stove, picking up a pan and pours the contents over the pasta. He squeezes juice from a lemon over the top and then grates a generous amount of parmesan before tossing it all together. After spooning some on a plate, he pushes it toward me.

"Eat up. You'll need your energy."

I look up, my stomach muscles clenching in a delightful way, but he's busy piling pasta onto another plate.

I unfold my napkin and dig in. It's delicious, but I'm not that hungry any longer, not for food anyway.

"This is good," I say dabbing at my mouth with my napkin before finishing off my first glass of wine. "May I have my second glass, please?"

He looks up and smirks before standing to retrieve the wine from the refrigerator. I try not to watch him as it only adds to my suffering, but it's impossible as my eyes hungrily follow him.

I look skeptically at the glass after he pours the wine. "If I only get one more glass, you could at least fill it."

He shakes his head slightly as he fills the glass. "You enjoy pushing the limits, don't you?"

Do I? "I don't think so." I take a sip of wine.

He glances up, his expression impassive. "Perhaps it's just my limits you enjoy pushing," he murmurs.

I squirm on the stool. I push *his* limits? I take another healthy sip of wine as he goes back to eating.

"How old were you when you lost your mother?"

His fork stalls halfway to his mouth before continuing. He chews, wipes his mouth and then takes a sip of his wine.

Okay. I guess I'm being too nosey, or maybe it hasn't been that long, and her loss is still too fresh for him to want to talk about her. I take another bite of pasta and chew thoughtfully. There are so many questions I want to ask. I have a sudden yearning to know him better.

When his fork clanks against his plate, I look up to catch his intent stare. "I was eighteen."

Oh. "That was young."

Something flickers in his eyes, and then he stands, laying his napkin on the counter. "Yes." He picks up his plate. "Finished?"

"Yes, thank you, it was delicious." I stand and hand him my plate. "Can I clean up… I mean since you cooked." I don't understand his expression when he turns toward me.

"I have a housekeeper, Caitlyn."

I gather up my silverware and our napkins, before walking around the counter. "Well, I can help you put the leftovers away." He walks over and takes the items I've picked up from me.

"I have a housekeeper. That is not what I need you for."

It's all I can do to keep my mouth from hitting the floor as I stare wide-eyed at him.

"Fuck!" He deposits the napkins and silverware on the counter. "I'm sorry, that sounded—"

I avert my gaze, looking anywhere but at him. After a moment, I give a sharp huff of my breath and turn to leave the kitchen.

"Cait." His hand encircles my arm, stopping me. He pulls me into his arms. "Hey." His hand encircles the back of my neck, and as he lowers his lips to mine, we both hear the sound of a phone ringing. Liam is suddenly glaring down at me.

"Is that my phone? Where did you put my purse?"

"Ignore it," he snaps.

I blink. Why is he irritated that someone is calling me? The ringing stops, but I at least want to check who is calling. "Okay, but I still need my purse."

My phone starts ringing again.

He drops his arms from around me. "Who the fuck is calling you?"

"I don't know Liam, but I need to check." When he continues to glare at me, I decide to follow the sound.

I find my purse and my clothes in the living room lying on the couch. My dress is neatly folded with my purse lying on top. I dig out my phone as the ringing stops, the call going to voicemail. The number calling is not one I recognize, probably a wrong number.

I turn and give a start of surprise to discover Liam standing in the doorway with his arms crossed over his chest, anger clearly displayed on his face.

"A wrong number."

His eyes narrow dangerously. "I told you to never fucking lie to me," he says softly.

"*What?* It was a wrong number."

"Don't insult my intelligence, Caitlyn."

My eyes widen in surprise. "You just insulted me."

His forehead creases with a frown. "I didn't insult you."

"Reminding me why I'm here was—"

He moves so quickly across the room, I only have time to take a couple of steps back in alarm before he's grasping my arms, hauling me up against his chest.

"Liam," I cry out softly.

One arm anchors me immobile as the other grasps my chin.

"I apologized. What I said came out sounding wrong. I don't want you cleaning up after me, Caitlyn, and you're not here for a convenient fuck!" I blanch at his words and push at his chest, suddenly needing to put space between us.

"Hey." He grips my chin a little tighter and tips my face up, but I don't look at him. "You are here—because I want you here." My eyes flash to his. He closes his eyes and leans his forehead against mine, his hand releasing my chin to cup the side of my face. I feel the tension leave his body as he simply holds me close.

"I need you here," he says softly. My eyes widen. The sudden rush of longing that I feel at his words is almost visceral in its intensity. He raises his head, his gaze delving into mine. His thumb gently strokes across my cheekbone and I unconsciously turn my face into the caress. The blue of his eyes is dark and deep, full of an unexplained emotion.

"It's been a shitty day, from the moment you left, and all I could think about was getting back here to you." His words reinforce what I sensed earlier from him, an almost desperate need.

"Really?" I breathe, almost afraid I'm dreaming, and if I speak too loudly, I'll awaken.

He nods slowly, his eyes moving over my face. "All I know is that when I'm with you, everything else fades away. I can forget all the shit that is happening. It's just you—and me." His voice is low and seductive as he watches me closely, his eyes holding mine captive in their fervency. He is so freaking hot, and he is simply, everything I've ever wanted. My heart feels as if it will pound its way right out of my chest. Surely he feels it as he holds me close.

My gaze breaks from his, lowering to his lips. I lick mine wanting, needing to taste him.

"When you look at me like that, darlin'—Fuck!" He scoops me up, his mouth coming down on mine in a hard, hungry kiss that ravages the last coherent thought I have left. My arms encircle his neck, fingers delving into his silky hair.

Ending the kiss, he strides from the living room with me in his arms. I press my face against his neck, inhaling his addictive scent, raining kisses up and down the column of his throat. His arms tighten possessively around me as we head down the hallway.

I'm frantically pushing his shirt off his shoulders, down his arms as we reach the bedroom and he opens the door. He releases my legs, his hands gripping my waist as I slide down his length. His mouth comes down on mine in another deep, passionate kiss that steals my breath.

Oh, I want him so much.

Liam breaks the kiss long enough to pull the T-shirt I'm wearing up, baring my breasts. I moan, biting my lip as his fingers pinch and pull at my nipples. When he leans down to draw a swollen nipple into his hot mouth, my knees almost buckle. His arm goes around my waist as he sucks and bites at the turgid flesh. Then his mouth is back on mine, nipping and sucking at my lips. His hand squeezes my bare bottom, holding me in place as he pushes his jean covered thigh between my legs, against my softness. My senses are reeling when he raises his head.

"The way your hard nipples feel against my chest, just might get you fucked before you're ready, darlin'," he says, his voice husky with passion.

I moan softly, my nipples are sensitive, slightly sore, and he feels wonderful as my bare breasts press against the hot, fevered skin of his chest. I grip his upper arms to keep from pooling at his feet, loving how the muscles bulge when he flexes and moves his arms. I slide my hands over his toned shoulders, down over his pecs and then back up. A shiver courses through my body knowing what this strong man is capable of and how his body brings such pleasure to mine.

I'm not sure at what point I realize we aren't in Liam's bedroom, but awareness of my surroundings eventually surfaces.

I pull away slightly. "Where... are we?"

I look around at the room I checked out earlier in the day when I conducted my tour of Liam's apartment. Dust covers still drape the furniture protectively, the only thing different is there is now a suspension of leather straps dangling from the wooden beam that runs the length of the ceiling.

Liam reaches out to grasp one of the straps that are part of the swing.

Holy hell!

Now I might not know much about the BDSM lifestyle, but even I have heard of sex swings.

"T-shirt off, darlin'."

I glance around the room, now wondering about the other contents. "What's under the dust covers?" I whisper, not sure if I really want to know.

"Arms up."

I raise my arms, unconsciously responding to his command. I shiver as the cooled air chills my skin and causes my nipples to harden almost painfully. Damn, it's cold. The air conditioning must be set really low.

"It's cold enough to hang meat in here," I say as his hands encircle my waist and he lifts me. His laugh is low, an immensely sexy sound that triggers a deep, intense yearning in the pit of my stomach.

"Grab the straps, darlin'."

The swing looks similar to a regular swing, but there are leather straps instead of chains, and the seat is a strap of leather.

I do as told, and Liam sets me on the wide strap, his hands holding me steady. I pull my gaze from looking above us where two large eyebolts anchored in the wooden ceiling beam support springs and the attached swing. *When did he hang the swing?* Liam slides my hands where he wants them on the straps, and my heart rate picks up with my nervousness. I don't know what will be expected of me and that, quite frankly, has me suddenly anxious.

And there is the fact I'm naked. I want to angle my arms over my breasts and cross my legs. Liam continually divests me of my clothes while he keeps his on. And though there's something hot about that, at times such as this, it leaves me feeling very vulnerable. Of course, right now he's only wearing a pair of sexy, low-slung jeans.

"Liam, I don't know about this."

He looks up from adjusting a strap, his eyes looking right into mine.

"I do."

He gives the swing a little shake, and I jerk in sudden fear of falling. He grins wickedly.

Bastard!

"Caitlyn, there's nothing to be afraid of." He returns his attention to the straps. "This is a sex swing."

"I know."

His eyebrows lift, and his mouth raises at the corners. "Do you now." I blush. "Been searching the internet have we?" He holds my gaze, and I swallow with difficulty.

"Cait." He looks back down to pull at a strap. "Do you trust me?"

"Yes," I whisper without hesitation. And I do. I've never felt safer than I do with Liam.

He looks up. "Say it."

I swallow as his eyes hold mine, ensnared in their blue depths. "I trust you, Liam."

He continues to hold my gaze, and then his face breaks into that panty-melting smile of his.

I blink slowly.

"Well now, we're going to have some fun, darlin'." He moves my braid back behind my shoulder, his fingers brushing against my neck. My breath catches in a soft gasp, drawing his eyes back to mine. He runs one finger slowly down the side of my neck, over my collarbone to the center of my chest. I gasp sharply this time as his finger continues its course down between my breasts.

The contracting of my stomach muscles is keen as he draws his finger straight down to my belly button.

I watch, my eyes locked on his finger, the digit wreaking havoc with my senses as he draws it over my pubic bone, through my curls. His hand forces my tightly closed legs apart enough so his finger can slide over my slit.

I whimper, my teeth coming down to bite my bottom lip. He releases the strap he's holding, the swing swaying slightly and reaches to grasp my chin, releasing the bite on my lip.

"This is all about enjoyment, darlin'."

I gulp. "For you...?"

His smile is blinding. "For both of us."

Oh, hell. When he smiles at me that way, there's no telling what I might let him do to me.

"Okay," I whisper. His eyebrow rises in silent question, and I nod.

"Okay," he says, leaning in to position a strap near the back of my head. I inhale deeply, my body pulsating in reaction to his sexy male scent. He pushes me back to rest more fully against the adjusted strap as he pulls another one more securely across my back. "Relax against the straps." His voice has taken on the commanding tone that seems to melt any resistance I might have as if it were butter.

Reaching up he wraps a strap with Velcro around one wrist, effectively binding my wrist to the swings support strap that I'm holding on to before doing the same to my other wrist. My arms are now secured above my head.

Panic sets in.

"Why are you tying my wrists?" I gasp softly as I pull against my bindings.

He places his hands over mine, and I immediately calm.

"There are several reasons but the main one is—it pleases me." He brings his face close to mine and breathes against my lips, causing my stomach muscles to clench almost painfully. "I like the control over you that it gives me." His voice is low and seductive.

He steps back, something in his demeanor changes perceptibly, and I watch as he reaches to pull an item from his back pocket. When he dangles a strip of black cloth in front of me, a frisson of dread slices through me.

I shake my head rapidly as he steps behind me.

"Yes," he says firmly as he positions it over my eyes.

"Oh, fuck!" I don't realize I've said the words out loud until Liam gives a low chuckle.

"Fuck?" he whispers near my ear. "Oh, yes, darlin', I *am* going to fuck you."

My back almost bows with the tightening of every muscle in my body, in anticipation of what he has in store for me. I think I'll hyperventilate as I sense him moving back to my front. This not being able to see shit is a little scary.

When he grasps one of my ankles and raises my leg, the swing shakes as my body jerks, my hold tightening on the straps.

"Relax, Caitlyn," he orders sharply. "You won't fall."

"Well," I gasp. "Warn me the next time you do something like that."

He pinches one of my nipples and I jerk again, sending the swing swaying. "If I wanted you to know what I was going to do to you, Caitlyn—I wouldn't have blindfolded you."

Oh, shit! I let out an unsteady breath.

He lifts my untethered leg, his warm hand encircling my ankle. He wraps me securely and then my legs are hoisted up and widely apart. This tips me back in the swing as I am spread open for him.

My heart is pounding again, and my breath is coming, in short, soft gasps. As apprehensive as I feel, it doesn't come close to how freaking turned on I am at the moment.

"Darlin', I think you like this," he says as he runs a finger from my clit to my opening. "Nice and wet." He presses his finger just a bit into my passage, and I jerk slightly, whimpering. My whole body heats with flush at how I must look.

I feel the air stir as Liam moves around me. "I love how you blush for me, sugar," he growls, bringing his mouth down on mine in a hard kiss that leaves me dazed when he releases me, moving around me again. I start shivering, and I honestly don't know if it's from the chilliness of the room or from my desire.

Liam grips my ankles, suspended above my head and then brings his hands down the inside length of my legs to my center. I cry out and jerk against my bindings.

Gah! If he doesn't take me soon, I'm going to perish, hanging right here on this swing. That'll be a sure scandal for Justice House.

Liam runs his hands back up the outside of my legs this time and I can't control my shudder.

"Liam, please," I whine.

He grips my waist firmly, giving a sharp pull, and I jerk forward, my center smacking against his jean covered erection. I moan, my back bowing slightly.

Oh! If he does that again, it just might be the answer to my prayers.

I feel Liam lean over me, his medallion barely touching, tickling across my mound. I cry out at the effect this causes deep in my core. He cups my breasts, then pinches my nipples sharply.

"Ahh!" The swing jerks and sways with my movements.

"Do you want me to let you come?" Again his voice sounds brusque, hard.

I give a short, breathy laugh. "Yes!" *Oh, please yes. Now.* I hear the sound of a zipper and the rip of foil.

"You look beautiful like this, sugar," he murmurs and then he's running his hands up and down my legs, over my bottom, squeezing firmly. I moan, my body moving with a will of its own, arching into his hands as they move over me.

"Are you ready for me, darlin'?" he asks, his voice husky.

I mewl an answer, my body shaking, quivering with my arousal, my gasping breath echoing off the walls.

He positions his erection at my entrance, before gripping my hips with a firm hold. He yanks me forward with a quick hard jerk, as he thrusts into me at the same time, burying himself balls deep. My body arches, and I cry out hoarsely, spasming around the invasion of his large erection. The pleasure of his possession is a sharp, exquisite pain.

"Fuck!" Liam growls. "So fucking tight."

He pushes against my hips, and I slide off his erection. He lets me go as far as the tip, and then he's jerking me back along his length, his balls slapping against my bottom.

I cry out again as my back bows.

"You want to come baby? Let's see how many times I can make you come."

A shiver runs down my spine as he grasps the straps of the swing next to my hips and sets up a relentless push and pull, slamming into me ruthlessly. I am so fully spread open to him that the depth of his penetration steals my breath with each hard plunge. He's had me on the edge of an orgasm since the episode in the garage, only to tease me repeatedly, withholding my release. Now, the force of his thrusts hitting against my cervix is a sharp sweet pain, and I grit my teeth against the unbelievable sensation as my orgasm lashes out with a vengeance.

My legs and hands pull against the straps as my body convulses, jerking about as I hang suspended in midair. I'm left breathless and limp as Liam continues thrusting at a punishing pace. I feel a sudden need to see him. I want this blindfold off. "I need to see you," I gasp. He changes the angle of his thrusts, and soon I feel my body respond as everything begins to tighten his strokes hitting that oh-so-sweet spot dead on.

Oh, no! Too soon. My head thrashes back and forth, and I grip the straps so tightly my fingers feel numb. I cry out as my body arches up sharply with my second orgasm.

I lose all track of time as Liam brings me to climax with what seems to be ruthless determination. The man never tires, never falters as he turns and pulls the swing, angling my body to his satisfaction and my deep pleasure. At one point, he unstraps and repositions my arms and legs, massaging each limb before strapping me securely again. He does not remove the blindfold, ignoring my pleas to do so. I love watching him when we have sex, and I feel cheated. In an odd way, the blindfold leaves me feeling disconnected from him.

Can a person die by orgasm? The thought crosses my mind as I come hard with one orgasm after another until I can no longer string two thoughts together or differentiate where one orgasm ends and another begins.

It feels as if hours have passed when he at last releases my limp legs, rubbing each one.

"Here drink." He places a bottle against my lips as his arm supports my back. I drink thirstily.

He releases my arms and massages each, keeping me supported against his body, and I turn my face into his sweat slickened chest, loving his musky, hot scent. When he lifts me up into his arms, I don't even have the strength to wrap my arms around his neck as my cheek rests against the medallion on his chest.

The blindfold is still in place as he carries me and then sets me down on a cold, hard surface. He pulls against the cloth at the back of my head and it falls away. I blink against the light.

Liam's face is at my level as he gazes into my face his eyes fervid with their intensity. His large hand cups the side of my face.

"How do you feel?" he asks, his voice gruff sounding.

I smile, suddenly feeling shy. "Good," I say softly, my voice hoarse.

The skin around his eyes tightens fractionally, and then he's leaning in, his mouth taking mine in a soft, warm kiss. I sway slightly as he pulls away.

"Can you sit here for a moment without falling off the counter?"

"Yes," I whisper. I think I can.

Liam steps back slowly and then moves to the open shower. I stare at his gorgeous body, muscles rippling as he moves, my eyes feasting on his fine ass. My stomach tightens. I am certain at that moment that I will never tire of Liam Justice.

I close my eyes, too tired to keep them open as I hear the shower come on. Then Liam is picking me up from the counter, cradling me against his chest as he walks into the shower with me in his arms.

I wake slowly knowing it's late by the amount of sunlight coming through the windows. I sit up and gasp when I see the time.

Damn. I flop back against the pillow. Liam keeps me up all night and then I sleep my day away. The thought of last night has me biting my lip.

Holy hell.

I squeeze my legs tightly together against the sudden lust that sweeps over me. Gritting my teeth, I suck in a deep breath.

Holy. Hell.

I'm smiling as I exit the en suite, fully dressed since Liam thoughtfully brought my clothes leaving them in the bathroom for me. I wonder, not for the first time, where Mr. Justice is. Not spotting my shoes or bag, I decide to look for them as I go in search of Liam. I find the missing items still in the living room, but a noise in the direction of the kitchen has me heading that way.

Liam's bent over with his head in the refrigerator, and I walk silently in my bare feet up behind him. I don't know what comes over me, because I'm not a grabby kind of girl, but I reach between his legs and grab him firmly.

He gives a loud "Whoa!" jumping straight up, and I step back grinning as he spins around. My grin quickly turns to an expression of shock when I see Bryce's surprised face.

"Cait!"

"Bryce! Oh!" I quickly back up. "I... I am *so* sorry!" I take another step back and then I'm practically running from the kitchen.

"Cait, wait!"

I'm slipping on my shoes just as Bryce catches up with me.

"Cait," he laughs "Don't worry about it."

I refuse to make eye contact with him. My face feels blistered with my blush. "I am so sorry," I say once more before I head down the hall to the elevator with Bryce right behind me.

Where the hell is Liam?

"Cait, honey, don't leave. It's okay, please don't be embarrassed." I might have felt better at his reassurance if he weren't laughing. "Come on Cait, it's fine, I liked it! You can feel me up anytime you want."

I huff a breath, truly irritated now.

The elevator opens, and I step inside. As the doors slide closed, I look up into Bryce's smiling eyes, alight with a wicked gleam.

Again, I don't know what comes over me as I flip him off.

I'm swatting at a pesky fly as I recline against my lounge chair, when Liam starts blowing up my phone with calls. Julie and I are soaking up rays beside the pool where she and Paul live, and she looks over from her reclined lounger.

"You aren't going to talk to him?"

I reach for my drink and settle back with a sigh. "Not right now." I take a long draw on the straw in my margarita. Julie made a pitcher to bring down to the pool with us and we're on our second glass.

"You're mad at him because you grabbed the crotch of his friend?"

I laugh. "No. I just don't feel like talking to him right now." I close my eyes letting the afternoon sun and tequila soothe my emotions.

"He's never there when I wake," I divulge, feeling her look at me.

"Yeah, but he has a business to run, right?"

"Oh, I don't mean it upsets me. I know he has responsibilities; it's just that... he's never there when I wake. It makes me feel—" I shrug.

"Abandoned?"

I look over at her. "Yeah, I guess." I'm not sure I want to try to explain that more than anything, it makes me feel—dismissed.

"Ladies, how long are you bathing beauties going to bake out here?" We both look up at Paul as he joins us. "Do you have a margarita to spare?" He pulls a chair from a nearby table over close to our chairs.

"Oh, we might be persuaded to spare one," Julie teases. She reaches out to her husband, who promptly enfolds her hand in his large one, bringing it up to his mouth to kiss her knuckles.

I sit up and reach over to pick up the pitcher to top off Julie's glass as my phone rings again. I hand her glass to Paul.

"You'll have to share with your wife unless you brought a glass with you."

"This is fine." He raises his eyebrows. "What's going on?" He nods in the direction of my ringing phone.

"Liam keeps calling, but Cait doesn't want to talk to

him. They had a wild night of sex, and she wants him to question his manhood, his ability, if he was all that good in the sack or not."

I snort a laugh. Julie looks over at me and grins. She stands and moves to sit in her husband's lap, wrapping her arms around him as Paul sips from her glass.

"Baby, I want a sex swing."

Paul and I both spew margarita.

I've just settled in bed for the night, my iPad balanced on my knees, when my phone rings.

"Hi."

He doesn't say anything at first, then he sighs heavily, and just the sound of his sigh causes an intense longing to be with him.

"Finally decide to answer your phone, darlin'?" His slow drawl has me biting my lip.

"Sorry, I was out with Julie."

"And Paul?"

I roll my eyes as I set my iPad aside. "Yes."

"Why did you leave, Caitlyn?"

"Your friend was there and—"

"You were invited, he was not."

I chew my lip, not saying anything. I wish I were with him right now. He sighs again, and I visualize him running his hands through his hair.

"I'd come get you right now,"—his voice is soft, husky even—"but you have a job, and if I brought you here, you wouldn't be able to work tomorrow, darlin'." Every muscle in my lower extremities clenches at his words. "And you need to be here about twenty minutes before the morning meeting." His voice has lost its soft, seductiveness, taking on his commanding tone.

"Why?"

"I need to speak with you and Holly."

"O-kay." An anxious knot forms in my belly. How can just his tone do that to me?

"And Caitlyn?"

"Yes?" I ask softly.

"I want you accessible to me tomorrow. No underwear." I sit up straight in bed. "You will make yourself available to me anytime I desire."

What?

"I don't care if you are in the middle of a discussion with a member, you will excuse yourself and come to me."

"Liam—"

"Do you understand?" His voice comes out clipped, hard.

Desire and need unleash with a fury within my body. I can barely answer when he growls my name.

"Yes!" I gasp.

"Good. Don't be late," he says brusquely and ends the call.

I sit stunned for a moment. I can't go to work and not wear a bra. Some of the men stare at me as if they imagine me with no clothes on as it is. I'm far from flat-chested and it will certainly be noticed.

Liam answers on the first ring. "Yes, Caitlyn." He sounds distracted.

"I can't go to work not wearing a bra," I hiss. I bear his silence and wait for him to say something, hearing the shuffle of papers.

"Wear a bra with a front clasp. If you don't have one, I'll have one delivered—"

"I have one!" I snap.

He'll have one delivered? Tonight? I glance at the bedside clock. It's after nine. On a Sunday night. Maybe he means in the morning but then that would have to be before seven. I'm suddenly annoyed knowing that he probably has a charge account with some women's lingerie store. Of course he does. I'm sure he's bought more than one woman sexy lingerie.

"I don't need you to buy me underwear," I say through gritted teeth before hanging up.

I bound out of bed and start rummaging through my closet as I fume with irritation. It would serve him right if I didn't show up at all for work the next day. I could call in sick. A thrill of excitement courses through me. What would he do if I did that?

CHAPTER TWELVE

Justice House is quiet as I walk the hall to Holly's office. I just pray I don't run into Bryce. I'm not in the mood for his teasing.

I finally found a dress just that morning near the back of my closet. One easily worn with no bra since there is an extra layer of fabric that drapes across the bodice. A black knit with a loose, layered skirt and a back that has a slit leaving the dress open from the buttoned neckline to the elasticized waist, giving a glimpse of my back. Perfect. Liam had better not gripe about the short length either I decide as I smooth my hand over my hair. I straightened it and it lies sleek and shiny over my shoulder.

I'd be lying if I said I wasn't excited and aroused by the thought of what Liam has in mind for me today. I glance toward his closed door as I stop outside Holly's office.

"Hey," I say as I walk in. She's already busy with paperwork scattered across her desk.

"Hi," she greets as she stands.

"Any idea what this is about?" I ask as we cross the hall to Liam's office.

She frowns and shakes her head. "Not a clue. He just

said be on time and to come on in when you got here." She knocks and opens the door, letting me enter first.

Liam stands with his back to us, legs planted apart. Very clear from his body stance that he's upset, his whole body is rigid. He's holding his phone to his ear, and he evidently doesn't hear us coming in because he's practically shouting.

"I don't give a damn what you have to do or how much it costs me! I want that bastard to die in that fucking jail cell; do you understand what I'm saying?"

I stop, surprised by Liam's words and the animosity in his voice.

"Liam!" Holly says sharply.

He turns a frown of annoyance on his face. He immediately looks at me, his gaze holding mine before those sharp blue eyes dip to run down and then back up my body. I swallow deeply, and my body tightens perceptibly in answer to that look. He's wearing sweats and a sleeveless T-shirt, still damp from his morning workout. He looks unbelievably handsome.

"I'll need to get back with you, but do what you have to to make this happen." He ends the call and moves to his desk, sitting down.

I'm processing what I've just overheard as he leans back in his chair, arms up with his fingers interlocked behind his head, his eyes still on me. He's trying to intimidate me. Or us. That's why he's sitting, leaving us standing. Is it because of what I heard? There is something serious going on with him and my natural instinct is to help, but I won't ask my questions in front of Holly.

"Thank you for coming in early," he says cutting into my thoughts. "I wanted to inform the two of you first that I'm implementing a new house rule,"

I frown. Why does he want to inform us first? I glance over at Holly and catch her wary expression.

"Because of the incident in the club Friday night—" My attention flies back to Liam meeting his gaze. "—I've decided that employees will no longer be allowed in the bar or In-Justice after their shift ends."

What?

"What?" Holly asks with alarm.

"You heard me," he says calmly.

"You can't do that Liam!"

"Why?" I ask, giving a quick glance at Holly.

"I'm dealing with the situation as I see fit." Our gazes lock briefly before he turns his attention to Holly. "And yes, Holly, I can do that."

"How is punishing your employees dealing with the situation?" Holly exclaims.

Liam's eyes narrow dangerously, but Holly doesn't seem to notice, or she just doesn't care.

"I had to revoke a membership this morning—"

"What?" I interrupt. "Not Marc's. He was trying to prevent the incident."

Eyes radiating blue fire slash to mine and I almost take a step back from the anger leveled at me.

"*Mr. Thomas,* has received a suspension of his membership." Liam's voice is deadly quiet, and I quickly decide I'd rather he yelled. He stands, coming around his desk to stand before me, and I swallow against the dryness in my throat under his icy blue glare.

"All of this could have been avoided if you would have told Bryce that, *handsy guy,* made you uncomfortable. Instead, the situation escalated into an altercation." Anger positively radiates from him.

"Liam," Holly says calmly. "Cait is new here. It's easy to forget some of the rules—"

"Except, this isn't the first time she has disregarded procedure, is it Ms. Shaw?"

Ms. Shaw!

Liam's eyes burn into mine and then he sighs heavily. Without another word, he strides across the room to the bar.

Damn. I've driven him to drink. *Before* the morning meeting.

Holly crosses the room following him. "Okay, surely there is another way—" she begins, holding her hands out in a placating manner.

"It's this way or I fire Cait."

I inhale sharply, and Liam's gaze connects with mine. I feel as if my heart plummets straight to my stomach. The thought of never seeing Liam again fills me with an indescribable pain. He must see that pain as he frowns.

"Liam, you change rules all the time—"

"And I changed the rules this time. Now enough! It's done." His eyes come back to rest on me.

"Liam, you're being ridiculous!"

"Excuse me?" His gaze is positively frigid when he looks back at Holly, his voice that unnerving, quiet tone again.

Why is he doing this? It seems so wrong. He treats his employees well, and to punish all for one person's mistake doesn't make sense. I recall what Bryce told me that night as we waited for Liam in his office.

Anyone involved in an altercation—

It's the rule—

The expulsion of *all* involved—

If he's doing this just so he doesn't have to fire me—I can't let him do it.

"Liam, I'm sorry, but you can't do this!" Holly's voice is strong and assertive.

"Holly, I love you—you are like a sister to me. But right now, you need to get the hell out of my office."

Holly's mouth drops open and then she's stalking toward the door, clearly pissed off.

"Tell Bryce to start the meeting," Liam calls after her.

I watch as Liam takes a bottle of orange juice from the mini-fridge and fills a glass. He holds the bottle up. "Would you care for some juice?" His voice is brusque.

"No, thank you," I say softly.

He downs the glass of juice in one long drink.

I take a deep breath to quell the worry that in my effort to set things right, I just might make things worse.

"Liam—"

"Don't start, Cait."

"Please don't do this. When your employees get off work, some of them want to have a drink, relax for a bit. It's not fair—"

"I said—enough." His voice is firm, and his eyes hold mine with a hard glare.

I bite my lip and almost back down, but I know I need to put this right. "I'm the only one who should receive the brunt of your decision, not your whole staff," I say softly. "I'm the one who should be banned—just me." I take a deep breath. "I promise you, that if you don't penalize everyone else—I'll abide by your decision and not give you grief over it."

Clear blue eyes regard me steadily. He seems to consider the idea for a moment as if giving it careful thought.

"Done." His tone is decisive as if everything is settled.

Huh? My eyes narrow suspiciously, a disturbing thought taking shape.

"Now come here."

Why would he want to keep me from spending time in the night club?

"Caitlyn, come here."

I mull this thought over as I slowly walk to Liam. He reaches out when I'm close and pulls me into his arms.

"I like this dress but it's too short."

I hiss in a breath, my eyes flashing to his amused ones. "You planned this out! This was your objective all along." My eyes search his. "You don't want me spending time in the club." I bite my lip at the sudden realization of what that means. And it hurts. I huff out a soft breath and push against his chest.

"Hey." He tips my chin up with one long finger, but I keep my eyes averted, not wanting him to see my hurt. "You can go to the club anytime, darlin'. With me."

My eyes flash back to his. "Only when I'm with you... Liam that doesn't make sense, why..." My eyes widen in surprise. *He's jealous?* "You... don't want me dancing with other men?" I say astounded and push against his chest again as I try to step back.

He laughs as he holds me with little effort, quickly bringing his mouth down on mine. I resist for just a moment, and then I'm melting against him. He deepens the kiss, one large hand moving to the nape of my neck, holding me firmly. The other cradles my bottom as he presses my body to his, his erection hard against my soft belly.

Warm lips slide across my jawline to my ear, biting the lobe as his hand slides up under the skirt of my dress, caressing my bare bottom. Right in my ear he murmurs, "I told you—no one touches what is mine." His hand grips my bottom firmly.

I moan softly, my hands sliding around to cling to his waist.

"No one takes from me what is mine." He brings his mouth back down on mine, kissing me deeply. His tongue probes my mouth boldly, limiting my ability to stand as my knees weaken. By the time he ends the kiss, leaning his forehead against mine, we're both breathing heavily, and I'm clutching his T-shirt to keep my balance.

"You are mine, every delectable inch of you." His breath is warm and spicy as it flows across my face. His hand encircles my throat, and he tips my head back as clear blue eyes hold mine with their intensity. "Are we clear on this?"

I breathe "Yes" as my hands move up under the back of his T-shirt. I try to lean in closer, I want my mouth on his skin, but his grip on my throat tightens, and he forces my head back once more. I gasp softly, closing my eyes. Why does this turn me on as it does? His control.

"Look at me," he demands. I look up, feeling slightly dazed. "You belong to me. I do not want other men touching you." I nod as much as I'm able with his hold on my neck.

His eyes narrow, somewhat menacingly. "If I have to remind you again, you won't like the consequences, darlin'."

My eyes widen, and I inhale sharply. Not from his words so much as the sudden, sharp clenching of muscles in my lower extremities.

His hand releases my throat to slide to my back, deftly undoing the button that holds the back of my dress together at the neckline. Pulling one side of the dress down my arm, he bares my shoulder and breast. My nipple puckers immediately, begging for attention.

"Very nice, darlin'." His soft, slow voice causes my heart rate to beat faster as his fingers close in a tight pinch on my exposed nipple.

"Liam!" I gasp, clutching at his back.

He rolls and tugs my taut nipple between his fingers as the fingers of his other hand dig almost painfully into my bottom. When his head lowers, I moan softly, arching my back slightly, presenting my breast more fully to him. But it's not my breast he goes for I discover as his mouth comes down on my shoulder in an open-mouthed kiss. I moan deeply, and when he bites down, I cry out softly, my body shuddering against his.

"Shhh." He licks at the spot as I bite my lip. He then nips and sucks his way across my shoulder, licking up the side of my neck as I tremble in his arms.

"Fuck you taste good," he says, his hand gripping a handful of hair at the back of my head, pulling my head back before taking possession of my mouth in another deep kiss. I slide my hands up into his hair, pulling gently, and he groans deep in his chest.

I whimper softly when he pulls his mouth from mine, not wanting him to ever stop kissing me.

"We have a meeting to get to, darlin'."

I push my bottom lip out in a pout, and he laughs softly, giving my nipple a quick pinch before pulling the bodice of my dress back up to cover me. I blush when he gives me a lascivious wink, before spinning me around to fasten my dress.

Fingers trail down the center of my back, from my nape, dipping beneath the material of my dress, to the base of my spine. My breath catches, and I bite my lip, my body shuddering with need. I want him, right here, right now.

He fastens the button, and then he turns me around to face him.

"Ready?"

I hear the suppressed laughter in his voice and look up to catch the sparkle in his eyes.

Why does he do this to me? He makes me want him with an intensity that has me forgetting everything but my need for him—then he leaves me hanging.

I huff softly and turn to deliver an elbow to his stomach. He grunts dramatically and then laughs. That laugh causes all types of reaction in my body.

"We need to go, sugar, we're late," he says as he heads to his desk.

"Liam."

He looks up, raising a dark eyebrow in question.

"You never had any intention of issuing a house rule forbidding employees in the club or bar after their shifts, did you?"

He glances at me but doesn't say anything as he opens a desk drawer.

"Did you even cancel that guys membership?"

He looks up again, his eyes as hard as his expression when they meet mine. "I most certainly did cancel Travis Holt's membership." He looks back down at the drawer. "He's lucky that's all I did."

I frown slightly. "What about Marc?"

Liam slams the drawer closed. "You're awfully concerned with another man, darlin'."

I snort softly. "I'm only concerned because he really did nothing wrong. I feel bad enough that his membership was suspended. If it had been revoked…" I shrug. I would have felt like shit. And I know I would have felt obligated, at the risk of alienating Liam, to make things right.

I start toward the door and as I reach it, I call over my shoulder, "I rescind my offer." I smile as I close the door, knowing it won't take him long, and he doesn't disappoint as he catches up with me in about five seconds. Oh, this is fun I realize as he pushes me up against the wall. He must think so too as there's a wicked gleam in his eye.

One large hand grips my arm as the other braces against the wall near my head. "What offer might that be, darlin'?"

My heart beat picks up its tempo. "To not go into the club without you." My voice sounds raspy, out of breath. His nearness, his scent is all it takes to kick my libido into high gear again.

"Sorry, sugar, but we made a deal."

I angle my lower body against his. "You made a deal with me too, and I didn't wear underwear, obeying your order."

He pushes against me, forcing me back to the wall, and I gasp as a burn ignites in my belly.

My voice is breathless as I say, "You need to follow through with your part of the deal, Justice."

His lips are so close. I reach behind his neck to pull him across that small space between us. He obliges, leaning down to capture my mouth, just as a door opens directly across the hall from where we stand and out steps Miranda. She freezes mid-step, eyes opening wide before they narrow with ill-concealed anger.

My hand falls to my side, and I try to move, but Liam's hold on my arm tightens. He stands up straight, but he doesn't make a move to step away from me. His forehead furrows into a frown.

"Why aren't you in the meeting?" he asks, annoyance evident in his voice.

Miranda pulls her murderous glare from me, and as I watch, her angry countenance transforms into feigned hurt.

"I..." Her voice breaks and then she looks away. "I forgot last night's settlement reports in the library."

She's good. She's able to put just the right amount of distress in her voice. Although, it might not be fake. I'm not sure how I'd act if I stumbled upon her and Liam in an intimate moment.

I look up to catch Liam's silent contemplation.

"Well let's go, we're late," he says.

He clasps my hand and takes off down the hall with Miranda following behind us. I can feel her eyes boring into my back.

When we reach the dining room, Liam waits for her and then opens the door. Every eye in the room turns our way as we walk in. Bryce is standing near the waitress stand with one foot propped up on the seat of a chair. His eyebrows lift in that cocky way he has.

"It's nice of the three of you to join us." He puts emphasis on *the three of you*, and I hear a snicker or two.

I put my head down and hurry toward where Holly and Joni sit.

"Nice to see you again, Cait," Bryce calls out. "I feel—happy—to see you."

I'm going to kill him I decide as several glance my way. My face feels on fire as I sit beside Holly. She gives me a questioning look, and I shake my head. I'll fill her in later; I don't want to draw any more attention than we already have.

The morning meeting ends and the day shift disperses as everyone goes about their various duties.

The day goes to hell after that.

Shortly after the meeting, Lara discovers someone has tried to shimmy the lock on one of the large antique file cabinets in her office. The ones that hold the membership records.

I remember thinking how difficult they might be to get into when I was in Lara's office while filling out new hire paperwork. And there is the fact that there are security cameras in that room. I've not seen Liam since the meeting, and I'm sure he and Mike are probably busy going through the camera footage.

Why would someone want to get a look at the membership files? I know why I wanted to. I wonder if Valerie's lawyer, who has taken over the running of the magazine in Valerie's absence, has decided to follow through with Valerie's plan to.... What? What exactly was Valerie's objective? She wanted information on Liam, that much was certain. And even though she wouldn't admit it, she was clearly looking for someone else within the clientele of Justice House. Other than that, I don't know much. But I do suspect that whoever she was looking for was someone important, and for unknown reasons she wasn't saying who or why.

So—it was personal. Pat said Valerie met with two men on the day Valerie assigned me to the Justice House. I no longer think that they were cops, I'm fairly certain that they were Private Investigators working for Valerie.

Is that why Valerie left town? I know it was a sudden decision on her part since Pat said she re-scheduled several appointments for Valerie that day. Had the investigators given her information that led to her quick departure? A sudden unease settles over me. What if something bad has happened to Valerie in connection with all this.

I look around the quiet dining room. I need to talk to Paul. And Joseph Case.

Why didn't I think of this before? Probably because all I can think about is Liam, from the very first moment that I saw him.

"Why so glum, young Cait?"

"Leon!" I laugh nervously. "You startled me."

"Is something bothering you?" he asks his eyes full of concern.

"What?" I frown. "Oh, no. I guess it's just too quiet, gives me time to daydream."

He studies me for a moment and not for the first time, I feel as if his eyes see more than most people's do.

"Where is everyone?" I ask in a bid to divert his attention.

He shakes his head solemnly. "We have never had this type of trouble at Justice House."

"Do they have any idea who might want to break into the files in Lara's office?"

"Someone who will be very sorry when Mr. Justice finishes with them."

I nod. Yes. I'm sure Liam is beyond angry. I remember how he responded to the stranger who'd managed to make his way upstairs. To my knowledge, they never did find out who the man was or how he managed to enter the mansion unnoticed.

Consequently, that is when Liam stepped up his security.

I look toward the door. "Leon, if you'll excuse me, I need to find Liam." I know he's curious at my sudden departure, but I don't want to take the time to explain. I need to talk to Liam.

He's not in Mike's office as I suspected. One of the security officers who work for Mike is manning the wall of monitors. He just smiles with a small shake of his head when I ask if he knows where I can find Liam.

I make a note of the time, knowing I don't have long before the dining room opens for lunch. As I near Holly's office, I hear her talking, and I'm surprised to see her husband Ryan here at this time of day.

"Cait, come in." Holly invites when I knock on her opened door.

"Hi, Ryan."

"Hi, Cait, how are you?" He leans against Holly's desk his long legs braced in front of him in a stance, not unlike the one Liam favors. In fact, there are many similarities between the two men.

"I'm good and you?"

He smiles. "Good."

He pushes away from the desk. "Babe, I need to be on my way." He reaches for his wife, pulling her into his arms.

"Um... I'll—" I nod toward the door and start edging that way.

"It's fine, Cait," Holly reassures me.

"I need to get back." I motion toward the door again. "I was just looking for Liam."

Ryan turns to look at me.

"I imagine he's in security with Mike," Holly says.

"He's out at the gates," Ryan informs, regarding me steadily.

"Oh... thanks."

I make my exit, hurrying back toward the dining room. I'll have to wait to speak with Liam since it's time for the dining room to open. As I pass by one of the day rooms, the door opens, and before I realize what's happening, a strong hand latches onto my arm, pulling me into the room.

With what is going on here at the Justice and my surprise, my self-defense training kicks in. I spin and bring the palm of my hand up under the chin of my assailant as my heel comes down on the top of a foot. I'm not tall enough to do much damage with the chin chop, but I know I'm inflicting pain on someone's foot. It all happens so fast before I have a chance to identify my assailant.

"Sonofabitch!" Bryce puts his hand to his chin and hops on one foot. "Fuck, Cait! I think you broke my foot!"

"What the hell are you doing? You're lucky I didn't aim lower!"

Bryce instinctively covers his crotch with his hand. "Damn! You're fondling me one minute and ready to put the hurt on me the next."

My eyes narrow, and I exhale sharply. "What Bryce?" I demand a little impatiently. I'm not going to apologize; he brought it on himself. "I have to get to the dining room, lunch is about to start." What the heck is he up to?

"Calm down. I just want to apologize." He gives me the boyish smile he does so well. It's all I can do not to grin back. As it is, I feel my face heat.

"Look at that!" Bryce laughs.

I'm not in the mood for his teasing, and I need to get to work. "Thank you, apology accepted." I turn to leave.

"Wait, Cait." Bryce laughs again. "That was not my.... Look, I was out of line earlier—upstairs and in the meeting. I shouldn't have teased you that way. I'm sorry."

For once, Bryce seems serious. I dip my head in acceptance. "Thanks."

He smiles. "It's just... you are so young, and you blush so beautifully, it's hard not to take advantage of that."

Okay. He's ruining his apology.

"I like you, Cait. You're good for Liam." Bryce levels his gaze to mine. "He's crazy about you and—he needs someone like you."

Oh. He's quickly redeeming himself.

"I haven't seen Liam happy with anyone this way in a very long time."

Oh.

I think Bryce has just become a friend for life. I step close and stand on tip-toe to kiss him on the cheek.

"Thank you, Bryce. I like you too." I smile shyly. "But I have to go." I step to the door and turn back. "Thank you."

"Cait?"

"Yes?"

"You're in love with Liam, aren't you?"

My eyes open wide, his question catching me by surprise. It's not really any of his business, and Liam is whom I should be saying this to, but... I feel Bryce has been honest with me, and I know he cares deeply for his friend.

I take a deep breath. "Yes," I whisper. *Whoa!* My heart

is suddenly pounding, and I feel a rush of adrenaline just admitting this to Bryce. I'll probably pass out when I tell Liam.

Bryce smiles gently. I turn, and as I open the door, I look back.

"Please... don't say anything."

"I won't, Cait. But maybe you should."

My shift is almost over, and I have yet to speak with Liam. I've seen him a time or two, but he was busy with the people from the security company. It's been an odd day at Justice House, and I am looking forward to going home.

I'm on my way back from turning in my shift report when I remember I need to talk to Leon. I head to the bar to find him talking to a young blonde woman.

"Ms. Cait," he says.

"Hey, Leon."

The blonde looks up, giving me a friendly smile. I'm a little taken aback. She's stunning, and I'm certain I haven't seen her before.

"Cait this is Emily Bronson, a club member. Emily, Cait is our new hostess."

She holds out her hand. "Hi Cait, I've heard good things about you."

I'm surprised, wondering who's been talking about me and if members take an interest in the hired help. "Thank you."

She laughs. "Holly's been giving me the lowdown on what's been going on around here," she explains.

"Have you been away?"

"Yes."

I pick up something in her expression, and her clear green eyes dim somewhat. A touch of sadness perhaps?

"Well, it's very nice to meet you Ms. Bronson, welcome back."

"Please call me Emily."

"Ms. Shaw, have you abandoned your station?" I turn at the sound of Liam's deep voice, looking up to catch his frown.

I blink. What's his problem? I glance quickly to the hostess stand, my eyes scanning the empty dining room.

"Oh Liam, don't be a grouchy boss!" Emily admonishes.

I start at her familiarity. But of course they know each other, she's a member of his sex club. My face heats at the realization that they may have had sex together. Kinky sex.

I turn to Leon. "I wanted to let you know that Mr. and Mrs. Ted Williams will be dining with us Friday night for their anniversary. I wasn't sure if you have that Montrachet that they enjoy on hand."

He nods. "I think I have a bottle or two, but I'll order extra. Thanks, Cait." He gives me an easy smile.

"Are you ready?" Liam asks Emily.

What?

"I am." She slides off the bar stool and grabs her clutch bag from the bar. She smiles at the bartender. "Later, Leon." Then she flashes me a smile. She really is beautiful and seems genuinely nice. "It was good to meet you, Cait."

"You too, Emily." I give her the best smile that I can muster, totally ignoring Liam, but I feel his eyes on me. When he says something to Leon, I turn to return to the dining room.

He's leaving with her? What is she to him?

As Liam and Emily walk past, I busy myself with the paperwork that I need to leave for Tansy.

"Bye, Cait," Emily calls as they leave.

"Bye, Emily." I smile brightly and stack the papers.

I want to follow them, see where they're off to. Are they going upstairs? I could never imagine the hurt and jealousy that courses through my body with a burning rage. I turn and walk smack dab into a hard chest. A tiny "oomph" escapes from between my lips, and warm hands encircle my upper arms.

"You should watch where you're walking Caitlyn." I look up to see that he's still frowning.

What the hell is he doing?

"I should be back in a couple of hours. Wait upstairs for me, Mike will let you into the elevator, and when I get back, we'll go out to dinner." He releases my arms, and before I can respond, he turns and leaves.

I look after him, too shocked to do anything more than stand there.

Is he kidding? I turn to face the room and catch Miranda's smirk.

CHAPTER THIRTEEN

HOLLY AND I FIND A table near a window in a little Italian restaurant that is a favorite of Holly and Ryan's.

"Thank you for coming out with me. A drink is just what I needed," I tell her.

I hold up my glass, and she raises hers to clink against mine, the crystal making a clear ringing tone as the two glasses meet.

"After the day we've had, I needed this too. And now, Ryan is going to be gone all night. I hate when he goes out of town."

"Is he working on a case?"

She hesitates before setting her glass down. "Actually... he's taking care of some business for Liam."

"Oh."

She takes the straw from her glass and places it between her lips as she studies me. "Is Liam why you're upset?"

I toy with my straw. "Sorry, I thought I was hiding it better than I guess I am." I smile wanly.

Holly laughs. "It's okay, you don't need to apologize." After a moment she asks. "Anything I can help with?"

"You can help me understand Liam."

Holly snickers. "He's a man. That could be an endless job."

As I sip my drink, the waitress delivers a couple of fresh drinks to our table.

"Here you go, ladies. Compliments of the two guys at the bar."

Holly and I both look. Two attractive men, dressed in business suits, smile and one raises his hand.

"Tell them thanks for the drinks, we appreciate the gesture. And please tell them that we are married and not interested in conversation… or anything else," Holly quips, looking over at me with a wink.

"No problem," the girl says as she picks up our near empty glasses.

"Thank you," Holly says.

"Smooth," I say as the waitress leaves us. "I probably would have sent the drinks back."

"Let's just hope they don't press the issue."

My phone rings, and I don't even look at it, certain it is Liam.

Holly gives me a raised eyebrow.

"He left earlier, with another woman. Then he had the—audacity to come back to tell me to wait upstairs for him and that he'd take me out to dinner when he returned."

"Whoa!" She frowns slightly. "He left with another woman? Who?"

I pick up my drink and down about half of the frozen concoction before answering her. "I don't know. Some blonde named Emily. She seemed nice, and she was friendly but…"

Holly sputters into her drink, dabbing at her lips as

she sets her drink down. "Cait..." She hesitates when my phone starts ringing again.

I let it ring, trying to decide if I should answer or not. Holly starts laughing, and then I'm laughing with her.

"He is probably pulling his hair out," she says as she tries to bring her amusement under control.

"You think?" I chuckle.

"Hon"—Holly reaches over to pat my hand—"Emily belongs to Bryce, I mean, they're engaged."

"What?" This totally floors me. "Bryce is engaged?" I ask, astounded at this information.

"Well, they are taking a break." She reaches to pick up her drink. "The stupid ass!" she mutters under her breath.

Finishing her drink, she turns to look for the waitress. "We need another drink."

"Yes we do," I agree as I catch our girl's eye.

As we sip our fresh drinks, I look pointedly at Holly. "So—Bryce and this Emily..."

Holly huffs with annoyance. "He's going to end up losing her if he's not careful. Emily is one of the nicest people, and she worships the ground he walks on. The thing is he's so in love with her, he thinks stupid."

"What happened between them?"

She hesitates.

"I'm sorry. I'm sure it's private."

"No, it's okay... I mean it is private but... it's just a long, sad story."

"I don't need a sad story tonight," I say, not able to keep the wistfulness from my voice.

"Hey! You and Liam are not a sad story." She leans into the table. "He's crazy about you."

"I'm not so—"

"Yes, he is. Bryce noticed first, kept pointing things out to me. It's so evident. He's never had a relationship with anyone like you, Cait."

Her words send warmth coursing through me. I've never had anyone such as Liam, and I'm certain I never will again. In my heart I know—he is the one. And—that's just too bad for me. My sudden elation fizzles.

I think Holly notices because she picks up her drink and nods toward mine. "Drink up! Let's tie one on."

I giggle and then down about half my drink.

My phone rings again. I know I should answer, but I don't know what to say to him.

When Holly's phone starts ringing with what she says is Liam's designated ringtone, we dissolve into laughter.

"Oh!" Holly gasps for breath and then points at me. "The problem with our men, is that they are too damn controlling." She nods as if agreeing with herself.

"Is Ryan... controlling?"

She looks up. "Pfft. He tries but"—she bats her eyelashes—"I like to keep him on his toes." She giggles. "The only place Ryan Phillips dominates me is in the bedroom."

I sputter into my drink.

"Don't let the suit fool you. He may look conservative, but that man can fuck for hours."

I start to laugh. This is a side of Holly I've not seen before. "Where did you meet?" I ask.

She chuckles a low, throaty sound. "At a cocktail party for the rich and famous. I thought he was hot, but I also thought he was some rich, smug lawyer with a stick up his ass. I was in a bad mood that night and just felt like giving him shit. He didn't take too kindly to that."

She smiles mischievously. "Within the hour he had me upstairs in one of the bedrooms fucking my brains out."

My mouth drops open on that bit of information.

"It's been lust ever since. He made me marry him the next month."

"Really?"

"Oh, yeah." She picks up her glass. "Lord, I love that man."

I smile.

She swirls the drink in her glass, eyeing me with a goofy grin.

"What?"

"Oh I'm just thinking about how you keep Liam all stirred up."

"I don't..."

"Yes you do, and I love it." She laughs out loud. "You're good for him."

"The thing is he confuses me." I use the hand holding my glass to gesture and some of the drink sloshes out. "Oops." I giggle and pat at the table with my napkin.

"You're drunk," Holly informs me.

"No I'm not."

We both think that's funny.

"We need another drink," Holly informs, waving her arm widely to get the attention of the waitress. "You need another one?" she asks me.

"Yeth."

Holly laughs so hard she almost upsets her chair, which in turn causes hysterical laughing on my part.

The waitress brings our fresh drinks. Setting them down in front of us she stands with her hand on her hip.

"The bartender is a little concerned about you ladies," she informs us. "I told him you were okay and you have someone picking you up before long?" She gives us a questioning look.

Holly and I give her blank stares.

"Yes!" Holly finally announces.

"Absolutely," I add, nodding emphatically.

"All right then." She picks up our empty glasses and returns to the bar area.

Holly's phone rings and we lose it again until the ringing stops, only to start again. This sobers us both a little.

"Maybe I should answer," Holly says. "He's probably having a fucking fit and—he tends to worry," she murmurs as she looks at her phone.

I suddenly don't find the fact that Liam is worried funny. "I'll call him," I say, fishing my phone out of my purse.

Liam answers on the first ring.

"Where the fuck are you?" his voice has that controlled, angry tone.

Damn.

"I'm having a drink with Hollys." She waves her hand. "She says hi." I giggle.

There's silence on the line, and I shrug at Holly. She giggles, and then slaps her hand over her mouth.

"Are you drunk?" he asks quietly. Too quiet.

"No! Well maybe a little. Wait, I'll ask Hollys." I look over at Holly. "Am I drunk?"

Holly snorts into her drink.

"Tell me where you are?" Liam asks in the same controlled voice.

Damn, if I don't love his slow, southern drawl. "I love your voice," I tell him.

I look up as some guy stops near Holly's chair and starts talking to her.

"Caitlyn, where are you?"

"You only use my full name when you're mad or annoyed at me, and I'm the one who should be mad not you." I promptly hiccup.

"Where are you."

"I don't know. I don't remember the name." I giggle again. *I must be drunk.*

"Let me talk to Holly."

"Can't."

I hear him hiss over the phone.

"She's talking to some guy. Wait! It's Holly and Ryan's favorite restaurant." I grin, feeling inordinately proud of myself.

"You two stay right there. I'm coming to get you," he growls, and my insides tighten in a most pleasurable way.

"I'm ready for you to come get me, Liam."

"You stay right there, do you understand me, Caitlyn?"

"Yes," I answer.

"What did I say?"

I giggle again. "We are to stay right here… because you are coming to get me."

I hear him speaking to someone, and then he says, "I'll be there in a few minutes."

The line goes dead.

"Okay then," I say, slipping my phone into my purse.

The guy talking to Holly leaves, and Holly looks at me just as our waitress sets down two steaming cups of black coffee.

"I'm supposed to tell you that, *Liam* said for you both to drink this coffee," she says, looking amused.

"Thank you," Holly says.

After she leaves us, Holly asks, "Is he on his way?"

"Yep." I sip at the hot, bitter brew and then set the cup down. We've been having fun, but neither one of us is past the point of pulling ourselves together. And—I have something serious to ask her.

"Tell me about him. About Liam."

She studies me for a moment, her amused expression at once guarded. "You love him don't you?" she finally asks.

I swallow against the dryness in my throat. "With all my heart." First Bryce and now Holly. If it's been that obvious to them, is Liam aware too?

"Liam had a… hard time, growing up." Holly takes a sip of her coffee. "His father, if you can call him that, was a hard man."

A hard man?

"Walter Justice was on the wrong side of the law most of the time, in and out of jail while Liam was growing up. He was a small-time hustler with a mean streak. Never there for Liam or Liam's mother. Abusive to them both, especially—when he drank."

Oh, no.

"Growing up in a small community, Liam had a hard time living down his father's reputation. I guess you can imagine how hard it was for him, having to deal with the constant gossip, humiliation—the shame he felt." She shakes her head slightly and smiles sadly. "He was so proud and so strong."

My heart aches at the thought of what Liam's life

must have been like when he was a boy. "You've known him a long time."

"We grew up together. The four of us have always been close, always there for each other. They're my brothers." She grins. "Of course, Bryce is the annoying, pain in the ass brother." I laugh with her in agreement.

"When Liam bought Justice House, he and Mike moved here, and it felt as if part of my heart was missing. When Bryce left, I really thought that I had lost them all forever. I enrolled in a local college and barely managed to survive. I'd lost my best friends. And then one day there was a knock at my door, and there stood Liam. He brought me here and this is where my life is now." She picks up her coffee and peers at me over the rim. "He is an extremely loyal friend."

That, I had already figured out about him.

"What about your family back home? If you don't mind my asking," I add quickly.

"My parents died when I was young. My dad's sister raised me and... it was not an ideal situation... for either of us."

"I'm so sorry, Holly."

She shrugs. "It's okay. They've been gone a long time now."

I pick up my cup and sip at the cooling coffee.

She stares at me a moment and then leans toward me. "There's something you should know, Cait." She holds my gaze. "As fiercely loyal as Liam is... if you hurt or betray him... you are done, dead to him."

I swallow uncomfortably. Does she suspect? I don't know what to make of what she's said, and then she continues.

"He will cut you out of his life as if you never existed."

She sits back and takes another sip of coffee. "Not a particularly good trait but—I think you need to know."

A curl of uneasiness creeps up my spine. "I'll keep that in mind." I respond softly.

When the back of my neck prickles, I know Liam has arrived. I turn and meet burning blue, dead on.

Holy hell. The man takes my breath away.

"Liam! Mike!" Holly calls out excitedly.

I stand and watch as the two men cross the room, Liam's gaze never leaving mine. When he reaches me, I walk into his arms, wrapping mine around his neck, not caring about the fact we are in a restaurant.

"Liam."

On tiptoe, I bury my face against his neck. He smells good. Intoxicatingly good. His arms tighten momentarily, and then he's releasing me, his hands gripping my arms as he peers into my face.

"Are you okay?"

"Yes." I nod.

His gaze flicks to Holly and then back to me. "Sit down, and drink your coffee."

"Can I take it with me?"

I think I see a flicker of amusement in his eyes before he looks at Mike, who then heads toward the bar.

"Let's go. Get your things together girls." His voice holds a measure of sternness.

I suddenly feel the intense need to be alone with him so we can talk. After what Holly told me, I'm anxious to tell him everything.

He hands me my bag. "Come on Holly," he urges.

"Oh, Liam! Don't be a grump," she says as she stands, looking around on the floor. "I can't find my shoe," she wails.

Liam sighs and pulls one of the chairs from the table to reach her lost heel, holding it out to her. He makes a come on motion as she slips the shoe on.

"Hold your horses!"

I can't hold back my giggle.

"Don't act so put out," she admonishes as she stumbles around the table. "I've picked your drunk ass up more than once."

"Yes, but I never put myself in danger as you two have."

What?

"Two beautiful women drunk on their asses, out alone."

"I'm not drunk," I say as he grips my arm and pulls me along with him as he starts for the front door.

"Just plain stupid, Holly," he says over his shoulder.

"Oh, don't be so—self-righteous!" she sasses back.

"Yeah, well you won't be so smart mouthed when your husband gets home."

I look back, and Holly stops, her expression almost laughable.

"You called Ryan?"

"Yes, I did." He stops us at the door where Mike waits holding two go cups.

"Why would you do that?" she hisses as we step out into the night.

The Land Rover sits right at the curb, and Liam opens the back door of the SUV for me. I slide in and look up to see him staring at my legs. His gaze slides slowly up my body to meet my eyes. I don't mistake the heat I see there, and my stomach muscles tighten perceptibly.

Whoa! One glance from this man, and I'm a goner. I bite my bottom lip and watch as Liam's eyes narrow.

"Buckle up," he says tersely and watches as I fumble with the seat belt before handing me my coffee. He shuts my door, and then slides in up front behind the wheel, adjusting the rear view mirror before starting the engine.

Holly slides in beside me.

"Liam, why would you call, Ryan?" she demands, tossing him a glare as she takes the cup Mike hands to her.

"Because you wouldn't answer your fucking phone!" he says, anger apparent in his voice, and it seems to shut Holly up.

I look up and meet Liam's eyes briefly in the rearview mirror, and then he looks straight ahead, keeping his eyes on the road as he drives us back to Justice House.

Liam doesn't talk or look at me again during the drive through town.

Holly and Mike are quiet too, and that's okay as I think over what Holly told me about Liam's father.

What I know now just reaffirms my high opinion of Liam. Growing up with a father who was an abusive alcoholic, losing his mother as a young man, and he still managed to improve his life. Most wouldn't have had the fortitude to pull themselves out of such dismal circumstances, but Liam not only survived, he thrived.

If not for the file Valerie has on Liam, I would have no idea just how far he has come. It's nothing short of amazing. In ten years, he has accomplished what most men don't achieve in a lifetime. And through it all, he seems to have managed to stay focused on the important things. He's kept lifelong friends close, and he genuinely cares and provides well for his employees. I've seen how club members and people outside of Justice House respond to him. He's well-liked and respected. He is a man who has it all and clearly enjoys his success and the life he has built for himself.

But I've sensed the loneliness in him and his underlying need. He said he needed me. That he could escape—with me. I study his profile, and I'm overwhelmed with the depth of my feelings for him. He has become so important and dear to me.

Essential even.

As we pull through the gates to Justice House, Holly looks over at me and grins.

"What?" I mouth.

She leans forward. "You can let us out at the club door, Liam."

Liam's gaze flashes to mine in the mirror.

"Yeah, I could use a drink," Mike adds.

At the last second, Liam turns the steering wheel and brings the SUV to a stop on the far side of the Porte cochere.

Almost before the vehicle comes to a full stop, Holly has the door flung open and tugs on my arm. "Come on," she whispers.

I release the seat belt and scoot across the seat to slide out on her side.

"Stay with me," she murmurs as she links her arm through mine and leads me toward the outside club entrance.

"What's going on?" I ask.

"You need to shake Liam up a little," she declares.

I glance back toward the SUV as the security guy greets and opens the door for us. Liam drives on toward the garage to park.

"But, I don't want to shake him up," I say.

"Trust me, Cait."

I sigh, not sure what she's up to.

"You know how he manipulated you with that whole scenario about making the bar and club off limits to employees?"

"You know about that?" I exclaim.

She laughs. "I figured it out after he didn't make the announcement. Knowing Liam, I reasoned it was to control you." She grins. "You're setting precedent here, Cait."

I shake my head at her as we enter the club from the foyer.

It's packed, as usual, and we make our way toward the bar amidst the crowd and strobe lights that pulse to the beat of the music.

As we wait for our drinks, the guy standing next to me at the bar, looks over and smiles. He says something, but the music is so loud, I just shake my head and shrug to let him know I can't hear him.

I'm relieved when the DJ takes a break, and the noise level drops to a low roar, but at least Holly and I can hear each other talk.

As our drinks are set before us, hands come down onto my shoulders. I step back against Liam and then realize it's not Liam when Holly's eyes widen in surprise.

Oh, shit! I have a sudden anxious moment when I think about Liam arriving to see another man's hands on me.

I spin around, and I'm shocked to see Paul.

"What... what are you doing here?" I give him a quick hug as he laughs.

"Good to see you too."

"I'm sorry, you know I'm happy to see you but..."

He laughs again, clearly amused at my surprise. "Liam invited us."

What? I really am surprised now. "Wait. Us? Is Julie here?" I turn to scan the crowd.

"I left her at the table talking with your friend, Bryce."

I'm reminded of my manners when Holly shifts beside me. "Oh, I'm sorry. Paul, this is Holly Phillips. Holly, my good friend, Paul Sims."

"Nice to meet you, Holly."

"Liam invited you?" I ask.

"Yes I did." Liam's deep, slow drawl has me quickly turning around. His gaze holds mine for a moment, his blue, blue eyes snaring mine captive with their intensity before he turns to Paul, offering his hand.

"Bryce settle you and your wife at a table?" Liam asks.

"He did, thank you. We appreciate the invite."

Liam waves his hand. "It should have come sooner."

Liam turns and surprises me when he pulls me against him. I press my face to his chest, inhaling deeply. I do wish we were upstairs, so I could thank him properly for inviting my friends. I just want to be alone with him.

"I'll help Paul find his way back to the table," Holly offers as she steps around us.

"We'll be there in a moment," Liam tells her as I look up, his eyes locking with mine.

With a backward glance, Paul follows Holly.

"Surprised?" Liam asks.

"Shocked." I smile up at him. "Thank you."

He gives me a knowing smirk. "I'd about decided you were going to miss the occasion." His hold tightens slightly. "You were gone when I returned, and you wouldn't answer your phone," he growls lifting an eyebrow in reprimand.

"You should have told me they were coming."

"Well now, that would have ruined the surprise." He grips my chin and leans in just as Bryce walks up.

"Hey, bro. Cait."

Liam pauses but doesn't look up, his gaze holding mine. "What is it, Bryce?"

"Churchfell is leaving. He wants to speak with you, says he has a slight problem."

"Of course he does." Liam now looks up at Bryce. "Give me a minute."

Bryce nods and moves further down the bar toward one of the waitresses.

Liam sighs. "Cait, I need to take care of business, and then I'll join you and your friends. I shouldn't be long." He levels his gaze on me. "I expect you to be here when I return."

It's as if my body starts humming in answer. "Okay," I whisper.

"Don't look at me that way," he growls. "Not here."

My lips part as I inhale sharply. "I'll try," I say softly. I turn, and then he's gripping my arm, pulling me back flush to his body.

I'm aware of people looking our way as Liam's head lowers, his mouth taking possession of what belongs to him. He grips the back of my neck, holding me just where he wants me, his kiss anything but gentle as he proceeds to brand me as his in view of every member watching. When he slowly releases my mouth, his eyes are dark with lust, and I'm clinging to his shoulders, reeling from his kiss.

"Break it up you two," Bryce growls. "Liam let's go,

Churchfell isn't going to wait all night while you play kissy face with Cait." Bryce looks over at me and grins.

I ignore him, as does Liam.

Liam runs his thumb across my swollen mouth as his tongue comes out to lick against his bottom lip. He draws his lip into his mouth as if wanting to get every last bit of my taste that might remain there.

My breath is indrawn sharply before I release a breathy laugh.

Liam's eyes gleam as his face breaks into that oh-so-sexy smile of his that just makes everything south of my navel melt.

"I'll be back to get you shortly," he warns. "Behave."

"You too," I shoot right back, and I think I catch a look of surprise as I smile and turn to go in search of Holly. On second thought—I turn back and stepping close, I stand on tiptoe to bring my mouth close to his ear. "I love you, Liam Justice."

I search his eyes, looking for a response. The look that comes over his face is either one of surprise or uncertainty. I'm not sure which. I smile at him then. A good teasing smile and turn to find Holly. Without a backward glance, I melt into the crowd.

That's not exactly how I planned to tell Liam that I love him for the first time but—the moment felt right. And I know I surprised him.

I just hope it was a welcome surprise. I bite my lip, an onslaught of doubt suddenly assails me, and I stop abruptly. People bump into me as I stand there, panic setting in.

"Cait!"

I look up to find Holly, Paul, and Julie looking at me.

Holly motions for me to join them. I take a deep breath and smile, hoping they didn't notice my near meltdown.

It doesn't take but a drink or two for Holly and me to have our partying mood and giggles back. Bryce has joined us, and he and Paul keep us busy dancing.

I keep looking up to the balcony. The man Liam went to speak with is with the private party going on up there. I'm ready for Liam to be down here with me, not up there with—who knows who. I have no doubt that Miranda is up there. She seems to be constantly involved in any party going on at the Justice, and she usually manages to be where Liam is.

"I'm happy you and Paul are here," I tell Julie during one of the short breaks the DJ takes that allows us a chance to talk and be heard.

"Me too," Julie says. "I've always wanted to come here. It was really nice of Liam to make the effort." She looks over at her husband.

I glance at Paul. He seems relaxed as if he's enjoying himself. I'm hoping this gesture of Liam's means that the subtle animosity between the two men is over.

I grin at Julie as the music starts again, and Paul, catching us looking at him, stands to claim his wife for a dance, giving me a wink.

Liam finally joins us, and I can feel his irritation that his meeting lasted so long. Bryce says something to him as Liam reaches down to take my hand, pulling me up from my chair. He shakes his head at Bryce and then leads me onto the dance floor.

I step into his arms, and he pulls me tightly against his length. My body quickly responds to the fact that his erection is pressing into my belly. I look up into eyes that seem to blaze with blue fire. My breath catches as his head lowers, and he buries his nose in my hair, inhaling deeply as his hand tangles in the length.

He smells so good. Just a whiff of his scent is enough to cause my stomach to clench. Surrounded by him, immersed in his scent is—heaven. I reach up to touch him, running my fingers over the stubble on his jaw. When he raises his head, my hand moves into his hair. His hand pushes against my bottom as he presses his erection against me.

"Liam," I moan, pressing my lips to the hollow of his throat. I'm oblivious to the bodies around us. It's just Liam and me.

His hand moves up to rest against my bare back that the slit in my dress allows. I tremble in response to his hand on my bare skin. When he takes my earlobe between his teeth, it's as if he's hit upon a direct line to my lower extremities. When he bites down, it's a jolt straight to my clit. It's all I can manage not to cry out.

"Please, Liam," I plead. I clutch at his back, my long moan pulls me from my sensual nirvana, reminding me we aren't in private, and we're practically dirty dancing in the middle of the club's dance floor. I loosen my hold on him, and my hands move to his shoulders as I tell myself to remember where I am.

Liam's quiet. He's not said a word. I'm assailed once again by uncertainty. What does he think of my declaration? Is he angry or maybe indifferent? As we continue to dance, he remains quiet—remote. I shouldn't have told him here, not as I did. He's probably thinking about how he's going to tell me, thanks, but no thanks.

When the music stops, I glance up. His bright blue eyes are watching me. I'm embarrassed that he looks calm and unaffected, whereas my whole body feels flushed, and I'm having difficulty catching my breath.

"Say something," I say a little irritably.

He jerks me closer, bringing his mouth to my ear.

"I want that luscious mouth of yours wrapped around my fucking cock, right now, darlin'," he rasps, his voice thick with lust.

I look up in surprise, swallowing hard at his words. I feel my face suffuse with heat. Without another word, he grips my hand, pulling me along behind him. It's as if a sea of bodies part for us as he heads for the door that leads back into the mansion.

CHAPTER FOURTEEN

"WAIT, LIAM!" I TUG AGAINST his hand, and he slows only to pull me against his side. "We need to say good night," I gasp, looking back in the direction of our table.

Liam doesn't slow as we continue through the door to the bar and restaurant area. I struggle to keep up as he walks quickly down the hall, and then he's pulling me into the storage room, the one where only a few weeks before, we shared our first—kiss. He flips on the dim overhead light, and this time when he shuts the door, I hear the unmistakable click of a lock.

I barely have a moment before he's unzipping his jeans.

"On your knees, sugar." His voice is gruff with arousal.

Oh! My knees almost buckle with my body's reaction to his blatant need. The thought of this strong man needing me, desiring me as I do him, evokes a strong response in my body. Knowing he couldn't wait for us to reach his office, inflames me.

I lower to my knees, and then he's gripping my hair roughly, pulling my head back.

"Hands behind your back, sweetheart."

I do as bid; desire to have my mouth on him, pooling with a hot need low in my belly.

He grips my chin with his free hand. "I'm going to fuck your mouth, and I want you to keep your hands behind your back, do you understand?"

"Yes." I'm suddenly panting. My erect nipples chafe against the fabric of my dress with each rapid rise and fall of my chest, heightening my arousal.

He releases his impressive erection in all its long, thick glory.

Holy Hell! I am more than a little intimidated, and as my body starts to tremble, Liam strokes my hair back with one hand and the length of his erection with the other.

"Suck, darlin'."

I swirl my tongue around the bulbous head of his erection. "Mmm..." I hum. Liam Justice tastes good. I lean forward as much as the hand clutched in my hair will allow and suck him into my mouth.

"Look at me," he commands, his voice already sounding tight with the control I recognize. I look up into a blazing blue fire. He releases my chin, his hand joining the other to fist in my hair.

"This is going to be quick," he gasps as he rocks further into my mouth. "Suck hard, baby."

I do, there's no way I cannot as natural instinct takes over and the strong desire to please him becomes a driving force as I draw him to the back of my throat.

"Fuck!" he growls.

He grips my hair to the point of pain as he begins to move, thrusting his erection deep into my mouth. I close my eyes and remind myself to relax. *Keep calm and breathe.*

"Keep your eyes on me!" I look back up as he thrusts deep, withdrawing quickly only to plunge deep again.

As my throat spasms around him, he stills, his head thrown back. A long, low moan erupts from deep in his chest as he holds my head still with my face pressed to his groin. Just as I start to panic at not being able to breathe, he pulls back. And then he's thrusting his erection in and out, sometimes deep into my throat, other times shallow as I continue to suck forcefully. His breathing is loud and raspy, labored as he grips my hair, his biceps bulging, holding my head just where he wants as he continues to fuck my mouth. There's no gentleness, only hard, fucking need.

His legs are braced apart, his whole body rigid, unrelenting with his movements. Just as I feel his body tense, he buries himself deep, his hands pulling my hair painfully. A growl erupts from deep in his chest.

My gag reflex has kicked in and I bring my hands to his hips, pushing against him. I feel the liquid heat shoot down the back of my throat as Liam cries out and stills.

He releases my hair, and I jerk free. He stumbles back against the door, and I fall forward onto my hands at his feet, drawing in great gulps of air.

"Fuck!" he growls loudly.

He reaches down, drawing me to my feet to pull me against his body. He holds me tightly, his large hand at the back of my head pressing the side of my face against his chest. I can hear his heart beating, matching the fast tempo of mine. He pulls back, looking down into my face.

"Are you okay, darlin'?"

I nod.

"Are you sure?"

"Yes," I whisper.

His hand caresses the side of my face and he leans down, his lips resting on my forehead. I lean into him, loving his arms around me. All too soon, he releases me and adjusts himself into his jeans. I step back suddenly feeling shy.

"Let's go."

He unlocks and opens the door, stepping out into the hallway. He holds his hand out to me, and when I join him, he grips my upper arm pulling me along with him. I'm relieved we see no one on our way through the mansion. I'm sure my hair is a wild mess.

The moment we walk through the door of his office, Liam turns to grip my upper arms; he walks me backward, forcefully pushing me up against the wall. I gasp at the surprise of his action as he looms over me, pressing my body to the wall and holding me there with his hard frame.

Oh, my.

I feel small—dwarfed by his size. It's a heady feeling, knowing I am so much weaker than he is. That I am under his complete control.

He rubs the rigid length of his arousal against my stomach. I'm not surprised he's ready to go again, and I'm more than ready. I bite my lip, moaning softly.

Gripping my wrists, he raises my arms above my head, bringing them together to hold in one of his large hands. His other, circles the side of my neck, his thumb pushing up under my chin, so my face tips up. He holds me this way as he brings his mouth down on mine, his hand sliding up along my jawline, holding me immobile. His kiss is forceful, rough and deliciously sensual. I feel need claw low in my belly as his tongue plunders the inside of my mouth, seeking, exploring. I tentatively bring my tongue to his, and I feel his erection become even harder between us. Liam licks and bites at my lips, sucking and stroking with his tongue as I writhe in his grasp.

When he suddenly releases me, I almost fall to the floor, but he grips my arm to steady me and pulls me across the room to the bar area. He abruptly leaves me standing as he turns to pour a drink from a decanter and then reaches into his mini fridge to pull out a bottle of water, setting it on the bar top.

I hate this feeling of uncertainty that I'm having. Perhaps it's Liam's detached attitude. He's said little to me since his meeting in the club.

He turns and looks at me, taking a sip of his drink.

"Take off your dress, Caitlyn."

I inhale sharply as my insides turn to liquid. With fumbling fingers, I reach up behind me for the button at my neckline, my gaze locked with his. I slide the dress down off my shoulders and hesitate before letting it drop, to pool at my feet. I'm naked save for my thigh high stockings and heels.

Liam's gaze drops to my breasts, and my nipples tighten and elongate under his smoldering stare. As his eyes move slowly down my body a tremor courses through me. He sips his drink his eyes meeting mine again over the rim of his glass. There's a salacious gleam there.

I close my eyes, biting my lip, willing myself to calm down.

When I hear the sound of something hard and sharp coming down on the bar top, I open my eyes and cry out with surprise as Liam grabs me. He quickly spins me to face the back of the couch, roughly pushing me against it. Taking my hands, he places them in front of me on the back of the couch.

"Do not move your hands," he commands in a hard voice.

Before I have a chance to respond, he's skimming his hands up the back of my thighs, moving them up over my bottom. He presses his hard body against my softness pushing me into the back of the couch, firmly holding me there.

"I have to remind myself, that this is all new to you,"—his breath is hot against my neck, bringing goose bumps to my chilled skin—"that you don't try to willfully displease me." His hands move to my breasts, cupping, and molding around their fullness, pinching and pulling at my nipples.

My back arches slightly. With his body wrapped around mine as it is, he allows me little movement. My heart rate escalates, and I try hard to control my breathing, which is loud in the room.

"But I also know I can't let you continue to blatantly disregard my authority."

I frown. "Liam, I don't—"

"Quiet."

When I try to turn, so I can see his face, his hold on my breasts tightens, and he presses me more fully into the couch.

He lowers his head close to my ear, his voice raspy. "You will not come, darlin'." His lips skim down the side of my neck to my shoulder. One large hand settles on my quivering stomach. "If you come before I give you permission—I will punish you."

Oh! I almost feel faint with the reaction his words

elicit in my body. I've only been able to have an orgasm for the first time in my life since I met him a few short weeks ago. How am I now supposed to be able to control them?

"Mmmm," he hums. "I almost hope... you fail."

Fuck!

He steps back and delivers a hard slap to my bottom. I jump and yelp.

"Upstairs now, darlin'."

I don't move fast enough to suit him, and he gives me another hard swat.

"Ow!" I rub at the sting on my bottom.

Liam heads for the elevator, and I quickly scoop up my dress, holding it to my front.

I step into the elevator, clutching my dress to my breast, and when I start to put it back on, Liam laughs, but there's no humor in that laugh.

"Don't bother," he says.

The doors open, and he holds his hand out for me to precede him.

"Are you mad at me?" Surely there's more to this than me leaving earlier.

He lifts that damned eyebrow again. "Should I be darlin'?"

My mouth drops open slightly. *Damn it.* I don't want my question turned back on me. "No."

He snorts softly. "After you, Caitlyn."

I don't want to turn my bare backside to him, so I sidle out of the elevator. When I look up, he's still standing in the door of the elevator, watching me. I blush and swallow uncomfortably. What puts him in these moods? And I know it's not only because I disobeyed him. Now that I think about it—

"I don't deserve for you to be upset with me," I say looking up at him. When he doesn't say anything, I continue. "You deliberately gave me the impression you were leaving with another woman!"

His brow furrows. "I was leaving with another woman."

"And I'm supposed to be okay with that?"

His face darkens with anger, and as I take a step back in alarm, he's on me, gripping my arm, bringing his face close to mine.

"I told you once, darlin', it isn't wise to rile me."

I believe him because right about now, he's scaring the hell out of me.

"I'm afraid, sweetheart, you have two transgressions to answer for now."

I frown. "What?"

He doesn't answer as he grips my arm tighter. He pulls my dress from my clutch, tossing it back toward the elevator, and then he's pulling me along behind him through the apartment. I can barely keep up with his long, angry strides.

"Liam, please. Why are you so angry?" My voice comes in gasps. When he doesn't say anything, I ask, "Wh-What are you going to do?"

He pulls me to a stop outside the room that I first suspected was a storage room. The sex swing episode changed that perception. My stomach muscles tighten at the prospect of another night on the swing.

He looks down at me, his blue gaze burning with an unfathomable emotion. His hold on my arms is forceful as he pushes me against the wall, stepping up against my body, pressing into me. His sexy, mind-fucking scent engulfs me. Fisting a hand in my hair he roughly yanks my head back as his mouth comes down on mine. He kisses me hard—ruthless, inflaming me with apprehension and need all at the same time.

I'm gasping when he releases my mouth and steps back from me. My nipples have tightened and they jut out proudly from my response to his nearness. I blush under his lustful stare. It's a little unnerving the way he's looking at me.

"I can't decide if I should punish you, or throw you down on the floor and fuck you until you beg me to stop," he growls.

I swallow uncomfortably. "Liam." I breathe his name. I know what I choose.

Suddenly, he's looming over me, intimidating me further with his size. His hand encircles my throat as he brings his face close to mine.

"You fucking belong to me!" he hisses from between clenched teeth.

I inhale sharply, my eyes opening wide. I've never seen him this way. This angry. "I know," I answer, my voice breathy.

"If I ever see you letting another man touch you—" He presses me back tightly against the wall.

What the hell?

I shake my head against his hold. "I haven't," I whisper.

His free hand moves between my legs to cup my sex firmly as he continues to hold me against the wall. "This—is mine."

His eyes are positively glacial. There's no warmth, none of the teasing affection he usually bestows upon me, just ice-cold blue.

"What's wrong?" I whisper.

"You tell me," he growls.

I frown, "You're so angry."

His hands drop to his side, and he steps back, releasing me.

"I'm always angry. Get used to it," he snaps before turning to head back down the hall to the living room.

I follow slowly, conscious of my nakedness, and I let my hair fall forward to cover my breasts. I lean half way around the doorway and watch as he pours himself a drink.

He's fully clothed, as usual while he has me naked. He's dressed in jeans and a white, button-up dress shirt, dark stubble shadows his jawline, and his hair is messy from running his fingers through it. My fingers positively itch to pull at those dark locks. He is the sexiest man I have ever known. Looking at him, as he is, in all his confusing anger, I know I am crazy in love with him, and I want to help him.

"No, you're not," I say.

He pauses to look up, his eyes moving over me. "I'm not what?" he asks as his attention returns to his drink.

"Angry all the time."

He glances briefly at me again. "Would you care for something?"

Okay. He doesn't want to discuss his anger. "Clothes."

He snorts softly before knocking back his drink, and then reaching for the bottle to pour another.

I take a deep breath.

He walks toward me then, unbuttoning his shirt as he crosses the room. My breath catches as he stops in front of me to shrug out of the shirt, draping it across my shoulders as his gaze holds mine.

His shirt is warm from the heat of his body, and I

want to reach out and lay my hands on his chest, his warm skin.

I slip into the shirt under his watchful eye. My whole body grows warm with flush as my senses come alive to the fact that he is half-naked now.

"You're not always angry, Liam." His eyes narrow as if in warning. "There's something wrong, something that's bothering you, and I know that it is important—"

He reaches to grip the front of his shirt, yanking me off balance so that I have to take a step forward.

"Do you want to leave, Caitlyn?" I frown. I don't have a clue what he means. He lowers his head, bringing his face closer to mine. "Do you want to leave—go home?"

My frown deepens, and I search his beautiful eyes. "No."

"Then shut the fuck up!"

My mouth drops open, and he releases his hold, turning to stride back to the bar. I feel as if he just slapped me. "I think I just changed my mind," I mutter.

Turning, I head for the elevator.

The son of a bitch!

I spin on my heel and head back. He hasn't moved from the bar, which pisses me off further.

"You are being an asshole!"

He turns to look at me, his eyebrows raised in surprise.

"You act like an ass to me when all I am trying to do is reach out to you. I know you're angry, but it's more than that, you're hurting." I'm pissed, but I know I need to calm down. "Since I first met you, you've been dealing with something, and I can see that. I haven't pried, even though you've often taken that anger out on me." I take a deep breath to steel myself against his blazing blue glare. "You get angry and use my body to alleviate that anger."

He blinks.

"What? You think I didn't notice?"

Even from across the room I can see the skin tighten around his eyes as he watches me warily. It would almost be funny if I weren't so mad.

"So, what's up with this, *You're mine, You belong to me, You better never let another man touch you?* You own me? Is that what you think?" He does own me. I know it, and he knows it.

I am trying to control my anger, but my breathing is quick and shallow now.

"Right from the start, you said no expectations. I understood that. I mean, I am smart enough to know that a man like you—and someone like me—" I close my eyes and shake my head. I'm not doing this right. I'm probably not making sense at all. When I open my eyes, Liam is frowning. "I understood what you wanted from this... relationship, even though... I wanted more," I admit softly. I'm suddenly not angry just—sad.

His expression doesn't change. No surprise to him, he's used to women wanting more.

"But then you started changing the rules, Liam, and I became more... invested." My eyes fill with tears. Damn it, I can't cry. I want him to take me seriously, and listen to what I have to say.

"I see when you're upset, when something is bothering you. I can tell when you're hurt and angry," I whisper.

I sniff. His silence is making something inside of me wither.

"Liam"—I take a deep steadying breath—"you said that I helped you get through what you are dealing with, so if... if sex is how you cope... all that you need from me... I can do that for you." He's frowning hard now, an almost pained expression on his face, and I feel a tear slide down my cheek. "But please, stop making me believe that there can be more between us." The last ends on a soft sob. "And if I screw up and forget the rules, asking why you're upset—Don't"—my angers back—"tell me to fuck off!"

I spin on my heel again and head for the elevator. I'm proud that I've held it together, and if I can just control the tears until I get out of here, I can let go then. Liam has a different idea though as he suddenly scoops me up into his arms.

"What are you doing? No! Put me down!"

I struggle, and I think I hit him on the head.

"Fuck, Cait!"

I wrap my arms around his shoulders and bury my face against his neck. "I don't want to cry," I cry.

"Shhh, baby, I don't want you to cry either."

I let loose then. I'm a blubbering mess as he cradles me in his arms. We remain that way until the tears subside, and then he carries me back through the apartment. He shifts me slightly and reaches to open a door, and then he's climbing stairs, clutching me tightly as he opens another door, and we step outside. I can smell the night air and feel the cool breeze on my skin. He's walking again, and then he sets me down, pulling my arms from his neck.

I look around as he steps away from me, wiping my nose on his shirt sleeve. I'm sitting on some type of bed, I think with a canopy above me. It's dark, but I see lights from buildings in the distance. Wherever we are, we're up high.

Small clear lights come on and there are a lot of them outlining the perimeter of where we are. There are also tiny twinkling lights in the potted exotic plants placed around the area.

I frown. I'm on a bed with a canvas canopy over the top, and white billowy curtain sides, almost like a tent. More of the same tiny lights outline the frame of the canopy. It's beautiful. The breeze blows gently, creating a twinkling effect with the lights.

I look behind me, and Liam stands at the other end of the bed. He's watching me.

"Where are we?" I sniff.

He steps close picking me up once more to step back to the head of the bed, sitting down, with me in his arms, his back against the iron headboard. "We're on the roof. It's my—I come up here sometimes."

I glance around us. "It's beautiful with the lights... and the stars."

"Yes." His arms tighten around me. "You can see more stars up here away from the street lights and—the glare of life."

I look up at him. He uses this place, this quiet place as a type of escape. "I love it," I say softly. A lone tear escapes, trailing down my cheek produced from the overwhelming emotions running rampant through me. I feel battered from the onslaught of emotions that I've had to deal with throughout this day. And my heart aches for this man I have come to love so deeply.

Liam uses his thumb to catch the tear. "I thought you were finished."

I sniff again. "Me too."

"Please don't cry anymore," he says gruffly.

"I'll try." I shiver slightly, pressing closer as the slight breeze picks up. Liam reaches over to pull the bed cover over me. "I-I need to get these heels off." I slip off his lap to sit beside him and pull up my leg to unbuckle the strap.

"Let me," he says as he leans forward pushing my fingers aside. He nimbly loosens the strap to slip off my heel. His hand massages my foot, and I grit my teeth to stifle my moan. He quickly reaches for the other foot, repeating the process. I'm unable to quiet my moan this time.

"Stockings?"

I nod. He turns and slowly slides a stocking down one leg and then the other, caressing each leg. I bite my lip.

I scoot back against the headboard and pull the blanket up, holding it back for Liam to sit beside me. He smiles wryly. When he leans back against the headboard, I scoot close against him.

"It's peaceful up here. I like it," I say softly.

We sit quietly then, listening to the wind rustling through the leaves of the tree tops. Much of the noise of the busy city night, one block away, is muffled up here. I lean my head on Liam's shoulder. I feel the need to touch him. Liam sighs deeply, and I look up to meet his gaze. His eyes look dark blue in the subdued lighting. A corner of his mouth lifts and he leans over to kiss the top of my head.

"I'm sorry."

"Thank you." I snuggle closer. "I meant what I said," I say softly. "If you need… if it helps—"

"Hey." I look up. He shakes his head and then he slides his arm underneath my shoulders, he pulls me in even closer. He suddenly slides down, pulling me with him until we're both lying on the bed. He turns on his side to face me, and I do the same.

"Cait... you have no fucking idea how much I need you."

Oh.

He leans over to place a soft kiss on my mouth. I lift my hand to trail my fingers across his jawline. His dark scruff is so soft. I frown. We really know so little about each other.

Liam smooth's his fingers across my forehead, and as if he reads my thoughts, he asks, "Do you talk to your parents?" He surprises me with his question.

"Yes, every Sunday. I call and talk to them. Occasionally, through the week but my mom... she stays busy with my dad and it's tiring for him... talking on the phone. He's an invalid." Liam's gaze meets mine. "He developed Chronic Fatigue Syndrome that leaves him bedridden and quite ill at times. It's a terrible disease that is nothing like its name implies."

"I'm sorry," he murmurs.

I shrug. "We never let ourselves dwell on the bad side of his illness. My parents insisted that we live as if his illness were an annoyance, not a tragedy."

"What do you mean," He reaches to tuck my hair behind my ear, his knuckles caressing my cheek.

"Mostly we just never fussed over what he could or couldn't do. They insisted that I never use his illness as a reason not to do what I wanted. After I left home, I realized that they made everything about me." I shake my head and give a little laugh, still in awe how they managed that without me realizing it.

"They weren't able to go to any school functions or other activities, but they made sure I attended everything I needed and wanted to. They were interested in everything I did and insisted on sharing every experience. My mom and I would have our evening meal in Dad's room." I smile. "I had to tell them everything that happened during my day." I grin at the memory.

"They pushed me to strive for what I wanted and to work hard for my education, encouraging me to be independent and to make my own decisions at a young age. They taught me to never feel guilty about leaving them and living my life." I smile wistfully. "My dad said the real tragedy in it all would have been if I'd become a prisoner of his disease."

"They sound very wise and loving."

"They are," I say softly.

"How long has he been ill?"

"Since I was twelve."

Liam frowns. "Twelve years," he mutters softly.

"Yes," I whisper. I know he's thinking of his mother. He looks sad. "You said your mother passed twelve years ago?" His expression is suddenly guarded, and it's silly of me, but that hurts my feelings. I lower my eyes, so he can't see the hurt.

He sighs heavily and rolls to his back, slinging his arm over his face. "Don't do that, darlin'."

"Do what?"

"Let my inability to open up to you—hurt you." He lowers his arm and turns his head to look at me.

"Do you open up to… any of your friends?" I ask my voice barely above a whisper. He's known Miranda a long time. Does he confide in her? I feel raw jealousy at the thought.

"I don't need to—they were there when the shit went down."

He reaches over and hooks a long curl of my hair, winding it around his finger. I watch as he studies it in deep concentration, a crease between his brows. "This is what you've done to my heart," he says softly.

I blink. "What?" I breathe.

"You've wrapped yourself around it darlin'." His mesmerizing blue eyes look up to capture me in their hypnotic glow.

I can't breathe. I'm caught in a blue net as the world around us disappears. Liam rises to lean over me, and then he's taking my mouth in a deep, slow kiss. My arms twine around his neck, and I reach up to run the fingers of one hand through his hair. He works the buttons of his shirt open and brings his mouth down to suck strongly on a taut nipple as his hand moves between my legs to my center. My back arches, and I moan as he sinks two fingers deep into my channel.

He bites down and then releases my nipple slowly from between his teeth.

Pleasure/pain.

I gasp softly when he lifts up slightly, his medallion landing between my breasts. It feels hot from his body heat and not for the first time, I feel as if it sears his mark on me.

"Fuck, I love how tight and wet you are for me."

I cry out softly as his mouth comes down to latch on the opposite nipple. His fingers spread apart inside of me, rubbing against my vaginal walls. He pulls his fingers out to slide along my slit, over my sensitive nub, massaging the bundle of nerves that lie in that tiny epicenter. He works me into a frenzy, sucking, biting, and pulling my turgid nipples as his fingers fuck me relentlessly.

"Don't come," he orders. I mewl softly as I writhe on the bed beneath him.

"Liam!" I cry as I feel my insides tighten. He stills the movement of his fingers, and I tighten my inner muscles around them.

His eyes glitter as he looks down at me. "You do not come until I say," he warns in a hard voice.

"Okay," I say softly. I pray that I don't.

I whimper as he pulls his fingers from between my legs and then quickly stands beside the bed. He holds my gaze as he unzips his jeans, his erection jutting out at me.

Coming back down on the bed, he lies on his back, pulling me over on top of him.

Oh.

"Sit up." His voice is husky, sexy.

I straddle him, and he quickly lifts me up and pulls me forward until I'm above his face.

"Up on your knees, sugar."

Holy hell!

I reach a hand out to grip the headboard to steady myself.

He spreads me open with his fingers, and when he raises his head to suck on my clit, I gasp and grab the headboard with both hands. He sucks and pulls the sensitive nub into his mouth, and I almost come right then.

"Liam!"

"Don't come, darlin'."

"Argh!" He sucks more firmly on my clit as it elongates. When he bites down, I cry out, and a shudder starts from deep within working its way up my body. My back bows, and I grip the headboard, holding on for dear life.

Don't come. Don't come. Don't come.

Liam sucks hard and it almost hurts. He's gripping my bottom painfully, but it helps me to center my thoughts there on that discomfort and not on the fact that I desperately need to come.

When his finger presses against my cheeks, pushing into my anal passage, I try to jerk away, crying out hoarsely. That does hurt and not in a good way.

Liam releases my engorged clit. "Hold still, Caitlyn!" He growls, his grip tightening on my bottom.

I mewl and lay my head on the rim of the headboard as I pant.

"I want you to hold still. Do you understand?"

"Yes," I whine. I'm biting my lip so hard I taste blood.

"Do not move and do not come," he says firmly.

"Liam, please," I beg in a whisper.

"You can do it, sugar."

He licks from my opening along my slit to draw my fully exposed clit back into his mouth. "Fuck!" he mutters around my clit. At the same time, he presses his finger back into my backside.

"Oh!" It hurts. I pant, trying to control my body's natural response to pull away. I fight it, but I still lean slightly up and away from the pressure of his finger.

"Don't move!" he growls.

His fingers slide over my opening, smearing my wetness between my cheeks. He does this several times before he presses his finger into me again. I don't know at what point it starts to feel good but when it does, it feels really good. My body no longer belongs to me. It's under its own rule. I can no longer control my movements. A fine sheen of sweat covers me, and the cool night breeze is the only thing keeping me from combusting.

My body moves against the firm thrust of his finger in and out of my anal passage.

I can feel Liam watching me as I grip the headboard. I'm on my knees, my head thrown back in sexual abandon. *Oh!* It feels so good.

"Liam," I gasp. "I need—" I cry with the intense pleasure.

He stills his hand, his finger still inside of me. He suddenly sits up, bringing his chest to mine. I cry out as his finger presses deeper. My nipples are almost painfully sensitive as he presses against them, the sensation only adding to my sensual overload.

"Are you ready for me to fuck you, darlin'?"

"Yes," I moan as I shiver with anticipation.

"How?" he asks gruffly, rubbing his chest against my nipples. I moan, biting my lip.

"Hard," I pant as I press back, taking his finger a little deeper.

"What else?"

I frown.

"Tell me, darlin', or it's not going to happen."

"Liam," I whine. He knows I'm embarrassed to tell him what I want.

He slowly begins to pull his finger from me.

"Please!" I'm really not sure what I want, I just know I need—more.

He stills. "Do you want my finger"—he pushes his finger back inside of me—"here?"

I cry out as my back arches.

His laugh is a low rumble in his chest, and then he pushes against my hips as he lies back.

"You're going to ride me." My eyes open to catch the

salacious gleam in his. "No condom." My eyes widen. "It's been long enough," he says.

He pulls his finger from me then and grips my hips to lift me. "Straddle me, darlin'."

Positioning his large erection at the opening of my sex, he raises up slightly to enter me just a little, just enough to bury the head of his erection. When I attempt to take him deeper, he grips my hips tighter, stopping me.

"Feel that sugar, right there."

"Yes," I pant.

"No deeper until I say—understood?"

"Yes." I close my eyes. He's going to drive me crazy.

"You take it deeper and—I'll fuck you hard."

My eyes fly open, and I can't stop my breathless giggle.

His sensual mouth lifts at the corners.

"What if I obey?" I ask playfully, swirling my hips, only to gasp at the sensation.

His hands move to grip my bottom firmly. "I'll fuck you even harder."

A delicious thrill runs through me, and I bite my bottom lip.

"You've been a good girl, not coming, so now, you do as I say, and I'll make you come like a fuckin' train."

My breath draws in sharply. His words in that sexy slow drawl are enough alone to make me come. My core clenches painfully, and I moan, my back arching, pushing my breasts forward.

"You are so fucking beautiful. Move up and down on my cock, darlin', no deeper than I said."

It's so hard not to impale myself on his length. But it is also immensely erotic to do as he commands. It drives me beyond madness as I follow his directions. Slow. Fast. And finally, permission to take him deep.

I cry out as his large erection stretches and fills me beyond capacity. "Oh, fuck!" I cry as I sit against his groin with him buried deep in me. My body tightens painfully around him. My nipples throb, and I can feel my heartbeat pulsating in my clit.

"Okay?" his voice is tight with control.

"Yes," I gasp between clenched teeth.

Gripping my hips, he raises me up, his hard, thick erection slides out of me slowly, dragging against my sensitized tissues. When he jerks me back down on his length, I almost come.

"Arghhh!"

Oh!

"Wait!" I gasp, leaning forward, resting my hands on his chest, my hair falling around him.

Liam reaches up to palm my breasts, squeezing firmly. When he bucks up with his hips, I groan.

"Please, Liam. I need to come," I beg.

"Do you, darlin'?"

He thrusts up into me again, and at this different angle, I'm no longer able to control my body as the spasms start. My inner muscles tighten around Liam as my back arches.

"Not yet," he warns before growling, "Up."

He guides me where he wants me, and as he grips my hips, he pistons up into me with an unbelievable force.

When he moves his hand between my legs, his thumb comes down on my over sensitive clit. My orgasm slams into me, no question of me being able to control my body at this point as uncontrollable tremors rack through me.

My whole body spasms, with one long, body contorting, mind fucking orgasm.

Before the quaking of my orgasm eases, Liam has me on my back. I cry out as he goes down on me, his mouth sucking on my clit as he penetrates both openings with his fingers.

My body arches up off the bed as I desperately yank at Liam's hair, trying to stop the sweet torture. His mouth on my clit is too much, too painful. I can't take it.

I panic at the deluge of sensations from his mouth and fingers as another orgasm hits, shredding my insides as it wrings cry after cry from me.

I can't breath as Liam rises above me, flipping me to my belly. He pulls me up onto my knees.

"Hands on the headboard." His voice is rough, raw near my ear as he presses against my back. He leans back, and I cry out when he smacks my bottom. Hard.

"I'm going to mount you now, darlin', fuck you hard."

I pant at his words. *My God, do other men talk as he does?*

My body is still shaking as he works his hard erection into my swollen channel. Moving slowly at first, his hand strokes up and down my spine. His erection is soon gliding in my slickness, and he begins to really move, slamming into me forcefully. He pounds me so hard, he raises me up off my knees with each powerful thrust, and I press back to meet each one. When he pushes a finger deep into my backside, my body shudders, and my cry of ecstasy signals my next orgasm.

I'm conscious of sobbing, the sensation of pleasure is beyond containable as shock wave after shock wave pound at me, and I fall into the abyss, screaming.

CHAPTER FIFTEEN

I WAKE WITH A START, SITTING up clutching the sheet to my breasts.

"Liam!"

"Shhh, I'm here," he says as he steps through the curtains that are ruffling slightly in the breeze. He has his shirt and jeans on, and I wonder what's become of my clothes. He quickly scoops me up into his arms along with the sheet, and I grab his shoulders, my arm sliding around his neck. He looks down, meeting my eyes—and there it is. That special energy that passes between us. I inhale sharply, but before I have a chance to ask if he feels it too, he's striding out to a chair, several feet from the bed. I look around noticing the beer bottles and bottled water on a small table placed alongside the chair.

He sits, cuddling me close, then wraps the sheet more fully around me. He reaches over for the water bottle uncapping it. "Drink."

I almost down the entire contents before handing the bottle back to him. He smirks, and then grips my chin, his mouth taking mine in a soft kiss.

"How long was I asleep?" I ask when he ends the kiss. My voice sounds hoarse.

He tucks my hair behind my ear. "A couple of hours.

You were plumb tuckered out, darlin'." He smiles wickedly, and I feel my face heat with my blush. Liam responds with a low, seductive laugh.

"Did you sleep?" I ask. His mouth lifts at the corners. I shiver slightly in the cool morning air, and he pulls the sheet up over my shoulder. I sit up a little straighter as a memory comes to me.

"Did I hear a phone ringing?"

He gives a short choked laugh.

"What?" I look up at him.

His eyes sparkle with amusement. "Security called, they were concerned. Seems they heard a woman scream but were unable to find anything wrong or out of order when they ran a search of the grounds."

I frown, and then I blush so hard, I feel light headed and faint. "Oh, no!" I would crawl off his lap and run if his arms didn't suddenly tighten around me. I bury my face against his shoulder as he laughs out loud.

His laugh calms to a low rumble in his chest. "They didn't know it was you, darlin'." He buries his nose in my hair and inhales deeply.

"The sun will be up shortly," he murmurs. "It's a glorious sight from up here."

I look up, but it's still fairly dark. I snuggle back against his shoulder. I love his arms wrapped around me, keeping me safe and warm. He kisses the top of my head, and we sit quietly watching the early morning sky, listening to the happy chatter of birds as they awake for the day. There's a slight glow on the horizon when Liam breaks the silence.

"My mother was murdered," he says softly. I sit up abruptly, my eyes wide.

Holy Hell.

He reaches over, picks up one of the beer bottles, and drinks deeply before setting it back down. "I came home from school and found her."

I gasp, already reeling from the fact that his mother was murdered. "Liam, I am so sorry," I breathe. My eyes fill with tears, and I swallow past the lump in my throat.

"She was strangled."

I feel my heart constrict, and all I want to do is wrap my arms around him. I sit there keeping my eyes opened wide, so the tears don't fall.

"Her killer's parole hearing is in a couple of weeks." He rubs his hand over his face. "That's why I've been busy the last couple of months, making sure the bastard stays in jail." I recall the phone call I overheard him on the day before in his office. It also explains the anger.

I lay my hand on his shoulder. "I'm so sorry, Liam that your mother was taken from you in that way. I'm sorry that you had to be the one to find her."

"I was late." The skin around his eyes tightens as he looks off in the distance, recalling the memory. "I was supposed to take her to the library with me, but I stayed after—" He shakes his head. "If I'd been there to pick her up as planned—" He closes his eyes, his face etched in pain.

I shudder. "You might have been hurt or—" I can't say the word.

He shakes his head.

"You can't blame yourself, Liam."

He opens his eyes. "I don't blame myself, Caitlyn, I didn't kill her!" He looks down at me with blazing blue eyes.

I blink at him. "I just meant—" I pull the sheet tighter around me.

He breaths in deeply, exhaling with a sigh. "I'm sorry." He strokes his finger across my bare shoulder, down my arm. "I don't blame myself. I just have a lot of—what ifs."

"You were so young," I whisper. I turn more fully against him and wrap my arms around his neck. Pressing my face against his warm skin, I inhale his delicious scent as his arms tighten around me.

I am stunned by his revelation, and my heart is heavy with the thought of what he must have gone through. But I'm also in awe of him. I can't imagine how he managed to pull through the ordeal of losing his mother in that way. And from what Holly told me, I doubt if his father was there for him.

"What did you do—after?" I ask softly.

"I was very close to my mother's parents, and I went to live with them. They helped me through the ordeal of the trial." He strokes my back. "They also helped me buy this place."

I lift my head. "They did?"

He nods. "They did. They thought it a good idea for me to get away from—all that had happened. Start fresh."

"Do they live close?"

He smiles sadly. "No, they're both gone now."

He doesn't say anything more, and I lean back against him processing all that he has said. The importance of him sharing this tragic part of his life is not lost on me. I know that if we are going to have any type of relationship, it is imperative to be truthfully honest and upfront with each other.

"Liam—" I take a deep breath, nervous about telling him why I came here to work for him, and terrified of the outcome. "I need to tell you something—"

"Look."

I turn in his arms to see the sun peeking over the horizon. It's breathtaking. Soft, muted shades of pinks, oranges, and blues blend into each other, the colors becoming deeper, richer, and finally radiant as the sun slowly rises.

"Did you mean what you said to me in the club earlier?" Liam asks against my ear before running his nose down the column of my neck to my shoulder.

I inhale sharply. "Yes. Very much." I hold my breath, scared of what he might say about my declaration of love.

"Well, that's good." He turns me in his arms before taking my mouth in a searing kiss. His hand pulls the sheet down around my waist, before molding around my breast, tugging on a sensitive nipple. I moan softly. He raises his head, his eyes glowing with a wicked gleam.

"I reckon it's time you moved in with me, darlin'."

Liam leaves for the morning meeting, and I savor a cup of coffee as I sit on the deck outside his bedroom. I can't stop thinking about the night we had. Liam's admission that I was part of his heart and the unbelievable lovemaking. I bite my lip. Sex with Liam is always incredible, but last night…

And now he wants me to move in with him.

Opening up to me as he did about his mother's death was definitely a good thing, but I'm still in shock over that revelation. My heart hurts for him. There's also the small nagging voice that keeps reminding me I need to tell Liam I worked for Query Magazine. And soon.

I hear a car door and I stand to look over the railing

and see Bryce walking up the driveway. He looks up and waves.

I finish my coffee and dress. I have several things to accomplish today before I have to be back here for work this evening, and I need to get back early so I can talk to Liam.

I hurry to the elevator. I want to make it out of Justice House before the morning meeting is over. This walk of shame I have been doing is getting old. Maybe living here would have its advantages. I grin. There could be several advantages to moving in with Liam Justice.

My purse is sitting on Liam's desk in his office, and I grab it up on my way out. I'm digging for my keys as I head for the back entrance when I remember I forgot to call for a cab.

Damn. I don't want to wait for the gate guard to call me a cab, someone's sure to see me and notice I'm still wearing the clothes I wore yesterday.

"Cait!"

I look up to see Bryce leaning against the door outside his office. "Bryce." I glance around wondering why he's out here and not in the meeting.

He pushes away from the wall to walk beside me. "Funny thing, early this morning," he says. I glance out of the corner of my eye. "I received a call about a woman screaming."

What? I feel my face warm, and I duck my head.

"You wouldn't know anything about that—would you?"

Damn him. I can hear the laughter in his voice.

The women's restroom is just ahead, and when we reach it, I murmur something about freshening up.

"I like the dress you're wearing," he says, laughing. "I meant to tell you that last night."

I open the bathroom door gritting my teeth, and Bryce's laughter follows me in. That man...

I stop abruptly when I see Miranda primping in front of the mirror. What the hell is up with ditching the meeting this morning? As I wash my hands, Miranda turns, leaning against the sink watching me with a smirk on her face.

I sigh. "Do you have a problem, Miranda?"

She grins outright. "Not anymore."

I dig through my purse for a hair tie and pull my hair up into a ponytail.

"I wouldn't get too secure in your position here if I were you."

"Why's that?" I ask as I smooth my hair back. She gives an unladylike snort, and I give her what I hope is a smug smile before turning to leave.

"You know"—she calls out—"He always fucks the hostesses."

I stop and turn to look at her with mock surprise on my face. "But you were never a *hostess*," I say, and then turn again, more than satisfied when I hear her sharply indrawn breath.

"Ha ha," she snips. "Well, if it doesn't bother you to be just another notch on his bedpost..."

I stop again and look at her. She's unbelievable. "Where are you going with this Miranda?"

She puts her hand over her heart, mocking me now. "I'd just hate for you to get the wrong impression of the situation."

I try not to smile, but it's hard.

"It's good that you keep your amusement," she says.

"While I find your concern—touching, Miranda, I think I'll be okay. But thank you."

"You don't believe me. You think you're the one don't you? You think he's in love with you." She laughs then. "Has he told you?"

"That's none of your business."

"Ask him about Melanie. She was the hostess you replaced."

I'd really like to shove that *replaced* where the sun doesn't shine.

"I know about Mel." I really only know what Tansy's told me, but Miranda doesn't need to know that.

"I bet you don't. Ask him. Ask Liam why she left."

She turns back toward the mirror giving her hair one last pat, and then she walks past me as she heads out the door, more than pleased with herself, sowing her little seed of discord.

I stand outside Liam's office. I'm pissed at Miranda but more so at myself for letting her fill me with doubt. I try to tell myself to ignore her, to just let it go. But I recall Tansy telling me that Melanie left suddenly, and If I'm going to consider moving in with Liam, I need to know.

I knock softly, not sure if Liam will be in his office or still at the morning meeting. I hear him call out for me to enter. He's sitting at his desk, head down, but he looks up as I walk in. He lays down his pen and leans back in his chair, hands behind his head. He's still in his morning workout clothes.

"Hey, baby." His salacious smile causes the usual reaction, a tightening deep in my core. I take a deep breath. I know if I don't get right to the point, his sexiness will have me sitting in his lap, all thought of what I need to know totally obliterated by his mouth and hands on me. I watch as the smile in his eyes fades to appraising.

"What can I do for you, darlin'?" he asks in that thick drawl of his, to which my body immediately responds. Will he always affect me this way?

"I... need to ask you something." My voice sounds breathy and—weak. I clear my throat.

He watches me further, his eyes cautious now as they try to assess the situation.

I give a nervous little laugh. "Did—did you sleep with the previous hostess, Mel?" I blurt before I have a chance to chicken out.

His glare is unnerving and I bite my lip, trying to compose myself by focusing on that little discomfort. When he stands, my pulse quickens, unsure of what he's going to do, but he only moves to stand in front of his desk, leaning against it with his arms crossed over his chest. His eyes narrow on me and I hold his gaze, determined not to let him intimidate me. Several moments pass, with neither of us saying anything, our eyes locked in silent combat.

"I take your silence as an affirmative," I finally say.

"Do you?" he drawls softly.

I take a deep breath. "So—do you sleep with all of your hostesses?"

He tips his head to the side, and after a beat, he smiles slightly—deceptively. "Sleep? No, I would say sleep is not the appropriate word, darlin'." I frown slightly, knowing he's toying with me. He's so good at it.

"Fucking." He nods his head. "Yes, I reckon fucking is a better description," he says in his smooth voice.

I swallow deeply and nod my head. "It's true then," I accuse softly.

His burning gaze narrows. "Not entirely," he says tersely. "I didn't sleep with all of the hostesses."

He shifts, and I watch the play of muscles in his arms as they uncross and he walks slowly toward me, stopping in front of me. I can't take his burning gaze any longer and I look away.

"Caitlyn." He sighs in irritation. "I fucked them," he says harshly. My gaze flies back to his. "I didn't sleep with them and I didn't date them."

"Were there others... other employees that you... " There's a perceivable hardening in his eyes and I take a step back. "You did." I can't keep the hurt from my voice. So much for him not dating the help. *Am* I just another notch on his bedpost as Miranda suggested? I feel a slight panic at that thought.

He reaches out, his large hand wrapping around the side of my neck, pulling me those last two steps back to him. So close my breasts brush against his chest, and I gasp softly as a jolt of desire enters my body straight through my nipples. They harden painfully.

His eyes pierce me with their intensity. "All the women in my past, I fucked," he says firmly. "I never invited them into my home nor were they ever allowed here in my office, and I sure as hell never asked anyone else to move in with me!" There's definite anger in his voice. "All I did was fuck them, Caitlyn." His hand is still on my neck and he uses his thumb to push up under my chin, his impossibly blue eyes blazing down into mine. "Now I'm sorry if that hurts you, but I can't change what I did when I didn't even know you."

"I know that," I say softly. "I just... needed to know."

"Well now you do!" he snaps.

There's a knock on his office door. He releases me but doesn't step away.

He shakes his head in exasperation. "What are you doing, Cait?" He asks in his slow drawl.

What *am* I doing? I'm an idiot, letting Miranda get to me. She knew I'd ask Liam and she also knew what his reaction would be. I played right into her scheme to cause trouble between the two of us.

"I'm sorry, Liam. I have no right to—"

Without warning, he yanks me into his arms. I only have time to gasp in surprise before his mouth comes down hard and insistent on mine. His is hot and demanding, punishing as his tongue boldly forces its way into mine. He fists his hand in my hair, and I moan, gripping the front of his t-shirt as he pulls my head back to better assault my mouth. His other hand slides up under the skirt of my dress to grip my ass. He holds me in place exactly as he wants me as he relentlessly ravishes my mouth, my senses. His erection is hard against my belly, his heat like a branding iron.

When he abruptly releases me, my world is spinning and I stumble forward, struggling to keep my balance. I am embarrassingly breathless, panting with the need he has ignited in my traitorous body.

He reaches out to steady me and then turns, walking back to his desk to sit; his eyes on me once again as he calls toward the door, "Come!" Then his eyes gleam wickedly. "Not you, darlin'," he says softly. I huff a breath and turn away from him.

Holy hell! I'm ready for him to take me right here, right now. He's made sure of that. I want to rub my breasts to ease the throbbing but instead I take a deep breath, willing myself to calm down before turning back around.

Mike stops mid-stride into the room. "Am I interrupting?" He glances between us.

"Yes you are, but Caitlyn and I can—resume our discussion later." Liam's eyes are still on me as he raises his brow, arrogance written all over his face. He licks his bottom lip before drawing it into his mouth. His eyes gleam when he sees my flush. He knows exactly what he does to me.

Embarrassed, I quickly head for the door, giving Mike a small smile as I pass by him.

"Cait," he says in greeting.

Once out the door I lean against it. Well, I never thought Liam was a saint, and the thought of him with others is not a pleasing thought. But he's made it perfectly clear that he wants me, and that is all that really matters. Miranda be damned.

I enter the doors of Query Magazine just shy of noon, hoping to lure Paul away for lunch. What I need to relate to him needs said away from anyone who might overhear.

After I'd gone home, showered and changed, I called in a picnic lunch from the deli across the street from the magazine. I plan to drag Paul to a nearby park. It's too nice of a day to eat inside.

I'm a little surprised to find the lobby void of people. There must be an employee meeting going on, and I hope it's not bad news about Valerie.

Query Magazine has a new receptionist, and she looks up as I cross the lobby.

"May I help you?"

"Hi. I'm Cait Shaw." I give her a smile, which she does not return. Geez. She wouldn't last a day if Valerie were here. Valerie is big on treating visitors to the magazine as if they were guests.

"I'm here to see Paul Sims."

"Let me check if he is available."

I wait patiently while she calls Paul, eyeing me speculatively.

"Cait!" Paul rounds the corner.

"Hey."

He gives me a hug. "Have you met our new receptionist? Cait this is Lisa Brown. Lisa, Cait Shaw. Cait used to work here."

"It's nice to meet you Lisa."

"You too Miss Shaw."

"You can call me Cait." I don't think she hears me; she's too busy ogling Paul.

"Lisa, you don't need to call when Cait stops by, just send her on back to my office." Lisa gives me a look, one that annoys me.

I step over and loop my arm through Paul's. "Ready big boy?" He gives me an amused look.

"Has Julie met her?" I ask as we head back toward his office. Before he can answer, I ask, "Where is everyone?"

"They're all in a meeting. Guess—"

"Paul wait until you hear what's been going on at Justice House!"

He stops. "What's been happening at Justice House?"

"Two nights ago someone tried to break into the file cabinets where they keep the member files."

He frowns.

"You know that I think Valerie was looking for

someone within the clientele of Justice House. Well, now I think her interest was on a more personal level."

Paul narrows his eyes in that way he does when he's not sure he agrees with me. He takes my arm and starts walking again, guiding me down the hall.

"I also think that either Joseph Case had something to do with the attempt of getting a look at those files or there is someone else looking for the same thing Valerie was."

Paul continues to frown. "What do you think is so interesting to everyone?" he asks.

"Well—I don't know, but you were the one who pointed out that some of the members might take drastic measures to protect their privacy."

It's my turn to stop, drawing Paul to a halt beside me.

"I haven't had a chance to tell Liam yet, but I think the attempted break-in is a two man job. I think there is someone working at The Justice who helped this—unknown thief—to get inside the mansion. Remember I told you about the man who entered Justice House a few weeks ago, the one who made it all the way upstairs. I don't think they ever found out who he was or how he managed to just walk right in without someone noticing him."

"So why do you think someone helped this recent intruder?"

"After the incident, with the guy upstairs, Liam beefed up security, hiring extra guards and implementing a state of the art security system. What if the person working on the inside knows how to shut down the alarm system?"

"What about the guards?" Paul asks.

"It wouldn't be hard to find out their routine, slip past and enter an unlocked door."

"I don't know, Cait."

"It wouldn't be impossible if they had a helper on the inside. There is information within Justice House. Information that Valerie was seeking, and if Joseph Case did not put someone else in there after I quit, then—" I raise my eyebrow. "What if Valerie's disappearance is connected to all of this?"

Paul nods, considering what I've explained, then he quirks his finger at me.

I frown. "What?"

He pushes the door open to the magazine's Media room.

"Let's ask her."

Bemused, I enter coming to a dead stop as soon as I see Valerie at the front of the room.

Paul chuckles as he comes in behind me, pushing me on into the room.

"What? When?" I sputter.

"She came in this morning," Paul whispers as he guides me to a couple of empty seats. "I was just getting ready to call you when you showed up."

"Where the hell has she been?" I look up at him, and he shrugs, shaking his head, clearly as puzzled as I am.

We sit through the remainder of the meeting as Valerie assures everyone that it is back to business as usual. As things stand, I have no business sitting in on the meeting since I'm no longer employed by the magazine. But there is no way I am going anywhere until I know where in the hell Valerie has been.

The meeting wraps up, and as the room clears Paul and I remain seated. As Valerie makes her way toward us, she's busy grilling Bob Welch, head of the Advertising Department.

"Bob, I'll need the reports on collections and publication by the end of the day," she says briskly, clearly dismissing him.

"No problem, Valerie. I'll have them to you before I leave tonight."

"Paul, Caitlyn, how nice of you both to be here for the meeting." She barely looks at us. "Come with me."

My eyebrows lift in surprise, and then I laugh. Good to know some things never change. Paul nudges my arm. "I don't work for her anymore, I can laugh," I whisper at him.

We follow Valerie to her office. Her presence in the building has already restored order where there was only a semblance of that order the last few times I was here during her absence. Valerie Sharp *is* the heart of this magazine. Whereas she might be brusque and short-tempered, she is highly professional and demands the same from her employees. And when you work in a high-stress workplace, you can take comfort from sound authority.

"Pat, step into my office please," Valerie says to her private secretary barely glancing at her.

"Certainly, Valerie." Pat looks questioningly at Paul and me. I lift my shoulder and give a shake of my head.

"Shut the door, Paul," Valerie commands as she strides to her desk.

"Caitlyn, I do not accept your resignation." Valerie opens a drawer in her desk as she sits, sliding what I assume is my letter of resignation across the top.

I almost laugh out loud again. "Valerie, you don't have to accept it." I sit in one of the chairs in front of her desk. "But that doesn't change the fact that I quit the magazine shortly after you left on your little vacation." She tilts her head. "And where have you been?" I ask.

"Pat, contact personnel to re-instate Caitlyn on the payroll—"

"No, Pat," I counter command. I glare at Valerie. She is not going to bully me on this. "I work for The Justice House, Valerie. I am not coming back to the magazine."

Valerie's eyes narrow.

"You work at The Justice because of me, Caitlyn. *That* is the only reason you are working there." She enunciates each word in that precise way she has of speaking.

"Easy, ladies." Paul holds up his hands. "No reason for either one of you to get upset."

Valerie leans back in her chair. "Paul—Pat, I'd like to speak to Caitlyn in private." When neither of them makes a move to leave, Valerie raises her eyebrow. "Now," she says forcefully.

The door closes with a click as they leave.

Valerie stands and moves to her corner liquor cabinet to pour us a drink.

"Valerie—where have you been?"

She hands me a glass and then returns to her chair. She downs half her drink. "I need you in Justice House, Caitlyn." She makes direct eye contact as if willing the answer she wants from me.

I take a sip of my drink. "I need answers from you Valerie."

She sits back in her chair, a begrudging smile on her face. "You remind me of my sister," she says. I'm surprised. I didn't know she had a sister. She's never spoken of a sister or any family for that matter.

"I am searching for someone," she finally admits.

And? I say silently. If she thinks that unsurprising

revelation is going to appease me, she's sorely mistaken. I remain silent, though.

"For several years now, I've followed this—*individual's* activities around the country, even into Mexico and Central America."

I set my drink down. "This person must be very important to you."

I see a flash of something in her eyes before she hides it. "Very." She finishes the last of her drink. "A year ago the trail led to Justice House."

Wow. "You've been very patient." The wrath of a woman scorned.

"I have to be. I made a mistake a few years back, and I've paid for it since."

"So, she's looking for an ex-lover to extract her revenge. Seems extreme but knowing Valerie—"

"I need you in Justice House, Caitlyn," she says again.

"Valerie"—I lean forward in my chair—"I quit the magazine because I couldn't deal with the aspects of the job. You know I was having a difficult time with the deception involved. Yes, in retrospect—I should also have quit my job at the Justice, I see that now." I take a deep breath, nervously looking away from her too sharp gaze.

"You've become involved with Liam Justice."

My gaze flies back to hers. "Yes," I say quietly.

She stands and moves to look out her window at the busy world going on outside of Query Magazine.

"Out of respect for you, I have never told Liam I was working as a spy at Justice House. I wanted to wait until you returned so I could tell you first. I felt I owed you that much. But, things have progressed between Liam and me, and I have to tell him now because I owe *him* that." *I just pray he understands.* Panic grips me again.

I should have told him already. I should have told him this morning.

"Valerie—where have you been? You had to know people would be worrying about you. For Pete's sake, the police were called in!"

"I was in a situation where I had to lie low. That's all you need to know."

I sigh. "Okay." I stand, knowing that's all I'll get from her. Gathering up my purse, I stare at her back, she's turned once more, looking out the window. I feel guilty. I'm not sure why, but I do.

"Thanks for everything, Valerie. I appreciate you giving me a job." I feel my throat closing up.

At the door, I turn back.

"Maybe if you met with Liam—explained your situation—" My voice trails off. Liam Justice would never let Valerie Sharp, editor of Query Magazine, anywhere near Justice House, let alone invade the privacy of his club members.

"Goodbye, Valerie," I say softly, but she doesn't turn or say a word.

Paul, and I have a quick lunch discussing our views on Valerie's return. Lying low? What does that mean, that she put herself into a situation where she feared for her safety? Paul thinks there is a lot more to the story, and so do I.

Now I'm hurrying out of my cab at Justice House. I wanted to get here early. Liam is going to hear what I have to say, whether he wants to or not.

The security guard nods as he picks up the phone as I walk by. It's a beautiful day, and the grounds of Justice

House are lovely. Flowers bloom in numerous beds, and the flowering ornamental trees give up their delicate scents to float on the warm breeze.

It's early enough in the day to still be reasonably quiet, but I know that will change once the dinner crowd arrives and then later when the nightclub opens.

I wave at Leon as I walk past. The two male members he's talking to at the bar look up and smile.

"Hi, Tansy." I pull out a chair to sit beside her. She's filling out her shift paperwork.

"Cait." She smiles. "You're early."

"I need to talk to Liam before my shift starts."

"He came by earlier and left a message for you. He wants you to come straight to his office as soon as you arrive."

She wiggles her eyebrows, and I laugh as I stand.

"I guess I'd better not keep the boss waiting."

I knock lightly and then walk in. I come up short, surprised, and then smile. It looks as if the whole gang is here.

Holly is sitting on the couch. Bryce and Mike are at the bar. When my gaze encounters Miranda's smug, evil smile, a frisson of unease makes its way down my spine. My eyes immediately seek out Liam. He's standing, his back to the room, at the large windows behind his desk, looking out to the front of Justice House.

He knows.

I can tell. Not from the way the others are looking at me, but because Liam is not. He always looks at me, as if he can't keep his eyes off me.

I need to talk to him alone.

It's only been a matter of seconds since I walked in the room, but it feels like an eternity as I wait, praying Liam turns and looks at me, willing him to ask me to explain. I suddenly can't breathe, and I feel as if I'm going to be sick, my hand goes unconsciously to my stomach.

"Cait?" It's not until he says my name for the second time that I look at Bryce.

"Yes?"

"Do you work for Query Magazine?"

I swallow against the nausea rising up in my throat. "No, I—"

"Yes, she does!" Miranda glares at me with ill-concealed hatred. "Valerie Sharp assigned her to investigate you, Liam!"

"Miranda, you may go now!" Holly's voice is sharp. "I'm sure you have—*duties* to take care of."

"No! I need to stay, and make sure she doesn't lie her way out of this."

"Get the hell out, Miranda!" Holly states more firmly.

Miranda looks to Liam for help as Mike holds his arm out and motions for her with the curling of his fingers.

"Liam?" Miranda uses her best hurt voice.

"Go," Liam orders without turning around.

I look quickly at him. *Please look at me.*

Miranda tosses her hair and flounces out in a huff. After the door closes, I glance at the others and then back at Liam.

"Please, Liam I can explain." I need to explain. He doesn't respond in any way.

"Explain, Cait," Bryce says softly.

I take a deep breath to steady myself, but my voice still comes out unsteady. "I did work for Query Magazine—"

"Oh, Cait!" I hear Holly say in a plaintive whisper as if she'd been holding onto the hope that Miranda was lying.

I glance at her quickly. "But, I quit the magazine a week after I started working here."

Holly glances at Liam.

"Why did you do that?" Bryce asks.

"Because—" my voice breaks. Damn. This is going to sound lame. "Because I'd been having doubts about what I did for the magazine, and I liked everyone here"—I meet Holly's gaze—"and—" I look at Liam's back. I can't say it in front of the others, but I'm hoping he knows I mean him, that that's when he and I started.

"Why were you investigating Liam?" Bryce asks.

"At the time I wasn't told specifically why, and I had my doubts about my assignment."

Please, Liam. Please look at me.

When no one says anything, I tear my gaze from Liam. "I suspected the real target was one of the members here at The Justice."

"You were the one who tried to break into the files." Mike finally speaks his voice angry.

"No," I say emphatically. I turn toward him. "I didn't, I swear." My gaze sweeps the room, meeting the doubtful stares of each one of them. Except for Liam. "Please, you have to believe me. I quit the magazine right after I started here. I *never* gave Valerie any information."

"A private investigator has been keeping tabs on you for the past few weeks," Mike informs me.

A Private Investigator! I know with certainty that is Miranda's doing.

Mike continues. "You have been documented going in and out of Query Magazine on numerous occasions."

"My friend Paul still works there."

I glance at Liam's back, and I think I see a tightening of his shoulders.

Mike reaches over for a file lying on the bar top. "At least one of those visit's was a meeting with Valerie Sharp's attorney, Joseph Case."

Holy hell.

"Was this meeting before, or after you quit Query Magazine?"

I can't breathe. I feel as if a noose is tightening around my neck. "After," I whisper, trying to push the panic back down. "But the meeting wasn't about—"

"Get out," Liam says in a deadly quiet voice.

"Please, Liam let me explain. That meeting wasn't about you or Justice House. Valerie was missing—"

He turns and levels blue eyes filled with a frightening rage, on me. I quell under the burning anger I see there.

"I don't need to listen to any more of this."

"Please! You have to know I would never do anything to hurt you!"

"You—are fired."

I shake my head. "Please," I whisper as I blink against the sudden tears.

"Get the *fuck* out of my house!" His shout reverberates around the room.

I blanch at the look of disgust he levels on me.

"Get her out of here!" he utters from between clenched teeth.

"Let's go," Mike says.

"No. I'll walk her out," Bryce says.

I'm barely conscious of Bryce taking hold of my arm as I watch Liam walk to the elevator. He doesn't look at me again as he enters and turns to hit the button that will close the doors forever against me.

He believes I have betrayed him.

I know my punishment.

I no longer exist to him.

AUTHOR BIO

Rivi Jacks has a lifelong love of books, and she is a true believer in holding onto a good love story. One reason her attic and barn are full of the books she has collected through the years.

She lives in the Missouri Ozarks on a farm with her husband, and when not writing or reading, she likes to take long walks down country roads, cook, fish, and spend time with family and friends.

CONTACT LINKS

http://rivijacks.com/

https://twitter.com/rivi_jacks

https://www.goodreads.com/book/show/19016508-sweetwater

https://www.facebook.com/pages/Rivi-Jacks/234024470093905

https://www.pinterest.com/rivijacks/

PLAYLIST FOR SEEKING JUSTICE

Stripper (Ribbed Music) ~ Sohodolls

Sexy Back ~ Justin Timberlake

Dark Horse ~ Katy Perry

Dark In My Imagination ~ of Verona

Fire Breather ~ Laurel

No One Like You ~ Scorpions

Sexy Silk ~ Jessica Cornish

Sing ~ Ed Sheeran

Love Don't Die ~ The Fray

Love Runs Out ~ One Republic

Stay ~ Rihanna

Blue Blood ~ Laurel

Let Her Go ~ Passenger

You Can Be The Boss ~ Lana Del Rey

Make It Wit Chu ~ Queens of the Stone Age

Made in the USA
Charleston, SC
08 May 2016